Treason at Ten

Also by the same author:

ROYAL VISIT TO TONGA (Pitkin, 1954)
THE FRIENDLY ISLANDERS (Hodder and Stoughton, 1967)
A GUIDE TO PITCAIRN (Ed. 1970)

KENNETH BAIN

Treason at 10

FIJI AT THE CROSS ROADS

Hodder & Stoughton
LONDON SYDNEY AUCKLAND TORONTO

British Library Cataloguing in Publication Data

Bain, Kenneth
  Treason at Ten: Fiji at the crossroads.
  1. Fiji. Political events
  I. Title
  996'.11

  ISBN 0-340-49093-4

First published in Great Britain 1989

Published by Hodder and Stoughton,
a division of Hodder and Stoughton Ltd,
Mill Road, Dunton Green, Sevenoaks, Kent TN13 2YA
Editorial Office: 47 Bedford Square, London WC1B 3DP

Photoset by Rowland Phototypesetting Ltd,
Bury St Edmunds, Suffolk

Printed in Great Britain by St Edmundsbury Press Ltd,
Bury St Edmunds, Suffolk

ACKNOWLEDGMENTS

I am indebted to the elected Prime Minister of Fiji, Dr Timoci Bavadra, for writing the Foreword to this book; and to his wife Adi Kuini Vuikaba, for enlightenment about customary matters in Veiseisei on which I have drawn.

My thanks are due for permission to reproduce certain copyright material: in Australia, *The Australian Financial Review*; in Britain, *The Times*, *The Independent*, Sir Raymond Firth and Mr Stanley Arthur; in Fiji, the Government Printer, the *Fiji Times* and the University of the South Pacific's Institute of Pacific Studies; and in New Zealand, *The New Zealand Herald*, *Auckland Star*, *The Dominion*, *The Dominion Sunday Times* and the *Otago Daily Times*. The publishers and I regret any unintentional omission or oversight and will gladly add an appropriate acknowledgment in any subsequent edition of this book.

My appreciation goes to Lord Goodman, June and Ronald Knox-Mawer, Derek Ingram of Gemini News Service and Tony Gould-Davies in London; to Rod Gates, presently New Zealand Ambassador in Japan, Carolyn McAskie, Canadian High Commission in Sri Lanka, Geoffrey Caston, Vice-Chancellor of the University of the South Pacific, Nick Hurley and Gary Wiseman; and to Graeme Baildon of Fulcrum Advertising, David Elworthy, Sir Henry Cooper and Ken Greville, in Auckland. Each will know why.

In common with journalists and friends of Fiji in many places, I have cause to be grateful to Dale Keeling and his colleagues of the *Fiji Independent News Service* in Sydney and in Fiji itself.

I have benefited from the judicious editorial interventions of Jane Osborn; and from the considerable skills of Margaret, who has poised her pencil at odd times in strange places and typed for me for close to forty years.

Finally, I must thank 'Atu, whose part in the proceedings is made clear but who would prefer it were otherwise; and Ashley, who first urged me to start and, from the safe distance of the Caribbean, nagged me until I finished.

No one, other than myself, bears any responsibility for my text that follows.

KENNETH BAIN

Sevenoaks, Kent
12 November 1988

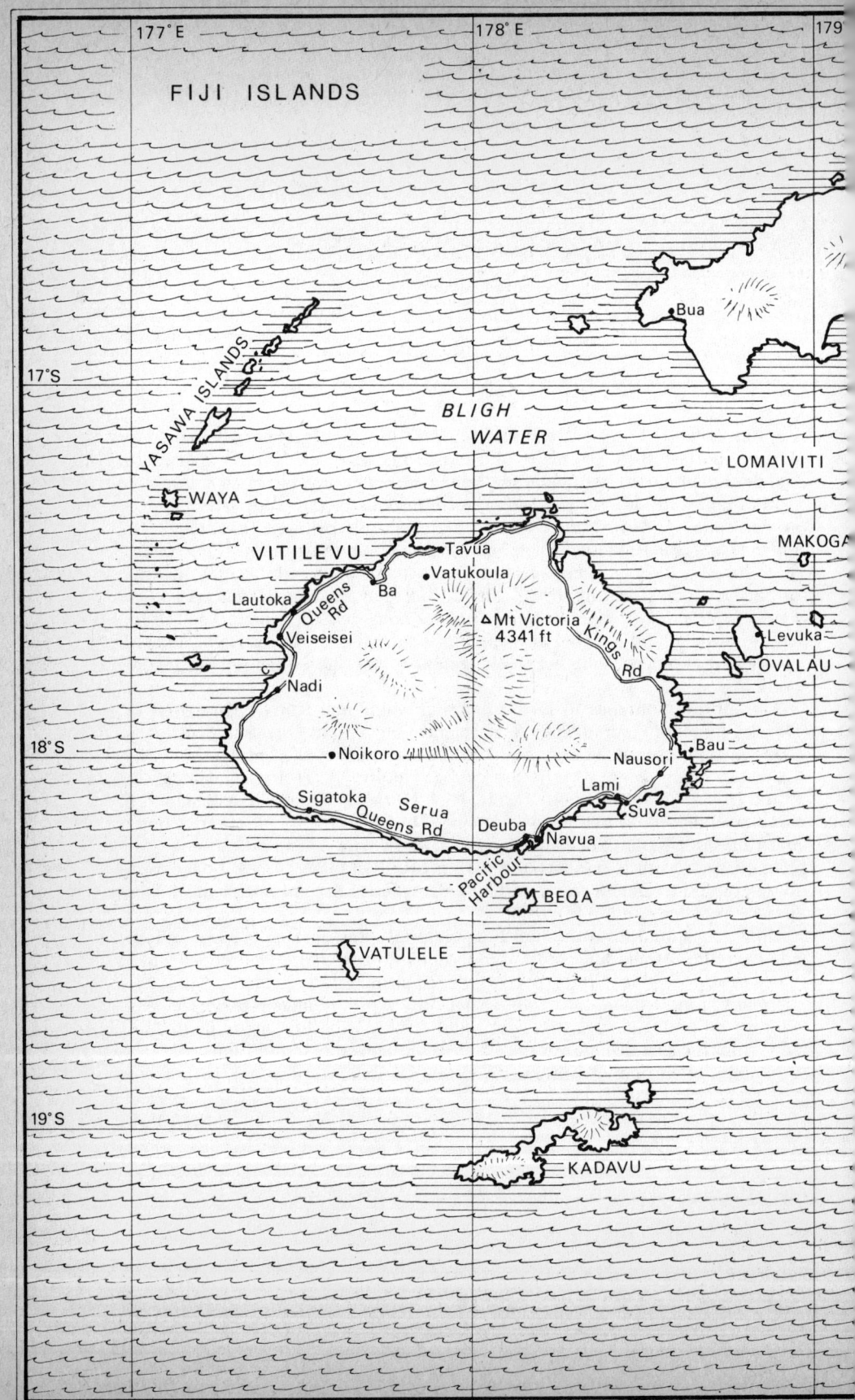

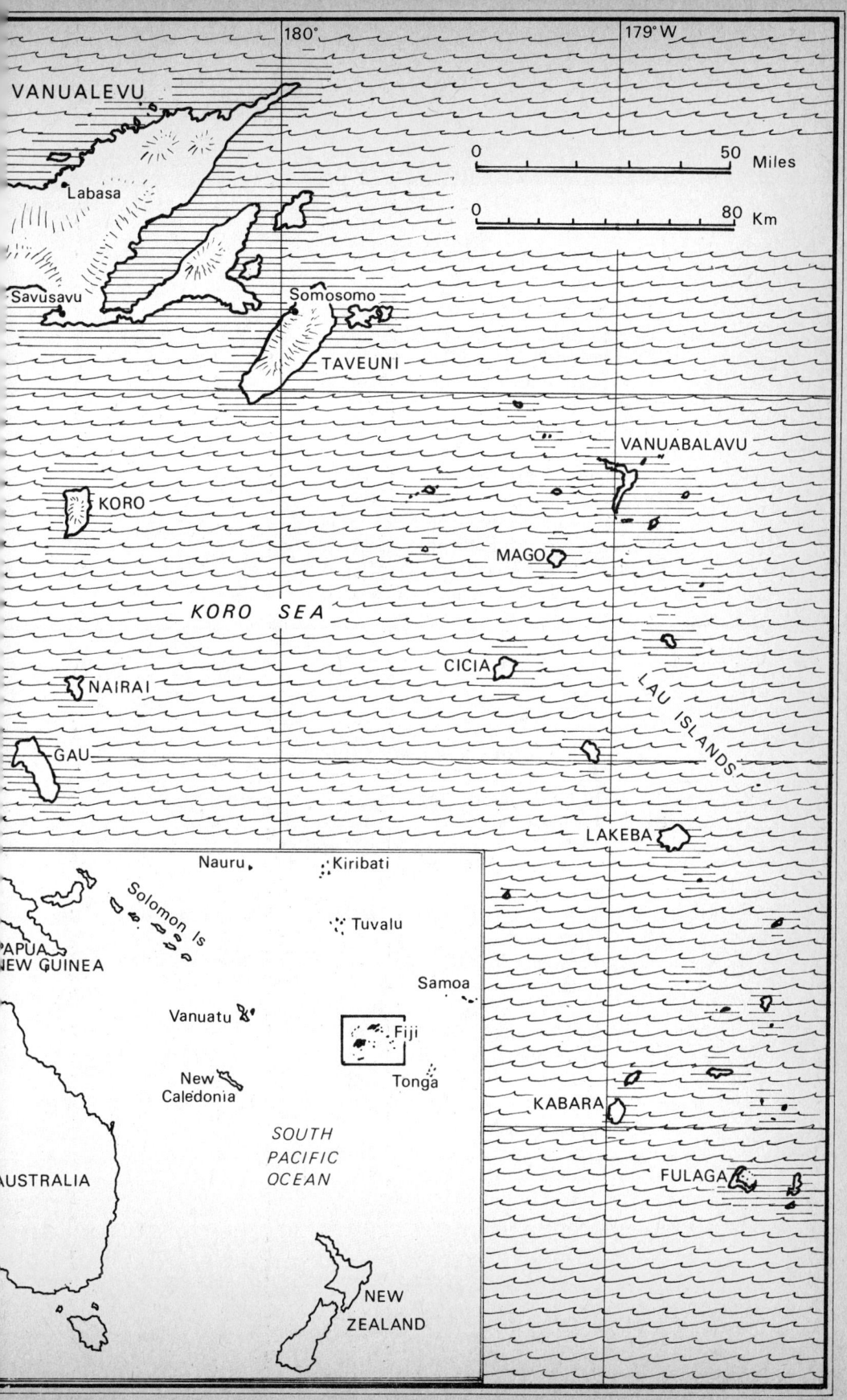

VANUALEVU

Labasa

Savusavu

Somosomo

TAVEUNI

VANUABALAVU

KORO

MAGO

KORO SEA

CICIA

NAIRAI

LAU ISLANDS

GAU

LAKEBA

0   50 Miles

0   80 Km

180°

179°W

Nauru

Kiribati

Solomon Is

Tuvalu

PAPUA NEW GUINEA

Samoa

Vanuatu

Fiji

New Caledonia

Tonga

KABARA

AUSTRALIA

SOUTH PACIFIC OCEAN

FULAGA

NEW ZEALAND

Fijian spelling

B is pronounced as MB in number
C is pronounced as TH in mother
D is pronounced as ND in tender
G is pronounced as NG in singer
Q is pronounced as NG in hunger
J is pronounced as CH in church

Examples:

Cakobau	is pronounced THAKOMBAU
Nadi	is pronounced NANDI
Magiti	is pronounced MANGITI
Yaqona	is pronounced YANGGONA
Tabua	is pronounced TAMBUA
Jioji	is pronounced CHAWCHI (George)

Glossary

Adi	:	The title for Fijian women of rank.
Bula	:	Fijian greeting: good day, good health, hullo.
Bure	:	Fijian-style dwelling house.
Kai vata	:	Kinsman.
Lali	:	Hollow tree trunk ceremonial drum.
Lovo	:	Earth oven. Sometimes also loosely used for the food cooked in it.
Maca	:	Dry, i.e. empty. Of the bowl when the mixed yaqona has been consumed.
Mana	:	Prestige, influence, authority. Used widely in the South Pacific.
Palusami	:	Taro leaves cooked in coconut cream.
Ratu	:	The Fijian chiefly title for men of rank.
Sevusevu	:	Ceremonial presentation or gift.
Sulu	:	The wrap-around body cloth used by both men and women.
Tabua	:	Whale's tooth. The most prized article of Fijian ceremonial presentation.
Tanoa	:	The large wooden bowl in which the yaqona is mixed.
Tapa	:	Bark 'cloth'.
Yaqona	:	Kava, in Polynesia. The ceremonial and social drink which is both the champagne and vin ordinaire of the South Pacific.

FOREWORD BY DR TIMOCI BAVADRA

The dawn of a new era came to Fiji in April 1987, when its voters exercised their democratic right through the ballot box to choose the new kind of government they wanted to administer the country. The election was a victory for a fledgling Coalition of parties over an incumbent government which had dominated the political life of Fiji since 1970.

The people's choice did not simply mean a victory for the Coalition of the National Federation Party and the much younger Labour Party. More significantly, it had emerged from the seeds of a new political consciousness and unity germinating among the ordinary people of Fiji's multi-racial society. The outcome promised to be a long-run triumph for the vast majority of our people: the poor, the unemployed and otherwise marginal. It was these people – drawn from all ethnic communities – whom the Coalition was, and still is, pledged to serve.

Sadly, it was to be a false dawn.

My time in office as Prime Minister lasted only until 14 May 1987 – thirty-two days in all – when the people's decision was gunned aside. At ten o'clock that morning, all members of Her Majesty's Government of Fiji were forcibly removed at gunpoint from a sitting of Parliament and taken into military custody. Thus, constitutional democracy and the democratic process were extinguished in yet another corner of the world.

I have very few sweet memories of that and the following days which led inexorably to a second *coup* on 25 September 1987, the declaration of a republic, and the abject departure of Fiji from the Commonwealth.

Images of the brutalities, intimidation and other forms of coercion directed at so many innocent people are difficult to erase. Equally vivid is my continuing concern about the economic crisis into which our country was plunged, prompting a surge in unemployment and poverty. I was also concerned about the carefully manufactured racism which spread its divisive, and destructive, tentacles through our society and has become a central part of the institutionalised fabric of public life.

What happened and is still happening in my country should lead us all to examine the motivations for human oppression and to ponder the inhumane indignities so often inflicted by those who call themselves civilized.

What a great divide there is between the selfless and the selfish when the retention of power for power's sake overrides all else!

I look back on one experience with encouragement. In a bid to crush our spirits while we were being held prisoner at the Prime Minister's official residence in Suva, the soldiers tried to separate Indian and Fijian Members of Her Majesty's Government. We linked arms together – all of us – and sat on the floor. As the soldiers gradually pulled us loose, we could see the shame in their eyes. From that day our unity as a human force has never been in question. Torn loose, perhaps; but never apart or overcome.

In a sense, that one event is symbolic of what our present struggle is all about – those who would separate us on arbitrary ethnic grounds will encounter a fight to the last breath, for the unity and multi-racialism that must be the basis of our future. There have been many such symbolic events. Each has renewed our strength.

Though small in size, our country has great natural wealth and beauty. Fiji's people – of all ethnic groups, ages and genders – are its most important resource. We have worked together in the past and learned from each other. We will do so again. And in doing so, will reclaim for our country the cherished values of justice, equality and freedom.

It is a very simple ideal. Many before me can claim to have held it. But our shared resolve to make that ideal a reality gives it (and us) a special strength. We will pursue that ideal; and by sharing it, feed that spark of hope within us all.

Treason at Ten was written by a New Zealander who has been a perceptive and knowledgeable student of Fiji and its people for most of his adult life. His working knowledge of the Fijian language has, over the years, sharpened his sensitivity to the complexities of Fijian politics and traditional culture.

Kenneth Bain held increasingly responsible senior posts during the last two decades of British colonial administration of Fiji. In 1970, he accepted one of the first diplomatic appointments – to London – for our newly independent country. His wife and two of their children were born in Suva; a third was born in Tonga. The South Pacific is in his blood.

The book provides a rare insight into the politics of the Commonwealth and broadens our understanding of its administration. Moreover, the events leading up to, and beyond, the departure of

Fiji from the Commonwealth highlight the international importance of the crisis.

The author's ability to portray the uncertainties and hazards of unsettling events as they unfold adds an extraordinary quality to his writing. Adi Kuini and I read a first draft in our village of Veiseisei in March 1988. It was a moving experience for us both. Thus, I was pleased to accept an invitation to contribute a foreword – not least because the author has told me things about myself, and others, that I did not know, or had forgotten.

With this book, Kenneth Bain has made an important contribution towards understanding the contemporary South Pacific and the wider world of human affairs.

Veiseisei
25 September 1988

PROLOGUE

There was an early teacher on one of the more remote and smaller islands of South Pacific Fiji. His school children were assembled in the village one early morning, sitting cross-legged on mats in the shade of the coconut trees. They were to the side and thus not in the line of a falling nut.

'It is time,' said the teacher, 'for me to tell you about your home in Fiji and the world beyond your reefs and seas.'

He drew a rough picture of the earth's land masses and oceans and then pointed at a large open expanse near the bottom. He placed a fingernail in the centre.

'You see this tiny spot, no larger than the eye of a fly. That is the size of your land compared with the rest of the world.'

When the children returned to their families with this extraordinary tale, the elders were incensed at such an insult. They went to the house of the teacher, clubbed him to death, roasted and consumed him: thus providing an early example in Fiji of what happens when the truth is told to those who cannot recognise and do not wish to hear it.

It is tempting to conclude that the behavioural extremities of a section of Fijian society in the course of 1987 are derived from and explained by an indisputably barbaric past. It would be mistaken to do so. There are other lands, not least Britain and the United States, where violence, arson and race aggression have no such intrusive origins – apart perhaps from the latter-day resentments of the poor and the deprived against the wealthy and the historically well positioned. In such conditions, racial animosity is not the basic cause of violence, but a potent added ingredient which can inflame the underprivileged and the less successful to strike out against the privileged and the diligent of whatever race.

The complexities of Fijian society, under threat of irreversible change in a pervasively commercial world, do not permit these dark issues to be categorised simply. The best that can sensibly be done at present is to observe and to recount rather than essay long-term analysis.

It used to be said that if you started in England and dug straight through the centre of the earth, you would as like as not come out the other side in one of the South Pacific islands of Fiji. Since there are some three hundred of them, the possibility, while never tested, is certainly there.

In my innocent if not blameless years of post-war colonial administration, when red still dominated the map of the world, there was, geographically, no more distant outpost of the imperial domain. And none where the sunset beating of retreat was performed with greater solemnity and devotion to a distant monarch: as the Union flag was lowered, that is, at the Queen Elizabeth Barracks of the Royal Fiji Military Forces in the capital city of Suva.

There was good reason. In 1874, the chiefs of Fiji, assembled in the old capital of Levuka on the island of Ovalau, had voluntarily placed themselves and their land under the trusted protection of their sovereign lady, Queen Victoria. As Tui Viti – Queen of Fiji – she and her direct successors thus became so entitled. For the chiefs of Fiji, it was their third time of trying to hand over to the British Crown their fragmented, war-torn and debt-ridden land: a process which had also included a similar flirtation with the Americans and which was in sharp contrast with the imperialistic escapades which had led to colonial acquisitions in other parts of the world, red-stained or otherwise. Anyway, it is an odd coincidence that the same colour should have been used to delineate the British Colonial Empire on maps as for the Marxist march to the aspirant goal of workers' world unity.

The first European discoveries of the islands of Fiji were accidental: by the Dutch sailor-explorer Abel Tasman in 1643 and Captain James Cook who sailed by the hazardous archipelago in 1774. Then, on 28 April 1789, off the island of Tofua in Tonga, Lieutenant William Bligh and eighteen officers and men of HMS *Bounty* were put by a mutinying Fletcher Christian into the ship's launch and left to their own resources. And what resources Bligh and his men proved to possess: for there began an open-boat journey of bravery, endurance and navigational skill without parallel in naval history. Bligh set off west for Dutch Timor, 6,000 kilometres away, through the uncharted reef-strewn waters of the Cannibal Isles, the name by which Fiji was justly known at that time.

From Southern Lau, Bligh penetrated the heart of the island group, charting his many discoveries of reef and island in great and lasting detail. Today, Bligh Water stands as a memorial to his navigation and seamanship: and his escape from pursuing Fijian canoes near the Yasawas.

To the Fijians, those early visitors were Kai Vavalagi, the men
from over the horizon. Sustained contact with these curious white
men was not to come until the sandalwood boom of 1804–10 and
the *bêche-de-mer* trade from the 1820s to the 1850s. Ships in
profusion came into the waters of the group with their cargoes and
traders, potential settlers and beachcombers, carpetbaggers and
drunks. Disease too. Initial acceptance of trinkets and nails for
timber was followed by demands for axes, knives and 'tabua' (whale
teeth). Thence to the musket and the white mercenaries in the Fijian
wars of the first part of the nineteenth century. Meanwhile, the
missionaries sought to convert the heathen and to cover the in-
decently bared bodies of the women of the noble savage with
all-enveloping Victorian raiments which were to become known as
Mother Hubbards.

A great oceanic triangle in the Central and South Pacific embraces
three distinct racial, linguistic and cultural groupings: Melanesia to
the west, Micronesia to the north and Polynesia to the east. The
Maoris of New Zealand represent the southernmost penetration of
Polynesia; Hawaii the most northern; and Pitcairn and Easter Island
the eastern extremities. Fiji, as we shall see, is the crossroads of
Melanesia and Polynesia. To the west lie New Caledonia, Vanuatu,
the Solomon Islands and Papua New Guinea, all of whose people
are black-skinned, fuzzyhaired and stocky. The Micronesians to the
north – Nauru, Kiribati, the Marshall Islands, the Federated States
of Micronesia, Palau and Guam – are pale-skinned and more spare
in build. They are atoll dwellers. Their faces carry visible indicators
of the Philippines and Indonesia. To the east of Fiji lie the two
Samoas, Western and American, the Cook Islands, French Polynesia, Niue and the last surviving Polynesian Kingdom of Tonga. Look
west and then east inside Fiji and you look at two different peoples
in one apparent racial entity. Look closer still and you perceive, in
a South Pacific island context, differences as deeply significant as
those between London and Cardiff, Edinburgh and Liverpool; while
miles of open ocean lie between.

Fiji itself is, of course, not a single-race land although there are
some today who wish it were and urge that it again become so. It is
not even a two-race land of Fijians and Indians. There are substantial
numbers of European settlers from Australia, New Zealand and
Britain, many long since in professional, commercial and political
life. There are Chinese and mixed Chinese–Fijian; there are
Tongans, Samoans, Solomon Islanders, Banabans from Ocean
Island, and what used to be called Gilbertese and Ellice Islanders.
There are Rotumans from an island north of Fiji proper whose

culture, language and social system are Polynesian and whose status is distinct from the rest of the nation. And there are those of a variety of mixed European and other blood. My wife is one – English, Tongan, Danish and Tahitian.

With all this racial enterprise, so to speak, Suva is today a cosmopolitan and colourful capital. Yet the country is not another Hawaii or even Jamaica. There are two races only today who really matter – Fijian and Indian. And while, to paraphrase George Orwell's *Animal Farm*, both races are equal, one is without question more equal than the other. Events in 1987 and 1988 were to demonstrate which this was to be.

PART ONE

'PARADISE' LOST

1

Thursday 14 May 1987

At ten a.m. in Suva, the face of Fiji was damaged beyond recognition; and no political plastic surgery would restore its shattered image. An army carrier drew up outside the Government Buildings. Ten elite soldiers with pistols, their identity concealed beneath gas masks, climbed down. The entrance road divides the heart of the executive, legislative and judicial organs of government from Albert Park, the hallowed home of rugby, cricket, soccer and hockey in the city. Sport it was not, as the soldiers moved fast up the ceremonial steps and crossed the hexagonal entrance lobby. They swung open the heavy wooden doors and entered the chamber where the newly elected House of Representatives was in early session. As they did so, a man with a great moustache in civilian dress arose from the public gallery and in a loud clear voice announced:

'This is a military takeover. Stay down and remain calm.' He then walked without haste from his seat until he stood before the newly elected Prime Minister, Dr Timoci Bavadra. His words are now enshrined in the new legends of the South Pacific.

'I am sorry, sir. Will you and all members of the Coalition Government please come outside with me. Now.'

Dr Bavadra sat silent and looked around him: at his stunned colleagues and at the immobile faces of the Alliance Opposition seated across the chamber.

'Very well. Under protest. Come along, gentlemen. Let us comply in a dignified and correct manner.' And he gathered up his parliamentary papers and proceeded to follow the man in civilian dress into the centre of the chamber, up the few steps to the public gallery and through the main doors.

In the road outside, two army trucks had arrived. Troops

3

descended and ushered in the Prime Minister, the Ministers of his Cabinet and all other elected members of the Labour–National Federation Coalition. Twenty-eight members of parliament were taken: Alliance party members remained behind, untouched. The trucks left for the Queen Elizabeth Barracks where armed soldiers, many masked, were on full alert. A sovereign government had been hijacked by the Royal Fiji Military Forces. The voice of the people had been stilled. Fiji had lost its political innocence.

The news broke a few minutes after the lorries left Government Buildings. A reporter of the commercial radio station FM 96 saw it all from the parliamentary press gallery. News editors in New Zealand, Australia and beyond reached for their files of Fiji background material to fill out such hard news as they could get: SHOCKWAVES OVER THE PACIFIC . . . COUP THREAT TO DEMOCRATIC TRADITIONS . . . FURORE IN FIJI . . . SHOWDOWN IN SUVA . . . REBELLION IN PARADISE: TELEPHONE LINKS CUT. So ran the first headlines, as jaundiced coup watchers wrestled with words and sought a new angle. They had it in the messianic, military Methodist Lieutenant Colonel Sitiveni Rabuka, the man in civilian dress, the third-ranking army officer. He was a veteran of United Nations peace-keeping in the Lebanon of 1980–81, whose bounce and charismatic, if erratic, confidence were to give him the aura of a Ronald Reagan at the start of his presidency. But the reality was different. He was no Reagan: just another half-colonel, leading another military coup, in another small and relatively unimportant country, usurping its constitution and the rule of law at the point of a gun.

Not quite 'just another country'; and not quite 'just another coup'. One in a country with strong and apparently enduring ties with the Crown, respect for human rights and an independent judiciary, a stable model of the democratic process for other nations, with a successful multi-racial society whose leaders and people had reached accommodation with one another. It was the communications hub for the South Pacific islands. The economy was buoyant and the confidence of foreign investors secure. The sudden coup thus seemed inexplicable until the forces at work were analysed and the tensions of recent weeks were probed beneath the surface. Whether the coup leaders realised it or not, the implications of their actions were to be of wide-ranging significance: for the Queen, for the Commonwealth, for the South Pacific region, and for the future livelihood and survival of people of all races in Fiji itself. The consequences were potentially dire and prospects bleak unless the coup could be reversed and the soldiers returned to barracks. Not much immediate likelihood of that – once such forces are unleashed, whether by a master sergeant, a sergeant major, a flight lieutenant or a lieutenant colonel: in Liberia, Uganda, Ghana, Greece, Turkey, Pakistan, Bangladesh, an array of Central and South American republics, or Fiji.

'An act of sheer hubris,' said one observer, 'by a self-indulgent pretender.' Hubris was not a word I knew, so I looked it up in two dictionaries. The combined definition was interesting: insolent pride or presumption. Arrogance, such as incites disaster. Pray God, said the afflicted, that it will not be so.

Throughout the day a series of placatory statements was issued by the coup leader. They did little to alleviate the confusion and fear which followed the events of the morning; and were of no comfort to the wives and families of the abducted members of parliament.

'You just can't imagine what we went through,' the Prime Minister's wife, Adi Kuini Vuikaba, recalled later. 'It was the most terrifying and agonising experience. I first realised something was seriously wrong when I received a call from Parliament from a police officer. He said there was a bit of a problem in the House of Representatives and my husband had been led off by Colonel Rabuka into armed trucks parked outside. I panicked. I got the children together because I expected anything. I thought the safest thing was not to leave the house but to wait for further instructions.'

The wait was to last thirteen hours. She had no idea where the prisoners had been taken, but thirteen hours later they were brought to the Prime Minister's official residence at Veiuto.

'Before they came, I received a call from Colonel Rabuka . . . He asked whether there was enough room in the official residence to accommodate the members of the team. He wanted my permission. I said, "Why are you asking my permission? I expected an order from you." Rabuka's reply was that I was still the lady of the house and he wanted my approval. So I said yes, I can accommodate the Prime Minister and all the rest of them.'

In the early evening, Dr Bavadra was permitted to telephone his wife.

'You know that they want to move us all to Veiuto. Do you think you can find room for everybody?'

The short answer was no; but Adi Kuini, the exhilaration of her husband's electoral victory shattered by the realisation of grave danger for him and his ministerial team and supporters, had not stopped to think of the difficulties.

'Yes. Of course. We will find sufficient mats and food. I have already told Rabuka.'

Shortly before midnight the captives were quietly removed from the military barracks and taken to the official residence of the Prime Minister. The army mounted mass surveillance of the house. Rolls of barbed wire were put out to surround the area and block off the entrance road. The first night of incarceration had been accomplished.

At eleven o'clock the next morning, the wives were permitted to see their husbands for a few minutes and to bring in changes of clothing and personal articles. Crowds began to gather outside the perimeter wire, as the news spread. They waved and shouted encouragement to those inside.

'There is complete peace and calm,' answered Lieutenant Colonel Rabuka. 'My Council of Ministers is in full control of government in this country. I reassure our nation, especially our Indian citizens and those of other races that the protection of their lives and properties is our top priority . . .'

When press publication was permitted to resume a week after the coup on Thursday 21 May, the *Fiji Times* produced a day-by-day summary of events during the period of its enforced silence. The following edited extracts take up the story of the captive parliamentarians and the confused events of the week:

Saturday 16 May
3 p.m.: A crowd gathers in front of the Prime Minister's residence in Veiuto where the Government members are being held captive. A prayer meeting is held with members of different religious organisations offering prayers. The military asks the crowd of more than a thousand people to disperse. When this fails, they line up trucks and army vans in front of the crowd, rev up the engines and inch-by-inch force the people to retreat. Singing the national anthem, 'Blessings Grant O God of Nations', the people back off with guns prodding their backs. Some guards, touched by the event, find tears running down their faces. People fearing that the captives will be removed stealthily at night to some other venue keep an all-night vigil at the junction to Vuya Road and Battery Road.

Sunday 17 May
3 a.m.: Guards disperse those still keeping vigil at Vuya Road.
5 a.m.: Six overseas journalists at the Courtesy Inn including Trevor Watson of Radio Australia have their rooms raided and their tapes and notebooks confiscated.
6 a.m.: The hostages are awakened at dawn and told that they

will be separated along racial lines. They decide to pray and sing hymns to prevent this.

9 a.m.: Guards enter the house to remove Indian MPs. A struggle ensues. The eighteen Indians are dragged out and thrown into five waiting vans and moved to Borron House (Rairaiwaqa). They stage a hunger strike for the day in protest at their separation and forcible removal.

12 noon: A prayer meeting is held in Sukuna Park, Suva, for the hostages. Leaders of the meeting, R. C. Sharma of Nausori and Amelia Rokotuivuna, are arrested. Sharma joins the Indian Coalition MPs at Borron House and Rokotuivuna is placed under house arrest.

Tuesday 19 May
Between 11 o'clock and midnight, all ex-government (sic) members are released from detention at both centres as people rejoice in the streets with vehicle horns blaring through the city.

The Prime Minister and twenty-seven other Fijian and Indian elected members of parliament had been held in custody against their will for five nights and six days. These words do not tell the human story. Adi Kuini recounted what she went through at a press and television interview immediately after her release:

'The days in captivity began in shock, but we were still treating it very lightly. It was only two days later that we began to realise its seriousness. It was fear of losing our lives. We had armed guards twenty-four hours a day. Any man could just pull the trigger and we would have been finished,' she said.

She recalled two incidents in particular. The first occurred on Sunday when the group was split along racial lines – the eighteen Indians being hauled off to Borron House and nine others, seven Fijians, one Chinese and one part-European, were left at Veiuto. 'At six a.m., we woke up the Indians and decided to hold a prayer meeting and sing hymns to prevent the soldiers from carrying out the separation. One hour later they began to be edgy and to lose their patience. Soldiers wearing masks walked in and the officer in charge said: "We can't wait any longer."

'Soon after that they called in a special squad and the struggle began. We all lay on the floor, arms linked together in resistance. They dragged away the Indians and people were falling on the roadside and thrown into the trucks. The Prime Minister and I tried to get into the van but they pulled us out. They had about five vans with armed guards on them . . . There was a lot of physical movement

7

and harassment by the soldiers. One of the ministers had a severe bruise on the neck the morning after.'

Adi Kuini described the slim figure of the Minister for Education, Tupeni Baba, hanging grimly on to the hefty frame of the Minister for Foreign Affairs, Krishna Datt, entangled with seven soldiers. She herself was linked to the diminutive Deputy Prime Minister, Harish Sharma.

'There was hardly any struggle. He was so light the soldiers just came and took him in,' she said.

As the Indians were carted off to Borron House, the Fijians left at Veiuto fell to praying. The Indians fasted throughout the day.

Monday night's terror began with the sudden arrival of a truck. 'Two mean-looking soldiers, armed, came in and started switching off lights and leaving only the verandah lights on. A few minutes after that – the Prime Minister and I were upstairs – six armed soldiers with masks stormed in. They told us to move into one room while others were ordered to stay in the living room. "You have to stay right here," they said, guns pointing at us all the while. The guards remained just outside the doorway all night, bursting in at intervals to check things out. It was the most terrifying experience. Doc and I thought we were going to lose our lives. We were saying goodbye to each other. We took out the Bible and started to pray. When we looked out of the windows we could see explosives being set up and police dogs running around. I lay with eyes open all night, expecting to die at any moment . . .'

When an army truck suddenly drove in just before 10.30 the next night (Tuesday) the Bavadras braced themselves for a second night of terror . . . 'I said, "Get ready for more hours of masked men and guns." Then I saw Colonel Wong walk in and from the expression on his face I could tell he had some good news. He had arrived with news of our release. It was just like . . . the feeling was so good that I can't express it in words . . . it was a mixture of both joy and relief.'

The prisoners fell on their knees and prayed in thankfulness for the mercy of their delivery.

2

The *Fiji Times*
14 October 1874

ANNEXATION DAY

Saturday the 10th inst. will long be celebrated in Fiji as the day on which these islands were annexed to Great Britain . . . At two o'clock precisely, about two hundred sailors and marines landed at Nasova from H.M. ships *Pearl* and *Dido*, and formed a square. About 2.30 p.m. the *Pearl* fired a salute, which announced that His Excellency the Governor had left the ship, and all were on the tiptoe of expectation. His Excellency and suite, accompanied by Commodore Goodenough, E. L. Layard, Esq., Hon. J. G. L. Innes, Esq., Attorney-General of New South Wales, Capt. Chapman, R.N., and several officers in full uniform, immediately on landing, proceeded to the Council Chamber, where they were received by King Cakobau. The King and principal chiefs and His Excellency Sir Hercules Robinson then signed the Deed of Cession in duplicate, when the King desired the Chief Secretary, Mr Thurston, to convey to His Excellency the gist of a conversation that had taken place in the early morning. Mr Thurston said:

'Your Excellency, before finally ceding Fiji to Her Majesty the Queen, the King desires to send Her Majesty, through His Excellency, the only thing he possesses that may interest her. The King sends Her Majesty his old and favourite war club, the former and, until lately, only known law in Fiji. In abandoning club law, and adopting the forms and principles of civilised societies, he laid by his own old weapon, and now, as Your Excellency sees, it bears upon it the emblems of peace and friendship. The King says that under the old law many of his people – whole tribes – passed away and disappeared, but hundreds of thousands still remain to learn and enjoy the newer and better order of things. With this war club, the King also sends his love and respects to the Queen of England, and says that he fully depends upon Her Majesty and her children who, succeeding her, shall become Kings of Fiji, to exercise a watchful control over the welfare of his children and people, who, having survived the era of barbaric law, are now submitting themselves under Her Majesty's rule, to civilisation.'

The King then handed the club to His Excellency, who said:

'I receive this club in the spirit in which it is tendered, and shall as the King desires, transmit it to Her Majesty, accompanied by a full expression of the King's wishes.'

It was, concluded the *Fiji Times*, 'a splendid conquest, without a contest; a freewill offering of which Great Britain may be justly proud!'

That was perhaps a slight overstatement, as a more celebrated journal loftily proclaimed a fortnight later:

The Times, London
30 October 1874

It is officially announced from New South Wales that Sir Hercules Robinson has accepted an unconditional surrender of the Fiji Islands, and we may conclude that this interesting group has definitely become part of Her Majesty's dominions. We cannot profess feelings of unmixed satisfaction at the intelligence. It was, perhaps, unavoidable that we should at last assent to the transfer of sovereignty so strangely forced upon us by the King, but we speak the thoughts of all sound politicians when we say that we should have been glad if the necessity of considering the offer had never arisen . . .

We shall have to walk with great circumspection to escape future trouble in relation to Fiji. The King has unconditionally surrendered the sovereignty of the Islands, but we know from experience, if experience on such a point were necessary, how difficult it is to ascertain with precision the authority of a King of such communities as that of Fiji . . . It is idle to apply to a half savage race the notions of political organisation suggested by the present state of Europe. We do not dwell upon the twenty thousand unreclaimed cannibals who inhabit the uplands of Fiji, and are content to treat this element of the question as non-existent . . .

All the land in Fiji is appropriated, but only as tribal, and not as individual, property and the notion of selling land was unknown among them until the pioneers of British civilisation tried to educate some of their chiefs to understand it . . .

The cession of sovereignty by the King, even if we treat it as a perfectly serious and complete transaction, leaves wholly untouched the question of land rights in the Islands, and one of the first cares of the Government of the new Crown Colony will be to ascertain the native customs and ideas relative to land rights, and to provide for the formalities and sanctions under which a transfer of tribal land might be recognised and enforced . . .

3 October 1932

After a lapse of fifty-eight years, King Cakobau's war club was formally returned to Fiji.

'I have it in command of His Majesty King George V,' said the Speaker of the Legislative Council, 'to present the club on his behalf to this House with the following message:

'"Since its presentation by King Cakobau to Her Majesty Queen Victoria this mace has had an honoured place among the Royal Treasures in Windsor Castle.

'"His Majesty now returns the mace for ceremonial use in the Legislative Council of Fiji, as a visible token of his abiding concern for the welfare of his Fijian people, of whose unswerving loyalty he is deeply sensible."'

10 October 1970

At a formal and dignified ceremony before a gathering of thousands at Albert Park in Suva, the instruments of constitutional government for the newly independent Dominion of Fiji were handed by His Royal Highness the Prince of Wales to the first Prime Minister, Ratu Sir Kamisese Kapaiwai Tuimacilai Mara. It was a moment of heady historic significance as the ultimate responsibility for the good government and protection of all the peoples of Fiji was passed back by the sovereign and by the sovereign Parliament to Fiji and its own institutions. Thus, ninety-six years after the chiefs had entrusted the administration of Fiji and given the protection of its people and land into the hands of Queen Victoria, her royal descendant relinquished that trust to the successors of the ceding chiefs in a Fiji that was different beyond the imaginings of those who had gone before.

So different as for it to seem incomprehensible that in 1643 Abel Tasman warned that the islands should be avoided as the natives were involved in almost constant internecine warfare. But was it so different? Maybe Tasman had the measure of Fiji after all. Could it be that the colonial era was just a hiccup in the historic evolution of a people whose elemental character was beginning to re-emerge in a confused challenge to and within the traditional chiefly social structure: a challenge dressed up as communal, racial or religious conflict of a kind that, in this century alone, has afflicted so many otherwise benign lands – Cyprus, Sri Lanka, New Caledonia, Lebanon, Israel, Ireland and other less salubrious sanctuaries of the human race? 'Tribal conspiracy in Fiji coup', the *Samoa Observer* had said.

It is too soon to be certain. The motivations for human action and reaction are rarely simple and straightforward. More often than not, a combination of factors and influences is at work; not least of these factors are timing, opportunity and a modicum of luck. Plus courage – or the absence of it.

As the Fiji celebrations continued into the night of 10 October 1970, a service of thanksgiving and dedication to commemorate the independence of the new state was held in London's Westminster Abbey. The sermon was given by the Right Reverend John Vockler, a former Bishop in Polynesia. He had this to say:

We look forward to the future with hope and in faith . . . Fiji must accept, as it has so far, the realities of its character as a multi-racial society and all of its citizens must strive for such an understanding of that character as will enable it to do what it well could do – and many of us hope and pray it will do – that is, set an example to our disordered world, of harmony and goodwill based on an acceptance of what is true and valuable in its diverse cultures. That will not always be easy, and impatience will tempt some to seek short-cuts to more immediate aims. If that temptation can be resisted, there will be built up a real and lasting unity: not uniformity; but a unity springing from an harmonious diversity . . .

With goodwill and a genuine desire for national unity, Fiji can show the whole world that it is possible for men and women of different races and religions to live together in harmony and peace . . . Fijian, Indian, Chinese, and white men can, if they give themselves to Fiji and her needs, enrich one another and the common life, by their own gifts and talents being placed at the disposal of all. Christian, Hindu, Muslim, and Sikh – if they will enter into a creative dialogue – can together, with respect for one another, build the spiritual foundations on the basis of which a great Pacific nation can grow.

But this will only happen if there is a genuine mutual respect which accepts the honesty and integrity of those from whom we differ, preserves the possibility of creative tension and of genuine difference of opinion. There is thus required of Fiji's citizens and leaders true tolerance and deep charity by which all can rise above self interest and seek the common good.

Five years after cession in 1874, the first shipload of five hundred labourers arrived from India to work in the developing fields of sugarcane, to plant, to cut, to transport and to crush in the factories of Vitilevu and Vanualevu. They were 'indentured' workers, committed for a specified contract period of five years to an assigned employer, housed in 'labour lines', paid a pittance and provided with a sea passage back to India, if they wanted it, five years after satisfactory completion of the indenture. Even from this kind of commercial bondage, most stayed on in the cane fields and factories. They were in the main from the United Provinces or South India. Their depressed living prospects in India itself offered no magnetic attraction to go back home to Calcutta or Madras. For almost four decades from 1879 until 1916, some sixty thousand made the same journey for the same purpose to become, in due time, small farmers on land on which they had little security or likelihood of acquiring it. Their numbers grew to such an extent that by the time of the 1956 national census, the immigrant Indians outnumbered the indigenous Fijians. By 1987 about half the population of close to three quarters of a million were ethnic Indians: lawyers, doctors, teachers, magistrates, accountants, nurses, tailors, shopkeepers, transport operators, building contractors, carpenters, taxi and bus drivers, cooks, clerks, mill workers, canecutters and money men of one kind or another. The Indian stake in the economy was not, however, universal, and most remained poor. Australian capital had run the sugar industry until it was nationalised; Australian companies still monopolised the gold mining industry and controlled much of the cargo-carrying shipping and air services; while the copra planters of Ovalau, Lomaiviti and Taveuni were an anachronistic reminder of the past commercial influence of early settler families.

With independence in 1970, the European dominance in government and commerce that was a feature of the colonial era passed into the oblivion of the sunset scotch and soda. Or four. From then on, the two main races came to the forefront of the social, political and economic stage. Those of mixed European and Pacific island blood rapidly changed gear as they discovered the desirable

13

affiliation to seek. Foreign investment capital switched from patronage of the Fijian to pursuit of his patrimony; while young, aggressive, often foreign-educated, Fijian commoners began increasingly to stamp their mark on the Fiji social and political scene; and to question the assumptions, pattern and style of Fijian chiefly leadership in a modern world. The reaction of the chiefs, adjusting as they had done to the requirements of a political system of electoral suffrage, was to seek to ensure that privilege and leadership by right of birth continued in parallel with the electoral process and the hustings.

There was a stumbling block. The development of a trade union movement was nurtured sporadically by Whitehall and the colonial government: tolerated, but viewed with suspicion in the sugar, gold and copra industry strongholds of European commercial dominance and influence. By the 1950s young Fijians, male and female, began to drift to the towns and often stayed on in breach of the regulation under which they, Fijians only, could by law be returned to their villages. Unemployment, overcrowding, social dislocation and money shortage in the new economy all began to inflame racial tensions and to increase urban crime. With no official minimum wage and no effective consultative machinery for achieving a job return sufficient to maintain an even basic family livelihood and housing, the situation became fraught with incoherent discontent and frustration. In a 1984 study for the University of the South Pacific, *Protest and Dissent in the Colonial Pacific*, authors Peter Hempenstall and Noel Rutherford concluded:

> The alienation of the Fijian working class in the towns, and the stresses caused by the high level of unemployment and the low level of wages, produced another phenomenon – a partial fusing of the various ethnic groupings of workers into something like a single proletariat with common interests and a common enemy – the employers, who were mostly, of course, white. The European community was totally unaware of the alignments that were developing. They believed that the Fijians were the most loyal and devoted of protégés who depended on their European allies to protect them from the more economically sophisticated Indians. Such a view was entirely tenable in the villages, but in the towns, especially in Suva and among the unskilled workers and unemployed, the platitudes were beginning to wear very thin.

> The development of a sort of alliance between Indian and Fijian workers, against all the predictions and expectations of the whites,

was no doubt the result of shared disadvantages and common interests. However, it required nurturing by a perceptive leadership before inter-racial barriers could be overcome. One leader, who had great influence among Fijians, was Apisai (at that time calling himself Mohammed) Tora, Fiji's first avowed communist. Tora had soldiered for the British in the Malaya emergency, but had been politicised by his experiences there and converted to the communist cause. On his return to Fiji, he became involved in the newly organised trade union movement, and when the Wholesale and Retail Workers General Union was formed in 1958, he became President of its North Western branch. Tora was an effective speaker and constantly exhorted his listeners that white businessmen were the enemies, not the friends, of Fijian workers. 'Fiji is a white man's heaven, but a black man's hell,' he told one audience. Tora, however, was in Lautoka on the other side of Fiji from the capital, Suva. In Suva, the President of the WRWGU was a Fijian chief, Ratu Meli Gonewai. Ratu Meli had great influence with the Fijian members of the union, but was essentially a moderate and conservative figurehead. Effective power in the union belonged to its young secretary, James Anthony, a man of mixed race with a Christian Indian–Irish–Polynesian background. He was, as he himself claimed, 'the brains behind it'.

The so-called 'disturbances' in December 1959 were organised by these men. The trouble arose from, or perhaps formed part of, the efforts to shut down Suva by the denial of oil supplies, except for essential services. The pent-up frustrations of the crowds who gathered in the streets and the potential damage to operations at Nadi airport, in the sugar mills, to public transport and to water supplies resulted in serious confrontation with the colonial administration and the police. Relations and confidence deteriorated and then vanished as statements and counter-statements inflamed rather than pacified the union leaders and their supporters. Requests for public meetings were denied. The temperature heated up as gangs began to roam and destroy when attempts were made to distribute petrol. Police riot units moved in; orders for crowd dispersal were given and ignored with jeering and catcalls. Tear gas merely set off rampaging crowds to leave a trail of destruction and looting behind. Stones, blocks of wood, concrete posts, the contents of shop windows (mostly from European-owned stores) were rained on the police.

A night curfew was only a breathing space after that first day.

The rioting continued into a second. Hempenstall and Rutherford again:

> The colonial administration had been taken completely by surprise by the events of Wednesday, 9 December, but when rioting broke out again next day, officialdom was better prepared . . .
>
> The Executive Council met and approved the issue of Regulations under the Public Safety Ordinance, including the granting to the police of wide powers of search and arrest without warrant, the calling up of the 2nd Territorials to assist the police, and the imposition of a 7.00 p.m. to 5.00 a.m. curfew. The most effective action of the government was, however, made through the medium of the Fijian chiefs. The Police Commissioner gave permission for a public meeting to be held in Albert Park at 2.00 p.m. at which, it was widely rumoured, Anthony and Mohammed Tora would address the crowd. People began moving towards the park at 1.00 p.m., stoning buildings along the way. The Labour Department came in for special treatment, its windows being smashed by cans of food, looted from Morris Hedstrom's Self Service Store. However, when the crowd gathered in Albert Park they discovered that they were to be addressed, not by strike leaders, but by the highest chief in the land, the Vunivalu, Ratu George Cakobau, and other leading chiefs including Ratu Edward Cakobau and Ratu K. K. T. Mara. Mr B. D. Lakshman, an Indian member of the Legislative Council also spoke to the meeting.
>
> Ratu George did not say very much but his words, coming from the most revered of Fijian chiefs, had enormous impact on his Fijian audience. He said:
>
> 'I do not want to stop your meeting. I want to speak of the damage you have done. You are not young, and you know right from wrong. But whatever you do, remember the name of Fiji. The reputation of the Fijians is up to you. That is all.'
>
> Similar short but solemn admonitions were given by Ratu Mara and Ratu Edward Cakobau. It was thus a chastened audience which listened to the last speaker, Mr Lakshman. When he sought an assurance from the crowd that there would be no more violence, he was given it unanimously. The crowd left Albert Park in an orderly manner and there was no further violence. The riot had ended . . .
>
> On the next day, Friday 11 December, the calm continued, and property owners began to relax and to clean up the mess . . . By this time, however, a new force was being thrown into the scales with the active intervention of the Fijian chiefs.

Britain had ruled Fiji for nearly a century through the 'Ratu System', whereby matters affecting Fijians were dealt with by their own chiefs. Through this system of 'indirect rule' the chiefs had not only preserved the authority they had enjoyed in pre-colonial days, but had augmented it. The chiefs had become part of the power structure of the colonial regime and to some extent beneficiaries of western capitalism. One of the factors helping to maintain their privileged position, and indeed the whole colonial system, was the fear felt by Fijians over the aspirations and ambitions of the large and growing population of Indians. An unspoken contract of mutual support existed between the Fijians represented by their chiefs on the one hand and the British Administration and western business interests on the other. The appearance of a coalition between Indian workers and Fijian workers combined as a more or less united proletariat against white domination and exploitation, was very disturbing to the chiefs. One of their leading spokesmen, Ratu K. K. T. Mara, described it as 'a revolution'. They moved quickly to use all their influence to suppress the violence, to end the strike, and to break up the new and unacceptable alliance . . . Ratu Edward Cakobau expressed his shame that Fijians had been led on by 'other people' who were using them for their own ends. The same theme was hammered home even more forcefully by Ratu Penaia Ganilau, the Roko Tui Cakaudrove, to admonish the people from Macuata, Cakaudrove and Bua. They were warned of other people with 'sweet mouths' who would lead Fijians astray . . .

The constant reiteration by the chiefs that the violence of the preceding days had brought shame on the good name of Fijians was a potent weapon. So too was the repeated suggestion that Fijians had been made the dupes of Indian agitators . . .

Strikes are one of the few means wage labourers have of protesting against what they perceive as exploitation. In the Pacific Islands wage rates persisted at levels providing only minimal subsistence at a time when in metropolitan countries they had risen dramatically . . .

As anywhere, once trade unions became established, strikes were likely to become a vehicle of protest. Fiji, however, was something of a special case. Indian workers had some experience of strike action. Fijians, on the other hand, with the exception of a few minor stoppages at the Vatukoula Gold Mines, had none. Moreover, when Fijians began to be involved in wage labour in the towns, strike action by urban workers was inhibited by the racial tensions between Indian and Fijian. Employers became convinced that they would never combine in a unified effort to win a better deal. The events of 1959 shattered this illusion. For a while, Indians and Fijians did unite in a common cause, and when they did the colony was shaken to its foundations.

The Fijian chiefs whose position and status was threatened by what they saw as an unholy alliance, moved quickly to break it up. Both the suppression of rioting and the negotiated end of the strike owed most to their intervention. Moreover, when the strike was over they sponsored the establishment of Fijian unions in all major industries, so that Fijians should not be 'corrupted' and 'led astray' by Indian 'agitators'. The consequence was that the co-operation between Indian and Fijian workers against white employers, which was the most significant aspect of the 1959 strike, proved ephemeral. Fijian workers were weaned quickly from their new found alliance, and the status quo ante was quickly restored. The wage earners of Fiji remain divided on racial more than class lines.

Or so it may have seemed, but the issues were becoming increasingly complex.

It took a week before a settlement was reached, an agreement was signed and the strike was over. The oil workers returned to work with an interim increase in wages pending an arbitration award. The high chiefs of Fiji had, by their prestige and acceptability, prevailed – in 1959. Opposition to their diktat had melted away. But the lesson had been learned as, much later, the action script still provided for some of the same players. Prime Minister Mara took Apisai-Mohammed Tora into the Alliance Cabinet; and, later still, Governor General Ganilau wrestled with the consequences of the dissolution of a Parliament which had seen the emergence of another alliance. It was one that again crossed the barriers of race, but this time with the more potent nationwide endorsement of the ballot box. A Labour–National Federation Coalition with a Fijian medical practitioner at its head and an Indian lawyer as his deputy presented a real and dangerous threat, not to the paramountcy of Fijian interests, but to the paramountcy of Fijian chiefly interests twenty-eight years later in 1987.

The crucial year of change was 1965. With the granting of a large measure of internal self-government to Fiji, the chiefs found themselves obliged to make the transition from leadership by birth and inherited status to leadership by electoral qualification and consent. Custom and politics had joined forces and, paradoxically, thus provided the germ of the separation to come. It is difficult now to believe that with the passing of Ratu Mara from long leadership of his country's constitutional government, there will again be an elected Prime Minister with comparable high chiefly status. The year 1987 was the watershed not only for democracy but for the Fijian chiefly system and social structure. A new and powerful factor had emerged in Fijian society and in Fiji as a whole: the army and the gun. Authoritarian obedience would not now just be expected. It would be ensured by being enforced: overtly and covertly.

On 21 April, Tora, having been re-elected to Parliament on 12 April, went to Dr Bavadra's village of Veiseisei in west Vitilevu. Speaking in Fijian, he gave warning that Fijians had been dispossessed in their own land and that it was time for them to strike out against their enemies. On 10 May, Tora was arrested and charged with sedition and inciting racial antagonism. The case was to become the focus of increasing inter-racial tension. Which, with his singular experience of such things, he was well qualified to calculate in advance.

A week earlier, the Lautoka offices of a law firm were set on fire. One of the partners was Jai Ram Reddy, former leader of the National Federation Party and appointed by the new Prime Minister to be Minister of Justice and Attorney General in the Coalition Government. Charges of arson were laid and a member of the Fiji Senate appeared in court to face them. He was Jona Qio, nominated to the Upper House in 1985 by the Great Council of Chiefs. No plea was taken and the accused was released on bail to appear again four days later. It was not to be. The 14 May coup intervened. And it was no coincidence that Senator Qio, like Tora, was one of the founder members of an extreme Fijian movement whose actions were to be of crucial influence on events in the months to come.

The day after Tora's speech, the Governor General warned intending demonstrators against the newly elected government not to break the law. So, perhaps, a march of over four thousand Fijians through Suva streets on 24 April was successfully negotiated as a peaceful but racially-charged anti-government demonstration. The following day a similar street march was held in Lautoka. This too was uneventful, but Tora warned of a civil disobedience campaign to come. On 6 May Fijian demonstrators were refused permission to hold a mass meeting in Suva to coincide with the formal opening of Parliament on 8 May. That day, nineteen of the twenty-four Alliance members boycotted the swearing-in ceremony, claiming that a crowd outside the party's offices in Suva had prevented their leaving. Three days later, on 11 May, they were sworn in without incident and the stage was set for the grand military intervention to save Fiji from itself.

3

Fiji – the way the world should be
– Tourism publicity slogan, 1987

Friday 15 May 1987: Coup Plus One

'Are you still going to Fiji?' they asked in Auckland when the coup was twenty-four hours old.

'Of course.'

'Do you think . . . well . . . do you think you'll get in?'

'I imagine so, if Air New Zealand is operating. I don't believe the problem is one of getting in. It will be one of getting out again in a week's time when the effects of all this have begun to bite. The Pacific is not Africa. There are no meandering land borders to cross; just islands with lots of ocean. So we shall see.'

But first I flew south from Auckland to Christchurch and Dunedin. It was an exercise in nostalgia. Below, at 8,000 feet, was the volcanic cone of Mount Egmont, the Fuji-like landmark of pastoral Taranaki and the source of the bitter winter winds of New Plymouth. Thence across an expectedly translucent Tasman Sea, to the coastal sounds of Nelson and Marlborough and on to the cathedral city of Christchurch. Early snows had already capped the upper peaks of the Southern Alps, that great divide between the plains of Canterbury and the wastes of Westland.

Further south still is Dunedin, the capital city of the Province of Otago. Not without justification, it likes to think of itself as the antipodean Edinburgh. I was born in the suburb of St Clair; and it was to its windswept beach that I first went. The trams were no more and the rush-hour traffic was like London at two a.m. The antarctic rollers still crashed and pounded on the sand; and I marvelled that I had, with a child's temerity, learned how to body surf in such unwelcoming waters.

On the radio in the motel bedroom that evening I listened for three hours as two tiny local commercial radio stations ran fevered

21

phone-ins on the Fiji coup. In Dunedin, at least, democracy was not dead. I slept badly. By Sunday, it would be Suva.

Sunday 17 May 1987: Coup Plus Three

TE 58 was scheduled to depart Auckland for Nadi at 16.05. It was a short-haul Boeing 767 on a shuttle to Fiji and back, the one-a-week Air New Zealand flight to do so. Auckland's international air terminal is not the busiest there is. Check-in was straightforward: a Frequent Traveller Club pass eased the way for first-class reception on an economy return excursion booking from London. I bought an open-dated ticket for the Nadi–Suva sector. TE 58 was due to reach Nadi at 19.10 and the last scheduled Air Pacific service for Suva was FJ 120 at 19.45, too tight for computerised confirmation. There were seats on that post-coup internal flight, but they could not be pre-sold at Auckland. A connection was possible, just – if TE 58 arrived on time and everything clicked, like immigration and baggage unloading. Not otherwise. Unless Air Pacific was running behind schedule. That was not unknown.

Passenger loading was prompt and at 16.00 the doors were closed. At 16.30 the captain apologised: 'We are missing one passenger. His baggage is on board, but you will appreciate that for security reasons we cannot leave at present.'

Indeed, but the omens for getting on to Suva with no confirmed booking out of Nadi were thus not good. Air Pacific might hold, if there were a few likely passengers, timetabled connection or not. It would depend on a number of things. Not least was the mislaid Samoan who clambered up the aircraft steps five minutes later and made his way, to the silent disapproval of 120 passengers, to his rear row seat. By 16.45 we were out over the Hauraki Gulf and away to the north, the Whangaparoa Peninsula below and the Coromandel hills to the east. Let there be tail winds, I muttered, as the captain revealed '. . . and fortunately our flight time to Nadi tonight should be only two hours and thirty minutes'. It might still be possible. A signal was sent ahead for Air Pacific: two arriving passengers wanted to go on to Suva. Timely, it transpired, since the flight was about to be cancelled. There were no other passengers.

The flight to Nadi gave time for reflection. There were plenty of questions, but at that stage, not many answers. How would it be, this new traumatised Fiji? So different from the one I first met as I stepped jauntily down the ship's gangway to colonial duty in the Fiji of 1949. That was thirty-eight years back into a largely forgotten past; and now, to many, an unlamented one.

Air New Zealand touched down only ten minutes behind schedule. The aprons were empty apart from one small Air Pacific de Havilland Twin Otter. That looked like FJ 120. I moved fast along the familiar open walkway in tropical darkness. Nadi, the sign said, in large letters (not Nandi as it is pronounced).

I am the first at the desk of the immigration officer.

'Welcome to Fiji.'

'Thank you.'

'How long are you staying?'

'About a week.'

'Have you been to Fiji before?'

I hesitate, tempted to say, 'Yes, for about twenty years or more.' What purpose would it serve? Never volunteer information unless there is good reason. And you can profit from it.

'Yes.'

There are no supplementary questions. Just the flourish of the stamp on the blue pad and another passport entry.

FIJI

Imm.Act 1971 Sect 9

Visitor

17 May 1987

Entered Nadi

Valid for one month only unless extended

'I hope you enjoy your stay.'

Comforting. Now for customs. Down the open wooden staircase to the baggage hall below. Empty. Ten minutes later some baggage begins to emerge through the black plastic flaps of the hatch and on to the rollers. The usual sense of mild relief when familiar suitcases come through; and wonderment that they are not in Tokyo by mistake. A trolley. Bags loaded. Green channel, not a customs officer in sight. I am in, unscathed. Big deal.

The height of the tourist season. The public concourse outside should be alive with voluble taxi drivers, handout holders, and pretty girls from the Visitors' Bureau or the Hotel Association anxious to latch on to the uninitiated and adventurously unbooked. It is sub-dued and near-deserted. I walk from International Arrivals to the Departures Terminal, past unlit windows, locked doors.

The concourse clock shows 19.35. The flight to Suva is operating and still open.

I put my cases on the scales and collect a boarding card. Armed soldiers stand behind the check-in desks for two international flights. The counter staff are nervous and jittery. Some are already beginning to shout. Weary passengers, checking in, shout back. Tempers heat and rise. The insults begin – race, colour, country, religion, sex – the extremities of human abuse provoked by exhaustion and fear of the visible guns.

'Where did you come from?'

'Sydney.'

'Is that where you live?'

'Yes but I am going to Honolulu tonight.'

'How long have you been in Fiji?'

'Seven days.'

'What is your work?'

'I'm a businessman.'

'What business do you do?'

'All sorts.'

'I asked what sort of business you do.'

'. . . I sell electronic equipment. You know, adding machines, calculators, that sort of thing.'

'What else?'

'Nothing else.'

'Please open your briefcase.'

'Very well.'

'What is this?'

'It is a report I have done. For my business, a sort of survey.'

'A survey of what?'

'Of Fiji.'

'Of Fiji? I shall have to take that for examination.'

'It is a market survey. That is all. Nothing to do with politics. Just selling more calculators.' The voice faltered. He was a little man, the right sort of victim for a bully. 'It is my only copy.'

'My instructions are that no reports on Fiji can be taken out by passengers now. None. None at all.'

The official took the document and threw it beneath the counter. There was a moment before the enormity got home.

The businessman was angry now, and frightened. 'You have taken my property without my permission and for no reason. This won't be the last you hear of this. I want your name and I want a receipt.'

'. . . and all passengers should now be on the aircraft . . .'

'No name. No receipt. I do not have any. You can leave now. Or, if you wish, you can stay back in custody while these papers are examined in Suva, isn't it?'

24

'Not me!' His breath came faster. 'I'll go, finally and for ever, from your goddamn country. Bloody bloody Fiji.' Then softly, as he moved past the emigration desk to the departure lounge, 'Bastard'.

'. . . I told you I left the cases with the man you say is now off duty. I saw him put them over there.' She was young and frightened and white. Her first time abroad, I guessed, and no longer on the holiday of her dreams.

'They are not there now,' said the Fijian soldier behind the counter. 'They have been taken away for examination. Or stolen. It is not my job. You have no receipt.'

'The man wouldn't give me a receipt. He refused. Like I told you – he just took the cases and put them over there.' She pointed. To nothing.

The soldier handed back the passport and turned away, no longer interested. The Indian airline clerk said gently:

'I am sorry. Here is your boarding card.'

'What about my cases? My new clothes. I can't just leave without them. You have ruined my holiday.' Tears came. Hysterics were close.

'The final boarding call was five minutes ago. They will be closing the doors. If you wish to catch the flight . . .'

'You fucking Indians and Fijians. You deserve each other. Beat each other's brains out for all I care, you black beasts. I hope your country rots in hell and you with it.'

'White bitch. Yes sir, can I help you?'

'. . . I told that other clerk, over there, the booking was made at the Qantas office in Suva. I was there. I did it myself. They entered it on the computer. You have my ticket with the confirmation endorsed on it. How long do I have to put up with this crap? Just give me a boarding card and seat number and let me get the hell out of here.'

'As I am saying, sir, Suva office is closed; we have no record of any Suva reservation, and the flight is overbooked. We are having computer trouble . . .'

'Bugger the computer trouble . . . That's not my problem.'

'I'm afraid there are a great many people desiring now to leave Fiji.' He pointed to the hundreds, mainly Indians, and the piles of nondescript baggage, in the departure terminal. 'I am putting you on the waiting list, but . . .'

'You will not put me on the waiting list. You will put me on the bloody flight. Give me the telephone. Get me the manager in Suva.'

'He is not there.'

'Well, get me the Nadi manager.'

'That is the same as Suva manager. He is not there too.'

'Well, wherever he is, get him. Just get him so I can clear up this stupidity now, and fast.'

'I'm sorry, sir. That I cannot do. I am putting you . . .'

'Look. If I don't get on that 'plane, you and Qantas will hear about this in big black dirty front-page ink. I have copy to file tonight and a strategy meeting tomorrow morning in Sydney. Did you get that? I am the press, you bloody little Indian man.'

The clerk blinked. His hands trembled a little. He put his fingertips together. He could take no more. 'I suggest you shut your big mouth, sir. You see those Fijian soldiers. They are coming over. They are hearing you shouting. I am now off duty. Excuse me, please.' He turned and slipped through the door marked 'Airline Personnel Only' and was gone.

'Qantas Airways announces the departure of its delayed flight QF 94 for Brisbane and Sydney. All passengers should now proceed to Gate No. Six and await further instructions . . .'

The boarding call for Suva came none too soon. That flight too was late. There had been some uncertainty as to whether Nausori airport flight control would be manned and the airport open for night landings. It is a twenty-five-minute flight south-east above the mountainous interior of Vitilevu, across the dividing line between the 'dry' zone in the west and the 'wet' zone in the east. A young moon made it possible, even at night, to detect the dramatic change in topography and vegetation which lies astride an island the size of Puerto Rico. We came in low over the serried iron roofs of the Indian township of Nausori, the Rewa river bridge visible to the right and the runway lights of the airport comfortingly ahead.

The small airport terminal building was deserted and quiet – none of the usual hubbub of perspiring taxi drivers with waiting cars, no Air Pacific bus and no one to meet me. I tried the telephone. There was no reply. In the dark and mounting gloom, an Australian voice said:

'Like a lift to Suva? I have a car.'

'Thank you. I would. My arrangements seem to have come un-stuck; and there is nothing else.'

'Right. Here we are. Bags in the boot. Get yourself inside. I'm in computers. You with the Government?'

'Used to be. Long time ago.'

'Official visit? On business?'

'No. Just, well, just sentiment and family: a daughter, son-in-law and two young grandchildren. You know, usual sort of thing, but not quite the usual circumstances for such a visit – as I expect I shall discover.'

'Good on yer.'

The journey was otherwise silent. Radio Fiji was off the air. There was no traffic until we reached Nasinu. The Samabula streets were empty. He dropped me at the Piccadilly Taxis stand. In spite of its name, it has for years been just a wooden shack with a telephone inside, opposite the Anglican Cathedral in Gordon Street. It is one of the oldest and most reliable of Suva taxi businesses. There was a solitary car and driver. I gave my destination in Tamavua and we negotiated a price. It was above the normal. I did not complain.

The Suva peninsula thrusts out, thumblike, from the coastline of south-east Vitilevu. Its fine natural harbour was not least of the reasons for the transfer of the seat of government from the old capital of Levuka on the island of Ovalau in 1882. The official hejira, the *Fiji Times* called it, as the Governor left for Suva on 30 August.

A mile or so offshore, the gentle white line of broken water breaches the reef edge. When the tide is low, the wide expanse of the exposed coral is a human hunting ground for myriads of trapped fish, sea snakes, molluscs and crabs. There is a break in the reef which marks the entrance to Suva Harbour; but navigation is far from straightforward, as the wrecks of fishing boats give constant reminder. The 1952 hurricane, the eye of which went directly through Suva, reached wind gusts of 170 m.p.h. When one of these blasts briefly touched 180 m.p.h., it broke the anemometer of the Royal New Zealand Air Force weather station at Laucala Bay. Then it was that the Union Steam Ship Company's passenger-cargo vessel *Tofua* of 5,500 tons dragged its anchors and slid relentlessly on to a sandbank. There was no gentle white line at that time.

The tropical island city of Suva is not in the same league as Singapore or San Juan; but it had become the preferred metropolitan centre of the South Pacific. Over the past twenty years, it has developed a style of its own whilst preserving some of the more historic buildings, gardens and avenues; and an improved standard of design and construction has given it some claim to modest distinction. It is diverse, colourful, sensibly planned and far from uninteresting. None of which looked possible when, in 1880, the *Fiji Times*, then in Levuka, fulminated about the frightful prospect of the replacement of Levuka by Suva as the capital of the new British colony:

> In resuming the question of the relative suitability of Suva and Levuka as the site for the future capital of Fiji, we would next direct His Excellency's attention to the general insalubrity of the situation.
>
> Upon glancing at the plan of the proposed city of Suva, the feature most prominently impressed upon the mind is that almost one-eighth of its entire area is represented by mangrove swamps.
>
> In close proximity to these fetid and pestiferous marshes, a town is laid out upon a plan which upon paper suggests nothing so forcibly as the idea of a dilapidated geometric spider's web after a strong gale.
>
> It is intended that, with the exception of the one business thoroughfare, the lanes and alleys, by courtesy called the streets, of this abortion of a city shall be but forty feet wide, and it is scarcely necessary for anyone to be gifted with a spirit of divination to foresee the consequences.
>
> Shut out from the sea breeze by their own tortuous winding, the byways of this rookery appear as though specially designed to retain the malarious exhalations which continually arise from these mephitic swamps by which the town is bounded, and the unfortunate inhabitants, condemned perpetually to inhale the contaminated atmosphere, must of necessity suffer in health even should they escape the very probable chance of pestilence or epidemic disease.

The taxi driver set off into Macarthur Street, Victoria Parade and Renwick Road. The banks, airline offices, travel agencies and arcade shops were dark and shuttered. The Garrick Hotel, scene of water-front revelry for over sixty years, was silent now. Then, up into Waimanu Road, past the Lilac Theatre, dubbed New Lilac after it had, in the 1960s, received a coat of paint and some less uncomfort-able seats; and on to the twists and turns before the Colonial War Memorial Hospital.

The driver slowed as pedestrians were picked out by the car lights. A crowd ahead – men, women and children, standing, waiting, subdued. A road block manned by armed soldiers stopping and searching the few passing vehicles. Barbed-wire barriers stretched across the road. Rolls of wire strewn around the entrance and driveway to an imposing stone mansion. Lights ablaze and silent, it stood beyond the reach of those keeping vigil outside the grounds. Memories flooded back. Known as Rairaiwaqa, it had been the Suva residence of the Borron family, owners of Mago island copra estate in Lau. As close friends of Ratu Sir Lala Sukuna, they had rented the house for twenty years to the distinguished first Fijian national leader. There he lived in aloof, but dignified, grandeur amid the rich staircase panelling, Persian carpets and polished floors, a complete man of two worlds. On his death in 1958 and the laying of his chiefly remains in customary state within the house, the mournful disharmonies of the davui or conch shell had sounded day and night until the body was placed aboard the *Adi Maopa* for Ratu Sukuna's last journey to his resting place in Lakeba.

Otherwise abiding silence. And silence again now. For a vastly different reason. Inside, in enforced detention that night, were Indian elected members of the Bavadra Coalition Government. A lugubrious fate for a residence which had, long after Sukuna's death, been given by the Borrons to the Government of Fiji and used by the Alliance for official VIP guests.

With a cursory glance in the taxi, the soldiers waved us on. At the Samabula police station, the car turned left, then right again at the top of Edinburgh Drive, the Assemblies of God Calvary Church, and into Princes Road. It is a much-used route out of Suva to the lush and elevated suburban pleasures of cooler air, eye-catching panoramas of land and reef-girt ocean, plus the compatible proximity of well-shod neighbours. The small-scale Beverly Hills of Suva, Tamavua now has need of burglar alarms and guard-dog protection: for on the fringe of these select surroundings is Tamavua village, a Fijian dormitory for Suva labour – perennially overcrowded with neglected and poorly built houses and a traditional haven for the tough, the rough and the alienated. It is not at night a place into which to venture alone.

I became uneasy. The street lamps were out and houses shuttered. The short access path was off to the left and down into the unlit bush. We had, I thought, missed it, when the car beam picked out a name plate on the side of the road – MILES JOHNSON – one of the directors of the *Fiji Sun*, lawyer son of a former commercial magnate and Legislative Council member. We turned slowly in, our lights ablaze. I got out, walking in the beam, and knocked. The large figure of Miles Johnson rose from his chair, peered and called out, uncertain and questioning.

'Can you tell me where 'Atu's house is?'

'Yes. Go back out, then right, and the turning is a few hundred

yards away. Just beside Ratu Edward's old house. You remember?'
  'Thank you. I do remember.'

One of the four notable chiefs of the Fijian people to follow in the
footsteps of Ratu Sir Lala Sukuna, Ratu Edward – Etuate Tugi
Tuivanuavou – Cakobau was born in Bau in 1908. The half-brother
of Queen Salote Tupou of Tonga, he was thus known by the Tongans
as Tungi Fisi (the Tugi of Fiji). His warm charm, innate dignity and
gentle courtesy were to win hearts around the world – in
the circles of rugby and cricket, in universities, schools and
teacher-training colleges, in war-torn jungles of the Solomons and
Malaya, and above all in his capacity to transcend race in his
wide-ranging friends and admirers. He was a significant and
successful breaker of racial divides in Fiji itself – always consider-
ate, never condescending, and the teller of stories in a manner
which often made the telling funnier than the story itself. In a
hotel lounge or a club he was rarely without a willing audience;
and it was invariably inter-racial. Not for nothing had he been
one of the founders of the Union Club in Suva where Fijians,
Indians, Europeans and part-Europeans met and mixed in colonial
days when it was the exception so to do.
  His son, Ratu Epeli Nailatikau, was outraged by the military
coup, in which he was replaced by the coup leader Lieutenant
Colonel Rabuka (the third-ranking army officer) as Commander
of the Royal Fiji Military Forces. Outraged, and notwithstanding
that he is the son-in-law of Ratu Mara, dismissed none the less.
Their relations were widely thought to have been less than cordial
for some time.

The car turned into the anonymous entrance, down the wooded
slope and to a double-storeyed concrete house in total darkness.
I walked around in the lights of the taxi. The garage was empty;
an unfinished meal with five places was on the kitchen table; the
beds downstairs were unoccupied. There were all the signs of a
hasty departure. It was an ominous start to the family reunion.
  We drove without speaking back down into Suva. The Tropic
Towers in Robertson Road had a room for the night. The whole
hotel in fact. I tried a call to England without success and gave
up. Tomorrow would do. Tomorrow – the day of the coup plus
four – I should have to begin to come to terms with a changed
and troubled Fiji. As 720,000 others had already been forced to
do.

7 May 1955

It had been a relatively easy first birth, the doctors said, as such births go. The verandah of the old colonial-style wooden hospital at Vaiola served as the labour ward. Delivery took place behind an ageing curtain. Easy? The contraction cries were audible in the night-locked village nearby. There, the old women awoke and nodded knowingly: 'Fonu's time come.' It was my wife's Tongan name, used universally there. Margaret is the English one.

Birth was accomplished at 1 a.m. I had become a first-time father. The Tongan clock is set at GMT plus thirteen, in accordance with the eccentric time zone established by the present King of Tonga – Taufa'ahau Tupou IV – in response to his yearning that his Polynesian kingdom should always be first in the world's day. Supposedly, the nine-pound four-ounce girl could have been the first baby born on 7 May 1955. So a Mormon missionary informed me with the eagerness of a latter-day saintly revelation.

After the christening in the great new Wesleyan church in Nuku'alofa, the child was taken in accordance with custom to the Palace in Nuku'alofa, there to be presented and held in the arms of Queen Salote Tupou. A name had been bestowed upon her by the Queen: 'Atu-o-hakautapu, the bonito fish from the sacred reef. The name of the daughter of a Tu'i Tonga (the spiritual line of Tongan kings) and not used in the Queen's family line for ten generations, was brought to the hospital from the Queen on the morning after the birth by her two daughters-in-law, Princess Mata'aho, now Queen of Tonga herself, and Princess Melenaite, the wife of Queen Salote's younger son, Prince Tu'ipelehake. The princesses came with fine mats and royal tapa cloth to express pleasure at our good fortune.

At fourteen months, the child was carted off on her first ocean voyage from Nuku'alofa to Auckland and from Wellington to the Port of London. The ship was the former royal yacht *Gothic*, one of four 15,000-ton passenger-cargo vessels deployed by the Shaw Savill Company on its United Kingdom–New Zealand trading travel route via the Panama Canal. With her father supposedly in charge, 'Atu was on the sports deck one afternoon when the ship rolled steeply in one of those Pacific oceanic surges that are far from pacific. He staggered in order to stay upright, then looked at his feet. The child was gone – with the roll – sliding to the ship's rail where, head through and legs dangling in overbalance, she was pulled back to safety. Just. At thirty-two in 1987, it was in effect to happen again.

In 1970, midway through her secondary-school years at St Cuthbert's College in Auckland, her inherited New Zealand citizenship sitting uneasily upon her, she was uprooted again to England. This was not just a few weeks' holiday. It meant not only the relinquishment of friends, but changes of school, school year, syllabus, climate, culture and environment. Cheltenham Ladies' College accepted the task of effecting this educational and sociological metamorphosis; and, surprisingly, was the academic foundation of the clever, impatient, caring social democrat who emerged with a leaving scholarship and a place at Oxford. At Wadham in 1974, she matriculated as one of the small intake of women, when the collegiate toe was first put into the uncertain waters of bisexual admission. She was amused to be sharing a staircase, bathroom and lavatory with the men – the embarrassments were theirs not hers – as the walls of tradition and donnish disapproval fell asunder around her. Absorbing with relish the liberalism and free-ranging life at Wadham, she drifted further to the left in inclination, politics and junior common room debate. The illustrious chiefly shadows of Ratu Sukuna and Ratu Mara, both men of Wadham, touched her little; and she would bridle if reminded that she was the first South Pacific island girl to go up to read Politics, Philosophy and Economics.

With Oxford behind her in 1977, the left-leaning trend continued at London University's Institute of Commonwealth Studies where, in postgraduate scholarship, she came under the influence of intellectuals and tutors with similar beliefs and inclinations. A year or so later, she started her longest, toughest period of concentrated and lonely writing and research. Her real identification with the fortunes of class and race had begun. Seven years later, she knelt before the Pro-Chancellor of the Australian National University formally to receive her Doctorate of Philosophy. Marriage to a Tongan husband, Sitiveni; two children, Siale and Anga'aefonu; labour protest marches; anti-nuclear demonstrations; the sweaty slog of Fiji field trips into the heart of the Vatukoula gold mines; and 150,000 carefully tailored words bound in Tongan scarlet and gold lay behind her.

It was 7 May again, this time in 1987; and unbeknown to those of us who celebrated at the graduation ceremony in Canberra, the Fiji coup was but seven short days away. Long since having relinquished her New Zealand nationality to become a Fiji citizen, she had, a year before, been appointed a lecturer in the department of sociology at the University of the South Pacific in Suva. Her time there, like that of democratic government in Fiji, could be running out. The guns were being oiled and loaded. She was to need all of her store of courage and rumbustious modesty to see her through the dangers brought about by her unshakeable belief in the rightness of causes, and that with rightness and sustained effort they will succeed.

Monday 18 May 1987: Coup Plus Four

Tomorrow was now today. Veni came in the Honda Civic, rusting, untidy and with tyres that would get nowhere in a British MOT test. Sitiveni is Tongan for Steven. Veni is the shortened version which the family uses. Like 'Atu, the children have Tongan and English given names. The Tongan ones are preferred for normal use. He was apologetic but warm and kissed me in the Tongan way, cheek against cheek. His bright bula shirt was wrinkled. He had come at short notice. He might not have slept.

'Good morning, Tolu'afe.' He employed my Tongan honorary title. 'I am sorry that we were away last night when you arrived. 'Atu and I were out with the children.'
'Ah.'
'In Samabula. With a few handbills.'
'Handbills? What about? For whom?'
'Just calling for the release and reinstatement of the Prime Minister and his colleagues. We were handing them out of the car as we drove around. We went home when we ran out of them.'
He smiled, but I detected a hint of uneasiness. Nothing clandestine looks quite the same in the light of day as in the comfort of all-protecting darkness. Even something so eminently reasonable.
'Did you see any soldiers?'
'No. I suppose we were lucky.'
'More than a little. And foolish.'
'You think so?'
'Yes. I have been here for only a few hours, but it seems to me that what has happened has not fully sunk in. A military coup is not a boy scout game; it is serious business. And highly dangerous, for anyone who grapples with it.'
We drove past Rairaiwaqa. The road blocks and barbed wire were unchanged; a new platoon of soldiers patrolled in their jungle green uniforms with slung automatic rifles; and the weary families of those inside the distant mansion still stood together at the side of the road.
'I suppose you are right. Maybe you should speak to 'Atu.'
'Maybe I should . . . Indeed I will.'

33

We had parted at Sydney Airport eight days before, 'Atu and Veni to return to Suva and I to Auckland. The formal splendour of the Australian National University graduation in the Canberra School of Music was now a world away.

The old Stinson house is a minor monument to past glories. It stands imperiously and imperially amidst its faded gardens on a high point in the Tamavua hills. From its cliff-edge security you look down on the little village of Solomon Islanders and to a grand sweep of the valley to the Lami river and Lami bridge, the greater Suva bay and the range of hills beyond.

The Stinsons were one of the early pioneer families to come to Fiji before and after cession to Britain in 1874. In 1905 the Stinson Company was set up. The eldest son, Charles Stinson, whose keen business sense was matched by blunderbuss singlemindedness, was a persistent advocate for the introduction of duty-free goods sales in Suva and at Nadi airport in the early 1960s. Known in his younger days, somewhat disparagingly perhaps, as Stinson the photographer, he became much more than that. Mayor of Suva for one thing and during this time needed no persuasion to give his family name to the parade in front of the Suva Civic Centre on reclaimed foreshore land.

The circular cream-washed concrete house has wide panoramic windows on both ground and first floors. It suggests the yearnings for old baronial trappings made possible by commercial success; and it was one of three or four houses built on the heights of Tamavua between the first and second world wars by European settler families of influence and money. Long since sold to an Indian property developer, it is still spoken of as 'the old Stinson house'. A fortunate convention, as events were to turn out.

'We are in our usual muddle,' said 'Atu, 'and I shall have to leave you soon to go to the USP campus.'

'Why?'

'My class will be there. I have a lecture to give this morning.'

'Are you sure that your class will be there; and isn't it just a little bit dangerous to do that?'

'Maybe, but I have some papers to hand over in town and I can't ring because the telephones are tapped and cranky. So I have to go. Rosa is here and will look after you.' Rosa was Fijian; 'Atu's loyal companion and help; and surrogate mother of the two children.

I unpacked upstairs in the peace and quiet of a glorious morning and the natural delights of the blue sea, the white reef line, the craggy hills and the cloud-scattered sky, unchanging and untouched by the human convulsion so close below.

We were virtually without news; but Suva seethed with rumour and conjecture that led inevitably to worry, uncertainty, confusion and fear. The *Fiji Times* and *Fiji Sun* had been closed down by the army the day after the coup. Newspaper staff were removed from their offices by armed soldiers. The buildings were occupied and surrounded by the military. Radio Fiji, the official station, was under strict censorship and military control. It broadcast only what was issued to it. FM 96, the commercial station, which had managed to get out the Governor General's first post-coup statement, was off the air, its future uncertain.

At a time of such desperate human worry and tension, the whole population of Fiji – spread variously through its coasts, hills, valleys, cane fields and its outlying islands, small and large – was dependent for information about what was happening in its own country on the short-wave broadcasts (only, of course, in English) of Radio Australia, Radio New Zealand and the BBC World Service. We kept Radio Australia on constantly. It jettisoned scheduled programmes in order to provide the best available up-to-date news to the people of Fiji, a service on which all came to rely. Eye-witness accounts of occurrences in Suva and elsewhere made their originators far from popular with the military regime. The stories filed by foreign correspondents were the direct cause of the increasing harassment, brutality and invasion of their privacy that many reporters and photographers were to suffer. They could have been in Lebanon or Chile or Haiti.

In the afternoon, I looked through the piles of pre-election pamphlets and speeches in support of the Coalition campaign which lay in open profusion on chairs, bookshelves, tables and desks. I got them together as evening came and 'Atu returned, her task accomplished before the inquisitive eyes of two observing soldiers.

'I think we should destroy these.'

'Why?'

'They are evidence of your support of a government that is now deposed. Your sympathies are known. Your activities listed. It is standard stuff in circumstances such as these to undertake a search of property occupied by sympathisers and workers. It is just a matter of time before they come; and there is not much of that left. We must get rid of them – and I am going to do so.'

She demurred. 'You can't just burn everything. I have some important material here.'

'Exactly,' I said, 'and that is precisely why it has to go. Plus diaries and telephone numbers. I am sorry but there is no other sensible course. So let us begin. We are losing time. Do some memorising. And nothing is to be kept in back pockets.'

The tropic night comes fast on the departing sun. I was anxious to get the fire lit and the process completed before the darkness drew attention in the village below to sparks and smoke. A fire at a time like this at such a house would be sufficient reason for curiosity and investigation. Irrespective of whether there was no trace of what was burned. I fed a stream of paper into the well of the barbecue and fanned out the smoke as best I could. It took a long, long half hour to do, while the gloom deepened and the sparks heightened. When the last papers were gone, I took bowls of ashes down into the garden, dug a hole and buried them, covering the place of their disposal with rubbish and dirt. Once the barbecue metal had cooled, all should be well.

I was sweeping the last remnants away from the concrete floor of the patio when the lights of a vehicle turned into the drive above. The house seemed suddenly floodlit. From inside, Rosa acted. Swift and decisive. Grabbing 'Atu and the two children, she thrust them without ceremony up the connecting staircase to the floor above and locked the door. I continued my now aimless sweeping. Rosa opened the kitchen window as four soldiers with automatic rifles jumped out of the back of the truck and came towards the front door.

'Bula,' she said, with the Fijian greeting, and smiled her wide-eyed innocent smile. 'Na cava?' 'What is it you want?'

'Is this the Stinson house?' They never ask for the person they are looking for.

'E sega. No,' said Rosa, looking puzzled. 'This house is owned by an Indian. Sa yawa tiko na vale Stinson. The Stinson house is far away.' And she raised her chin vaguely towards Suva in the fashion Fijians adopt when showing the way. To point is impolite.

The soldiers were uncertain. 'Ko cei oqo? Who is this?' They turned to me.

'E dua na vulagi ga,' she replied with admirable presence of mind. 'He is just a visitor. Vavalagi qase.'

I continued my sweeping, intent on ensuring that even the slightest comprehension of the Fijian language should not be suspected. It had rusted away anyhow.

The soldiers climbed back on board, turned the truck around, drove off up to Princes Road and went off into the night. The first invasion had been repelled, but it was a sombre 'Atu we found upstairs. We spent the rest of the evening listening with increasing despondency to news from Radio Australia of the confusion in Fiji:

The Coup Leader: '. . . To the Indian community, I feel very deeply for your welfare. You belong here. You are part of our history and our future. Please be assured you have absolutely nothing to fear from this administration . . . I appreciate fully your sense of insecurity and loss . . . join me in my prayer for a future of peace, unity and love . . .'

The Royal Fiji Military Forces: 'The penalty for treason in all Commonwealth countries is death, and if this has to be my destiny, then I will accept it.' These were the words of the Head of State and Commander of the Royal Fiji Military Forces, Brigadier Sitiveni Rabuka, as he addressed officers and men . . . at the Queen Elizabeth Barracks, in Suva today.

The Fiji Ministry of Information: 'Lieutenant Colonel Rabuka was sworn in as the chairman of the Council of Ministers on Sunday night by the Governor General. Other ministers will be sworn in at 9 a.m. Tuesday . . .'

The Governor General: '. . . It is impossible for me to recognise the legitimacy of the Council of Ministers.' His statement made four demands on the military regime: the troops to return to their barracks; a restoration of a free press and radio communications and the lifting of all press censorship; the release of all people detained by the military regime; and the return to barracks of all troops not engaged in the maintenance of public safety . . .

With perplexing lack of consistency, if he was not under duress, the Governor General went on to grant the 'prerogative of mercy to those implicated in the illegal seizure of power'. The decision was taken in accordance with his judgment that 'no useful purpose would be served by vindictiveness which might hinder the complete restoration of legitimacy'.

To listeners of these confusing statements one question stood out: it was then, was it, forgivable and officially pardonable for the military arm of a democratically elected government to remove all the members of that government from the exercise of their parliamentary and executive responsibilities and to hold them in captivity against their will and for this to be smiled away with a mild rap on the knuckles by the headmaster admonishing errant schoolboys five days after their act of gross treason?

Between the bulletins, Rosa rocked with laughter as she told and retold the story of how frightened she had been; but how she had got rid of the soldiers by describing Grandpa as 'just an old European man!' Sort of true, I was forced to admit.

We ran watches throughout the night but otherwise slept well. The instructions to the soldiers would be less imprecise for the next visitation.

4

Fiji is a symbol of hope for the rest of the world
– The Pope in Fiji, February 1987

Tuesday 19 May 1987: Coup Plus Five

Dawn was unwarming, humid and comfortless. The cloud mass over
the hills was already heavy and threatening.

The banks in Suva reopened. As the hurricane shutters came
down from entrances, there was a frenzied rush to the counters.
Armed guards were at every door, inside and out. Foreign exchange
transactions were still suspended. Stocks of Fiji currency soon ran
down. The telephones in the Reserve Bank vaults kept ringing.

I cashed a sterling traveller's cheque for £100. Thirty minutes to
reach the counter and another ten for the transaction. Conversation
was stilled. There were listening ears. Silence was prudent. Mine
was the only white face in the queue. There were none among the
multi-racial tellers, clerks and typists, working in open plan behind
the counters.

It was not always thus. There was a time in the colonial days when
the Australian and New Zealand banks in Fiji declined to employ
'local' staff as tellers and typists. Couldn't be trusted, they argued,
to maintain confidentiality; and anyway they were not good enough
to do the job. Have to maintain standards don't we? So, at considerable cost, callow young men and girls were imported to do these
basic banking tasks and housed in bachelor quarters in Suva. An
errant clerk who was misguided enough to be seen keeping company
with a Fiji girl was sent back to Australia. Tut tut, management
said. There were rules forbidding it, as all staff well knew. So a
sea of Australasian young expatriates sat confidently behind the
typewriters and the adding machines.

The change had not come about without a struggle. The managers
of the banks then in Fiji – New South Wales, New Zealand and
Australia and New Zealand – met quarterly with the Government's

39

Financial Secretary. In 1959, with the colonial Government in full charge, the agenda for their meetings first included the item 'Localisation of banking staff'. It met with the combined objection of the bank managers on the instructions of their respective head offices. But it was soon to change: the racial monolith of banks was to be demolished and the arrival of the Bank of Baroda from Bombay helped to step up the tempo.

It was a similar story at Nadi Airport. In 1960, the Fiji delegate to the South Pacific Air Transport Council meeting at the Chateau Tongariro in New Zealand introduced the same subject. His technical adviser, the Fiji Superintendent of Civil Aviation, was a Yorkshireman. 'I have taken sharp-toothed Africans like bloody monkeys out of trees and turned them into air traffic controllers. Nadi Airport is a piece of cake compared with that,' he told a disbelieving New Zealand Department of Civil Aviation. As the Administering Authority of the airport at the time, the department fought change for years until it, too, was forced to concede defeat and began a reluctant programme of local recruitment and training. One early Fijian airport terminal manager was Nacanieli Uluiviti. Maybe it helped that he had once struck six sixes and a four in one eight-ball over during a cricket match in Suva. Not, however, against the bowling of Richard Hadlee. It all seemed a century away, I reflected, in the banking queue.

Throughout the day, Radio Fiji continued to edify its listeners with an unrelenting stream of pop music. It did, however, announce that the Great Council of Chiefs was due to assemble at the Suva Civic Auditorium; but gave no indication as to what the council was to discuss. During the morning, crowds of Fijians began to gather and take up positions sitting cross-legged on mats on the lawns of Sukuna Park nearby. Fijians have an infinite capacity for patient waiting in circumstances such as these; and those who do are quiet and respectful in deference to the chiefly personages whose deliberations proceed within.

There was an ugliness in the atmosphere on this occasion, different from any I had known. On the arrival of the Governor General, in his capacity also as the high chief of Cakaudrove and Taveuni, there was a wave of booing and hissing from the assembled Fijians. To behave so was a gross insult to his customary rank and as the Queen's representative. It symbolised the violence done to custom and tradition by the coup; and the subterranean strains of anti-chiefly sentiment now unleashed, whatever the coup leaders might say.

At Nadi Airport, across to the west of Vitilevu and in Bavadra territory, there was an attempt to hijack Air New Zealand flight

TE 15, which had come in that morning from Los Angeles en route to Auckland. The first such incident experienced anywhere by New Zealand's international airline, it resulted in the suspension again of all flights in and out of Fiji. They were not to resume for seven months. Air New Zealand management and crews, rightly or wrongly, judged Nadi Airport to be insufficiently safe, while waning traffic and union action continued to justify an overfly Fiji policy.

So too with 'Atu: she was no longer safe in her own home and had to be out of sight in a place of security. It was one thing to conclude this, but quite another to persuade her of it and to make the arrangements.

The arrangements were necessary first. Persuasion would come afterwards. I walked to the Reserve Bank building in Pratt Street. This grand – for Fiji – concrete and glass edifice is the country's highest building. There are steps to a modest but tasteful entrance lobby with token security checks for access to the rest of the building. This is achieved by means of a 'speaking voice' lift, a modern computerised marvel, thankfully unique in Fiji, which unnerves the inexperienced when first encountered. The bank itself occupies only three floors, the rest of the fifteen floors being let to desirable tenants. Desirability is determined in accordance with advance judgment about prospective reliability in paying the rent on the due day. The New Zealand High Commission appears to have satisfied the examiners and occupies three upper floors. Within hours of the coup on 14 May, it had given sanctuary to William Sutherland, his New Zealand wife and two children. Sutherland was a part-European and had been a lecturer at the University of the South Pacific until the election of the Bavadra government to office in April. He had been involved in the Coalition campaign and shortly after electoral victory, Dr Bavadra announced Sutherland's appointment as Secretary of his private office. There were critics of this decision, not least from the Civil Service itself. It was a new-style post with no established existence and the appointment may have been procedurally unorthodox. Prime Ministers, newly elected or otherwise, are, however, not usually deterred by such considerations; and Sutherland had assumed his duties before the coup. While there were those who thought that his flight into hiding was a little premature, there was no doubt that he was an obvious target for the military regime.

Housed in the High Commission and not seen outside since the coup, Sutherland's acceptance was the precedent I needed to plead the cause for similar treatment of 'Atu. There was, however, a complication: her renunciation of New Zealand citizenship. The New Zealand Government might conceivably take the view that this removed any obligation there might otherwise have been on its part to give her shelter. But, if she was no longer a New Zealand citizen, I was. The case was duly made and agreement given for her to be received as a political refugee. Magnanimity had prevailed.

The arrangements completed, I went back to Tamavua. The soldiers had come a second time, fifteen minutes before. 'There's no one here,' Rosa had said. 'Only me and the children. You can see. Siale there. The baby Anga'aefonu there. And I am too busy to talk to you.' She continued to peg the washing on the line outside the house.

'We shall come back again,' they had said, as they left. 'If not today, then tomorrow.'

It was a war of attrition. 'Atu returned from the university as the sun sank below the cloudless hills and harbour.

'I think,' I said, 'that you must begin to face reality. You are forced to make a psychological leap in your comprehension of what is happening around you. There is now a convulsion from which there is no present return to what went before. Your idealism must be adjusted to the reality of your family and children.'

'Nonsense,' she said. 'You are becoming melodramatic. Just because a few inexperienced soldiers have come here. You don't seriously think that I am going to be frightened away from my home and job.'

'If not now, then you will be,' I replied, 'when it is, perhaps, too late. From now on, all contacts and telephone conversations must be abandoned. Arrangements have been made for you to go to ground forthwith. We must now start to consider how this is to be done and when.'

Agreement was slow, grudging and then it was qualified. 'Temporary acceptance only. Just an interim move. Don't think that I am going to make any permanent choice or decision, because I am not.'

Step by step, I said to myself, take things slowly, each stage at a time. One thing will lead to another as events worsen. She will come to realise, perhaps, that there is a point where courage becomes obstinacy and avoidable martyrdom is self-defeating.

Wednesday 20 May 1987: Coup Plus Six

Overnight the rains came in on the tradewinds. The clouds lay thick, black and oppressive on the hills across the harbour, a backcloth of menace to the relentless sheet of water that poured from the skies.

Tropical rain is like none other. It comes in sheets, solid and sustained. Hot-season rains bring an enervating humidity, too. Mildew grows in patches on the walls and seems to penetrate the best of anti-fungicidal paints. In the clothes cupboards, under the arms of shirts and dresses, sweat stains succumb to a clammy fungus. Inside and out, shoes acquire an amorphous green film. As the mosquitoes drone and lurch all night against the netting around the bed, you ponder how so much water can pour from the heavens straight and heavy, with such relentless fury. It may ease before the dawn, bringing out the toads to the grassy swamps around the house. The clean shirt sticks to your skin and is wet through before the buttons are all done up. It is not unusual to put on a second clean one at midday and a third in the evening.

It was one of those mornings-after as we got silently into the car and ventured out to the Princes Road. I sat with 'Atu in the back; Rosa in the front, looking comfortably Fijian; Veni driving.

We took nothing in the car apart from 'Atu's bulging handbag, an empty shopping basket – and the children. It was to look like a family expedition to the Suva market. Just as well. Outside Rairaiwaqa there was an army road block. A glance over the car's interior and a reassuring smile from Rosa was sufficient. The main hazard was the central police station compound, immediately opposite the Reserve Bank building. It was alive with uniforms. Veni stopped the car in a side road. 'Atu and I got out and walked round the corner, past the little Indian food stores and across to the entrance steps. She was in her usual early morning disarray, hair adrift, blouse loose, flip-flops and bare legs. Not, at first glance, a figure of interest to the minions of the military regime – or so I hoped on that hundred-yard walk through the crowds. Up the steps to the foyer, the security book signed, into that irksome lift and up to the tenth floor. 'New Zealand High Commission' it said on the glass door.

'I feel silly,' said 'Atu. 'Are you sure that all this is really necessary? I don't want to be parted from the children.'

'Better to feel foolish and be safe,' I think I replied, 'till we see what the next moves are . . .'

. . . 'Good morning. So here she is. Come this way.'

He opened a door into what looked like a large empty reception room. It was L-shaped with glass all round, a splendid vantage point to view the comings and goings in the police compound, on Victoria Parade in front and the Suva wharves and shops of Renwick Road on the other side. There was a refrigerator, a few chairs, a table and the coolness of efficient air conditioning. It had an enveloping normality about it.

'So here you are,' he said again, 'and here you may stay for the present. I'm afraid you will have to provide everything else that you need. There is a toilet through there and if you speak nicely to the girls in the filing room, I'm sure they'll let you make coffee. You'll have to arrange your own food. No going outside now you are in, unless it is agreed beforehand. The High Commission telephones are tapped, we assume, and you should not use them. Your acceptance here should be kept confidential so long as that is possible. You should not attempt contacts with anyone other than your family without consulting us first. I hope you will be reasonably comfortable. I am sure the High Commissioner will want to see you in due course. I understand that his daughter is one of your students.'

'Thank God for small mercies and the long arm of coincidence,' I thought, as I expressed our gratitude. Now the details – mattress, sheets, pillow, writing materials, books, toothbrush, changes of clothing, food.

'Before you and Veni set off to do all this,' she said, 'would you mind taking this envelope to the university entrance in Laucala Bay Road? Hand it in at the office beside the barrier.' She took a brown envelope from inside her blouse.

I hesitated. 'It is not that I am unwilling to do as you ask. Just that . . . well . . . we agreed you would bring nothing, absolutely nothing, with you. What exactly is inside it?'

'I know. I'm sorry. It's all right. You needn't worry. It's an essay I marked last night after you went to bed. It's due back in the department today!' She flashed me an innocent smile and giggled like a feckless schoolgirl. 'I have to keep up with my academic responsibilities, you know. In spite of . . .' She was serious again. 'In spite of all this!' We looked out of the window and down at the police compound. A convoy of trucks was arriving. One by one they disgorged scores of Indian men, women and children. Silent and huddled together, they stood, sat or squatted under the eye of armed police around the compound and the barracks above. What had they done? Where were they from? Why were they there? We were soon to learn.

'All right,' I said. 'Let me have it. I'll go now and get on with the shopping. Veni will bring you some clothes and night things.'

'Don't worry about the mattress,' she called after us. 'I'll sleep on the floor. I'm a sort of Polynesian, remember. And bring me some Proust to read.'

Some chance, I thought, and went out again into the street below in search of food. It would be necessary to do this on several occasions without incurring the curiosity of building watchers and, more importantly, the inhabitants of the police compound opposite. The curry take-away on the corner was the easiest. Quicker too than the Chinese equivalent next door. My food-bearing entrances were as unobtrusive as I could make them; but it is not entirely possible to carry powerful South Indian curry unobtrusively. That first day a lurking and vaguely familiar figure from the past oiled his way in my direction on the steps of the Reserve Bank building. He sniffed, then glanced at the paper parcel I was transporting into the building. He was of mixed race with an ambivalent and undistinguished civil service past. So where did he stand now? And was he a street-watching informer? Just a take-away curry carrier I was not, he would conclude, and report in the establishment across the street.

'This would never have happened in our day, would it?'

'No,' I said. 'I suppose it wouldn't. But then a lot of things that should have happened in our day didn't.'

And I went on, foolishly smug, into the lobby of the Reserve Bank, an eddy of pungent curry behind me.

I can never walk down Victoria Parade in Suva without being stopped every fifty yards or so as ghosts from the past emerge from the young crowds. They are ageing now. Recognition may not be immediate. An act of interpretation is necessary to cover the intervening years; and names of former colleagues and staff are not always in the forefront of the mental computer screen.

There was no doubt about the bent figure finding support from a pillar outside the airline office. It was Kau, a human pillar himself of the old Colonial Secretariat and the personal messenger of the Great Man. For over thirty years, Kau had sat quiet and reflective outside the Colonial Secretary's office to be aroused from time to time by a peremptory Oxbridge instruction: 'Kau: Take this by hand immediately to Mr X.' Never, please. Or, 'Would you?' Or, 'Thank you' afterwards. It was just as well that Kau's command of English was insufficient for him to decipher the subject and text of the Personal and Confidential telegrams or letters that lay between the open folds of the buff official envelopes. His sustained loyalty was touching, his honesty complete, and the light in his eyes enough for those who had occasion to remember and, at times, reward him.

Kau's political innocence was in stark contrast to his Arab counter-parts I had known in Gaza in 1946. The queues of petitioners to see the District Commissioner, the Arab and Jewish district officers – or me – never seemed to diminish. The reason was that they didn't move much. Until, that is, payment was made to the duty messenger at the rates approved for passing through to each of the officials concerned and the access barrier was moved aside. As the youngest and most junior of those of supposedly magical power and beneficial decision within, I rated the lowest 'bakshish'. Which was acceptable. How tedious it would have been to discover that there was no charge at all to get in to me. 'The beardless youth who has come among us,' said the village elders at my first tangle with a Bedouin blood feud.

Kau came forward smiling, calm, warm.

'Bula saka. Hullo, sir. It is good to see you again. I often think of you and the children and our days together. Times were better then, not like now. I am old. Perhaps that is lucky for me.'

'Yes, Kau. It is good to see you too. I am glad that you are well. And how are Filipe and Manoa and Saimone and Bogi and Petaia and Savou . . .?' A handclasp, an embrace, and I moved on.

It was an afternoon of vicious brutality in Albert Park and elsewhere in Suva, the first unbridled release of racial aggression. Fijian youths went on the rampage, burning, looting, stoning and assaulting non-Fijians, mainly Indians and their families. In Suva's Albert Park, below Government House and beside the central Government Buildings, a thousand Indians gathered for mass prayer following the release from custody of Coalition ministers and members of parliament. What happened was orchestrated thuggery as inflamed gangs descended on the crowd. A truck went by and spades were thrown out for the rampaging mob to use. Steel pipes were taken from another. Men, women and children were bashed and beaten with sticks, rocks, spades and forks as they fled for cover in trees, on the steps of nearby hotels, and in government offices. Outnumbered policemen watched until, after ten minutes of wanton violence, soldiers arrived. A mob leader demanded that the Indians be dispersed and that such assemblies be forbidden in future. 'Indian gatherings like this are a form of provocation and intimidation,' he told reporters. The realities were already distorted and the truth a hostage to brutality.

As more personnel-carriers arrived to rescue the terrified Indians, the gangs turned away to rampage through the streets of Suva. At the market, they bashed up Indian vendors and destroyed food stalls. Quickly, Suva's Indian shops were barred and barricaded and the streets became silent; while the trucks we had seen brought the shaking victims of mass assault into the police compound below the Reserve Bank building. There they stayed huddled together in silence and fear.

And with the silence there came the sound of massed male voices.

We looked from the windows, past the Sacred Heart Cathedral and up Pratt Street from where it seemed to be coming. Then, serried ranks of young marching Fijians came down the hill singing, if singing it was. An old tribal war chant: 'We are going to fight. Will you fight us?' It was eerie with malevolent menace. As the first rows of marchers came into full sight, they broke ranks on both sides, chased, caught and punched any Indian in sight. Then, they threw them, human rag dolls, to the ground and on the steps of the cathedral, and moved on, leaving a battlefield behind. Cars were overturned and wrecked, rocks smashed through unprotected windows. Cries of the injured came up to us from the carnage below; and our tears flowed as we watched, helpless and unbelieving, the wrecking of human life outside.

Three soldiers came out of the police compound. It seemed deliberately too late. They stood together in the middle of the road and pointed their guns straight into the crowd. Suddenly, ferocity died. The beaten limped or were carried silently away. The street was quiet again and empty. It might never have been.

But the violence continued to erupt in various parts of Suva as the crowds waited for the outcome of the meeting of the Great Council of Chiefs. Their patience had its reward. Lieutenant Colonel Rabuka emerged on the balcony, arms aloft and fists clenched, to proclaim, 'Sa noda na qaqa': 'We have won. Victory is ours. I shall not agree to anything that will destroy the aim of the coup.'

A great shouted scream arose from three thousand voices. From the deep gut of a warrior race, it became now an alarum, a rallying cry and a promise of militancy to come. There are few things more threatening than a wolf pack with the ways of sheep.

We agreed to disperse for the night. Veni and the children went to the home of a Samoan friend. With some inner doubts, I went back alone to the house in Tamavua. It was a broken night. I was restless and uneasy as the sirens blared from the police cars racing up and down Princes Road. And there was the beating of the lali, menacing and relentless from Tamavua village, designed to unsettle and then to unnerve.

5

Thursday 21 May 1987: Coup Plus Seven

The sirens penetrated my subconscious in the deep that comes before the dawn. I pushed aside the mosquito net and stumbled to the side of the window. The darkness was now tinged with grey. Lights swept down the drive to the house and an army vehicle stopped outside the garage. Six figures in jungle green and face masks and with automatic rifles jumped down and went to key points around the house. There were no orders and no conversation. Then, as I watched from above, they moved back into the truck and drove away. I wondered why. It could only be that, looking through the windows, they had seen no one asleep in the bedrooms on the ground floor and had not bothered to try to enter upstairs where I was, alone.

I showered and dressed in the half light. Then gathered my clothes and repacked the suitcase. The sun was coming up as I finished. It held the prospect of a glorious dawn. I made a cup of coffee and went out, in sulu and bare feet, to the balcony to look for the last time at the reef scene of harbour peace below. As I did so, a small pick-up hurtled down the driveway, lights off, driven by a teenage Indian with another holding precariously on to the cab roof in the back. It turned agonisingly outside the garage at the bottom and shot off up again in one movement. The boy screamed one word: 'Go!'

It seemed timely advice. My hands shook a little as I pulled the zip of the suitcase and clipped it shut. I went down the staircase, closed the front door behind me and put the bag on the back seat of the car. I pulled out the keys and put one in the ignition lock. It did not turn. Another. Same result. A third and the engine fired, faltered and stopped. Was the battery flat? Was the car out of petrol? All those failed 'perfect crime' stories came back to torment. Fourth try. Away she went. Tissue please for sweating palms. Brake off. Engage reverse gear. Move out backwards. Turn. Then forward in low, up to Princes Road, turn right and off down the hill to Suva.

Gently does it. Don't hurry. Drive normally. Stay composed. Get your story ready. Anticipate the secondary questions. Appear ignorant of all things Fiji and Fijian. Copies of *Fiji Beach Press* on the back seat. Airline ticket. The typical tourist. 'Oh what a beautiful morning, oh what a beautiful day . . .'

I found a room in an empty Town House. This modest hostelry may have seemed an odd choice: it is across the road from the side of the main Suva police compound and barracks. Arriving guests can – or could – be edified by rows of drying undergarments hanging Kowloon style outside the windows. It is not wise to complain. One hundred yards away in Pratt Street are the Sacred Heart Cathedral and the Reserve Bank Building.

'A room with a view,' I had requested like thousands before in Venice, Sydney or Rio. A view, that is, of the right windows on the High Commission floors. We had arranged that if she wanted to communicate urgently, she would do the customary thing in such circumstances – put a towel outside the window. A blue one for me to come over urgently; and red as a danger warning of any kind. It was a bit obvious and maybe rash to do this in face of the police compound. But I couldn't think of anything better at the time – and maybe we could rely on a Kowloon laundry extension across the road not rousing attention. It turned out to be right. We had a trial run on my return to the Town House where I put out a white shirt for a moment so she could see where I was. She pulled her towel in and waved. I slept secure, doors locked and barred and not caring any more about the comings and goings of police traffic outside.

Friday 22 May 1987: Coup Plus Eight

The *Fiji Times* and the *Fiji Sun* had come back to the news stands after an absence of six days. 'At last the shroud of darkness is lifted,' said the *Times* optimistically. 'Let's end this nightmare. Now we plan to give you the news as it happened, without embellishment or emotion. The Governor General and Lieutenant Colonel Rabuka have assured newspapers of the freedom to publish. We hope for our readers' sake it continues.' And for theirs too, perhaps.

Indeed, in one respect the news was not without hope. The lead item was the release from custody late on Wednesday evening of Dr Timoci Bavadra, his wife and his colleagues. 'It is great to be free and return to my home,' he had said outside his Laucala Beach Estate house. 'On Tuesday night, I didn't think I was going to make it when masked gunmen rushed into our bedroom. They pointed their guns and harassed us. They said they were there for our protection. Can you believe that?' Dr Bavadra then told the large crowd:

'The main reason for the coup is that we have done in four weeks for poor people what the Alliance could not do in seventeen years. It was the Alliance fear of total extinction which led to the coup. The call for a change in constitution is almost beyond imagining as no one has complained about it in the past seventeen years of Alliance rule. I am very sorry that Ratu Mara, the chief advocate of the Pacific way, has remained silent after announcing that democracy is alive and well in Fiji. I wish it were.'

We had a planning committee meeting in the morning. Planning for departure, that is. Exodus and how to accomplish it. There were four essential ingredients: documentation for adults and children; transportation by air or road from Suva, a two-hundred-kilometre journey to the international airport at Nadi in western Vitilevu; airline reservations and tickets; and money. In addition, there were questions of what to pack and what could go and what should not. Arbitrary decisions were going to be needed, together with some rough justice.

'No papers,' I said again, 'no election pamphlets and no newspaper or magazine stories. No cameras, photographs or tapes. No lecture notes or USP-headed paper. No thesis copies or research drafts. No letters from friends or colleagues. No telephone numbers or address books. Just passports and tickets.'

Tickets to where? That had to be determined first. It boiled down either to New Zealand or to Australia; and in a real sense the decision became one of which airline was flying where and had available passenger space on which day. At one point, there was a report that Air New Zealand was putting on a special flight from and to Auckland; but that did not materialise, apparently because air crew were unwilling to fly to Nadi. In the end, I made a reservation with Qantas for Sydney. It meant giving names, but it was a risk that had to be taken sooner or later. You cannot manipulate such things in a small place where everyone is known to everyone. Anyway, passports had to be shown for the purpose of satisfying the airline about entry into Australia.

Qantas has its managerial office in the Reserve Bank building. I went below and found a shaking and shocked secretary. A part-European, she had just come in from lunch. Walking by Morris Hedstrom's main Suva store, she had seen Fijian gangs abusing Indian women. Three children were plucked from the hands of their mothers and thrown into Nubukalou Creek. The youths ran off laughing and shouting at the exhilaration of such splendid sport.

'I can't believe what I saw. It was dreadful. This is my country and my town. It is not somewhere else.' It was hard for her to turn back to work and airline reservations, but she did so. The computer clicked away and offered seats from Nadi to Sydney on the joint Qantas/Air Pacific service the following evening, Saturday 23 May. I hardly hesitated. 'Yes. And thank you.'

Less than twenty-four hours to do everything else: that was as it should be. Longer might be too long.

I agonised over the business of how to get from Suva to Nadi. Nausori is Suva's airport and the air journey to Nadi takes twenty-five minutes. But the twenty kilometres by road from Suva to the airport is through a notoriously unstable area of predominantly Indian roadside houses, already the target of attacks by youths from Raiwaqa, Samabula and elsewhere. And I didn't fancy waiting around in public view for an internal flight. It would be an open invitation for informers to inform and for instructions to be sought and boarding at Nadi stopped. There was more than sufficient time to alert police, immigration and any units in the west. The only alternative was the longer journey by road from Suva to Nadi Airport round the south coast via the Queens Road. It would take three hours. Three hours for anything to go wrong – dry petrol pumps, engine failure, nails on the tarmac, stoning, robbery and military or police road blocks. With a Fijian driver and escorts, it might be done. Plus some bluff and a bit of effrontery. A favourite civil service summing-up phrase is 'on balance'. It seemed to me that, on balance, by road to Nadi it had to be.

So it was agreed. Veni was charged with finding transport, not initially thought to be a difficulty – Rosa's brother-in-law Tui drove a van three times a week to Nadi – and getting passports in order. Rosa was allocated packing and preparing food and drinks for the journey. There would be no stopping for that. The bushes would have to do for the other things, children and adults alike. I set off after airline tickets and money. Seventy-five minutes elapsed while four tickets were written out and three credit cards were checked and used. Those who waited behind me were edgy and impatient. Seats were already at a premium. We had been fortunate. The bank changed Fiji dollars into Australian without demur. It put up the shutters on its foreign exchange desks soon after. I worked out rendezvous details and timings for the next morning, together with a 'wet weather programme' if the city erupted overnight or the Suva–Nadi road journey had to be reconsidered. Progress was reviewed in the afternoon. We were tired and irritable. The strain was beginning to show. Partly, I suppose, because 'Atu continued to resist the whole idea of 'running away'. In the end, she agreed only to temporary departure and would give no promise of anything more. It was enough – for the moment. We had no time for philosophical debate. The reality was in the streets.

Some disconcerting discoveries then came to light. Veni's Tongan passport provided for multiple entries into Australia. 'Atu's Fiji one did not. The children were both born in Canberra. They held Australian passports; but Siale's had run out and not been renewed. Both 'Atu and Veni were the possessors of outdated driving licences. Rosa's Fiji passport would expire at the end of June and could not be extended since the passport issuing office had closed its doors. Operation Exodus was at the point of frustration for these absurd reasons. I exploded in annoyance. Not so they. 'Keep calm,' they said. 'It'll all be right on the night.'

I doubted it. With hundreds of Indians queueing up at the New Zealand and Australian High Commissions, it was hardly the time to seek 'special concessions'; but we managed to get a New Zealand entry visa on Rosa's passport in spite of the fact that it was to expire so soon. There was no hope of getting her an entry for Australia in time, so her departure had to be abandoned, a cause for much heartbreak. We sought the assistance of 'Atu's hosts to intercede with the Australians for the rest. They did so, but in the event Veni had to spend several crucial hours sitting around in the Australian High Commission while a hundred and one other things remained to be done. He finally got 'Atu's passport stamped late in the day and a piece of paper for Siale, giving him right of entry into Australia for one journey.

I went through a sombre and shuttered Suva to dinner with the Vice Chancellor of the University of the South Pacific where we heard the announcement of the membership of the Governor General's Advisory Committee. When I got back, the transport arrangements to Nadi had failed. By midnight, no replacement had been found.

6

Saturday 23 May 1987: Coup Plus Nine – D Day

My telephone jerked me awake. 'Look out of the window.' It was
a male voice I did not recognise. Australian.

'Yes. Got it. Thank you.' Flapping gently from a tenth-floor
window of the Reserve Bank building was a blue towel. I threw my
clothes in the suitcase, went down the staircase to the lobby and
checked out. With the sort of purposeful stride you conjure up at
such times, I walked across the crowded entrance of the police
compound, up the steps of the Reserve Bank building, through the
lobby and into that hateful lift. 'Floor 1, Floor 2, Floor 3 . . .' the
disembodied voice droned away.

She was rested, smiling and ready. 'I thought you were never
coming. I'd better get the towel.' She opened the window, pulled in
the towel, gave it a kiss and stuffed it into an already overloaded
satchel. 'Meet your anonymous Australian. He's just flown in – to
help.'

'Hullo. Where's Veni?' I asked, exasperated. 'And the transport
to Nadi? Where are the children, Rosa, the luggage? For Pete's
sake, fill me in.'

'Don't fret. Let's go. Have I got everything? I must say thank you
to the High Commissioner.' She went off clutching four pieces of
nondescript impedimenta. It was nine o'clock. The time agreed for
the start of the crossing to Egypt. Into the lift and down again to
the lobby.

'Hi, 'Atu. You off somewhere?'

'Sure. Usual place,' she replied. And smiled at me. 'Just one of
my students.'

'Do they call you 'Atu?' I asked aimlessly as we went down the
steps. The street was alive with police and soldiers. Something was
afoot. We moved with nervous normality through the crowds.

'Here,' said the Australian. 'Get in, mate.' A taxi was at the
kerbside, the engine running, an Indian driver. By a circuitous route,
we reached the Southern Cross Hotel. In the driveway – 'before

your very eyes', as Arthur Askey used to say – was a middle-aged minibus. It looked like half of Suva was inside – Veni, Rosa, Epeli, Tui and the two children, Siale and Anga'aefonu, plus creaky suitcases bound with rope, cartoned packages, picnic baskets, towels, oranges, bananas and pineapples.

'Come in, Grandpa,' said Rosa cheerfully. 'Are you coming for a picnic with us at Deuba?' We squeezed in amid all this paraphernalia. The engine started. Sounded OK. The driver was Fijian and beside him in the front seat was a stately Fijian of advancing years. He was dressed in a grey jacket, grey sulu, and – I looked more closely from behind – a clerical collar. He turned. 'Shall we set off now?'

'Yes,' I replied. 'Yes. Yes, please.'

The driver let in the clutch. 'Just a moment,' said Veni. 'I want to take a photograph!' He got out with his camera. A policeman walked towards us.

'Don't tell me the Southern Cross Hotel is now a military installation and can't be photographed?'

My sense of humour had departed.

The policeman looked casually at the overburdened minibus, nodded to the clergyman and went into the hotel. Veni clicked and clicked again. I looked out of the side window and, upside down, made out the words emblazoned in large letters on the side of the minibus: CENTRAL METHODIST CHURCH OF FIJI NAMAKA CIRCUIT.

Thank God for God, I thought, and for that well-known Methodist lay preacher, Sitiveni Rabuka. And too for the people of Pitcairn who, as they set off in their longboats from the side of a freighter rolling wide in the Pacific swells, sing to the departing ship:

> 'Safe in the arms of Jesus
> Safe on that distant shore . . .'

Amen. In Egypt. Or Australia. Or wherever. And be it a merciful deliverance. Should be. There appeared to be appropriate sponsorship at hand.

'When and how did you get hold of this vehicular inspiration?' I asked.

'At about four o'clock this morning. We were up all night running around Suva chasing up leads and knocking on doors. By chance, after the consumption of a lot of kava and the passing of a fistful of dollars, we did a deal with these representatives of the Almighty.'

So, the coup notwithstanding, Fiji was still Fiji. Even though we had agreed on two vehicles – one as luggage and scout car in case of road blocks or incidents on the way. The second with most of the

passengers. But this was better. Worth some voluntary churchgoing
if all went well. Come to think of it, we looked so scruffy and
ill-organised that we might just pass for displaced missionaries moving house.

We set off on a diverted route out of Suva. The Walu Bay Bridge
was under repair and was not taking ordinary traffic – even that of
the church. Soon we were past the President Hotel on the right and
the Tradewinds on the left. Then up into the hills at speed on the
sealed surface of a well-surveyed road which made a mockery of the
swirling dust and sickening bends of the past. There was a small
crowd in the Navua flats as we reached the Deuba beach hotels and
the Pacific Harbour resort. It melted away as we approached, with
shouts of friendly recognition. The children slept in ample warm
Fijian laps. We entered the Serua hills and I remembered suddenly
another such journey years before.

It was 1946. I had set off with police car escort from Gaza to
Jerusalem. The convoy travelled at a pre-determined speed twenty-
five yards apart. We were armed, with scanners watching to left, to
right and in front. All went well until we passed Latrun, the detention
centre housing at that time in typical old British colonial style Moshe
Shertok, Ben Gurion and Golda Meir. The hills rose sheer and
brown as the road upwards began to twist and turn. I looked up. At
the top, just visible, on a peak ahead was a solitary figure, a flag in
hand. As he swept out of sight, the flag fell. We rounded a bend.
Fifty yards ahead lay a small bridge over a dry gully.

'Move,' I shouted to the driver. 'Fast.' We slewed over the wooden
planks of the bridge and up the other side. Slewed again and as the
bridge exploded, the air blast caught us. The plunger had been just
too late. We didn't look back. We were too anxious about the road
ahead.

They were times when you stopped your car if you spotted a
discarded sardine tin by the roadside ahead; when near invisible
wires were drawn tightly across an empty stretch of road to net a
car; when nails were strewn to puncture tyres and immobilise;
and when, months later in a crowded Oxford Street in London, I
instinctively fell prostrate on the pavement as a car backfired nearby.
A foolish feeling followed; but the nerve ends still tingled.

They tingled again as there was a loud crash and the Methodist
Church van slowed to a halt. We had all been in soporific meditation.
The driver got out, went down the road and picked up the back door
which had just fallen off. Replacing it in position, he gave it a healthy
kick with a sandalled foot. There was a satisfying click and we were
off again.

'Give me Anga'aefonu?' said 'Atu. 'I've just got to empty my boobs. I'm dribbling.' She opened her blouse and a contented baby proceeded to the infant version of meals-on-wheels. Pretty good flow of milk, I thought, given that crash. Or perhaps because of it?

So to the Coral Coast – Korolevu, Korotoga and the beach hotels – and across the single-track Sigatoka road bridge with its traffic lights at each end. There was a substantial crowd blocking the route through the town. Banners said 'Bavadra, Bavadra' and 'We demand Coalition Government'. Someone was haranguing the throng through a loud hailer.

'What's this?' said 'Atu. 'I must get out and see. And anyway, I want a pee.'

'No. Absolutely no. We cannot – must not – stop here. We've got to get on.' I smiled at the back of the clerical collar which thankfully showed no sign of wanting to disembark. Among all those Indians.

'Oh all right. The bushes then. But you are a bully.'

In the long slog of the Momi hills, we opened the thermos flasks and handed round the pineapples.

'Why are we still in this car?' Siale asked suddenly. 'I thought we were going to Deuba for a picnic. We've passed that.'

'I know. We're sort of having it in here. And then we're going in an aeroplane. So that'll be fun, won't it?'

'No. Aeroplanes are boring. Unless you are flying them. Can I fly this one?'

'I expect so. We'll ask when we get there. Have some more pineapple.'

We were now in the dry zone of Vitilevu. The rain forest and humidity had gone. The pine plantations and sugarcane fields had taken over. The backcloth of hills in the interior was craggy and stark. Brown dust lay across the baked surface soil in the beginnings of a drought which was to last for months. We passed a booster power station. The army guards sat above the road, playing cards, rifles nearby. The driver waved. The soldiers waved back. The merriment of rustic recognition and passing relief from boredom. Soon we were into the touristic tawdriness of Nadi town where, nearly forty years before, I had chaired its embryonic Township Board. Narewa village which had spawned some of Nadi's finest Fijian cricketers, lay to the left across the river. The Gujerati electrical and tailors' stores were closed, wooden shutters up. It was one o'clock. Not far now. Navoce and Nakavu villages. The great brooding hills of the Nadi hinterland ahead and to our right. Then a left turn at the airport access road. A deep breath: 'Nadi International Airport. Domestic Departures. International Departures.' This was it. The last bit had arrived. The hard bit. Would the documentation be OK? Would the bookings be on the screen or had the computers failed again? What military presence? What checks or restraints on departing citizens of Fiji or Tonga or Australia? Would there be a gentle tap on the shoulder at the exit clearance desk? 'Just a moment please. Would you come this way?' It had happened to me – in Honduras and in Liberia – but it was unpleasant to have such sensations in an adopted land. Flight check-in had not begun. This meant standing around in the open concourse with stacked baggage, waiting. There was no alternative. We rehearsed the story. The university was on vacation. Just a brief holiday visit to relatives, then back again at the start of the new semester. Innocents – and, we hoped, innocence – going abroad. The desks opened for business. The concourse now resembled Hong Kong's Kaitak at midnight.

I hovered at a distance while Veni checked in. 'Atu, Rosa and the children had been despatched to a corner of the rudimentary restaurant at the end of the airline counters. It was close to the point of entry for departing passengers. Epeli and Tui sat with them, cheerful, comforting, bodyguards of normality. Curry and roti all round.

'Baggage, please,' said the Indian clerk. 'On the scales. Where are your security clearance stickers? You have to have them or I cannot accept your baggage. Yes, I know that there is no notice about it, but it has only just been started since the Air New Zealand hijack. You will have to take your baggage over there' – he pointed vaguely – 'and come back.'

We zig-zagged through the throng to a roped-off area in the furthest corner. A hundred people were ahead of us. It took forty minutes. Then back to the check-in desk. The baggage, bursting at its ancient seams, was mercifully accepted, the reservations were confirmed and four boarding passes were issued.

'I've been seen,' said 'Atu. 'Soldiers have been over here. Tui got rid of them. When in hell are they going to board the flight? I think they've gone for instructions.'

I went for a walk. Another thirty minutes went by before the first boarding call. The flight had landed from Sydney and the few incoming passengers would soon be queueing at the domestic flight desks.

'You are not safe until the aircraft is cleared and airborne. You can be taken off at any time before that. So in the departure lounge, keep your eyes open and limit your conversation to essentials.

Give no reason to anyone for your departure or indication of your movements. Assume the harassed mother role.'

'That won't be difficult.' She smiled.

As they went through to the official exit clearance desks, a group of armed soldiers burst through the concourse and in through the 'for departing passengers only' door. Rosa stifled a scream, hand to her mouth. The crowds of Indian travellers watched, nervous but quiet, children bewildered and wide-eyed. The soldiers went past the desks without a glance and rushed on. A near thing. Or was I seeing danger where danger there was none?

Examination of passports and departure forms was agonisingly slow. An additional form had to be filled in. Further delay for its completion. Then a wave through the glass doors and they were out of sight. We went upstairs to the observation deck where there is a view – from fifty yards – of a short open way through which both arriving and departing passengers pass. It offers a brief moment for a first arriving gasp of joyous recognition or a last departing tearful wave. Fijians and Indians, like Jews and Arabs, have more things in common than those which divide. One is emotion. Another is the extended family. In the Fijian language, 'brother' includes the European concept of 'cousin'. The Fijian equivalent of 'cousin' is roughly a second cousin. Still a close relation. At Fiji airports, twenty or more Fijians will farewell or welcome a family member. More for high-ranking personages or respected elders. As for Asians, anyone who has been tempted into Bombay or Colombo airports will understand what a departing or arriving Fiji Indian does to family routine, schooling, office jobs and ageing grandparents.

As we watched from the observation deck, the reason for the sudden flurry of activity became clear. I had five seconds, after seventeen years, to recognise from those fifty yards the handlebar moustache of the unseated Commander of the Royal Fiji Military Forces, Brigadier Ratu Epeli Nailatikau, returning from Australia. To what? Reinstatement, suspension, house arrest, quiet retirement or leadership of a counter coup? I could only guess. But one thing was certain: his soldiers didn't know either. As a diversion, it couldn't have been better timed. It would absorb the attendant military and occupy the erratic telephone lines to Suva. Lesser matters, such as the inquisition, harassment and delay of departing airline passengers, would be abandoned. Or suspended long enough for boarding to be accomplished.

It seemed an age starting. First, the departure of an Air Pacific flight to Tonga was announced. The stately figure of the Minister of Education, Langi Kavaliku, moved into sight, followed by his flock of USP students and others in Tongan dress. A Polynesian pied piper at work. Then a long interval before a dribble of Sydney-bound passengers began to emerge along the walk-way and down to the waiting Qantas 747. We spotted the Sutherland family. They too had come by road from their sanctuary in the New Zealand High Commission in Suva. Then another seemingly long wait.

'There's 'Atu now,' said Rosa suddenly. She had been glued to the wire fencing. 'And Siale. And Anga'aefonu. And Veni. They've made it.' She waved frantically.

'Not yet,' I replied. 'The aircraft is still on the ground. Until it is cleared and in the air anything can happen.'

Rosa, now silent and exhausted by the strain, went off into a corner of the observation deck. There she sank down on her knees and wept.

Two soldiers went to the aircraft. It was hard to watch. Would they return with anyone? If so, who would it be? It was William Sutherland. He was searched and questioned about the reasons for his journey. In these uncertain early military days, he was then allowed to return on board.

The aircraft was finally airborne an hour and a half after its scheduled departure time. I hired a red Mini. Three large Fijians and I drove back along the Queens Road to Suva as the sun fell below a placid and innocent sea. The warming presence and support of Rosa, Epeli and Tui was an enduring part of Fiji and the Fijian people that neither the military coup nor Taukei extremism could destroy.

7

Monday 25 May 1987: Coup Plus Eleven

It was now necessary for me to sort out my own onward travel arrangements. Air New Zealand, on which I was booked, was still not flying to Nadi; and although decisions about what to do were being taken daily, there seemed no indication of an early change of mind on the part of the company and its crews. Passengers were being transferred to Air Pacific, Qantas, CPAir or Continental and sent in whatever direction was available.

The airline office in Victoria Parade was open but empty. As I went in, I caught sight of a familiar figure from the past. She had come to Suva from New Zealand in the days of the Pacific flying boats of Tasman Empire Airways Limited or TEAL as Air New Zealand used to be. She had done air bookings for us on a number of occasions over the years. Seeing me, she emerged from behind a glass screen and invited me behind it.

'How good to see you again. But what a time. I am officially retired, of course; but I still do a bit of travel work and they give me a space here.'

Her eyes gleamed and she leaned forward, conspiratorially. 'I approve of the coup, don't you?' She assumed my agreement, and went on. 'After all, who wants to be governed by a lot of Gujeratis?'

'I didn't realise . . .'

'Oh, yes. Bavadra is just a front. You know who is really in charge, don't you?'

I didn't, but it wasn't timely to say so. I was more concerned to get a flight out – somewhere.

I was due to go north to Honolulu and Los Angeles, but there was nothing available that was flying. So I went south-west to Sydney, east across the Tasman Sea to Auckland, thence the long haul north to Los Angeles and London.

Thirty-three hours at a stretch in the economy class of identical Boeing 747s is neither the most sensible nor the most relaxing way to travel. Mass air travel for any distance is bad enough. Unduly

60

prolonged, it creates the walking zombies who emerge from their flying machines; while the shallow smiles and the we-look-forward-to-seeing-you-again-soon farewells result only in a fierce determination to do no such foolish thing.

I slept a lot over the weekend, as my body clock sought to adjust after the savage dislocation inflicted upon it. It seemed an age since the first 'Now just lie back, relax, and enjoy your flight'; and André Previn had urged us to listen to 'the London Symphony Orchestra playing Haydn's Symphony No. 100 in G, conducted by me'.

Before that was my own solitary journey back again by road from Suva to Nadi. I had retained the rented Mini. After some blissful singing from an overflowing Sacred Heart Cathedral opposite the Town House, I went for a drive on a serenely sunny Sunday morning. Suva was all silence and peace: a Miltonic 'calm of mind all passion spent'. Out in the harbour, the sea rushed and crashed on the reef as timelessly as ever.

That evening Fijian customary generosity took over as Rosa, Epeli and Tui prepared a farewell lovo. Before we ate, there was a formal sevusevu of yaqona; and we drank till they cried 'maca'. (The bowl is empty. The yaqona is finished.) There was an exchange of thanks and appreciation. By nine, I had left the house at Tamavua for the last time.

The drive to Nadi next day was strangely uneventful – until the end. And then what happened was entirely unexpected. I had an hour or so in hand. On an impulse, I decided to drive past the airport along the coast to Veiseisei village. I had known it well when I was District Officer in Lautoka in 1949–50. It is the chiefly home of the Tui Vuda, of some historic significance in the west of Vitilevu and more recently an agreeable showplace for visiting tourists. So, impelled by another bout of compulsive nostalgia, I drove there. Only then did I half-recall – was it so? – that Veiseisei was also the village of the deposed Prime Minister, Dr Timoci Bavadra.

By the roadside, as I stopped the car, was a Fijian girl of about ten years.

'Is this Dr Bavadra's village?' I asked her. I could see no soldiers. Was I mistaken?

'Yes,' she said, 'it is.'

'Is he here?'

'Yes.'

'Do you know where he is now?'

'Yes.'

'Will you take me to him?'

'Yes.'

61

I got out of the car as she skipped away leading me into an old but new Veiseisei. She stopped outside a modest Fijian-style house from which there was a buzz of conversation. Then a ringing telephone. She went in. A moment later, an elegant Fijian lady came to the door and greeted me.

'I am 'Atu Bain's father. I came officially to Veiseisei many times in the past. I am just leaving Fiji from Nadi airport. I wonder if I may pay brief respects to the Prime Minister before I do so.'

She went inside and returned a moment later. 'My name is Kuini. Dr Bavadra's wife. The Prime Minister will be very glad to see you. Please come in.' I went in between the posts of the open entrance. Dr Bavadra was seated cross-legged in the Fijian way on the floor of his house with about twenty people. There was a solitary telephone in constant use. It was then that I discovered that I could cease being a father and be myself.

'I remember when I was at Queen Victoria School, you brought an Old Boys cricket team to play when I was there.' He was bubbling with pleasure. 'You were one of our cricketing idols. We all thought we should learn how to play a straight bat like you and Philip Snow and the other District Officers we saw play. And then you captained an otherwise all-Fijian Suva team to play in Lautoka. That was a match to remember. I want to introduce you to all these people. They will remember that hook for six off Ratu Meli Qoro.'

And the Prime Minister did so. Within seconds, there were ageing men in the group who came and shook my hand and said they had played cricket against me either in Lautoka or in Nadi or in Suva. As the years slipped away, in the warmth of that welcome lay the Fiji I knew and thought had been lost.

It was all agreeably informal; but the meeting had a deeper purpose. Conversations flowed fast in Fijian and English. What should we do now? Will the sugarcane be cut or burned and the mills closed down? Should we plan protest marches? Close down transport? What statements should be made? How can they be got out to the people? Should the west secede from the rest of Fiji? Why has Ratu Mara not spoken out? Should Dr Bavadra attend the South Pacific Forum meeting in Apia? Or telephone Bob Hawke and David Lange? Or Margaret Thatcher? Or the Queen? Even if the telephone is tapped.

The British High Commissioner had a long conversation with Dr Bavadra from Suva. The telephone was on the mat in the centre of the floor. With its long flex, it was answered by whoever was nearest to it from among the seated gathering. Adi Kuini wrote down the number for me on a note I still have: a lined page torn from a child's school pad. Promising to see the Commonwealth Secretary General in London immediately after my return to England, I took my leave and with me my first impressions of the physician-cum-Prime Minister whom I had, for the first time, met. That is, if we ignore those unduly adulatory recollections of a Fijian schoolboy.

8

Race is a fact of life
– Ratu Sir Kamisese Mara

Monday 1 June 1987: London

In the morning, I travelled by train to Charing Cross Station and walked, as I had done most week days from 1974 to the end of 1979, into the Strand, left to Trafalgar Square, on to Cockspur Street and Barclays Bank, then across below New Zealand House to Pall Mall. This time it was not past the great clubs of London to Marlborough Road: but left again to the British Council and the Wool Secretariat and No. 2 Carlton Gardens. There, the top echelons of the Commonwealth Secretariat had moved to enable structural work to be done on its headquarters at Marlborough House. That building was last used as Queen Mary's royal residence and made over on loan to the Commonwealth Secretariat on its establishment in 1965. The British Ministry responsible for the upkeep and maintenance of public buildings had long been worried about its weight-bearing capacity. The accumulation over the years of heavy document-filled cabinets was but one of the problems. There was a more intriguing question: whether the Thatcher Government having, it was suggested, lost real interest in the Commonwealth as an effective world policy institution and regretting the entrenchment of its Secretariat in one of the great royal buildings of London, was in fact signalling 'enough is enough'.

'Yes,' said the head porter, 'we are here temporarily, but we don't know for how long.'

'No,' I replied, 'I suppose not. There is sometimes nothing more permanent than the temporary. So we shall see. Meanwhile, it seems very elegant and gracious to me.' And I went up the circular staircase of the former home of Lord Kitchener.

The first Commonwealth Secretary General was the distinguished Canadian Arnold Smith. It was he who in 1974 had invited me to

64

join the senior staff of the Secretariat. A year later in 1975, Shridath Ramphal was selected by Commonwealth Heads of Government to succeed a reluctantly departing and in some respects disillusioned Secretary General, who had perhaps identified himself too closely in a personal sense with the Commonwealth vision. In any event, it was time for the Commonwealth equivalent – albeit smaller and more restricted in money and scope – of the United Nations Secretariat, to be headed by a man of the Third World.

Ramphal came to be a clear and unequivocal choice, competition having been elbowed aside in the wake of a timely journey through African countries by Sir John Carter, then the High Commissioner for Guyana in London. An international lawyer of repute, Ramphal had been appointed Attorney General and Minister of Foreign Affairs in the Burnham Government of his native Guyana. He had already made his name as an advocate of the interests of Caribbean sugar-producing countries, when the Commonwealth Sugar Agreement was coming to an end with Britain's prospective entry into the European Economic Community. That was far from all: his skills as an orator, his capacity to reduce complex issues to simple equations and his powers of negotiation and conciliation were already established in the minds of many. He was thus an outstanding Commonwealth man of the moment.

Today, he is in his third five-year term, having been a contender to succeed Kurt Waldheim as the United Nations Secretary General. Why he failed is another story; but one theory is that the major world powers did not want an energetic, innovative, successful international figure to deal with. Was he thus too good? Was he of the wrong race? Did he come from the wrong country for some? Or were his expectations pitched a bit too high? However all this may be, there were many who felt that what the United Nations had lost, the Commonwealth had regained.

Ramphal's immediate response to the news of the Fiji coup was loud and clear: he unequivocally condemned the destruction of the democratic process by armed soldiers, the assumption of illegal authority by the army and the unlawful detention of the newly elected Prime Minister and his colleagues. He called for an immediate return to constitutional government.

'Do you not agree,' asked one television interviewer some days later, 'that the action of the Australian and New Zealand unions in refusing to work exports to Fiji is wrong and should be condemned as unhelpful to the people of Fiji?'

The Secretary General replied, 'It is the coup that should be blamed and not the unions whose actions were merely a response to it.'

65

The strong line taken at this stage by the Secretary General was of comfort to Dr Bavadra. An Australian Broadcasting Corporation radio interview with Ramphal in London, transmitted by Radio Australia from Melbourne, was heard by the deposed Prime Minister just before I saw him at Veiseisei. To convey Dr Bavadra's appreciation of the broadcast was a first object of my meeting with Ramphal. The second was to provide him with an account of the events in Fiji during my week there. The third was to offer a personal analysis of the situation; while the fourth was to ask, on Dr Bavadra's behalf, for the mediating weight of the Secretary General to be put personally into a Commonwealth initiative for Fiji.

Near the end of the year, I looked back at a discussion note I handed over at this meeting.

General atmosphere in Fiji: Confusion, fear, terrorising of and assaults against defenceless Indian families by uncontrolled Fijian mobs in urban areas and long queues at the Australian and New Zealand High Commissions in Suva. Contrary to some press reports, business and domestic life is a long way from normal. In my view, the situation is not serious, it is grave. All that has been done since the coup is to paper over the cracks . . .

The economy: Air New Zealand and Qantas have eliminated or reduced calls at Nadi. Air Pacific flights have been markedly reduced. Virtually no passengers are flying in. The high-quality hotels on the south coast of Vitilevu are empty. Staff of all races are being laid off. The sugar crop is not being cut in any part of Fiji. There are historic examples of cane burning as the ultimate Indian protest. If this happens now and the army is sent in, the results could be horrendous. New Zealand and Australian trade unions have refused to load goods for Fiji and food supplies are already being seriously affected. External aid is being withheld and investment will dry up. If all this is sustained, the economic outlook is bleak.

Reactions in the region: . . . We await what happens at the South Pacific Forum meeting in Apia. Assuming an absent Fiji is discussed, my present guess is that New Zealand and Australia will, broadly speaking, be able to persuade the Melanesian countries to join them in condemning the coup. The Polynesian countries where the chiefly structure of society is more closely akin to that of Fiji will be more reticent.

The wider significance: The shock waves of the Fiji coup and its aftermath are arguably comparable to the effect in the Caribbean and beyond of events in Grenada in 1983. It is not necessary for me to allude to the implications for the Commonwealth . . .

Analysis of the recent election results: The Labour–National Federation Coalition is the first truly inter-racial party and government in Fiji's history. That was its strength and has been its weakness. Its success at the polls represented a class struggle, not a racial one. Fijians were divided but, in the west, widely supported Dr Bavadra. In the east of Vitilevu, urbanised Fijians wrested traditional Alliance-held Fijian national seats away to the Coalition.

It was not strictly an Indian-dominated government. The deposed Cabinet consisted of fourteen Ministers; six elected Fijians, six elected Indians, one elected part-European and one Indian appointed Senator (Attorney General). It was a talented team. The racial composition of the parliament is fixed by a Constitution and is thus unchanged (twenty-two Fijians, twenty-two Indians and eight General).

The issue was and is both a dynastic one within the chiefly structure of traditional Fijian society and a challenge to chiefly control through the ballot box. There is no question of any threat to the ownership of Fijian land or rights because the 1970 Constitution and related legislation entrenched these so well that any tinkering is almost impossible; and could not conceivably be initiated by the Bavadra Government. The ordinary Fijian does not know this. Thus, ignorance has been exploited and fears inflamed. It is reasonable to conclude that so long as the complex electoral arrangements under the 1970 Constitution meant the perpetuation of the Mara Alliance Government, then democratic electoral practices were acceptable since they coincided with the chiefly traditions of leadership and power. When this was put to the electoral test and rejected, the trouble began and the Indians have been made the scapegoats.

Ramphal was amenable to the suggestion that his personal intervention might be critical, but concerned about timing. During the week, the South Pacific Forum had been meeting in the capital of Western Samoa, Apia. Fiji was not officially represented but three of Dr Bavadra's Ministers, Tupeni Baba, Krishna Datt and Joeli Kalou, two Fijians and one Indian, had gone to lobby delegates in order to enlist the support of the Forum countries. These included Australia, New Zealand and all the independent island territories – Polynesian, Melanesian and Micronesian. The outcome was agreement to a possible mediating role for the Forum and a proposed mission to this end to Fiji led by Prime Minister Hawke of Australia.

First reports suggested that the Governor General of Fiji had turned down this initiative; but the reports were not conclusive and there was still the possibility that a Forum-sponsored visit of some kind to Fiji might take place.

The Secretary General's conclusion was that, for the time being anyway, he ought to await the outcome of the South Pacific Forum proposal. As he pointed out, it was the appropriate regional body for such first action. 'In any event, how do I get into Fiji in present circumstances?'

It was a crucial question: he could go only if formally invited by the de facto Government of Fiji via the Governor General. Such an invitation would need the prior consent and support of the four key figures: that of Dr Bavadra could be assumed; that of Ratu Mara and Colonel Rabuka could best be sought if the Governor General, as the Queen's representative in Fiji, had instructions to seek it. He would himself be hard put, it seemed to me, to adumbrate opposition to his Queen's wishes.

I thus urged the immediate intervention of the Palace. The Queen was the Head of State in Fiji. Her Majesty's personal support had already been given to the Governor General in a message which had been sent to him for the meeting of the Council of Chiefs assembled in Suva four days after the coup. It read:

> I have been following with close interest and sympathy the events of the last few days, and it grieves me that the peaceful and harmonious development of Fiji as a democratic and multi-racial society has been so suddenly and sharply disturbed.
>
> I know you are now in consultation with my loyal Council of Chiefs, and I pray that together you will find a solution which will be in keeping with the traditions of democracy, tolerance and loyalty.

In not specifically expressing her concern for the return to office of the elected government and the electoral principles enshrined in the Constitution, the Queen avoided entering the political arena in Fiji as its sovereign head.

But the Queen is also Head of the Commonwealth. She holds this office, if it can be so described, by virtue of the unanimous wish of the heads of government of participating countries, whether they are republics with their own presidential head of state, as twenty-five of the forty-nine then were; or recognise the Queen as their head of state, as eighteen then did; or have their own constitutional monarchies or hereditary rulers as six do. The position is not vested in the British Crown and thus does not automatically pass to the Queen's heir.

The Queen would be going to Vancouver to open the biennial meeting of the Commonwealth heads of governments in October. In this capacity, the Secretary General was her principal adviser and mentor. For him to be permitted to intercede in Fiji on behalf of Queen and Commonwealth, the weight of the Queen's authority and prestige in the eyes of the high chiefs of Fiji was, I believed, the only means by which the essential persuasion would be successful. A further burden would thus rest upon the Governor General. My note again:

> Proposal for discussion: . . .The Commonwealth Secretary General will already have considered whether he should seek to intercede directly in Fiji. I believe he should. A visit by him would be the essential first stage . . . Perhaps the Palace could put this to the Governor General on behalf of the Head of State.
>
> . . . The first objective of such a visit would be to frustrate adoption of a patchwork new Constitution now being prepared which would perpetuate racial enmities, heighten the prospect of communal violence and do permanent damage by disadvantaging the Indians to an unacceptable degree.
>
> The approach might be made on the basis of 'the Pacific way' which Ratu Mara has been an exponent of in the past and could hardly now decline if made in the name of the Queen and the Commonwealth Secretary General. The initial plan might be for separate mediating meetings with the power axis – the Governor General, Dr Bavadra and Ratu Mara – with the object of a joint meeting thereafter.
>
> The Secretary General might then propose that an appropriate group visit Fiji to review the Constitution in the light of current circumstances, with terms of reference which would take account of the status and aspirations of all races with particular weight to the traditions and place of the indigenous Fijians. The latter concession to the objectives of the coup might be dependent upon the acceptance of the restoration of the elected government for, say, a period of one year to enable new constitutional proposals to be drawn up, debated and accomplished legally.

If all this was to be achieved before attitudes in Fiji became too entrenched and thus irreversible, speedy action and agreement between the Secretary General and Buckingham Palace was essential as a first step. It was an argument that Dr Bavadra himself was soon to pursue in London for what seemed the one remaining hope for the restoration of his Government and of what the press, and even Ramphal himself, quaintly and wistfully referred to as 'the return to normalcy'.

'And what of Ratu Mara?' asked the Secretary General.

The former Prime Minister had made no public statement since he conceded election defeat on 12 April. Absent from Parliament at the time of the coup, he had remained silent thereafter. So rumour and speculation increased. The likelihood of his complicity in or prior cognisance of the coup spread far and wide among the population of Fiji. Not only there. The role allegedly played – or not played – by Ratu Mara became a key question for perceptive and searching reporters and might, some thought, have been a factor in the rough and ready treatment accorded to many of them by the army.

The New Zealand Herald is published in Auckland, not only the country's largest and most sprawling city but also the biggest agglomeration of semi-urbanised South Pacific Polynesians in the world – Samoans, Tongans, Niueans, Cook Island and New Zealand Maoris – all gravitating over the years to opportunity and bright lights, and too many to indebtedness, overcrowding, alcohol, customary rootlessness and crime.

On Friday 15 May and Saturday 16 May, the two days immediately after the coup, the *Herald* carried the following editorials:

FIJI'S UGLY, RACE-BASED MILITARY TAKEOVER

The seizure of power by an army colonel in Fiji is a Pacific disaster and a Commonwealth crisis. Even if power were restored to the legitimate Government within hours or days, nothing could be the same again. The hope was that democracy had taken sturdy root. It is now exposed as shallow and fragile.

Since Fiji attained independence in 1970 it has lived under the rule of Ratu Sir Kamisese Mara and his Alliance Party, a grouping that crossed racial boundaries but kept power in the hands of indigenous Fijians. The ethnic Indians, who now outnumber the indigenous Fijians by 347,000 to 330,000, have accepted this state of affairs with patience and a general absence of major friction.

Last month, however, the country elected a coalition of the Indian-dominated National Federation Party and the union-backed Labour Party. The coalition grouping gave Indians, for the first time, access to power; there were only seven indigenous Fijians among its twenty-eight members of Parliament.

The signal now seemingly given to the world is that where the

Indians were prepared to live peacefully for seventeen years under Fijian dominance, the Fijians were not prepared to suffer more than a month of the Indians . . .

The situation certainly tests the pious platitudes New Zealanders hear so often about stability in the Pacific. Here, right next door, is the sort of situation which some people imagined only far away . . .

DEMOCRACY BETRAYED

With the overthrow of democracy in Fiji has come the downfall of the man who nurtured and sustained it in surpassing fashion since the country attained its independence in 1970 – the former Prime Minister, Ratu Sir Kamisese Mara. It is not high political office that he has lost to the coup; that went in the general election that swept out his party a month ago. What he has forfeited since the Army seized power on Thursday is his personal credibility and mana.

Beaten by the ballot, Ratu Mara spent four weeks in opposition and then, in a contemptuous gesture to democracy and constitutional government yesterday, joined the so-called Council of Ministers of the new military strongman, Colonel Rabuka. The overthrow of the legitimate Government by force was a treasonable offence; by joining those who committed it, Ratu Mara looks suspiciously like an accessory after the fact – if nothing worse, for his action assuredly invites accusations of complicity in the coup.

His motives are as suspect as those of his new master. Colonel Rabuka says his actions were prompted by fear of further racial disturbance and bloodshed. But apart from one sketchy report of the murder of an Indian bus driver by an ethnic Fijian, there has been no sign of bloodshed, and the marches of protest against the election outcome seem to have been demonstrations within acceptable limits.

The colonel says he did not want to see the Army – composed almost entirely of ethnic Fijians – called out against ethnic Fijian protesters. That explanation must drastically diminish any hope among the Indian populace of its receiving much protection from the new regime.

Moreover, although Ratu Mara may believe that he personally is the best man to hold the country together – and thus is duty-bound to make his skills available to the military council – the electorate showed a month ago that it thinks differently. And in democracies the electorate decides such matters. The pity of it is, as Mr Lange has pointed out, that Ratu Mara did not use his influence and prestige in support of the constitutional processes before the coup was staged.

Yet if Ratu Mara has betrayed democracy, the Governor General, Ratu Sir Penaia Ganilau, has displayed constitutional propriety and personal courage of conspicuous degree. Now reported to be under house arrest, he has stoutly defied the military takeover, and has proclaimed his assumption of executive power and declared a state of emergency.

In Ratu Ganilau's fortitude lies probably the best hope that the numbed Fiji populace, when it recovers from its shock, will recognise where its best future lies.

As rumour compounded rumour about the former Prime Minister's possible involvement, Ratu Mara, in late May, set about telephoning the Secretary General from Suva. He was not initially successful. Ramphal, already aware of the rumours, needed time and took it, to decide what sort of line he should take.

When they did speak, he learned that Ratu Mara, worried about the reports of his alleged involvement in or endorsement of the coup, wished 'to put the record straight'. The conversation went something like this:

'But are the reports true?'

'Absolutely not.'

'Then why haven't you said so?'

'I have, but they don't report me.'

I pondered this for a moment. On Saturday 23 May, the *Fiji Times* reported what it described as Ratu Mara's first public address since he conceded defeat at the April election. He told supporters outside the Suva Civic Centre the previous day that he had been accused of staging the coup or of having had a hand in it.

'I have denied this many times, but I suppose the suspicion would always be there,' he said.

Indeed. But denial of complicity, true or not, was one thing. Failure to denounce the enforced overthrow of a democratically elected government on the part of a man who himself had been elected to office as Prime Minister under the same Constitution in four separate elections since 1970 was quite another matter.

None of this in itself is, of course, evidence let alone proof that Ratu Mara either sanctioned the coup or was privy to the intentions of its leaders beforehand. It was his sustained silence about the coup and his acceptance of appointment as Minister for Foreign Affairs under the Rabuka-led 'Council of Ministers' that was called into public question – first and foremost by the Prime Minister of New Zealand, David Lange.

On Tuesday 7 July the *Fiji Times* entered the debate with this editorial:

THE DEAFENING SILENCE

Multi-racialism or multi-culturalism, has served this nation well as a state policy.

It helped to create a dynamic and vibrant society. Fiji prospered economically and socially in so rapid a fashion that it became a model . . .

Multi-racialism recognises the inter-dependence of one community on another. It requires co-existence based on a sincere recognition of and respect for each other's rights and needs.

That these unwritten rules were observed over the past seventeen years was our biggest blessing . . .

But recent events have cast a dark pall on the country, raising questions about just how secure and deep were the bonds of multi-racialism. The ugly head of racism has reared itself, shattering the image of a happy paradise.

Has multi-racialism become a dirty word? And is it dead as a state policy?

Why are all the advocates of this policy maintaining a stony silence now?

The most deafening of all is the silence from that champion of multi-culturalism, peace and harmony, Ratu Sir Kamisese Mara. The country, and indeed the entire world on whose stage he has been a notable player, are waiting to hear him say just precisely where he stands.

As the country hurtles along the road to bankruptcy, it is time for all those leaders who built their political careers on a platform of multi-racialism to come out from their cocoons and proclaim loudly whether they now find it expedient to throw overboard the values that they have been preaching so long.

There is one further point to be made. The traditional role of the chiefs of Fiji may have been under challenge; but it remains difficult to believe that the third-ranking officer in the army, a commoner and one whose high chief was, coincidentally, the Governor General himself, would have undertaken such draconian action as the abduction of the elected Prime Minister and his Fijian and Indian ministers from a sitting of Parliament without at least a tacit nod of chiefly endorsement for his actions. It would just not make either customary or political sense. Furthermore, in his many public utterances in the aftermath of the coup, Lieutenant Colonel Rabuka sought to set great store by his respect for the customs and traditions of the Fijian people, chiefly and otherwise.

It must have been an intriguing golf game between Ratu Mara and Lieutenant Colonel Rabuka that Sunday before the coup. Two other men played with them at the Pacific Harbour course, said one report from Suva, but they were not identified. Past Lami, the hills of Serua and beyond Navua, the Pacific Harbour resort was a discreet forty kilometres or so from Suva. As always, the golf club was the sanctuary of the elite.

The conjecture could not be stilled, either inside or outside Fiji. At a press conference some forty-eight hours after the coup, the New Zealand Press Association reported, Lieutenant Colonel Rabuka went so far as to confirm that he – a Methodist lay preacher – had indeed played golf the previous Sunday with Ratu Mara. He had settled his coup plans before the game, but did not, he said, reveal them during it.

'How very sensible,' remarked one observer, 'to withhold advice of the timing of his destruction of democracy in Fiji so that knowledge of its occurrence could be denied later by the one man who might have turned the tide had he been so minded.' Admiral Poindexter, on the evidence of his testimony to the Washington Irangate enquiry, would have approved.

With a degree of editorial tongue-in-cheek, *The New Zealand Herald* noted: 'Ratu Mara was this week awarded an $87,500 prize for his role in "disaster prevention and preparedness".

'The award was announced on the day of the coup. The prize is the newly initiated United Nations Disaster Relief Organisation Prevention Award.'

It was thus interesting – if nothing more – that the former Prime Minister was away from Suva and not in Parliament when the abduction took place; and that his son-in-law, the Commander of the Royal Fiji Military Forces, Brigadier Ratu Epeli Nailatikau, was in Perth, Western Australia, a distance from Sydney in the east roughly equivalent to that between London and Moscow and a further 1800 miles to Fiji.

While these circumstances were at least a convenience to the coup planners, perhaps a more important consideration was the fact that, slowly but surely, the newly elected Bavadra Government was settling in, showing signs of seeking to heal wounds and of implementing sensibly and constructively the pledges in its electoral manifesto. It was all beginning to go too well for comfort. So, if this process was to be successfully disrupted, action to do so could not be long delayed. There would appear to be no other compelling reason for the timing of the coup since, economically, it could not have been more unfavourable. It was the start of the main tourist season and not long before the sugar mills would begin to belch. To await the completion of the cane cutting and crushing season would have meant deferment of military action until the latter part of the year. By then the new Government would have become entrenched, but the Indians would no longer have the one powerful economic weapon in their hands: the year's standing crop of sugarcane.

The timing of the coup showed a massive ignorance of or indifference to the consequences to the economy, the hardships to be visited on the population without racial distinction, the potential ruin of countless lives and the growth of physical harassment and victimisation. With it, perhaps for ever, went the good name of Fiji and its reputation for multi-racial tolerance and relative harmony, which Ratu Mara had himself done so much to foster.

In the afternoon of Tuesday 19 May, Suva was subdued and nervous. In Renwick Road, I met by chance an old and valued colleague from the past, a Fijian commoner who had risen through intellectual skills and dedication to a post of high responsibility and influence in his country. He is a man of humility, dignity and courage. We spoke of the coup and its origins.

'It is surely not, as portrayed, merely an ethnic outburst,' I suggested. 'Isn't it more a dynastic struggle within Fijian society itself and a convulsion generated at least in part by chiefs for their own ends?'

'Yes,' he replied, 'I am afraid it is. And one aspect of it is very very sad.'

The tears welled in his eyes. 'All that Ratu Mara has achieved over the past twenty-five years will be forgotten. He will be remembered now only for what he has done and what he has not done this past week.'

9

Sunday 7 June 1987

While I was not despondent when I left the Commonwealth Secretariat on the afternoon of 1 June, I was not exactly overjoyed
either. The South Pacific Forum idea seemed likely to founder. In
any event, what could it hope to achieve? Was Bob Hawke, a Prime
Minister of unorthodox credentials for this purpose, likely to have
any lasting influence; or would he be just another politician without
any real insight into the complex issues at work in Fiji? And like
Margaret Thatcher, he was soon to face a general election – in his
case, 11 July.

The gentle Pacific murmurs of sympathy in the wings of the
meeting of the South Pacific Forum in Apia were one thing, the
realities quite another. So the notion of a Forum-sponsored visit
faded from view and the days went by. As they did, the feeling
grew among political Fiji-watchers that governments would fall back
on the old placebo when basic principles are at stake.

A standard press release might read like this:

> After extensive consultation and consideration, and bearing in
> mind the sensitivity and special nature of the problems involved,
> the Cabinet has today concluded that the resolution of the current
> difficulties in . . . is best left to those directly involved: the people
> themselves.
>
> In view, however, of the links that have historically bound our
> two peoples so closely together, this Government will continue to
> give all available support that is within its power. Ministers remain
> confident that a satisfactory solution will be found in due course
> if those in positions of responsibility continue to be given appropri-
> ate trust and encouragement.

For the rest of the week, the news from Fiji remained far from
comforting.

On Saturday afternoon, the telephone rang and an operator's

voice said, 'This is Melbourne Australia calling.' A Seventh Day Adventist pastor announced himself. He had just arrived in Australia from Fiji and had travelled on the same aircraft as Dr Bavadra and his wife. He had been given my telephone number and asked to tell me that they would arrive at London Heathrow by Qantas Flight 1 on Sunday 7 June. That was tomorrow.

A dozen questions tumbled over each other as I put down the telephone. In what circumstances had they left Fiji? What was the purpose of their journey? Were they alone? Had they been able to bring out any money? What appointments, if any, had been made? Where were they to stay? Had transport been fixed? Had the British High Commissioner in Suva been told and the Foreign and Commonwealth Office in London alerted? Had Heathrow Security accordingly been advised? How would Dr Bavadra be regarded for reception purposes, both at the airport and in the eyes of Buckingham Palace? What security facilities would be provided during the visit?

Was it for me to attempt to deal with these questions and should I go to the airport? It is a sensible bureaucratic practice never to volunteer services – especially for those matters which are not within one's personal control, and certainly not on a Saturday afternoon in Britain. The one thing I could and did decide, however, was to go to Heathrow next morning.

I opened a desk drawer for a current British Airways world timetable. Melbourne–Sydney–London. Qantas daily. Arrival time: 06:55 hours. Ugh.

The M25 is London's orbital motorway. It is a far from unqualified success; but, for many, it has made driving to Heathrow a shorter and more easily accomplished journey: notably at six on a Sunday morning when you can have the motorway virtually to yourself.

Even at that sort of hour, Terminal 3 was awash with arriving travellers. The early morning of each day is the time when the big inter-continental Jumbos come in, minute after minute, from all over North America, the Indian sub-continent, the Far East, South America and Australasia. Qantas, like every long-haul carrier, queues up for a landing slot in the traffic-control arrivals pattern; and then discharges its daily passenger load with a high degree of timetable reliability. Thereafter, they are to all intents and purposes on their own.

Would this apply to Dr Bavadra and Adi Kuini, I wondered, as I drove through the Heathrow tunnel and into the Terminal 3 car park? Would they be spirited away in an anonymous black limousine; or would they be obliged to clear Immigration and Customs and then wheel out their own luggage through the green channel exit door like most everyone else? The rules for the reception of arriving and departing state guests and government visitors at London's airports are precise and efficient, provided that the procedures for starting the machinery involved are set in train in good time. Saturday afternoon for Sunday morning was not in that category without a high-level diplomatic entry point; and I was no longer properly placed to press the button.

When a formal inter-government request with proper notice is received by the Foreign and Commonwealth Office in London, the welcome mat will be put out at the door of the arriving aircraft for visiting heads of state and government, immediate members of royal families, cabinet ministers or their equivalent and high-ranking international and national public servants. But a line is drawn. Who qualifies and who does not is described in information notes sent out from time to time to high commissions and embassies in London. None the less, the daily numbers of arrivals and departures to whom the special facilities are extended at the London airports can run into scores – including the prolific retinues and families of some exotic visitors. Each of those for whom the procedural tap is turned on will be formally received by a 'meeter and greeter', on behalf of Her Majesty the Queen or the Secretary of State for Foreign and Commonwealth Affairs, as the case may be. There will perhaps have been an early awakening and drive from Tunbridge Wells for a retired group captain who has had to mug up on the dynastic intricacies of an oil sheikhdom, the unfamiliar ranking titles of Nepal or Malaysia, the debt rescheduling problems of Brazil or recent events in South Korea.

Upon disembarkation, the official party is taken to the terminal's VIP suite where passports and baggage checks are quietly taken from anxious aides for rapid informal clearance. Depending upon the status of the visitor, the staff of the ambassador or high commissioner of the country concerned will be fussing about the transport, the seating priorities in the cars and the fact that extra persons have turned up in the retinue without prior notification but with considerable extra baggage. There will be some sweating over the moment to seek final agreement to the details of the day's programme; and last-minute checks at the hotel to ensure that the suites that have been allocated are set up and ready as they should be.

It is not always so. Ratu Mara, as Prime Minister of Fiji, came to London in 1972, a year or so after independence. He and his wife, Adi Lady Lala, had been booked into a penthouse suite at his

78

hotel. All the arrangements had been checked and double-checked. Everything went swimmingly until the manager of the hotel turned to unlock the door.

With a flourish, he declaimed, 'Do come in, Prime Minister.' But the door would not budge. The security arrangements had been so good that a special lock had been installed by the hotel's security man, who had the keys. Sadly, he had not been told the time of the official party's arrival and was thus not there to re-open his carefully protected accommodation. It took half an hour for him to be found. A tired and irritable Prime Minister was not amused to have to wait. Those of us with some degree of involvement in the matter found it desirable to attend to other urgent work during the waiting time and thus keep out of prime ministerial firing range.

In the Hillingdon Suite, as it now is – the Alcock and Brown Suite, in the past – of Heathrow's Terminal 3, coffee and biscuits will be served on immaculate china and, unknown to most visitors received there, the British Airports Authority will bill the Foreign and Commonwealth Office for the service extended on its behalf to every such arriving and departing visitor. The 'meeter and greeter' will say his formal farewells and get into his Ford Escort for the drive home, his day's work done. Or more often, he will pull out his notes for the arrival of – who next? In this case, Sunday 7 June, the present Prime Minister of Fiji perhaps, the coup notwithstanding?

I thought it hardly likely. There would have been no request from Fiji itself for the extension of the usual courtesies – even if there were courtesies which could be regarded by the protocol-consumed Foreign and Commonwealth Office as appropriate for a short-term Prime Minister in such unpromising circumstances. No one is more skilled than the English at giving the cold shoulder.

Before leaving home, I had lingeringly fingered outdated diplomatic passes which gave entry to the inner sanctums of the security zone of Heathrow: one was issued when I was at the Fiji High Commission in London and the second during my time at the Commonwealth Secretariat thereafter. These documents were supposed to have been handed in when the appointments came to an end; but whoever does that? Maybe I could use one of them to get to the aircraft door itself. It used to be possible. I wondered whether it still was. But no. It was not worth taking a chance and hardly a sensible thing to greet a Prime Minister, deposed or otherwise, from the arms of two large security guards.

So I went to the main arrivals concourse of Terminal 3 and peered around through the hubbub. At the end of the walkway from the Customs exit was a bunch of TV and still cameras, with men jockeying for position – arguing, complaining and flourishing press cards to unimpressed policemen who were trying to move them on. I walked over and joined in, fingering my British Virgin Islands driving licence. It was in machine-produced plastic with a nice colour photograph and an impressive official stamp. It worked wonders throughout the next hour. No one looked at it carefully, and even the *Sydney Morning Herald* seemed to be impressed by the fact that the Caribbean was at last taking an interest in the affairs of the South Pacific.

'You are, presumably, waiting for someone,' I ventured to a nearby photographer.

'Yeah, the deposed Prime Minister of Fiji: Timossi Bavardra.'

'Ah. I'm in the right place then.'

'Know 'im?'

'Yes.'

'Good on yer. Tell us when he comes out?'

'Certainly.'

'Give us the nod!'

'Yes.'

'Rick – joker here knows Bavardra.'

The *Herald* took a hand: 'Who do you work for? Some outfit in the Caribbean?'

'Yes, in a kind of way.'

'Stringer?'

'No.'

'Strong silent type, I can see.'

'Not really.'

'Where did you meet Bavardra?'

'In Fiji. Just back. "Bavahndra" actually.'

'Better note that. Thanks. What's it like, Fiji I mean?'

'Not good.'

'I'm not really surprised. All those bloody Indians. Don't really blame the army bugger.'

Not 'all those bloody Indians' stood behind us, but there was a quiet somewhat tense group of about fifty people. Most of them were indeed Indians, but there were some Fijians and one or two white faces as well. A row of placards held by those in the front line read FIGHT FOR FIJI. Not particularly sensible advice, I thought, in the current military circumstances of that country. But the general idea seemed to be on the right lines.

There was a pause in the emission of arriving passengers from the Customs exits. And then suddenly and without notice, Dr Bavadra and his wife emerged with a security guard. I slipped forward and just had time to say 'Welcome to Britain, Prime Minister' when they were engulfed by reporters, photographers, the assembled Fiji parishioners and an aroused and curious public in the arrivals concourse. Dr Bavadra was swept away and out of sight between flashing cameras and thrusting microphones. I took hold of Adi Kuini's arm and propelled her gently forward as best I could. She had long since lost sight of her husband and must well have wondered suddenly what now was happening. She confessed later that she had been worried by the sudden and unexpected human avalanche. The kerbside press conference over, the Prime Minister and his wife were installed in a black Mercedes. There were moments of brief farewell before they were driven away, alone.

Terminal 3 returned to normal – whatever that is at Terminal 3. And I met for the first time Jai Ram Reddy, former leader of the National Federation Party and Attorney General in the Bavadra Government; and Dr Tupeni Baba, the Minister for Education. Both had preceded Dr Bavadra to London.

So far as I could tell, there was no representative of the Fiji High Commission present when Dr Bavadra and his wife arrived at Heathrow on Sunday 7 June. There were no official calls paid on him at the hotel; no assistance given him with transport, meetings, office services or security. The High Commissioner was Sailosi Wai Kepa, a Lauan lawyer and former magistrate and Director of Public Prosecutions, whose wife and the wife of Ratu Mara are sisters. Asked by a London newspaper about his attitude towards the deposed Prime Minister and the announced purpose of the visit to London, he was reported as replying:

'I have been instructed by Suva to treat him just like any other Fiji citizen.'

When told of this, Dr Bavadra smiled wryly and said, 'Well, at least that would be a change for the better.'

I had been to call on the High Commissioner some months before the April elections. The Labour/Federation Coalition was then in its infancy. I had asked him how he assessed it.

'It is,' he had said, 'genuinely multi-racial and winning a growing amount of support. But it has a long way to go and little prospect of success.' There were some able leaders among them, he conceded, but like others, he dismissed Timoci Bavadra as purely a figurehead. He clearly believed that the Indians were smart enough to realise that their only chance of electoral victory and political power lay in accepting nominal Fijian leadership.

That leadership was to prove to be far from nominal. And it did the Indian cause no harm to discover it.

10

Sunday 7 – Wednesday 10 June 1987

The timing of Dr Bavadra's arrival in London was less than ideal.
Beyond his control this may have been, but the fact remained that
Sunday 7 June was a mere four days away from the United Kingdom
1987 general election. It was thus the final campaign sprint to the
British electoral winning post. Not only were press, radio and
television subjecting their subscribers to something approaching
election news overkill; but in-situ politicians and rival candidates,
both close to exhaustion, were interested in little else but the ballot
box outcome on 11 June. Less so, the eager journalists in London
of the ABC, AAP, NZBC, NZPA, Reuters and their colleagues.
They had other editors to satisfy and other minds to occupy.

The concentration for the final days on the parochialism of the
poll meant that non-election news and issues, however compelling,
had little chance of serious political attention. Or public exposure –
as the jargon has it. It was something that Dr Bavadra, so recently
elected to office himself, could understand – but need not
accept.

The British Government, it could be said, had no direct responsibility in the aftermath of the Fiji coup. That would not have been
the reaction of a government of France. The French retain close
links and influential ties with their former colonies. Whatever their
motives, they do not happily allow the establishment and consolidation of a system of government repugnant to or incompatible with
la belle France. Ninety-six years of British colonial rule of Fiji and
seventeen years of independence, however, meant some enduring
sentiment, overseas aid and technical assistance; plus a watchful eye

on regional implications and security. Nothing special or unusual in
that, in ex-colonial British philosophy. So the formal response would
be that Fiji was an independent sovereign state, wholly and exclusively responsible for the conduct of its internal and external affairs.
Sympathetic noises might be uttered to Dr Bavadra from a modest
ministerial or diplomatic level, but not much more.

The British Government was, however, one thing. Her Majesty
the Queen and the Palace quite another. I studied the facts again:
forty-nine separate independent countries recognised the Queen as
titular head of the Commonwealth, irrespective of their individual
constitutional arrangements and whether or not they had a separate
Head of State. Australia, New Zealand, Fiji, Tuvalu, Papua New
Guinea and the Solomon Islands were among those with the Queen
as Head of State. Two fellow Melanesian South Pacific island countries, that is.

Her Majesty was advised, as the need arose, by her ministers in
each of the countries of which she was also Head of State. But in
the absence of a de facto Prime Minister of Fiji, the dissolution of
the elected Parliament having effectively removed Dr Bavadra and
his colleagues from ministerial office, the Governor General would
tender that advice on his assumption of executive authority for the
administration of Fiji shortly after the coup.

There were precedents of a kind for the exercise of executive
authority by the sovereign through her representative, following the
military overthrow of a constitutional government recognising the
Queen as Head of State. In March 1967 the Queen was the head of
the lawful government of Sierra Leone when army officers took
over, dissolved the House of Representatives and all political parties.
The Governor General was obliged to leave the country. The most
durable Governor General of all is Sir Paul Scoon of Grenada.
Appointed in 1978, he survived the eruptions of 1979 when Sir Eric
Gairy's Government was overthrown and succeeded by the People's
Revolutionary Government of Maurice Bishop which suspended the
1974 Constitution. In October 1983, when Bishop was murdered
and violence broke out, the Governor General facilitated the intervention of Caribbean and American forces. He presided over an
Advisory Council from November 1983 until a General Election
twelve months later. Constitutional continuity on the spot resided
in the person of the Governor General. In this respect, the Fiji
Constitution was no different.

The implications of the dissolution of the Parliament of Fiji, lawful
or otherwise, were to shadow Dr Bavadra throughout his visit to
London and thereafter. The nature of his reception – or lack of it –

at Heathrow Airport was a portent. The next question would be his status at the Palace.

The popular press in Britain got an angle and plugged it, notwithstanding election preoccupation – or perhaps as passing relief from that preoccupation:

QUEEN SNUBS DEPOSED FIJI PRIME MINISTER

Dr Bavadra was initially dismayed, but not deterred.

'The Queen must see me,' he said publicly. 'After all, she is my Queen. She cannot refuse me.'

But refuse she did, and it was left to Sir William Heseltine, Her Majesty's Private Secretary, to explain why. It had been suggested that the Queen's decision was taken on the advice of the Governor General, as Her Majesty's representative in Fiji. Whether or not that was so and, if so, whether such advice was given without duress, is not material; and it is reasonable to suppose that, irrespective of the formal nature of the triangular relationships, expressions of view about this and related matters also made their way from the British High Commission in Suva to Whitehall and the Palace during the sensitive days of that London week of June 1987. Throughout, in the background, was the Fiji High Commission in London, outwardly distancing itself from the delegation's visit.

Dr Bavadra's first reaction was to decline to talk only with Sir William Heseltine. As the democratically elected Prime Minister of a loyal Commonwealth country, he had not journeyed across the world after enforced incarceration in his own land to be fobbed off with a private secretary, however courteously welcoming. So, at first, he said no. And it looked for a time to be both his first – and his last – word.

The Commonwealth Secretary General then took a hand. At short notice, he left London for Barbados where, with some twelve heads of governments from the Caribbean, he attended the funeral of Prime Minister Errol Barrow, the second Barbadian prime minister to die in office in two years. There Shridath Ramphal learned of Dr Bavadra's negative reaction to the Palace response to his request to see the Queen and to the notion that he see the Private Secretary instead. From Barbados he urged that the opportunity for such a meeting not be rejected: any meeting was preferable to none, and could lead to another.

It was a timely intervention; and Dr Bavadra pondered the advice overnight. Next day, he had changed his mind. In the event, either he or his ministerial colleagues went to the Palace office for meetings with Sir William Heseltine and the Assistant Private Secretaries on three separate occasions. The political leaders of Britain might be absorbed with a general election. Buckingham Palace was not. And perhaps it helped a bit that the Private Secretary was an Australian.

Dr Bavadra was gratified by the performance of the reserve players. Sir William and his colleagues could not, he said, have been more helpful. He was impressed by their understanding of Fiji and their constructive sympathy. They were ready to see him at short notice at any time during his week in London; and the meetings were set up with a minimum of fuss. He was assured that his submissions and concerns would be laid immediately thereafter before Her Majesty the Queen, who was following events as they unfolded in Fiji with close attention – based on first-hand personal knowledge of its leaders and people. The fact remained, however, that he was denied the royal access he sought and deeply believed he was entitled to. The rebuff was there, whatever the constitutional and legal niceties. He was forced to return home without the comfort and support that an audience with the Queen herself would have given him. It would have meant that his royal Head of State regarded him still as the elected head of Her Majesty's Government in Fiji. There are some who now wonder whether, given those relatively early days in June 1987 and in the light of what was to come in Fiji, the Palace decision will stand the test of time.

Throughout the week the Governor General in Suva was kept informed by the Palace of the discussions and the delegation's efforts to persuade the Queen to intervene in support of the restoration of her democratically elected government of Fiji. So indeed it could be said that at this stage Dr Bavadra got through to the Queen's representative via the Palace. Unusual, but in this case it was so, in a sort of way.

The Coalition campaign for the Fiji 1987 general election had been run on a financial shoestring. Not so the long-established Alliance Party with its big-business support, including that of much of the Suva Gujerati business community. The Alliance was believed to have booked up taxis a year ahead for bringing in voters to the polling station booths. This was beyond the resources of the Coalition. Its financial crises were on a different level – like running out of filing clips and writing paper at some of its polling station booths. But, *mirabile dictu*, it had won. So now, what approach to its spending would its ministerial delegation adopt in the heady, if short-lived, financial freedoms of London and elsewhere outside Fiji? Extravagance is a temptation to which many, exhilarated by first-time electoral endorsement, have succumbed.

The answer was: with an unimpeachable sense of responsibility. No trail of financial profligacy was to be left behind. There were no hired chauffeur-driven limousines, no chandeliered receptions, no lavish dinners, and no nocturnal partying. It was serious, all-consuming business from start to finish. The costs were being met by the London committee which had organised Dr Bavadra's transport from Heathrow Airport to the hotel – itself a relatively modest hostelry in Queensgate. The delegation brought no support staff as such, not even a secretary or typist. The London committee did the best it could to help. The hotel's facilities for communications and paperwork fell short of the five-star chain class. All telephone calls, in and out, had to pass through an old-fashioned switchboard and operator. There was a single telephone in the small public lounge where most discussions were held and action planned. There was no security. Visitors came, overheard and departed. Some to return, to sit and apparently read a newspaper. Two bedrooms were entered without authorisation by the hotel to 'fix' bedside telephone faults that did not exist. The pace was frenetic, changes of plan exhaustingly frequent, and orderly discussion difficult. Co-ordination and record-keeping were rudimentary. Attention to administrative detail was not always consistent. Enthusiasm and energy were unbounded. Optimism prevailed.

There was no apparent allocation of tasks or responsibility. Some-how, someone seemed to deal with transport and meetings; someone else with finding a typist in the hotel and preparing drafts in time; yet another would be answering, sotto voce, the stream of press and other calls which kept the telephone in constant use. One expected rest day never eventuated, because an unscheduled meeting at the Palace arose and had to be prepared for. The commonest sentences began, 'Doc, would you look at this'; or 'Doc, have you seen that . . .'; or just 'Doc . . .' Every so often gales of laughter relieved the tension. And, of course, it was all in a mixture of English and Fijian. It was hard to believe that these were some of the men who had been taken at the point of a gun from a session of Parliament and held in enforced detention until only three weeks before. And that their departure from Fiji itself had been surreptitious and hazardous.

In the dank mid-June London drizzle, taxis were used, but for essential purposes only. Otherwise, it was public transport. The hotel lounge became something like the claustrophobic waiting room of a small railway station to Dr Bavadra and Adi Kuini. Largely silent, she stayed observant and concerned, the isolation preying on her nerves. Meals were haphazard and often just sandwiches and coffee or soup. With his personal asceticism and sensitivity to cost and how it was being met, Dr Bavadra set a standard of self-restraint which was followed without question by his delegation.

There was Jai Ram Reddy, Attorney General and nominated by the new Prime Minister as a member of the Senate on 12 April. He was a quietly impressive, somewhat aloof, man – calm, lucid and sparing of intervention. When he did speak, he was logical and persuasive. He spent much of his time listening and drafting: but there were moments when he would allow himself the indulgence of a barely perceptible smile.

In contrast was Dr Tupeni Baba, Minister of Education, and until recently a lecturer at the University of the South Pacific in Suva. He it was who had, surprisingly, beaten the popular former Deputy Prime Minister, Ratu David Toganivalu, in the hitherto safe Alliance Fijian National seat of Suva, by a majority of 550 in a poll of 24,887. The centrepiece of Tupeni's handsome sculpted face was his dazzling white teeth set between wide and open lips. He was a natural communicator, enjoyed mixing it with the press and could, he believed, be mesmerising, as his long fingers flayed the air to emphasise his points. His engaging impetuosity put him in the forefront of debate. And he relished both the preparation of public speeches and the delivery of them.

On the morning of Tuesday 9 June, Joeli Kalou, the Minister for Labour and Immigration, arrived in London. Short, bearded and stockily built, he would have been at home in the front row of the national rugby team. He had been to Geneva to represent Fiji at a meeting of the International Labour Organisation. Formal advice of his attendance had been sent by the Government of Fiji before the coup. When he presented his credentials at the ILO headquarters in Geneva, he was shown a subsequent telegram withdrawing his accreditation. It was in the name of erstwhile Trinidadian James Maraj, the Secretary for Foreign Affairs in the pre-election Government and of the post-coup regime. Joeli was a puckish likeable man with a New Zealand university, teaching and union background. Undeterred by his enforced defrocking, he sought out a friend at court and was duly accepted as an observer to the ILO meeting. He then lobbied enthusiastically in the corridors for worldwide trade union support; and, hospitably embraced by the ICFTU delegation, got himself put down to speak on the Fiji situation a week later. His enterprise rewarded, he was to return to Geneva for this purpose.

'. . . in a mixture of English and Fijian.' Not English, Fijian and Hindustani?

87

In the days after the coup, the agency wires ran hot as correspondents and stringers filed stories for radio and TV bulletins, the daily press and weekly news magazines. The first South Pacific military coup was a major news item throughout the Commonwealth and beyond. As tourists streamed out, overseas newsmen streamed into Fiji, many to the sanctuary of the Travelodge in Suva. It was comfortable and well placed for their purpose – immediately opposite the imposing grey stone edifice of Government Buildings which house the Parliament and the judiciary, the law courts and most ministry offices. In front of the main entrance is Albert Park, named after Queen Victoria's consort and the home of Fijian rugby, Indian soccer and part-European hockey; together with cricket which, mercifully, embraces them all. The Park – the word being used in an antipodean sense of sports ground – had been the scene of one of the worst incidents of mass violence and intimidation in the post-coup period of racial animosity.

It used to be said that to write about a country you have to be there for either a week or a lifetime. Nothing in between made sense. In the first circumstance, you might get away with the superficial and even the trivial. In the second, you were assumed to have acquired judgment, penetrative skill and interpretative wisdom. Hopefully without attitudes. All that remained was whether you had the capacity to impart these things; and, if so, whether anyone else was interested when you did.

It is no longer entirely the case. There are now highly talented, widely read and travelled investigative journalists who rapidly come to terms with the common-denominator crises they are sent by their employers to describe. The good journalist is no more the mere recording instrument for events he witnesses or conferences he attends. He is commentator on, and instant analyst of, what he observes and hears. World television has such material every day. Much of it is acceptable in the transient terms of the daily newspaper or news bulletin. What it lacks, however, is the reflective depth which takes account of the special complexities of an individual society. There is, for this, neither the time nor the money. Thus to some newsmen, the Fiji coup was just another example of a worldwide trend – religious and racial intolerance, social and economic instability, and human incapacity to handle human problems without rancour and violence. What was new and newsworthy was that the horizon of the human tragedy was pushed outwards to embrace an island country of the South Pacific for the first time.

All newsmen, local and foreign, worked under great strain and risk. Press cards seemed to be an incitement to harassment by soldiers, police or groups of aggressive young Fijians, rather than a protection. Their hotel rooms were broken into by the army; tapes, cameras, typewriters and recorders were seized. Some were abused, arrested, held and released. Some were threatened with being shot for attempting to take photographs. The Radio Australia correspondent and a New Zealand television newsman were deported. It was quite clear why. The local reporters – Fijian, Indian, European and others – did the best they could to uphold the traditions of impartial reporting of what they saw and heard. It was far from easy. They suffered even worse victimisation and pressure. Objectivity was sorely strained.

However experienced and versatile they may be, suitcase correspondents do suffer from having to make instant judgments and to meet filing deadlines while events unfold. When there is room for differing interpretations – and events moved fast in Fiji – they must occasionally succumb to the over-simplified if not the wholly inaccurate. So it was that two quite separate assumptions came to be perpetuated in news reports at this time; and were not apparently questioned in either case.

The first was to describe the indigenous Fijians simply as Melanesians. While this is basically true, it is not the whole story; and to leave it like that is to omit a fundamental aspect of the racial equation of the election and the coup.

Fiji is the racial divide of two South Pacific cultures – Melanesian and Polynesian. Fijians are, in widely varying degrees, a mixture of both. Those in the north-west of Vitilevu and the interior are pure Melanesian – darker, stockier and with a more egalitarian social structure than the Polynesian. In the south-east of Vitilevu, Cakaudrove and Taveuni, the skin colour is a little lighter, the hair less fuzzy, the physique more imposing. The chiefly structure and Polynesian social and political influences are stronger. In the eastern islands of Lau and Lomaiviti, Polynesian physical characteristics and social influences prevail. There are villages today where the descendants of the marauding Tongan adventurers of the past still live; where houses are built in the Tongan not the Fijian style; and where dress and the first language are Tongan not Fijian. It is here in these small, relatively isolated, communities that the chiefly system is at its most durable. It is here, in Lau, that you find many of the best cricketers in Fiji; the creamy-skinned and most elegant of Fijian women; arguably the finest dancers; and some of the best-educated and most articulate of Fijian men and women. Lakeba is the chiefly island of Lau and Ratu Mara is its king.

The second point was of greater substance. It was the reiteration of the phrase 'the new Indian-dominated Government' and the conclusion that it was this which had, overnight, caused the 1970 Constitution to become inimical to Fijian interests generally and an intolerable threat to Fijian paramountcy, in particular. Was the phrase a fair description of the outcome of the April 1987 election?

Throughout much of its tenure of office from 1970 to 1987, the Alliance Government put out *Fiji Today*, an annual publication of the Ministry of Information. This was its description, in 1981, of the electoral system:

'The principal aim of the electoral system is the ensurance of a racial balance in the legislature. By this balance, multi-racial harmony is guaranteed in a country where the original inhabitants are outnumbered by the immigrants.'

Had anything really changed?

The constitutional arrangements for communal and multi-racial electoral voting were not simple, but they were well tested – in five successive general elections since 1970 – and understood. Each voter had not one, but four, votes, to be exercised separately and, in the case of three of them, inter-racially. It was an inspired barrier-crossing system. The first vote was for a communal candidate – Fijian, Indian or General (the latter being the 'others', European, Chinese, and mixed race). The remaining three votes were for Fijian, Indian and General candidates in 'national' seats where voters of all races made their choices. It was fashionable in the 1970s to talk of this as 'cross-voting'. So Fijians voted for Fijian, Indian and General candidates in such constituencies; Indians voted for Indian, Fijian and General candidates; and General electors did the same. These devices meant that to be elected, a National seat candidate of any race had to capture votes from the others in order to emerge on the top of the constituency poll. The population distribution by race was not, of course, even. The urban and the largely Indianised sugar centres of population on Vitilevu and Vanualevu differed greatly from the almost exclusively Fijian-populated smaller islands.

The 1970 Constitution provided for an elected Parliament of fifty-two members: twenty-two Fijians, twenty-two Indians and eight Others. In the April 1987 election, the twelve Fijian and three General communal seats were won by the Alliance; and all twelve Indian communal seats by the Coalition. The national seats resulted as follows:

	Coalition	Alliance
Fijian	7	3
Indian	7	3
General	2	3

So the Coalition of the Labour and National Federation parties won twenty-eight seats and the election. The Alliance total was twenty-four seats.

But there was a snag. There were only seven Fijians out of twenty-eight seats in the victorious Coalition. Worse, it was claimed by their opponents, there were nineteen Indians. The balance had been destroyed and the frailty of the Constitution revealed!

Yet, was it an 'Indian-dominated Government'? It was not an Indian-dominated Parliament because that was constitutionally impossible. Racial representation, as distinct from party support, was unchanged in the new Parliament. It was, however, an Indian-dominated majority party with Fijian leadership and support, just as the Alliance had always been a Fijian-led and dominated party with European and Indian support.

When it came to the selection of his Cabinet, Dr Bavadra moved with circumspection. Six of the seven Fijian members of parliament were appointed to be ministers. They were given the most sensitive portfolios – Fijian and Home Affairs, the Public Service, Lands, Labour and Immigration, Agriculture, Education and Rural Development. Seven of the nineteen Indian members were appointed ministers; there was one minister of mixed race and an appointed Attorney General, Jai Ram Reddy, who had not stood for election on this occasion. So, racially, the Cabinet broadly reflected the population figures by race; and 6–7–1 ratio could, as the Commonwealth Secretary General observed in June, hardly be said to justify the racial dominance attributed to it.

But said it was; and the myth became perpetuated in the light of the crucial switch of urban Fijian communal votes from the Alliance to the Coalition. So, too, the awesome conclusion that class might indeed have triumphed at the polls in a totally unforeseen way.

Yet, if racial composition of the Cabinet was sensibly balanced, was it seen to be so? Maybe not. There were three Fijians in the ministerial delegation in London and only one Indian. Fijian and Indian customary dress manifestly differs; but custom and comfort in chilly London are not necessarily compatible. So initially jackets and long trousers suitable for the climate had been brought and were worn by the Fijians. There was a case for relinquishing personal comfort for their appearances on the public platform at Brent and Leicester; and especially, for the formal meetings at Buckingham Palace and with the Commonwealth Secretary General. So suits were abandoned and the sulu reinstated by the Fijians. This was the mid-calf-length wrap-around skirt, with bare legs below and strong sandals with no socks. It was a style perfected years before by Ratu

Sir Lala Sukuna in London and at Lake Success, New York, where, on formal occasions, it was topped by a stiff white shirt, black tie and short-cut black jacket. A nice combination of two worlds and one which was not exactly 'Indian-dominated'.

There was yet a further point. On the day of Dr Bavadra's arrival in London from Fiji, I returned home to welcome friends from the Caribbean. Elihu Rhymer was one of them. A man of engaging charm and wit, he is a compulsive interlocutory provocateur. He is also President of Air BVI, the airline of the British Virgin Islands, and Chairman of the BVI Tourist Board. He it was who raised the question of the Fiji coup and its implications for the Commonwealth.

'I am not really surprised. You cannot expect an indigenous people to stay outnumbered and outrepresented in their own country and not object to it. And when they see a new government elected which will result in the loss of their land and their likely racial subjugation, they are going to complain about it in one way or another, aren't they?'

I sought to respond, but where to begin? 'If you believe this, either the situation has been misunderstood or it has been deliberately misrepresented. Perhaps both. The Prime Minister is a Fijian, there is a racially balanced Cabinet . . .'

He looked astounded. 'You are telling me,' he said, 'that the new Prime Minister of Fiji is not an Indian?'

'Yes, I am. He is a Fijian. A medical doctor, in fact.'

Elihu frowned. 'Do you know that throughout the whole of the Caribbean – I speak from recent personal knowledge – it is believed that Dr Bavadra is an Indian and that that is why the Fiji army took action? Black Caribbean people understand and sympathise with that. They don't want no Indian domination either. What you say makes it all very different and much more complex.'

'All very different and much more complex.' Indeed it was, I thought, as Dr Bavadra considered the need for a small but urgent public relations exercise to establish his true racial credentials and to dispose of some unexpected misconceptions about them. The Caribbean had inadvertently done the South Pacific a modest service.

In the late afternoon of Wednesday 10 June, the Commonwealth Secretary General and his wife entertained the Fiji delegation to tea at their Mayfair residence in Hill Street.

With the Palace snub story still going full bore, the attention of the press turned again to the principal executive of the Commonwealth to elicit what his reaction would be. News of the time and place of the meeting had been ferreted out; and when Dr Bavadra and Adi Kuini arrived at the Ramphal residence by London taxi, the press were there in force outside the entrance. There they were to wait with understandable impatience throughout the two-hour meeting inside.

Shridath Ramphal and Timoci Bavadra were meeting for the first time. Ratu Mara it was with whom Ramphal had been dealing as Prime Minister of Fiji for the twelve years of his office since 1975. He was, of course, well used to adjusting to changes in the faces of Commonwealth leaders and their policies – Australia, Canada, New Zealand, India, Guyana, Trinidad, Jamaica, West and East Africa. It was in the essential nature of political life and those who serve it.

The supporting Secretariat staff were an Assistant Secretary General and a number of heads of divisions – international affairs, legal and public relations, all of whose contributions might be needed. Introductions were informal and quick; and Shridath's sunny smile was already at work as he welcomed the delegation to his inner sanctum.

'Not everyone gets in here, I can tell you. So there must be something special about this meeting.'

It was good relaxing stuff. And those relatively new to the diplomatic hustlings of London felt welcome and at ease.

'I have, as you know, just returned from Barbados. I was able to speak about Fiji with Caribbean prime ministers who had gone there for Errol Barrow's funeral. They had many questions about the Fiji situation and they were all delighted to learn that I was to meet with you today. So you have the implicit support and encouragement of my part of the world. Together with one or two others I know of.' .

Dr Bavadra spoke with intensity and emotion about the situation he had left in Fiji and the circumstances in which he and his colleagues had been able to make their odyssey to London. He described the rampant fear of physical violence; the unthinking ruin of the economy in prospect; and the destruction of a tolerant way of inter-racial life which he and his colleagues had sought to uphold. He spoke too of his wish to avoid seeing Fiji sucked into the vortex of big-power world politics.

'You have been criticised,' said the Secretary General, 'for wanting Fiji to become a non-aligned country and thus not to be directly attuned to the policies of the Western power alignment.'

'That is so,' agreed Dr Bavadra.

'It is a sorry comment on the world,' Ramphal went on, 'that if you want to be non-aligned politically, there is something insidious about that. It would seem to be sensible for the smaller countries to derive influence and negotiating clout from being together in a common cause – for peace – but it does not appear to be seen like that.'

Much more was said by Dr Bavadra and his colleagues between the coffee and the smoked salmon sandwiches; and the Secretary General was entreated to initiate dialogue, discussion and consultation within Fiji itself, with the direct and positive encouragement of the Head of the Commonwealth, Her Majesty the Queen.

There was the question of what to say to the press and, as is customary, a draft press release – a short one in this case – had been prepared in advance for consideration. It was drafted by and with a Commonwealth Secretariat slant, as Ramphal made clear. It did not quite seem to fit the bill as the Fiji delegation saw it. So none was issued and it was left to Dr Bavadra to do what he could and to say what he felt right to those who had waited outside the door in Hill Street for so long.

Timoci Bavadra has an interesting technique for responding to press questions he either does not like or is not disposed to answer. When asked such a question, he simply remains silent. But not understanding this on the first occasion, the questioner repeats the question. The silence will then continue until the nonplussed enquirer tacitly admits defeat and abandons what he asked.

As the door opened on to Hill Street and the Fiji delegation prepared to depart, the microphones were thrust forward, cameras were raised and voices competed.

'How have your talks gone with the Secretary General, Prime Minister?'

'Fine, thank you.'

'What did you discuss?'

'Everything we could think of.'

'Will you be going to the Palace again?'

'Yes.'

'Do you expect to see the Queen?'

'If I am going to the Palace again, it is always possible.'

'Are you returning to Fiji?'

'Of course.'

'Will you be seeing the Governor General when you do?'

'I expect so.'

'Do you believe that you will return to the office of Prime Minister of Fiji?'

Silence.

The question was repeated.

Still silence.

'Dr Bavadra, I asked you whether . . .'

'Thank you, gentlemen. I think it is time for us to leave now.'

I do not think that Margaret Thatcher would get away with this, even if she were to want to. Perhaps Dr Bavadra won't for long either. But for the present he appeared to do so; and it was singularly effective.

Failure to plead, the lawyers would call it, I suppose.

11

Saturday 13 June 1987

Before leaving England to begin their long journey home to the South Pacific, Dr Bavadra and Adi Kuini escaped from the rigours of London to Sevenoaks in Kent. It was their one day of relaxation and privacy away from the hotel lobby, the newsmen, the telephones and the eavesdroppers. The chill of a wet June day did nothing to dampen their pleasure at the peacefulness of the garden and the resplendence of the spring flowers.

He talked and then fell silent for minutes on end, which was as it should be in such circumstances. He recalled his early formative years in Fiji and New Zealand; those like Macu Salato, who had preceded him in medicine; his time on loan to the Government of the Solomon Islands; and the help and encouragement he had received from Charles Gurd, a consultant physician of distinction and erstwhile Director of Medical Services in Fiji. As such, Gurd also held the even grander title of Inspector General of the South Pacific Health Service. His brusque but warm Bristolian directness had put many a struggling Pacific Island medical man into the right niche in his chosen profession. And so Dr Bavadra came to spend some years in medical and physical isolation in Lau, the chiefly seat of Ratu Mara and the man who was to be his arch political rival so many years ahead.

He asked me how I thought things would turn out. It did not seem to be a day for misplaced optimism, however well intentioned.

I paused, as any sensible observer does at such moments. 'All the stark realities of an indifferent world suggest that the guns will prevail and that the people will lose. At least in the foreseeable future and unless you can get everyone concerned round the conference table and keep them there.'

The most influential and durable court confidants in Fijian society are said to be those who give advice which coincides with that which the chief wishes to hear. And Fijians are not alone in that. There are countries where senior civil servants, having ascertained the predilections of their political masters, proceed to advance all the reasons why the politically preferred course should be adopted. It leads to a satisfactory working relationship and a quiet life.

'That could mean that democracy and the judgment of the ballot box may be at an end in Fiji.'

'Yes,' I replied, 'it could.'

He reflected in silence. 'I cannot accept that. I have a feeling that it will all come out right. But I concede that it will not be easy.'

I did not demur. There is all the difference between the pessimism of the intellect and the optimism of the will. You cannot disabuse such simplicity and strength of faith when there is deep-seated belief that destiny is at work.

For perhaps it was. A kind of quiet messianic steel comes through from Dr Bavadra. Together with compassion. Maybe it was not for nothing that the Vikings of the Sunrise, the ancestors of all Fijians, who first arrived long ago from a land far to the west in a great canoe, came ashore at the village of Veiseisei, on the south-west coast of Vitilevu, the home of Timoci Bavadra. To be in the direct line of such a legend of origin is akin, for purposes of identity, to being descended from the Founding Fathers of America.

Although they were, respectively, from the western and eastern extremities of Fiji, Dr Bavadra and Ratu Mara initially shared a common professional background. They both went, at different times, to the University of Otago medical school. While Timoci Bavadra completed his medical studies, Ratu Mara did not. It was not his doing. Not a long way from qualifying, and already an overseas student of more than ordinary promise, he was called back to Fiji on the instruction of the Fijian leader, Ratu Sir Lala Sukuna, to be prepared for wider fields of human – and chiefly – responsibility than medicine. He was shipped across the world to Wadham College, Oxford, where Sukuna had been the first Fijian to read for an Oxford degree. Mara became the second. He distinguished himself in cricket and athletics as well as scholarship.

With Oxford successfully behind him, he was later despatched to the London School of Economics in order that the future leader of Fiji would be appropriately grounded in a basic understanding of Third World economic development principles and practices.

As yet, he was far from mentally and emotionally settled. Appointed as an Administrative Officer in the Colonial Service in Fiji – a grade normally reserved for expatriate preferments – he was not reconciled to being paid less than, to him, crass young Oxbridge men who, on importation, received an inducement allowance in addition to the local salary.

Mara set about challenging this and other examples of discrimination, as he saw it; and he entered into protracted correspondence with the Colonial Office and the Fiji administration. Two uneasy and obstinate antagonists then locked horns; and Mara, being refused full equality of treatment, demanded to be transferred elsewhere, to wit the Gilbert and Ellice Islands Colony where, as an expatriate, he would thus, he argued, qualify for the additional money. He was concerned too about wider questions, not least being the policies of the Fijian Administration and the future prospects of the Fijian people.

At the Suva end of all this was Paddy Macdonald, Colonial Secretary and administrative head of the Fiji Civil Service. No one had a greater devotion to his files or a longer mental filing cabinet of the short-sighted precedents set by others. For him, the paper war could never be lost. Giving in to hard-luck cases meant bad and potentially embarrassing decisions. None such would be pinned on him, if he could avoid it. Mara got his first real taste of British-style bureaucratic obfuscation.

Macdonald was the original colonial workaholic. He would go to his office on Christmas Day and park his black car with its A1 number plate so that he was known to be there. In his elevated office in the clock tower of Government Buildings in Suva, he found it possible and desirable to draft amendments to the Civil Service General Orders at the height of a major hurricane. Not always easy in his own personal relationships, Macdonald did, however, recognise similar complexities in another man, albeit of a different race. He spent many patient months – writing, arguing and persuading – as he tried to keep Mara on the rails in England and, so he hoped, on his return to Fiji.

Lengthy and voluminous correspondence developed between an agonised and increasingly frustrated young Mara – the Colonial Office intervening and uttering soothing noises from time to time – and a patient but irritating mentor in Suva. These highly charged exchanges were kept in a special file and locked in Macdonald's personal office safe. The key remained in his pocket at all known times. That is, except when he was on leave in England and I, as Acting Colonial Secretary for a period in 1963, became the temporary custodian of it. After perusing the file during one illuminating weekend, I was not reluctant to return the safe key to its substantive owner on his return to duty. I had not added to the correspondence in his absence.

When Ratu Mara himself came home, he was far from reconciled. He eschewed Fijian society for a time and sought that of a number of Suva cricketers with whom he played social games on Sunday mornings. He took over the captaincy, as of right, of the Lau cricket team in the Suva club competition. That talented side became temporarily demoralised; and their naturally gifted batsman, Ilikena Bula, went to pieces for a time as efforts were made to harness his natural gifts in ways not then exemplified in his captain. Chiefly autocracy in a cricket team of allegiant commoners was not always the most satisfactory of Fijian combinations.

The great majority of Fijians are Methodists and many, the Bauans in particular, declined to play cricket on Sundays. No such problem for Mara and his friends, who were Roman Catholics and Anglicans. So Sunday morning social cricket on Albert Park in Suva became a regular occurrence with much drinking before, during and after; and the excitable laughter of the players began to penetrate the hallowed portals of the Grand Pacific Hotel beside the sea wall across Victoria Parade. It worried more than the Colonial Secretary: it upset many Fijians who found it difficult to believe that this could be the talented and dignified young chief who had been sent to the University of Oxford. The problem was solved – or rather sidestepped – by his postings to the old capital of Levuka and to Ba. It was there, in the heart of the Indian cane-growing districts of Western Vitilevu, that Ratu Mara had his first real taste of the realities of the sugar economy in what was to be the bailiwick of Dr Bavadra. But that was all in the future.

The tribulations that marked his homecoming constituted a phase of his life that he was perhaps to forget as, much later in independent Fiji, he gave up alcohol, veered towards vegetarianism and was increasingly impatient with the convivial aberrations of some of his more gregarious Fijian ministerial colleagues.

But while they forgave, many young Fijian commoners did not entirely forget, as they reflected upon the behavioural and financial stresses of chiefliness and its relevance to leadership in modern government or business.

The question of where Dr Bavadra went after his London visit was one of priorities. Should he go elsewhere to seek additional support; or should he go straight back to Fiji – to an uncertain reception by the military regime? The number of international telephone calls increased – in and out. Should it be Washington because of the alleged CIA involvement in the affairs of Fiji? Or Canberra, where Don Dunstan, the former Premier of South Australia and Fiji-born, was taking a hand to set up meetings? Or Wellington, since through-out New Zealand there had been the greatest initial political and popular response and sense of outrage? Or India, to enlist the aid of the Government of India in promoting or supporting a Commonwealth initiative both immediately and at the Heads of Government meeting in Vancouver in October? Perhaps a combination of all. Delhi alone and not Canberra and Wellington would not be viewed approvingly either within or outside Fiji. The Indian High Commission in London had confirmed that its Government would extend appropriate recognition to its visitors from Fiji. A not entirely unexpected approach in the circumstances, but potentially counter-productive.

Dr Bavadra, however, thought that Rajiv Gandhi's statement condemning the coup, and the fact that the Indian Prime Minister had sent envoys to the UK, Australia and New Zealand to argue the case for economic sanctions or 'some positive action' to defeat the coup, had been enough.

'What more could India do?' he asked. 'It would be preferable anyway if the Commonwealth acted unitedly rather than as individual countries.'

The pros and cons of the options were bandied about in the hotel lounge, as the travel agents came and went. One permutation foundered on the limitations of the airline schedules; another, because new considerations emerged or new personalities appeared late on the scene to suggest yet further elaborations – Washington for three days not one, including a fund-raising dinner à la US; Los Angeles and then Vancouver where, in both places, Fiji communities were anxious to meet with Dr Bavadra and to assist as best they could in his restoration to prime ministerial authority. So provisional bookings of halls and hotels were made and deposit deadlines set while answers were awaited. While one set of possibilities was being examined and its implications thought through, another two would come in and have their enthusiastic advocates. Airline bookings were made and cancelled or lapsed.

The media men in London attempted to follow all this with a degree of, at times, ill-concealed exasperation – particularly since it could not be fully explained to them that there was good reason to withhold travel and thus arrival details of the delegates. Their security was of greater importance. So, with bookings to Melbourne and Sydney on Qantas Flight 2 out of London on Sunday 14 June, it was not possible to confirm to an Australian Broadcasting Corporation reporter in London whether or not Dr Bavadra would be flying that night and arriving in Australia two mornings later. What kind of public relations is this, you could hear him saying, despairingly, to himself.

Throughout, there was one key factor: no commitment to travel would be made without a firm time and date for any meeting proposed in Canberra with Prime Minister Hawke; in Wellington with Prime Minister Lange; and in Washington with the Senate and House Foreign Relations committees. In the end it was to Washington and to Wellington that Dr Bavadra finally decided to travel after just a week in England.

He had been amused by British newspaper headlines the previous day. One had him 'limping home spurned by Britain'. Another, that he was 'left to ponder the meaning of democracy'. It was curious though to contend, as one story did, that in the week which had seen the re-election of a British prime minister, the attractions of the Westminster model of democracy 'must have seemed less than compulsive' to him. The reverse was the case.

'One must look at the issue; and the issue,' Dr Bavadra had said in Brent Town Hall a few days before, 'is the destruction of democracy in a Commonwealth country. We are all for democracy, aren't we? After all, there are elections here this week.'

In fact, the not unfriendly press stories did Dr Bavadra no great disservice. That he should be thought, in Fiji, to be unhappily 'limping home' was no bad thing. He might thus be judged as less of a force to contend with. On his return, his life and those of his colleagues could be a little less unsafe as a consequence; and time for regrouping and consolidation would have been gained. His valedictory letter to the Commonwealth Secretary General revealed his hopes and his expectations:

Before I leave the United Kingdom, I must express to you my deep appreciation and that of my ministerial colleagues, for your sympathetic reception of the Fiji delegation and for your wise counsel to us. As you know, I very much hope that your early personal intervention in the current circumstances of Fiji will be possible; and I am delighted that your good offices and the services of the Secretariat in London will continue to be available to us in our struggle to bring about the restoration of legitimate democratic institutions and stability in Fiji . . .

PART TWO

'PARADISE' NOT REGAINED

12

Tuesday 16 June 1987

So, from London Heathrow, Dr Bavadra and Adi Kuini set out, like Mr Smith in the Hollywood film forty years before, to Washington: there, hopefully to enlist the interest and support of the appropriate congressional committees in an exposure of the clandestine activities of American intelligence operators in yet another destabilisation game in yet another part of the world. The visit was very nearly frustrated entirely because Adi Kuini's passport was found to contain no American visa. Attempted without it, arrival at US Immigration at Dulles International would have been even less welcoming than Heathrow. Obtaining it over a weekend in London from a hard-pressed United States Embassy in Grosvenor Square was going to be far from straightforward – for anyone, let alone a party burdened with the special circumstances of Dr Bavadra and his wife.

The principal orchestrator of the Washington journey was James Anthony. The erstwhile trade union leader in Fiji cum latter-day academic and lobbyist in Honolulu, Anthony had flown to London from Hawaii at the end of the week to 'lend a hand'. And quite a hand it was, if his business card was anything to go by:

Militarization & the Arms Race in the Pacific
Pacific Marine Resources & Ocean Politics
Media Imperialism & the Politics of Telecommunications
Cultural Exchange

J M ANTHONY, Ph.D
Pacific Research & Information Network

Anthony had an interesting background in more than one respect. First, there was his unusual Christian Indian, Irish, Polynesian parentage. Secondly, he had been one of the fighters for workers' interests in the formative years of the trade union movement in Fiji; and, together with Apisai Tora, he it was who had led the protests

105

which had resulted in the civil disturbances of 1959. As a consequence of a piece of colonial sleight of hand, he was later found a place at the newly established East–West Centre of the University of Hawaii.

Prospering in these relaxed surroundings, Anthony wrote a book about the 1959 events in Fiji which he now modestly describes as 'bad'. Nearly thirty years on, he has become a mellowed entrepreneur with a capacity for persuading his listeners that he has the tortuous corridors of American congressional power within his grasp and influence. He is far from alone in claiming that.

Anthony set about phoning congressmen acquaintances in Washington about the visa problem. Early Monday morning, he went off with Adi Kuini to get passport photographs taken and then go on to the visa section of the American Embassy. Anyone who has ever attempted to obtain even a non-immigrant visa for the United States at the height of the North American tourist season will know what he faced. What should a deposed Prime Minister do in these circumstances when he is provided with no diplomatic or host country help? At midday they returned, visaless, to the hotel, no congressional or other form of persuasion having routed the system. By the end of the day, however, after several further hours of waiting at the end of long circuitous queues of hopeful applicants to visit the Land of the Free, they re-emerged tired but triumphant. Lawful entry into the United States was now possible and airline bookings to Washington were duly made for departure the following day.

There, the disappointments continued; but the optimism remained outwardly intact. At a press conference, Dr Bavadra urged Congress to enquire into alleged American involvement in support of the defeated Alliance Party in the April elections and in the 14 May military coup. Washington is a hard-nosed city with an appetite for allegations about unconstitutional activities of the executive or the off-beat sex life of the men of Capitol Hill. 'Once the scent of scandal is in their nostrils, the bloodhounds go for the jugular,' a victim of pursuit was once quoted, unbelievably, as having said.

Fortunately or unfortunately, Dr Bavadra had no such titillation to draw upon to excite the editorial interest of the TV networks or the press. Supplicants of Senate and House Foreign Affairs committees' time have a hard job anyway and especially in this case with a Coalition Party manifesto for the Fiji election which seemed akin to the New Zealand Labour Government line in being unwelcoming to US nuclear-powered naval ships.

The Fiji cause was of limited interest to Washington and it made little impact; but the delegation did its best. James Anthony described one US Embassy man in Suva as a 'barefoot Ollie North', the second best-known lieutenant colonel in Fiji in mid-1987.

The staff member concerned was said to be director of the Suva office of the US Agency for International Development. Dr Bavadra asked for a congressional probe to determine whether the coup was an official US Intelligence operation; or one conducted by a private American military assistance group associated with the Iran/Contra affair; or a combination of both. He had summoned the American Ambassador to the Prime Minister's Office in Suva on 20 April to protest against alleged destabilisation efforts linked to the Central Intelligence Agency. A sum of $US200,000 was alleged to have been made over to Apisai Tora, at this time a leading member of the Taukei movement, which backed the coup, and a former Alliance Government minister.

Dr Bavadra drew attention to the presence in Fiji, shortly before the coup, of US roving ambassador and former Deputy Director of the CIA, General Vernon Walters, and of retired US Army Major General John Singlaub. Believed to head a group known as the World Anti-Communist League, Singlaub was reported to be a central figure in the clandestine network that funded the rebels in Nicaragua when official US Aid was restricted by Congress. Dr Bavadra said there was evidence that Walters and Singlaub had been in Fiji before, during and after the coup. They were believed to have stayed in The Fijian Hotel, 130 kilometres from Suva, when the conference of a regional conservative group known as the Pacific Democratic Union, co-chaired by Ratu Mara, was being held at the time of the coup. It was conjectured that they were the other two unknown golfers in that Sunday game before the coup.

The story was carried in a limited way in some Australian and New Zealand newspapers, but its accuracy could not be established. It was all a bit vague. Prime Minister Lange publicly discounted it; the US Ambassador in Australia denied it. True or false, the South Pacific was, however, awash with rumours of this kind and of supposedly related Libyan activity in the area. The closure by the Australian Government of the Libyan bureau in Canberra at about this time merely added to the conjecture.

'HOPE FADES FOR FIJI'S OVERTHROWN GOVERNMENT'. This was the headline to the report from Wellington in *The Independent* of London on 23 June 1987:

> After two weeks travelling the world in search of support for his ousted government, Fiji's Prime Minister, Dr Timoci Bavadra, seems to have reached the end of the road.
>
> He received little joy in London, where his Queen declined to

see him. He cancelled plans to go to Canberra when Australian Prime Minister Bob Hawke used his involvement in an election campaign as an excuse not to see him.

In Washington his claims of American involvement in last month's military coup quashed any chance of backing from the Reagan administration. Yesterday, however, he backed away from earlier statements.

Although there had been 'a lot of allegations', he admitted he had no proof that the US participated in his overthrow . . .

While putting on a brave face afterwards, Dr Bavadra betrayed his feelings with answers to two questions at his press conference. Asked if he was confident of his personal safety when he returned home on Thursday, the Prime Minister, who was arrested at gunpoint with his government in Parliament on 14 May, said: 'Well, I can only find out when I return to Fiji.'

Asked if he could continue to work with the Governor General, who had promoted the coup leader, Lieutenant Colonel Sitiveni Rabuka, to full colonel, granted him a royal pardon and suggested a new uncontested election to change the constitution, Dr Bavadra paused for a long time before saying: 'Yes, I suppose.'

His Attorney General, Jai Ram Reddy, laughed and said: 'You can put your own interpretation on the long silence.'

In New Zealand itself *The Press* of Christchurch put it: 'OUSTED PM FAILS IN N Z BID'.

Crude, but broadly true. The story itself revealed Dr Bavadra's disappointment – but not, as yet, any admission of psychological defeat – in the country whose initial response had been the most vocal in denunciation of the coup.

Now, in Wellington, five weeks after the coup, Prime Minister David Lange made clear that his talks on 22 June were 'with Dr Bavadra' and that New Zealand did not recognise him as Prime Minister. The New Zealand Government supported the efforts of the Governor General to find a constitutional solution to the Fiji crisis; and he urged Dr Bavadra to go back and co-operate with these efforts: 'He should bring his political forces to work for a constitutional solution that was acceptable to all, did injustice to none, and restored Fiji's good name.'

Some task: to be told to go home and seek to restore confidence and stability for the economic and human chaos that was none of his making. The dissolution of the Fiji Parliament by the Governor General, said Mr Lange, had given Dr Bavadra a new status of being a substantial contender in Fiji rather than the office holder of Prime Minister of Fiji.

'If there was a constitutional dissolution of Parliament he ceases to be Prime Minister,' Mr Lange said.

'Whether the dissolution had been legal was for the Fijian courts, not him, to comment on,' Mr Lange said.

'Dr Bavadra, however, did have a considerable standing in the affection of New Zealanders because he had been deposed. That was why he was a guest of the New Zealand Government . . .'

It was a far cry from the New Zealand Prime Minister's first public reactions to the coup.

David Lange began to be of sustained interest outside the South Pacific region when, as Prime Minister, he took a stand on two separate matters. First, there was the *Rainbow Warrior* affair in Auckland harbour in July 1985; and, second, the prohibition of visits of nuclear-powered or nuclear-weapon-carrying vessels to New Zealand ports, with its consequential rupture of relationships and implicit treaty obligations under the Anzus Pact. These actions endeared him neither to Paris nor Washington, both of which thus joined for a time with Moscow in irritation with the petulant politician from Down Under.

The *Rainbow Warrior* investigation with its revelations of 'Spycatcher'-style covert operations and sabotage by the French became a running sore in both France and New Zealand; but the nuclear ship business was more profound and fundamental to Lange's personal beliefs and to New Zealand Government foreign policy and defence. It not only resulted in a serious and continuing rift with the Americans: it threw up differences in New Zealand's relations with both Australia and Britain.

Lange relished the publicity that came his way as a consequence; and was ever willing, it seemed, to put his views before the television cameras of whatever country. As a lawyer, he was not deterred by the polemics of debate – indeed, he appeared to welcome every opportunity to be challenged and to respond. He came across as a man of conviction and courage; a David who had successfully taken on the American Goliath and survived the threatened reprisals.

That was the image abroad. Inside New Zealand, however, the view, I found, was somewhat different. In Auckland, one politics-watcher said to me: 'He enjoys advocacy in debate almost as if it were an end in itself. But you never know for certain what his conclusions are going to be; and they may not be quite what he said on the same subject a week before. He changes his mind with disconcerting frequency; he makes promises he does not keep; he gives undertakings he does not honour. And so he cannot always be trusted.'

New Zealand honey, like New Zealand pottery, is favoured by the discerning, it is said. The not-so-sweet Manuka Mixed Flowers is produced by the Waitemata Honey Company on the East Coast Road, a few miles north of Mairangi Bay. It was there, on Thursday 14 May, that I was admiring a newly acquired two-kilo pack, when the telephone called me.

'Have you been listening to the radio?'

'No, why should I?'

'You should. There's been a coup in Fiji.'

'Nonsense. They don't have coups in Fiji. You must have got the country wrong.' And ungraciously, I went back to the precious honey I was committed to transporting 12,000 miles to Sevenoaks.

An hour later, the telephone rang again.

'I didn't get the country wrong. There *has* been a coup in Fiji.' Petulant but triumphant, my niece rang off.

I turned the switch. It was about noon. I became one of thousands in New Zealand, Australia and the neighbouring islands who were stunned by what they heard. At first disbelief, not wanting to accept that the democratic process in the South Pacific had been crucified. Then the reality: the newly elected Prime Minister Dr Timoci Bavadra, and all twenty-seven other Coalition Party members of parliament had been abducted during a sitting of Parliament in Suva by armed soldiers of the Royal Fiji Military Forces and were being held in detention by their leader, Lieutenant Colonel Sitiveni Rabuka.

As the details began to emerge, local radio stations in Auckland and throughout New Zealand abandoned their scheduled programmes for continuous phone-in programmes about the Fiji coup from early evening until well into the next morning. There was no other major topic of conversation on radio or television. The events in Fiji and conjecture about what seemed likely to follow dominated news time for weeks to come.

In the beginning, Prime Minister Lange's statements were clear and decisive. He deplored the armed destruction of a democratically elected government on the doorstep of his country; he reflected upon the dangers to the stability of the South Pacific region as a whole; and, initially, he did not entirely rule out the possibility of military intervention as, no doubt, the staff of the Department of

External Affairs nervously searched out their files on Grenada 1983. He had spoken by telephone, he recalled, with Dr Bavadra after his April election victory. His impression was of a modest, strong and resourceful man in whose hands the political leadership of Fiji could be safely entrusted. What had now happened was thus so much more tragic and unacceptable.

The following day reports carried David Lange's first and most outspoken denunciation of Ratu Mara's suspected complicity in the coup: his action in immediately joining the Rabuka Council of Ministers was 'treachery'. There was no evidence explicitly linking the former Fiji Prime Minister with the coup. It was, however, he said, clear that the instigators of the coup had sought Ratu Mara's support, which he had willingly offered them. He had pledged allegiance to the Queen (Ratu Mara is a Privy Councillor) but had been instrumental in bringing about a rebellion in one of her countries. Ratu Mara's continued silence since the 12 April elections had allowed planning for the coup to proceed.

'I believe a word three or four weeks ago from Ratu Mara in support of the constitutional process would have averted all this.'

By contrast, Prime Minister Lange applauded the initial statement by the Governor General which condemned the 'unlawful seizure' and promised 'to restore the lawful situation'.

'It will now,' Mr Lange said, 'be for Fijians and those who are leaders in this to determine whether they propose to cast aside not just the post-independence tradition, but what has really become very much the fabric of Fiji's way of life for a very long time.'

With similar condemnatory statements from Prime Minister Bob Hawke from Canberra, Dr Bavadra could not have expected more rapid political support from his two neighbouring Labour governments. But it was not to last. Perhaps it was a legitimate change of assessment and thus policy; perhaps it was a recognition that the problems thrown up by the coup were more complex and deep-seated than first perceived and thus required reappraisal; perhaps it was the appalling possibility, much aired in public debate, but discounted by the governments, of the use of Australasian armed forces as a last resort to restore law and order. Perhaps there were other weighty considerations – not least from Fiji itself – which led to back-tracking on Lange's part and to the emergence of an ambiguity that provoked the ire of the New Zealand parliamentary Opposition. Not the least significant circumstances might conceivably have been in Lange's own electorate of Mangere in Auckland – where growing rumbles of criticism could be heard from his substantial number of Polynesian voters. For how certain it is that the imminence of a general election will re-focus the political mind on the sensitivities of the constituency. So it was that the New Zealand Government's changing reactions of policy began to cause concern to Dr Bavadra in early June.

'A running commentary on Fiji affairs by the New Zealand Prime Minister has us totally confused,' said a spokesman for Dr Bavadra on 10 June. 'If he made just one statement a week, we might be able to keep up with his various positions.' His comments followed Mr Lange's reported statement praising the former Prime Minister (Ratu Mara) as working valiantly for a solution to the crisis.

'How does this match up,' the spokesman asked, 'with the earlier accusation of treachery by Ratu Mara for joining the military regime of Colonel Rabuka? First, Mr Lange questions the constitutional propriety of the dissolution of the Fiji Parliament. Now, by implication he endorses it, by saying that Dr Bavadra is no longer Prime Minister; and that we should rely on the Governor General, who dissolved Parliament in the first place.'

It was thus not surprising that the New Zealand Prime Minister was later accused by the Opposition of inconsistency. In what are usually described as heated exchanges, their Deputy Leader, George Gair, asked the Prime Minister 'to interpret his flexible principles and ambidextrous tongue, by saying whether he was for or against the coup'.

'Whether I am for or against the coup is a question asked by a man who cannot eat a banana sideways,' Mr Lange appears to have replied.

It was an unfathomable observation to the uninitiated and no apparent answer to the question put. Was it to be 'Auld Lange Syne' for the 15 August New Zealand General Election, as *The Economist* captioned a photograph of the Prime Minister in July? The world was soon to know. A month later, the voters of New Zealand gave their verdict – a forty-nine year drought-breaking second successive victory for a Labour Government; and the return of the Lange administration initially with an identical majority of fifteen seats.

It had been a politically active year in the South Pacific. The Fiji election of a Labour Coalition in April and the coup in May; a Margaret Thatcher-type third consecutive victory for Bob Hawke's Labour Government in Australia; a protracted election in Papua New Guinea with fifteen parties and 1493 candidates for 109 seats; and a new Premier in the Cook Islands following a unanimous vote of no confidence in doctor-sailor-latterday politician Tom Davis. No such nonsense in Tonga where the King appoints the Prime Minister and duly installed his younger brother in the post twenty-odd years ago.

David Lange was understandably elated by the margin of his success, especially as some traditional National Party seats in affluent constituencies came close to unexpected defection to Labour. One – Wairarapa – did so on a recount. By a matter of seven votes, Labour's majority was increased to seventeen and later to nineteen. He was, however, conscious of criticism of oral abrasiveness during the campaign and wary of publicity overkill. It seemed time to review some long-standing arrangements. Two days after the election, the Prime Minister announced the breaking of a tradition dating back forty years to World War II. He was, he said, ending routine post-Cabinet meetings with the press because 'they are always adversarial and that is no good for either of us'. In future, he would hold them only when he had something in particular to say or when there were a number of requests.

Jim Bolger, the Opposition leader, said that Mr Lange's advisers had clearly decided that packaged news presented through a propaganda team was safer than letting the Prime Minister face difficult questions from reporters. With unconcealed acidity, *The Dominion* in Wellington put it this way: 'From now on encounters with the press will be at his majesty's pleasure!'

Of greater significance was the re-elected Prime Minister's decision to relinquish the post of Minister for External Affairs. It was a subtle move, for by doing so, he could distance himself from the immediate local and regional problems resulting from events in Fiji, while still attending as Prime Minister meetings of Commonwealth Heads of Government and the South Pacific Forum.

The matter of delegation is one of the not so simple skills of administration. There are areas where precise application and definition is possible; grey areas where it is not; and still others where attempted definition is undesirable. Just because there is a problem, I have been informed by a legal mind, does not mean that there is always a solution. Perhaps.

The approach of one chairman to his chief executive will be 'get in touch if there is a difficulty you can't resolve. Otherwise cope. If I don't hear from you, I'll know you are doing so.' In those circumstances, the lucky chief executive – or permanent secretary with his minister – will never have a problem he can't solve. Another chairman will want to be consulted about everything and will be engulfed in minutiae as a result. He will seek to ensure that he is never discovered – by his colleagues, the press and his friends – to be unaware of and thus out of touch with what is going on in the company or ministry of government. He it is who is to be in the public eye and be seen to be in charge. The smaller the organisation or government, the greater will be the centralisation; and ministers will tell civil servants what to do rather than expect to receive their advice. This applies widely in the smaller Caribbean island governments; and as many of the ministers have once been public servants themselves, they are probably better judges of the quality of the advice that such civil services may render than any outsider.

Delegation goes downwards. Responsibility for decision-making, upwards. In all bureaucracies, from the desk officers to the Secretaries of State or their equivalent, all live with the daily problem of upward referrals and decisions about what should be placed in the black ministerial box. And what, for a variety of reasons, need or should not. They are not always right, as events in Washington DC suggested in 1987. The two-way traffic problem is one which presidents and their chiefs of staff do not escape either.

The other Lieutenant Colonel of 1987, Oliver North, kept much of North America glued to its TV sets as the national soap opera – the congressional Irangate enquiry – ran on and on before the arc lamps and the rolling cameras. Yes, he said earnestly, he had submitted on more than one occasion to Admiral Poindexter, the White House National Security Adviser, that the President should in his opinion be informed of the money-for-hostages deal and the diversion of funds from the sale of guns for Iran to the Contras of Nicaragua.

'Done,' said the Admiral in a marginal file note, when he had not and did not. It was desirable, he later argued, neither for the President to know, so he could make an 'honest' denial later that he did not know, nor for North to know that the President did not know.

When the hearings were over, the President said 'No,' he did not know, like he had said right from the start, but he ought to have known and it was wrong not to tell him; but he did not say what he would have done if he had known.

So also with a former elected Prime Minister of Fiji. He did not know either, he has maintained; but, equally, he did not say what he would have done if he had known of the coup before it took place. At least what, generally, he did and did not do since the coup is known to all.

13

Wednesday 24 June 1987

Timoci Bavadra and Adi Kuini arrived back in Fiji from London, Washington and Wellington to a rapturous welcome, if little else, by many hundreds of supporters at Nadi airport; and they enjoyed a triumphal progression to his coastal village of Veiseisei, fifteen kilometres west of the international airport. On 30 June, after party consultation in Ba, he met with the Governor General to give his response and that of his colleagues to Ratu Penaia's proposed steps on the long road back to democracy. The atmosphere was far from reassuring. New powers had been promulgated under the emergency regulations enabling the interim government to seize land, buildings, transport and crops. The screw was being tightened.

'The proposal for constitutional reform and two further elections designed to entrench permanent political supremacy and dominance by the Fijian race amount to racial apartheid and are thus unacceptable,' announced Dr Bavadra with refreshing candour. Instead, he suggested tripartite discussions between the Governor General, Ratu Mara and himself; and he protested vigorously against sustained harassment, threats and intimidation of people in the Northern and Western divisions. He refused to meet with or talk to Rabuka. The scars of his enforced confinement and of the violence to his principles were still too deep.

Any lingering hope was thus killed of an early resolution of the political crisis. He was now revealing that he was no mere front man. Here was a Fijian leader who by his own actions was ready to show that humanity is what matters, not race; and that it is people who are important, not their genes. It was believed by some that his objective was to bring down the Fiji economy. No single act on Dr Bavadra's part was needed to achieve that. The leaders of the coup had seen to it already. It took Fiji thirty years to build up the tourist industry to its mid-1987 level of significance in the economy as a whole. And less than thirty minutes to dismantle its fragile structure. It was a lesson long since learned the hard way by other countries:

Jamaica, Grenada, Seychelles, Uganda, Cyprus, Haiti and Lebanon. Now the unthinkable had happened in the South Pacific. A week after the coup, the plush hotels of the south coast of Vitilevu were deserted as guests fled prematurely or failed to arrive. The bars and restaurants were empty and silent. Staff of all races were placed on short time or laid off entirely. Taxi drivers vied for a solitary weekday fare; and the roads carried but a trickle of local traffic.

It was not just the tourist industry that suffered. That was not at the core of the canker. Six weeks after the coup, on 29 June, a 17.75 per cent devaluation of the Fiji dollar was announced by the Reserve Bank. Overseas investments by residents were suspended and foreign exchange facilities for intending emigrants were restricted for an indefinite period. Its purpose was partly to attract tourists back with cheaper holidays. Petrol and diesel prices were raised at the same time. Stringent foreign exchange controls looked to be imminent. The queues at the bank counters lengthened.

Meanwhile, the season's crop of sugarcane remained uncut in its most vital month. Because of a series of stoppages, coupled with 'politically inspired' labour walkouts, the Fiji Sugar Corporation closed its mills for a month. The experience at the Labasa mill had been warning enough. A mass protest by the whole workforce at the behaviour of increasingly unruly soldiers was followed by arson and sabotage. The Lautoka mill was shut before it opened. The cane stock was barely enough to keep the huge plant crushing for a couple of hours. The $F200 million a year industry was at a standstill. The ultimate Indian self-denial had begun. Civil disobedience could become civil war through the economy, as the cane farmers and mill workers confronted the gun.

Not only the present year's crop was at stake. Indian farmers said that if the army harvested the cane or forced them to do it at gunpoint, they would not plant or cultivate the new crop for 1988. 'We are the backbone of this country. We are not going to have everything we have worked for taken from us. If we have to take the country's economy down to get what is right, we will do it.'

It was a time of explosive high tension. Fijians set fire to Indian homes in one sugar-growing area; fights between Fijians and Indians broke out in another and Indians began to burn their own crops, the desperate last resort to economic masochism.

The New Zealand Herald, towards the end of July:

To a Fiji colonel accustomed to having men jump to his bidding, a takeover of the Government may have seemed straightforward. But the colonel and his chiefly backers are now receiving a painful double-lesson: in politics, people respond best to fair treatment; in economics, confidence is vital . . .

The cane crop is deteriorating and some of it is being burned. The chiefs point blandly to Indian lack of co-operation and say little about intended Indian disablement. But it must have dawned on Fijian leaders that all the colonel's guns and all the interim government's emergency powers have not achieved a harvest.

In just a few weeks, the Army and the chiefs have crippled the most promising economy of any Pacific small nation. Given their purpose, they may not care that they have stoked inflation and brought hardship on many people. Even if devaluation and other moves restore part of the tourist trade, all peoples in Fiji will pay a price for the economic innocence and political foolishness of the soldiers and the chiefs.

Mark Sturton, a macro-economist from the University of Sussex, had gone to Fiji in 1970 and become a Fiji citizen. After a period at the Central Planning Office of the Ministry of Finance, he joined the Reserve Bank and had just been promoted to the post of Director of the Research Department when the coup-inspired disaster devastated the Fiji economy. At first saddened and then disillusioned, Sturton left the Bank and Fiji in mid June. The brain drain was under way.

In May, the Fiji foreign reserves stood at some $F180 million. This was the 'low' point of the annual cycle before the sugarcane was cut, crushed and shipped abroad. By the end of June, six weeks after the coup, the reserves had dropped by a third to about $F120 million. Thus, if imports and consumption continued at the same price/volume levels, and exports dried up to a trickle of gold and coconut oil, the reserves would be exhausted by about September. Devaluation was one way of reducing imports, albeit the price of such action was increased inflation and hardship. The objective was to encourage import substitution by raising the price of imports in local currency.

The problem was not straightforward. Fewer imports would mean idle docks, laid-off labour; shortages and thus higher prices of spare parts, tyres, public transport and power supplies; erratic telephones, deteriorating roads and bridges; increasingly bare shelves in the supermarkets and queues for cakes of soap or rice. Australian wine would gradually disappear and so would Japanese electronics. The deprivations of Guyana would have reached Fiji. In the rural areas of the main islands, it would mean a return to a subsistence economy; and in the towns, urban decay, unemployment, robbery, violence

117

and intimidation. Property values would plummet. The movement of supplies would only be possible with security escort. Gun law would prevail.

The foreign reserves equation was only part of the difficulty. The massive escalation of government spending on the operating account was equally disturbing. Early in the second half of the year, the Reserve Bank warned that unless expenditure slowed, the overall deficit for the financial year would reach $F100 million. The budgeted deficit of $F77 million had been bad enough: the sort of thing that, in Washington, President Reagan was facing as the stock markets of the world crashed and the American dollar plunged remorselessly down. In mid June, the bank raised its minimum lending rate from 8 per cent to 9 per cent; and increased the statutory reserve deposit ratio for the commercial banks from 5 per cent to 6 per cent.

'FIJI: THE WAY THE WORLD SHOULD BE!' So the tourism slogan of 1987 had read. There was now a sardonic twist. At the beginning of July, Reserve Bank Governor Savenaca Siwatibau warned that local residents might soon be required to realise foreign assets paid for with exported currency and to repatriate the proceeds to Fiji. What did this mean and how could it be enforced? The practice was that qualified approval only was given for the export of money from Fiji. A maximum of $F5,000 per adult was normally permitted in any one year; and there was a proviso that residents might have to bring such money back if so required. Failure to comply could mean legal action and future refusals.

Some senior civil servants were involved in promoting the movement for Fijian racial supremacy in the period before the April 1987 elections. With the victory of the Labour–Federation Coalition, they feared – they said – the loss of their jobs. A month later, in the immediate aftermath of the coup, the bravado of demagogy took over. Finding themselves in a novel situation of gun-law and with the imagined feeling that they personally had achieved something great and lasting, they lost all sense of reality and responsibility. 'We are in charge now,' became their watchword. But the passing weeks increasingly raised the question, 'In charge of what?'

The brain-drain message echoed Jai Ram Reddy: 'If they wish to do all this, then they can take the responsibility for putting it all back together again. We are not going to be here to help remedy their self-destruction.' So concluded doctors, architects, engineers, accountants, lawyers and academics – many of those with saleable and thus exportable skills. A university teacher cannot continue to lecture if he or she is subjected to threats, and offices are searched and papers confiscated. A doctor will not continue to work in circumstances where he is ordered by a soldier with a gun as to whom he is to treat next – as happened at the Colonial War Memorial Hospital in Suva in the early days after the coup.

At the beginning of September, a Fiji Teachers Union survey revealed: 'At least 225 teachers have emigrated since the May coup. They include mathematics and science teachers. Most are Indians who have gone to New Zealand.' Under what circumstances and for what duration was not made known.

There are those who believe that few Fijians are naturally good analysts of situations and the consequences of actions or decisions. Were it not so, the prospect of economic disaster which directly flowed from the coup would surely have been of sufficient potency to call pause before it was too late. Anyone who has watched the Fijians in the Hong Kong Rugby Sevens and against France in the 1987 World Cup will know that they are natural intuitive responders. This is their special flair which they disport with feckless abandon of the principles of rugby discipline. At its best, it can be breathtakingly entertaining; at its worst, it can be wayward and lackadaisical.

The coup brought in its wake the headiness of unaccustomed command of the nation and supposed control of its resources. It blurred vision of the economic wreckage and human suffering which an experienced analyst would readily have foreseen.

As a community of traders and retailers, the Gujeratis, not least among the Indians of Fiji, suffer no such limitations. The Gujeratis do not waste time. Everybody else may be asleep but they are in the shop. There is a simple cost/benefit equation: if the cost is too high and the benefit too low to be endurable, they will stream wherever they are in hundreds to diplomatic missions and airline offices. As the nomadic urge took over, this they duly did in Suva. Families throughout New Zealand and Australia, Britain and India itself moved fast to help in the evacuation and resettlement. The transition was relatively painless and the losses not significant, for while the Gujerati is acquisitive of money, he is not of land and other fixed – in this case depreciating – assets. And he is quicker than most to perceive the winds of adverse social and thus economic change.

Asian migrants of modest background often find themselves resented or barely tolerated wherever they go. Are they their own worst enemies? If so, why? One possible explanation, visible on High Street corners of western cities, is that they work long, late and on Sundays: in contrast to the 'lazy locals'. But so do the Chinese who, apart from Malaysia where their immigrant numbers make matters different, do not seem to arouse the antagonisms attributed to Indians and Pakistanis. Maybe it is that the Chinese are disposed to intermarry, can be more flexible about their own traditions, learn the local language more readily, mostly eschew political power and do not have personal habits or practices repugnant to the accepting indigenous people. In the case of the Fiji Indian, the hovering figure of Mother India reproduces something of the fratricidal stratifications and customary divides of the country of their origin; a monetary acquisitiveness generally alien to Fijian society; and sometimes a sharpness of practice which makes fools of the economically naïve and the socially underdeveloped. Or so those who were first in Fiji believed. And came then to resent. 'The Indians have the taxis and the buses,' said Rosa. 'The Fijians travel in them.'

It doesn't then take much to foment frustration into violent action – when a ready-made one-race rapacious soldiery is at hand to undertake it – against a people who gave little support to a colonial government in time of war in stark contrast to those who did.

The Fijians of the north and west live more easily with Indians than the Fijians of the east. In the west there are rural Fijians – in the interior, on the coasts, amid the harsher climate of the cane fields and the gold mines – who understand the deprivations of the Indian cane cutters and mill workers, their fragile dwellings and breadline family life. The two races live in proximity, if not side by side. While they rarely intermarry, they intermingle increasingly and interrelate through the common denominator of the soil. This is not the case in the east. At its extremity, in the outer islands of Lomaiviti and Lau, there are few Indians. Hurricanes apart, life is lush, largely Polynesian and relatively isolated. Insulated some might say. In eastern Vitilevu, semi-detribalised Fijians, poorly housed, often footloose and relatively moneyless in a harsh urban economy, resent the apparent material comforts of the hi-fi shopkeepers and transport operators and the rewards of rank and authority. When aroused, they can be persuaded to rampage against those of whatever race who appear to have by right or superior skills what they do not. And, basically, that is housing, food and opportunity. Thus, they remain easy prey to the art of sophistic rhetoric.

The country with which Fiji has had the closest links – and in the past, severe dynastic rivalries – is the Polynesian Kingdom of Tonga. Its capital, Nuku'alofa, is but 400 miles south-east of Suva, the distance between London and Edinburgh or Auckland and Wellington. With a historic policy of non-involvement in the broader affairs of the wider world, Tonga maintains a pose – for totally different reasons – not altogether unlike that of the Cayman Islands in the Caribbean. The policy is designed to reinforce the survival of the last Polynesian kingdom. Its social structure is chiefly and feudal; and some Tongans affect an aloofness and quiet superiority towards the problems of their South Pacific neighbours. Tonga now has modest regional or international influence. Indeed, little is sought. Its official representatives may be disposed not to attend the colloquies to which they are assigned. If they do, their silence about the topic under discussion may be, it has been said, because they have received no instructions as to what to say. When instructions were sought on one occasion, the bewildered Tongan delegate was told by his Minister: 'Tell them nothing. It is none of their business.' This was an historically accurate reflection of Tonga's approach to foreign policy, post-nineteenth-century intervention and near dominance of Fiji, that is.

So when the Tongan sovereign speaks about the affairs of a neighbouring country – especially Fiji – it is noticed. In September 1987 the King, then on a visit to the French nuclear-testing atoll of Mururoa, was reported to have said about the Fiji coup:

'I would have acted like Colonel Rabuka, if I had been in his place. He simply had no other choice, as the Bavadra Government instructed him to maintain order, which meant that he would have had to order his Fijian soldiers to fire on Fijian demonstrators. So the only way to avoid such a tragedy and maintain peace was to overthrow Bavadra's Government.'

Asked to comment about race relations in Fiji since the coup, King Taufa'ahau Tupou added: 'If I were an Indian living in Fiji, I would take my family with me and leave the country. And that is precisely what the Indians are now doing.'

121

14

10–20 July 1987

By late June Dr Bavadra was becoming increasingly frustrated by the absence of confirmation of the visit he had sought by the Commonwealth Secretary General to Fiji. The South Pacific Forum meeting had come and gone. The possible Hawke-led Forum mission of intercession to Fiji had indeed been stillborn. What had happened to the Palace-supported Commonwealth initiative? I sought to find out and telephoned Moni Malhoutra, the Assistant Secretary General on loan from the Government of India, who had sat in on Dr Bavadra's meeting with Ramphal.

He was in no doubt as to how matters stood within the Commonwealth Secretariat. 'A visit to Fiji by the Secretary General is at present out of the question. It is clear that they do not want any outside interference and involvement.'

'They?' I said. 'Who are they? And how has such a conclusion been reached after Dr Bavadra's urgent representation and their discussion only a fortnight ago?'

'I have been on the telephone to Dr Bavadra,' he replied, 'and explained the position to him. The matter was clinched by a visit this week to the Secretary General by the Governor General's personal emissary.'

'And who was that?'

'Someone called Thomson.'

'Old or young?'

'Old.'

'Ah. Ian Thomson.'

'Yes.'

'You are quite sure?'

'Of course.'

'So you are doing nothing?'

'Not on that front, no. But we are considering in what other ways we can help.'

'Such as?'

'Constitutional advice and drafting. That sort of thing.'

'Thank you, I quite understand,' I said and put the telephone down. I did indeed. The pass had been sold, the opportunity lost.

It was not to be recovered. The apparent lack of an effective approach to the Governor General plus the time lapse from the initial urgings at the beginning of June and Dr Bavadra's London visit, had resulted only days later in a loss of momentum sufficient to consolidate resistance to a personal initiative by the Commonwealth Secretary General. It was now a classic recipe for inaction.

The regime in Fiji had, of course, been at work, although a report from Suva said that Sir Ian Thomson, a former administrator and Independent Chairman of the Fiji Sugar Industry, had had meetings in London on behalf of the Governor General. He had conferred with the Minister of State at the Foreign and Commonwealth Office, Lord Glenarthur, Commonwealth Secretary General Ramphal, and the Queen's Private Secretary, Sir William Heseltine. The purpose of these meetings was reported to be to brief the British Government and the Commonwealth Secretariat on action taken by the Governor General since the 14 May coup. Maybe it was pointed out that Britain did have its own High Commissioner in Suva; and that Fiji was no longer a responsibility of Britain; while the Commonwealth Secretariat had information available to it from all Commonwealth government representatives in Fiji. At the same time, the interim Fiji administration issued a statement about a mission undertaken by James Maraj, Secretary for Foreign Affairs and former High Commissioner for Fiji in Australia. According to this, Maraj had seen the Australian Governor General, Sir Ninian Stephen, ambassadors of twenty-one countries accredited to Fiji from Canberra, his Australian opposite number and other officials including senior staff of the Australian Prime Minister.

The waters were being muddied as families became divided on matters of principle and conscience. For the son of my old friend and colleague, Ian Thomson, was Secretary for Information in the post-coup administration and later the Governor General's secretary and spokesman. This did not prevent his name from appearing on a list of Fiji passport holders prohibited from leaving the country after the second coup on 25 September.

July was a significant month as events unfolded in Fiji. Rumour compounded rumour and, provided you didn't seek to do it at a public meeting, there was plenty to conjecture about: not least the possible severance of links with the Crown and the creation of a Republic of Fiji. In his public statements or responses to journalists the coup leader seemed to be developing a talent for teasing eager reporters; and either caring little for the effect of his inconsistent utterances or knowingly making them. By 10 July, reports indicated that Fiji might well become a republic. True or not, it was obviously one of Rabuka's options and he played on the nerves of the people of Fiji – perhaps also his own staff and the Civil Service – with some skill. An ABC journalist in Sydney received a fax of a leaked document from the Fiji Crown Law Office which spelt out the preparations for declaring Fiji a republic. The indicative date at that stage was 22 July. There was good reason. It was the day before Dr Bavadra's case challenging the legality of the Governor General's dissolution of Parliament was down to be heard in the Supreme Court. A republican flag and new national anthem were said to be ready. If all this was indeed intended, the negotiations then in process for a Constitutional Review Committee and its terms of reference were a pantomime to buy time for the main objective.

Talk of a Fiji republic was becoming widespread. Ratu Mara had recently been speaking about this on the radio. The impression was growing that the Queen could somehow still be Head of State. The Fijian people appeared to be being misled into thinking that if Fiji became a republic, the link with the Queen under the present Constitution would be unchanged. Even the coup leader seemed to think so. Or said he did. It is possible that there was deliberate confusing of the Queen's two roles in respect of Fiji – as Head of State and Head of the Commonwealth respectively. The newly qualified lawyer son of the former Prime Minister and a staff member of the Crown Law Office, was reported to be visiting Fijian villages discussing a draft new constitutional instrument with Fiji as a republic.

Meanwhile Ratu Mara himself was on a journey around the Far East with six military staff seeking to acquire arms, armed personnel carriers and helicopters, the money for the purchases in South Korea and Taiwan allegedly coming from United States sources. Colonel Rabuka was said to be setting up battalions, five hundred odd in each, in the main centres of population on Vitilevu and Vanualevu. There were more trade union arrests.

Krishna Datt, Minister for Foreign Affairs in the Bavadra Government, and an appointed member of the Constitutional Review Committee at the time, was taken by soldiers to the Fiji military forces headquarters at Queen Elizabeth Barracks in Suva two days before the review was to begin and held in degrading circumstances for twenty-four hours. He was one of about nine people who were outside Government House the previous day and were threatened by the military with guns at their heads. 'Your time is coming,' he was told. This was the first occasion since the release of the members of the Bavadra Government from detention after the coup that a former Minister had been held in custody by the army and not been taken to a police station.

The former leper hospital on the island of Makogai was rumoured to be under preparation as the permanent detention centre for Dr Bavadra and his political colleagues. It seemed an entirely feasible possibility to me.

I was moved on 12 July to do some more crystal-ball gazing for the Commonwealth Secretary General:

(a) The progressive arrest and detention of members of the Bavadra Government may be expected.

(b) The 'Queen's Loyal Council of Chiefs' will be used as the vehicle for constitutional change and the creation of a Republic. The Council could become the effective one-race new 'parliament'.

(c) Ratu Mara will become President (but on what basis remains to be seen) with Colonel Rabuka as Commander of the Army. The Governor General will disappear into retirement in Cakaudrove. Mara will move into Government House.

(d) The future of Fiji as a member of the Commonwealth must now be in doubt.

(e) Fiji will become the American South Pacific nuclear base. Land is being acquired. Work has begun at the Fiji Royal Naval training depot outside Suva.

(f) The celebration of the Republic will unleash widespread anti-Indian terrorising and communal violence to an extent not seen in Fiji since the tribal wars and the cannibalism of the nineteenth century.

(g) A further devaluation of the Fiji dollar can be expected.

As events in 1987 turned out, it was not a fully accurate forecast. But the substance was proved correct and consistent with the basic objectives of the coup and the Taukei movement leaders. They were clear enough for those with eyes to see. But it was to have no real effect. There was not much stomach for action. As was to be demonstrated.

A week later, on Sunday 19 July, we entered upon a day of curious confusion. Dr Bavadra telephoned me from Suva. He wanted to speak with Malhoutra. Could I track him down?

'I'll try,' I said, 'but I understand that he is in Nairobi and Harare for the next three to four weeks.'

He was at the Nairobi Hilton. I telephoned him there. No answer. I left a message asking him to call me in England and then went back to Dr Bavadra. It was close to midnight in Fiji.

'I have just received some very disturbing news,' he said. 'Ratu Penaia's term as Governor General has finished. He has been fired. The Council of Chiefs is assembling and the meeting begins in Suva tomorrow. I want to advise the Commonwealth Secretary General of all this and Sir William Heseltine at the Palace.'

'Right,' I replied, my mind in turmoil. 'I suppose we can assume that the Governor General will himself have told the Palace, unless he was prevented from doing so. I will keep trying Nairobi.' I took the Suva phone number and rang off.

Then, too late, questions began in my mind. Ones I had failed to ask. Our conversation had been guarded and stilted. We had assumed that we were not alone on the line. How was the Governor General fired? I assumed by the coup leader. Was a letter delivered to him? Was it at the point of a gun? Was Government House occupied? Was the Governor General under house arrest? Could he be contacted by telephone? Had he in fact been able to advise the Palace by telephone or telex? Where was he now? Who would be the next occupant of Government House in Suva? What would be his title? And not least – had the news of the sacking of the Governor General been confirmed by Dr Bavadra with Ratu Penaia himself? I should have asked that, but I suppose at 12,000 miles distance you don't query a Prime Minister, deposed or otherwise, about the accuracy of such weighty intelligence. Anyway, I didn't.

In mid-Sunday afternoon, Malhoutra came on the telephone from Nairobi. I gave him the news.

'I will pass it on to the Secretary General who is here, and come back to you.'

Half an hour later, the telephone rang again. This time it was Ramphal himself.

'The situation looks bleak,' I ventured.

'I entirely agree,' he replied. 'But the strange thing is that it has not been on the news. And Bill Heseltine knows nothing of it.'

'It was late at night in Suva when Dr Bavadra called me. He had only just heard. Maybe an announcement is being deferred until the Council of Chiefs is informed when it meets in Suva tomorrow morning. There were others present while Dr Bavadra spoke.'

'I'll speak to Bavadra at his breakfast time in Suva,' Ramphal concluded.

At 7.30 p.m. the Director of International Affairs at the Secretariat telephoned me. What he had to say was a relief in one way and far from it in another. It had been explained that the information passed to me was based on a misunderstanding and was incorrect. Separate checks before this had indicated no knowledge of 'any recent development of significance.'

I was put out, mainly because of my own failure to ask the necessary supplementary questions at the right time before sounding alarm bells all over the world; and partly because Dr Bavadra had not come back to me himself. That was a first and pointless reaction. Where lay the reality? What had happened in Suva between midnight on Sunday and eight o'clock Monday morning? There were two plausible scenarios. At distance from the scene of action, it was only possible to conjecture which was which. The first was that a genuine mistake had been made and that Dr Bavadra's information to me had indeed been found to be inaccurate. He would have had to establish this between the hours of midnight on Sunday 19 July and daylight on Monday morning 20 July, before Ramphal telephoned him from Nairobi. Was this plausible? Was it likely? Was there another explanation?

The other conceivable set of circumstances was more dire. Had Dr Bavadra's conversation with me from Suva been tapped? Was it desired by what the press called 'the Fiji Regime' to withhold formal sacking of the Governor General so it could have major impact when the Council of Chiefs assembled in Suva on Monday 20 July? So was the news that Dr Bavadra had originally given me an accurate reflection of intent at the time and not a mistake as he had told the Commonwealth Secretary General?

If it was, why should he have said that it was a mistake? The most likely explanation was that he had been under restraint with a gun pointing his way when Ramphal spoke with him in the early hours of Monday. A pre-dawn raid by soldiers might have been ordered; and this might have happened anyway to effect his detention under house arrest during the meeting of the Council of Chiefs.

And why should Council members again be called together from all parts of Fiji at no mean cost? One likely reason was to agree a submission to the Review Committee for changes in the Constitution which would entrench Fijian paramountcy in political terms and deprive any other race, whatever its numbers, of electoral representation based on such considerations. A second purpose might flow from the first: that in addition to the constitutional question, the Council of Chiefs was being assembled to approve and supposedly thus to formalise the legitimacy of the establishment of a Republic of Fiji and the nomination of its first President.

If the Queen did not know that the Governor General had

effectively been removed from office, then there might be no occasion for her to send a special communication to this meeting of Her Majesty's loyal Council of Chiefs. The postponement of the sacking of the Governor General would not only enable the news to be announced at the meeting and, by implication, the action to be endorsed; but it would also eliminate the possibility of any persuasive message from the Palace to the Council meeting about links with the Crown, the post of Governor General and its incumbent.

Finally, if the information about the end of Ratu Penaia's term of office as the Queen's representative was wrong on the evening of Sunday 19 July, would it be equally wrong one, two or three – or eighty-eight – days later?

At the end of the week, on Friday 24 July, Dr Bavadra came on the line again from Suva.

'Can you tell me generally how things are going?' I asked.

'I am now hopeful that goodwill and good sense may prevail. The Council of Chiefs has adjourned until Monday. I was permitted to address them. I was given a very good reception. There was a hostile crowd outside when I arrived, but I was not deterred by it.'

'Does this mean that there is a possibility of putting the clock back in the full sense?'

'It is too early to say, but I am a bit more optimistic. It is all what you said – discussion, discussion and keeping the dialogue going and open.'

The month of July in Fiji had not started well. It was to be increasingly marked by intimidation, military harassment, arson, looting, burglary, assault, victimisation of women and threats to the press. At the beginning of the month, three former ministers of the Bavadra Government – Tupeni Baba, Navin Maharaj and Satendra Nandan – were arrested as they prayed in a Hindu temple in Suva and the congregation was dispersed by soldiers.

'Now we have to get permission from the army to pray,' said Maharaj. 'I will ask no one but God for such permission.' As Baba is a Fijian and thus not a Hindu, it was not unreasonable to conclude that the meeting of the three former ministers was not exclusively in pursuance of spiritual salvation.

Schools began to close as parents kept their children at home following rumours of security problems. Indeed, the schools could not guarantee the safety of pupils. Civil unrest continued with reports of a riot north of the capital, the burning of canefields in the west and concern by the military over what it said were 'politically motivated' crimes. Radio Fiji reported that more than three thousand tons of cane standing in fields had been set alight near the sugar town of Ba. A mass shutdown of shops saw about fifty people arrested. Most of them were store owners who refused orders from soldiers to open for business. An army spokesman later said the arrests were made under the emergency regulations which gave wide-ranging powers to crack down on 'economic sabotage'.

15

An early British resident in colonial New Zealand was one James Busby. With status but no power, authority but no means of enforcing it, and thus with a disposition for many words but few deeds, Busby was named by the hostile Maoris as 'a man of war without guns'.

No such sobriquet could remotely be ascribed to Sitiveni Rabuka or Ratu Màra. With the establishment of a republic of Fiji and a chiefly assumption of the presidency, the first twentieth-century South Pacific island despotism would have arrived. The guns were there in plenty and the will to use them was apparent to all who had had the misfortune to be forced to look down the wrong end of the barrel. The logic of the coup would have been completed and its actions 'legitimised' by the agreement of the Great Council of Chiefs to sever links with the Crown and effectively disenfranchise non-Fijians.

The use of such a body for high-level Fijian advice was justified by virtue of the historic procedure adopted for the voluntary cession of Fiji to Queen Victoria in 1874 and the 'handing back' of the colony to the successors of those chiefs in 1970 by Prince Charles on behalf of the Queen. The Council's proceedings were virtually all in the Fijian language. One of the complaints since 1970 was that the Independence Constitution of that year had never been translated into Fijian. Quite so, but to do the lot would have been some task for even the most skilled of linguists and translators. No South-Pacific island language – or any other of comparable environmental and etymological limitations – can readily embrace the theological concepts of Christianity, let alone the modern marvels of science, medicine or economics, or the legal language of constitutions. After all, French has been hard put to find alternatives to simple invasions such as 'le parking, le weekend, and le sex'. Arabic has had to make do with a splendid circumlocution for the railway engine: it is in essence 'the machine that runs on the track of iron'. And could an air traffic controller land an aeroplane in an African click language?

Not much chance then for a Pacific island tongue with a complex Western constitution.

There are two levels of the problem – the philosophical and the practical. The second is easier. You simply adopt the foreign word and change its appearance a bit so that it looks more or less authentic; or you seek to describe in circumlocutory terms as in the Arabic example. Dr Bavadra's first name is Timoci or Timothy; rugby becomes akapulu in Tongan; Minister is Minisita; Steven is Sitiveni; and aeroplane in Fijian is waqa vuka or flying canoe.

The first principal of the Pacific Theological College in Suva was George Knight, a Scottish Presbyterian of erudite mind with the skill of the true scholar in being able to turn a complex idea into a simple expression. But even he ran into difficulty as he sought to teach the spiritual concepts of the Christian faith to his students from the Pacific islands. In 1967 he wrote about the linguistic difficulties they faced:

It is far from easy. Words such as grace, justification, reconciliation, conscience, devil, church, covenant, lord, stewardship, trinity, crucify, gospel, comforter, heaven, sin, ransom, redeem and many others simply don't exist in many languages. A Polynesian language, on the other hand, may have several hundred words for palm-tree or coconut . . .

God, in Tongan, is any object of fear, such as a shark. Congregation, in Samoan, means 'Council of elders and chiefs'. The ordinary people seem to have slipped out of sight here, wouldn't you say? The Tongan language has two words for 'he', one for an ordinary man, one honorific for an aristocrat. Which pronoun then should you use in the phrase 'He ascended into heaven?' Was he still the carpenter of Nazareth, or was he now one with God?

God, of course, has a lot to answer for: be he Jewish, Christian, Muslim Sunni or Shiah, or in the many manifestations that constitute Hinduism. It is only in the latter that there is no distinction between the sacred and the profane. Relief indeed for the carnally inclined. History is cluttered with campaigns entered upon and fought with the spiritual fervour of the zealot from the Crusades to the Allied and German troops who spent Christmas Day in the trenches of World War I beseeching the same heavenly endorsement of their respective causes. Might may be right; but it is not a bad idea to pretend to spiritual sanction of temporal policies, as the Afrikaaners well know. A white God, of course – but for the African churches, what colour is God?

Colonel Rabuka was in his Methodist church pulpit not long after the coup, seeking forgiveness of sin and promoting the practice of doing unto others what you would that they should do unto you. Throughout the service, uniformed and armed soldiers stood guard. So, brothers, believe in me – or else.

During the month of July, that versatile and fearless black cleric Desmond Tutu, Archbishop of Cape Town, called upon international banks not to renew loans to South Africa. It seemed to be an advance warning, because he went on to say:

'A time could come when it would be justifiable to overthrow an unjust system violently.'

Maybe so. But no one could justifiably claim divine support for the violent overthrow of a just system. That is until Lieutenant Colonel Rabuka did so in Fiji; and then pretended that what he had destroyed was unjust. Thus promoting the unoriginal thought that decisions of any kind and complexity which are in our favour are sensible and just; while those that go in the opposite direction are manifestly unjust. It is what every retreating batsman knows when the umpire has raised his finger for lbw, run out or any other form of 'unfair' cricketing dismissal.

The linguistic difficulties in respect of spiritual expression were matched by temporal ones: as a group of visiting British parliamentarians found in Tarawa, the capital of what was then the Gilbert Islands, at about the same time as George Knight's newsletter. They sought to explain to the assembled Gilbertese leaders and aspirant leaders the admirable and, as they believed, universally exportable concepts of the British parliamentary system within the Commonwealth.

'In the House of Commons at Westminster,' said their leader grandly, 'we have a largely two-party system of parliamentary representation.'

He paused as his words were interpreted into Gilbertese for the benefit of his listeners whose command of English did not extend this far.

'The majority elected party forms the government which determines the policies it considers right for the administration of Britain. The minority party is the Opposition – Her Majesty's Loyal Opposition, to give it the full title which we employ.'

He paused again for the interpreter, but this time there was evidence of some puzzlement and side comment among the listeners;

and the interpretation seemed to be a good deal longer than the original statement.

'Is anything wrong?' he asked.

The interpreter looked embarrassed. 'I am having a little difficulty in explaining what you have just said about the Opposition.'

'I don't see any difficulty. What I said was perfectly clear.'

'Yes,' replied the interpreter. 'In English, it is. But not in Gilbertese. The only word for "opposition" in Gilbertese is "enemy". And a number of those present do not understand how it is possible for Her Majesty the Queen to have a "loyal enemy" . . .'

The English language is deficient in its capacity to find a word to distinguish indigenous Fijians and ethnic Indians. The problem has been solved in Malaysia, which became Malaysia after the expiry of colonial Malaya. The Malays remain Malays and the Chinese Chinese; but all citizens are embraced by the word Malaysian which has no distinctions of race or origin. It identifies common citizenship.

There is no accepted equivalent in respect of Fiji, although there have been attempts to find one. 'Fijisian' was one possibility but was not acceptable to Fijians and sounds ugly. 'Fiji Islander' was a strong contender and would have my vote, thus embracing persons of all races and leaving the ethnic groups to call themselves whatever they wanted – Fijian, Indian, Rotuman, Chinese, part-European and so on. Again, this did not find favour with many Fijians; nor, of course, did any description of persons of all races in Fiji as Fijians.

The Fiji Constitution of 1970 was hammered out after years of preparatory and formative debate. It attracted the attention and contributions of numbers of specialist constitutional lawyers and was finally agreed by a British Government delegation and one from Fiji consisting of every member of the Legislative Council of the day, amid the splendours of Marlborough House in London. Its sizable complexities reflect not just the legal minds which worked upon it; but the imaginative provisions for plural and cross-voting that were in it. It is not altogether surprising that in 1987, the 1970 Fiji Constitution still remained untranslated into Fijian – or Hindustani too, for that matter.

Many of the letters to the British, New Zealand and Australian newspapers at this time sought to draw analogies from other countries. The consensus was that no fair and lasting formula had yet been devised to provide for the interests of racial, religious or tribal minorities, while safeguarding the 'legitimate paramountcy' of the majority. It was only necessary to look to Northern Ireland, Cyprus, North India and Sri Lanka for example, to perceive this. The emergence of a similar problem in the South Pacific was thus understandable if equally insoluble. Or so it was contended.

The circumstances of Fiji are, however, entirely different. The indigenous people were given entrenched constitutional protection, own 83 per cent of the land which cannot be alienated and are not exposed to a one-man one-vote ballot box. Marginally outnumbered though Fijians may be by the immigrant Indians, Fiji remains as economically dependent on Indian energy and enterprise as it was when Indians were introduced in the years after cession in 1874.

Understandably, this does not make Fijians love Indians any more. Indeed, the exclusivity of many Indian practices in marriage, religion, culture, language, education, food and personal habits, has entrenched aversion at some levels from the one towards the other. Envy of the money-making skills of many Indians is never far below the surface of Fijian opinion.

It is necessary to look to Malay/Chinese Malaysia for a human parallel for Fiji – and, of course, the Malaysian Alliance Party was a model for the Fiji Alliance, a grand political concept for inter-racial harmony and co-operation built on the platform of racial and religious tolerance by Ratu Mara over twenty years. The 1970 Constitution embraces all the conceptual protections for human rights and dignity that can be conceived to prevent man doing evil unto man; and it is entirely proper for Ratu Mara to take credit for being one of its principal intellectual architects.

There is protection of Rights to Life
of Personal Liberty
from Slavery and Forced Labour
from Inhuman Treatment
from Deprivation of Property
for Privacy of House and other Property
of Freedom of Conscience
of Freedom of Expression
of Freedom of Assembly and Association
of Freedom of Movement
from Discrimination on Grounds of Race, Place or Origin, Political Opinions, Colour or Creed
of Persons detained under Emergency Laws.

It is all in Chapter II: Protection of the Fundamental Rights and Freedoms of the Individual: fourteen pages out of a total of eighty-four.

What the Constitution does not do is turn fine words and concepts into lasting mutual respect; and it does not ensure that one political party will retain power for ever. What Constitution will? But the egocentric adherence to office of one political leader is a different matter and not peculiar to Fiji.

Authoritarian power is, of course, self-perpetuating. The longer it lasts, the more consolidated it becomes. And the more consolidated it becomes, the longer it will last. Durability is all. Not public morality or accountability. 'Power,' Henry Kissinger is said to have said, 'is the ultimate aphrodisiac.' Together with money, I suppose you could add, since the one may lead to the other.

Has any political leader ever relinquished office willingly? Public power is heady and compulsive whatever politicians may say to the contrary; and in some countries it can accumulate sizable financial benefits. Entry into public life is a voluntary act, not forced upon anyone. It thus demands a special sort of sustained self-interest plus boundless staying power, as Margaret Thatcher has so clearly demonstrated. Whether it brings with it simple contentment and a balanced family life is another matter. But over a period of time, it can certainly breed an immutable belief in indispensability. So that when political eclipse comes, as surely it one day will, extravagant responses can result.

One such was that of a Caribbean Chief Minister who found himself without sufficient support to continue to command a parliamentary majority. A new leader was duly appointed; but the outgoing Chief Minister refused to be outgoing. He proclaimed that he was still Chief Minister, irrespective of what might be announced to the contrary. Each day, he turned up in his office as if nothing had changed and sat, an increasingly lonely figure, behind his desk. The rallying call failed, however, to rally what was necessary. No staff came to seek his instructions or to perform the services he had come to expect. So while he clung to being Chief, he had no one unto whom to Minister. In the end, the police had to be summoned; and with a degree of embarrassment not hitherto known to affect policemen, ushered him out of the office, protesting to the last.

No such histrionics accompanied the departure from office of Ratu David Toganivalu after his electoral defeat in April. Moving up over the years from various ministerial posts with the Alliance

Government and a close, if at times exasperated, supporter and confidant of Ratu Mara, Ratu David found himself joint Deputy Prime Minister in the years before the 1987 election.

When Ratu David departed the political scene, he did so in a dignified way. In a *Fiji Times* interview after his defeat, he said:

> For people like me who have spent more than twenty years in politics and who were instrumental in establishing and formulating our Constitution, it is not easy to bow out completely. But we helped form the Constitution and we have to uphold it, so I hold no bitterness.
>
> On people who were bitter and hostile about the defeat, he said that the Government was not the personal property of anyone and no one should think it was.
>
> It is only human to get disappointed, but we must not let emotions rule our lives.

It is tempting to conjecture whom he meant in his reference to the Government not being the personal property of anyone; but if it was Ratu Mara himself, then the initial response of the former Prime Minister to parliamentary defeat was equally magnanimous and conciliatory.

In an official statement issued on Sunday 12 April from the Prime Minister's official residence in Suva, Ratu Mara said:

> Fellow citizens, we have come to the end of a long, hard campaign. You have given your decision. That decision must be accepted. While I am naturally disappointed at the outcome, I am proud that we have been able to demonstrate that democracy is alive and well in Fiji.
>
> I wish the new Government well in its endeavours. We must now ensure a smooth transition to enable the new Government to settle in quickly and get on with the important task of further developing our beloved country.
>
> I know how hard many of you worked and the disappointment some of you must feel that the Alliance has not been returned to government.
>
> It is important, however, that you now put that disappointment behind you. The interests of Fiji as a whole must always come first.
>
> There can be no room for rancour or bitterness and I would

urge that you display goodwill to each other in the interest of our nation.

Fiji has recently been described by Pope John Paul as a symbol of hope for the rest of the world. Long may we so remain.

16

20–28 July 1987

The second meeting in two months of the Great Council of Chiefs lasted eight days. The original expectation was for two; but there could be no certainty of this.

The shorter the meeting the greater the likelihood of pushing through a resolution for major constitutional change. Especially with the hundreds of aggressive and arrogant young Fijian men and women – the Taukei movement supporters – who remained outside the meeting throughout its proceedings and sought to intimidate and ridicule those who counselled moderation and caution. Among those who did were the Governor General Ratu Penaia and Dr Bavadra, both of whom urged a full and thorough assessment of the political and economic consequences of radical change in status and racial representation in the electorates.

The Council continued in session throughout the whole of that week in an atmosphere of tension in Suva. Many Indian stores stayed closed and barricaded as if a preliminary hurricane warning had been issued. Perhaps in a way it had. In the evening there was an eerie silence in the streets of Suva. Bars and restaurants were largely deserted and staff left to go home early. It was possible to walk through the city and hear only one set of footsteps echoing back from the buildings opposite. A self-imposed curfew prevailed.

The proceedings of the Council came to an end on 28 July. It then emerged that its members had drawn back from the republican brink. Monarchical counsels prevailed in the end, but it had been touch and go. The Governor General had urged the chiefs to maintain support for parliamentary democracy and not to sever ties with the Crown. So had Dr Bavadra, snubbed in London or not. At a crucial stage there was a reminder of the chiefly oath of loyalty to the Queen, hallowed with the kind of tradition since cession to Britain in 1874 that the chiefs were otherwise at pains to uphold.

Diplomatic activity was at last stepped up, as the critical nature of this meeting became recognised. The outcome would go a long way towards determining whether Fiji became a republic in pursuance of the coup and thus stayed in or went out of the Commonwealth; and what its future constitutional and electoral arrangements were likely to be for all communities.

Advisory body the Council might be, but it had already become a kind of surrogate parliament. It was, however, faced with the fundamental question of the means by which a change to republican status could legally be accomplished in the absence of an elected parliament. And any move to oust the Governor General – inevitably by unconstitutional means – and to set up a republic, would have serious implications for the continuing acceptability of Fiji as a member of the Commonwealth. South Africa had departed in 1961 because of its apartheid policy and practices. Whither Fiji? Within a week of the coup, the Commonwealth Secretary General had pointed out these dangers on British television.

'It would amount to a move against the Queen,' he had said.

So, indeed, it would – and very nearly had. And might still do, I reflected in England at the beginning of September.

Britain, the United States, Australia and New Zealand had separately and jointly waged a quiet but determined diplomatic offensive to dissuade the chiefs from taking the republican road. They emphasised the international price of such action; and the Governor General was left in no doubt that if a new constitution were to disenfranchise the Indians or exclude them from the enjoyment of fair representational rights, then a South African parallel would inevitably be drawn by other Commonwealth countries, not least, of course, by India.

There was, in late July, at least one Fijian voice of influential realism. The Governor of the Reserve Bank, Savenaca Siwatibau, not himself of chiefly birth, stated emphatically: 'Fiji already has an internal deficit of about $F93 million because of the coup. Declaring a republic would turn the country into an international leper.'

The most vocal support for a republic had come from the coup leader, Lieutenant Colonel Rabuka, and from the extremist Taukei movement. They threatened riots and killings if they did not get the changes they sought. It was widely believed that even if the Council of Chiefs rejected the republic notion, that would not be the end of the matter. The Taukei clique would surely continue its efforts to ensure that permanent political control rested with Fijians alone and was subject to no external accountability, however nominal and remote.

At this time, the American Chargé d'Affaires in Suva took a deep State Department-vetted breath and went public: 'The creation of any system in Fiji which does not respect and protect the rights of all its people, regardless of its label, should not expect support from the United States.'

He could not speak for others, but perhaps he did.

No such public statement had been reported from the American Embassy in Suva in the aftermath of the May coup. It was understandable why, given the widespread assumptions – well-founded or otherwise – about US-sponsored involvement in the April 1987 Fiji elections and support for the Mara-led Alliance Government. If Fiji were to replace New Zealand as a bastion of American nuclear protective strategy in the South Pacific, it would need to be a country with sufficient political and economic stability in its own right to be able to accept and thus absorb a large and controversial United States nuclear presence, with the capital investment this implied, without a serious prospect that all could turn sour.

Thus, the warning to Fiji by the United States Chargé d'Affaires could be read as less a plea for human and political rights than a pre-condition for his Government's investment and support. If the equal partnership of the Indians in the future of Fiji were to be permanently denied, the economic and political base for a large-scale United States commitment would be at risk.

New Zealand and Australia apart, the responses of other governments had been muted since the early days after the coup. The loss by yet another country of its political virginity was like all such misadventures, sad but predictable. It had to be lived with. Join the club, said the cynics.

The erratic nature of the neighbouring international reactions was apparent in the ambivalence that followed in the wake of the coup. Condemnatory statements were issued immediately by many national leaders. After all, elected politicians can hardly be expected to find any joy in the downfall of their kind, especially when, for the first time, this takes place a short distance across the sea. It was too close for comfort. But to condemn initially, and by implication to condone thereafter, are different matters. Why was it, one observer asked, that in the weeks after the coup, no government with direct interest in sustaining the stability of Fiji and its policies was sufficiently moved to indicate its disapproval by the downgrading of its mission and the despatch home of at least some of those from Fiji accredited to its own capital? Diplomatic isolation of a 'pariah' island regime would have been both a clear signal to the world and, more importantly, to the coup leaders. Britain may well recognise states, not forms of government; and contend that it could not very well withdraw recognition of a country where its own Queen was also Head of State. None the less, Britain was the colonial power for ninety-six years and thus had a special position if not a residual responsibility. To many the feebleness of its political responses in the weeks after the coup was akin to that in respect of Grenada in 1983 where British pussyfooting at the time of the tragic events at the end of that year was looked upon with disdain throughout the Commonwealth Caribbean.

Professor Sir Raymond Firth, whose anthropological credentials in respect of the South Pacific are considerable, made the following observations in the course of a letter to *The Times* (7 June 1987):

. . . One can understand how the Governor General may have felt that some form of accommodation to force majeure was the only option left to him. But this should not gloss over the fact that a properly elected government has been ejected by a display of guns in the Fijian Parliament, and replaced by a quasi-legitimate advisory council which includes the military leader of the coup.

Within the Commonwealth, such an issue of legitimacy is of paramount importance, and one expects some clear statement of principle from the British Government. The situation may have to be endured, it should not be approved, or ignored.

Stanley Arthur, the second British High Commissioner to Fiji after independence in 1970, thought otherwise.

. . . There is no more reason to expect 'some clear statement of principle from the British Government' than from the governments of, say, Barbados, Bangladesh or Kiribati. Britain has no special responsibility in this matter. (The fact that the Queen of Great Britain is also Head of State of Fiji is, of course, irrelevant.)

The Commonwealth as a whole might be expected to make some comment, since obviously an important constitutional point arises when the Head of State of a Commonwealth country refuses to see the properly elected prime minister of that country. At the very least, it raises the question whether the Head of State takes the advice of her Prime Minister, or of her representative, the Governor General . . .

Responsibility to explain her action must rest with the Queen herself, since no one else can do so, and comment rests with the Commonwealth as a whole. But there is no reason why the British Government should take it upon itself to pronounce unilaterally on the subject.

It seemed, simplistically perhaps, to me that the British Government should pronounce, unilaterally or otherwise, on the matter, and should make its actions match its words. If it condemned the hijacking of aircraft on their lawful international business and refused to negotiate with the hijackers, it appeared to be not only logical, but also essential, that it should state its views and policy with promptness and clarity when the elected government of a former colony and friendly Commonwealth country had been similarly hijacked. One, too, with historical links with the Crown. Whatever may be thought of its overseas policy in other respects, France, it has to be said again, would not have been bothered about the refinements of which Crown was which. Its approach would be essentially pragmatic – to ensure the continuance of its own interests, realistically and singlemindedly.

While it remained true that no Commonwealth government had formally recognised the new regime, political equivocation and expediency seemed to prevail beyond the shores of Fiji. That is, until the American statement and the evidence of rising concern, expressed publicly over two months after the coup by Britain, Australia and New Zealand, about the possible establishment of a republic in Fiji.

There was, of course, nothing intrinsically repugnant in the idea of a Republic of Fiji. After all, there were a variety of constitutional bedfellows among the forty-nine member countries of the Commonwealth at that time. Indeed, for only eighteen of them was the Queen Head of State, while twenty-five were republics. Australia has flirted with republicanism and isn't the United States one itself, whatever lingering notions some Americans might still nurture about the desirable trappings and grandeur of the suzerain concept? And in September 1987 the newly elected Government of Mauritius, a reinvigorated sugar and tourism success story, was reported to be about to become a republic. No problem there. It would go about it by lawful means and in accordance with accepted Commonwealth procedures.

It was thus not the creation of a republic as such that was the problem, but the means by which it would be engineered and what was feared following the severance of links with the Crown: the massive disenfranchisement of the Indians of Fiji through the entrenchment of the dangerously oversimplified philosophy of 'Fiji for the Fijians' and the mindless brutalising of Indians over the years that could result. If the Indians, like the Israelites before them, thus sought to flee en masse from the land of their tribulation, where should they be permitted to go and under what conditions? Would

New Zealand be moved to relax its immigration rules for humanitarian reasons? If so, for how long and in what numbers? And with Auckland already the largest urban centre of Pacific island population and culture, would not the racial problems of Fiji merely be transferred to New Zealand itself – less than a month before the New Zealand general election of 15 August, where David Lange's own electorate was to be found in the Auckland suburb of Mangere?

In mid June the New Zealand Minister of Immigration was reported as having told the annual meeting of the Wellington Ethnic Affairs Council that:

> New Zealand would not be an avenue for the Fiji military to achieve its reprehensible objectives . . . The military coup has wrecked years of nation-building and carefully balanced constitutional mechanisms designed to protect the special interests of different groups.
>
> For permanent migration to New Zealand, normal criteria would continue to apply. Temporary visitors' permits might be extended for up to three months for persons from Fiji already in New Zealand and who were unhappy about returning there for the present.

The *Auckland Star* editorial on 20 July took the point: ' . . . The New Zealand Government appears to have lost interest in Fiji. Coincidentally, the loss of interest began about the time queues of Fiji Indians started forming at this country's High Commission in Suva . . .'

Canada with its sizable population of Fiji Indians in British Columbia and its more relaxed approach to such matters might be a possible escape route for some. Australia would be hawkish and likely to distance itself; while the United States, the mecca of all mass migratory hopes in the past, was no longer willingly a human dumping ground for the world.

The Council of Chiefs had done its best to remove any doubt about its racial partiality. The chiefly formula for constitutional change sought to give Fijians perpetual authority and power; and to deprive Indians for ever of acceptable parliamentary status and influence.

It was a question as to whether its messianic pronouncement could be that of 330,000 indigenous Fijians to 350,000 immigrant Indians and 40,000 others. That apart, if it were to be accepted, the Senate would be abolished in favour of a single parliamentary chamber of seventy-one seats, an increase of nineteen. Thirty-six seats would be inalienably reserved for Fijians, plus four other members nominated by the Prime Minister, who would always be a Fijian chosen by the Fijian members of parliament. Of the thirty-six Fijian seats, twenty-eight would represent the fourteen Fijian provincial councils and would be selected from the nominations of district councils. The other eight would be chosen by the Council of Chiefs which would also have power to veto legislation, by what precise procedural machinery was not addressed; Indian representation would remain at twenty-two, with four Muslim seats, and General seats at eight, one going to the Banabans of Rabi. Racial cross-voting would be abolished; all voting would be communal and would be confined to non-Fijians. In the Cabinet, four portfolios would always be held by Fijians: Home Affairs, Foreign Affairs, Finance and Fijian Affairs. The Chairman of the Public Service Commission, the Judicial and Legal Services Commission, the Police Commission would all be Fijians. Racial balance in the public service, long a pious hope, would be mandatory. Additionally, the chiefs recommended, with faltering selflessness, that proprietary interests in mineral and other resources should be returned to the landowners instead of being vested in the Crown. Unsurprisingly, they asked that dual citizenship be prohibited, as it is already.

What did all this mean? That all Fijians would be deprived of the right to vote directly for the Government of their country; that Indians would be consigned to political oblivion; that Fiji would move inexorably along the path of racial bigotry and economic suicide; and that the American Chargé d'Affaires had been disappointed.

The Chairman of the Great Council of Chiefs and Adviser on Foreign Affairs to the Governor General, Ratu Josua Toganivalu (the brother of the former Alliance Deputy Prime Minister) did his best. 'The proposed system,' he said, 'follows the traditional Fijian way of choosing people for office.' Had nothing been learned in the ninety-six years of colonialism and the seventeen years of independence?

A former Alliance MP, Kolinio Qiqiwaqa, accused the Council of Chiefs of 'still living in the medieval age . . . today it is aggressively championing the cause of discord, strife, decadence, retrogression and possible genocide.'

The views of the Great Council of Chiefs were not necessarily the last word, although they would be influential and significant when the Constitutional Review Committee met. That was the next stage in the proceedings and it was to this committee that the chiefly conclusions went for consideration.

A review of the Constitution seemed to be an understandable device for the Governor General to adopt in the aftermath of the coup. It was, if nothing else, a good bureaucratic holding exercise. In this instance, however, it was more than that. In the light of the April 1987 election result, there was a case to argue on behalf of Fijian interests. The Constitution of 1970 was not intended to be the means by which Fijian representation in Parliament was so heavily outnumbered by Indian. That weakness needed to be remedied. But by how much? There would not always be a Timoci Bavadra to pilot the inter-racial ship with such idealism and self-denial. Constitutions are for principles, not for personalities. Or they should be. And they are not immutable. As with any other man-made precept, their fallibility is subject to re-examination and re-appraisal in the effluxion of time. So, 'Let it be done' was not an unreasonable response if the coup reflected something more than crude racial hatred or chiefly tribalism.

Something more indeed. For consideration at the July meeting of the Great Council of Chiefs had been a variety of options and discussion papers. One such paper invited support of the notion that the definition in the 1970 Constitution of Fiji as a 'sovereign democratic state' be amended by the deletion of the word 'demo-cratic'. It was the shape of things to come.

The Chairman of the Fiji Constitutional Review Committee was Sir John Falvey. His team was faced with eight hundred or so written submissions. Falvey had come to Fiji from New Zealand in the early 1940s to join the colonial government. It was a short-lived episode in his life as he moved on to the firm of Cromptons and legal practice in Suva. Long-time legal adviser to Fijian institutions, politician, investment counsellor and golfer, Falvey was one of the ideological architects of the Mara-led Alliance Party. He became its govern-ment's first Attorney General. In 1963 he had shared with Ratu Mara and the Federation Party Indian leader A. D. Patel, portfolio appointment to the Executive Council on the introduction of the membership system of government, that colonially conceived transit camp and training ground for ministerial office and independence. Falvey's appointment as Chairman of the Constitutional Review Committee was recognition of his skills of negotiation and compro-mise and, it was also thought, of his clear alliance with the Alliance.

The terms of reference for the review went through the customary tug of war before being finally agreed, if infelicitously worded, as follows:

To review the Constitution of Fiji with a view to proposing to the Governor General any amendments which will guarantee indigenous Fijian political interest with full regard to the interests of other people in Fiji.

To call upon and hear the views of the public of Fiji on the subject.

To begin hearings on 6 July 1987 and conclude hearings on 24 July 1987.

To deliver to the Governor General the findings and recommendations of the Committee by 31 July 1987.

To assist in the process, the Commonwealth Secretary General duly despatched a legal draftsman.

The committee's sixteen members were nominated by the Governor General, the Great Council of Chiefs, Dr Bavadra and Ratu Mara. It was heavily weighted with supporters of the Alliance. From the beginning, there seemed little prospect of an agreed report; or that it would be finished by the set date.

The review was being undertaken in circumstances of continuing racial tension, unrest and duress. The coup leader was a member. When he appeared at the meetings of the Review Committee, he did so with soldiers who remained throughout the proceedings. He made it clear what would happen if he did not get his way: the army would join the Fijian people in a 'widespread revolution' if Fijians did not achieve political control of parliament. He planned to increase the strength of the army to five thousand troops and to prepare it for fifteen years of tension. He wanted a helicopter surveillance division and a crack anti-terrorist unit for the fifteen-year 'calming period'. If the Constitutional Review Committee rejected the reforms proposed by the Great Council of Chiefs, there would be large-scale civil unrest.

'I have had feedback from our soldiers out in the areas. The people in the villages now sense that victory is coming their way. I would have a hard job controlling the army because we might just go out and join them. Three thousand soldiers with arms fighting for what we want. I wouldn't stop them. I would lead them and I won't be taking orders from anyone. The ousted Coalition probably doubt that such an uprising is possible. Just like they didn't believe a coup was possible. I am trying hard to persuade the Taukei movement not to resume its campaign of civil disobedience because they did not think that the reforms recommended by the Council of Chiefs went far enough. They are even more capable of violence now because they have gone so far. If they destroy Fiji and demolish the cities there will be a very big costly reconstruction programme. As long as the Council of Chiefs' reforms are adopted, the army is prepared to deal with such civil disobedience. We will have to be tough even if it means shooting some of our people.'

And if the recommendations of the Council of Chiefs were not taken on board by the Constitutional Review Committee and adopted, what then? A constitution was being drafted, an ABC journalist reported, which would be a blueprint for martial law, dictatorship and detention without trial. Military-sponsored republicanism would be installed in Government House in Suva; and a new flag would be raised to the masthead – in scarlet and gold, the colours of the Royal Fiji Military Forces . . .

The British Trades Union Congress meets in annual assembly to debate the movement's past, present and future. On many such occasions, the question of arbitration, as a means of solving employee–employer disputes, comes under examination in this public forum of the brothers.

At the 1987 conference in Blackpool, a delegate seemed to get to the heart of the matter:

'Yes,' he said, 'I am perfectly prepared to go to arbitration, but if the award is one I do not agree with, I reserve the right not to accept it.' He would get on well with Colonel Rabuka.

There was a degree of relief at this time for the economy. The cutting of sugarcane began in mid-July. Dr Bavadra had announced to the Indian cane growers and mill workers: 'You have made your point. Now you should take account of your families and your livelihood.'

As the mills in Lautoka began to belch their belated smoke, the emergency regulation giving the interim government power to seize land, buildings, transport and crops was revoked – 'in view of the growing mood of national reconciliation and reconstruction', a Government House spokesman said more than a little optimistically. The crush was nearly two months late and there could be no certainty about planting for 1988.

It was true that Continental Airlines had stopped flying to Fiji because of lack of business; that Air New Zealand was still overflying; that five hundred workers were laid off in the garment industry; that more than two thousand lost their jobs with construction firms as the future began to look increasingly bleak. None the less, the Governor of the Reserve Bank felt able to say on 3 August:

147

The Fiji dollar will strengthen sooner than expected. Its recovery depends on a quick solution of the political crisis. Foreign reserves which fell by fifty per cent following the May coup are now stabilising. Sugar is being harvested, the tourist industry is recovering and gold exports are at a record level. We are breathing easier now.

On the same day, however, exporters were advised to get cash or a firm letter of credit before sending goods to Fiji. The warning came from the Export Institute and was backed by the Auckland Regional Director of the New Zealand Trade Commission. 'There are still accounts outstanding for goods exported to Fiji. For anyone trading with Fiji, caution is the name of the game and everyone should work through a major bank,' the regional director said.

Two days before, Lieutenant Colonel Sitiveni Rabuka, having earlier been promoted to Commander of the Royal Fiji Military Forces, was 'officially sworn in as Commander in Chief of Fiji's security forces'. This put him in full charge not only of the army, but also of the police, and removed the Governor General's formal authority over the Army Commander.

'In a ceremony usually reserved for paramount chiefs and royalty,' said Reuters, 'more than two thousand soldiers, sailors and police joined traditional dancers to mark Colonel Rabuka's appointment as Commander in Chief.' He took the opportunity to proclaim: 'I know that if the Fijians do not get what they want through the Governor General's path, there will be rioting and perhaps killing.' It seemed an adequate-enough indication of his approach to the work of the Constitutional Review Committee, which had been locked in confrontational debate for nearly three weeks.

This sort of talk did little too to comfort an anxious and economically hard hit public of all races, many of whom in the urban areas were living in unremitting fear of intimidation, violence and general harassment. It kept alive apprehensions of the Taukei leaders' intentions following a speech given by Taniela Veitata. Standing in the April election for the Alliance, Veitata polled close to ten thousand votes and vanquished his two opponents with ease. His Fijian communal constituency significantly included Tamavua and suburban Suva.

'The Taukei movement was formed because of fears that Fijian interests would be endangered under the Bavadra Government. The military coup forestalled plans by the Taukei movement to burn Suva and kill Indians,' he said in a public meeting at Labasa. 'Our plans had to be called off when Colonel Rabuka carried out the coup. Burning and killing were phases of a Taukei plan to restore leadership to Fijian hands following the Coalition victory in the election. The first phase was a march by nearly six thousand supporters in Suva on 24 April, which passed off peacefully. Indians have excelled in business and education and held high positions in both Government and the private sector. Leadership was the only thing left for them to take away and once they have that, we Fijians are finished.'

The sole Indian among the judges of the Supreme Court, Justice Kishore Govind, determined that it was time for him to speak out. At the opening of the August Criminal Sessions in Suva, he condemned harassment of Fiji citizens by the security forces and warned the authorities 'no matter how high you are, the law is above you. No civilised society can afford to tolerate a continuing situation where citizens' rights and freedoms, guaranteed by the Constitution, are being violated in the name of authority.'

He recalled a recent assurance by his colleague, Justice Rooney, that the people's constitutional rights had not been extinguished by the public emergency regulations which gave the security forces wide powers of arrest.

'Yet in spite of this clear and unequivocal assurance, we read every day of citizens being harassed, of being arrested at unearthly hours, of being subjected to ill treatment and not being charged with any offence. We read of their being accused of distributing leaflets enjoining citizens to petition the Governor General for the restoration of democracy and of making anti-coup statements. How a petition to the Governor General or statements condemning the coup, which His Excellency himself described as illegal, can ever be anti-social behaviour defies logic and sanity,' he said.

Govind went on to observe: 'The right of assembly has been bestowed by the security forces on a chosen few. Supporters of the Taukei movement were permitted to gather in a downtown park every day recently; but permits for rallies by the deposed Coalition Government supporters were refused "for security reasons".'

Chief Justice Timoci Tuivaga, a Fijian from Lau, added that Govind had spoken on his own behalf, having advised him beforehand, 'but we would not quarrel with what he said'.

A few days before, on 29 July, in the Supreme Court, Justice Rooney had reserved his decision on a Crown application to strike out the action brought by Dr Bavadra that the dissolution of Parliament following the coup was unlawful. The phraseology used to describe Dr Bavadra's claim was 'frivolous and vexatious'. Hardly either, one might say.

Meanwhile, problems were beginning to emerge between Rabuka and the Taukei movement. The Taukei leadership believed Rabuka should have left it to them to direct Fiji's future. Instead, he had become, as one commentator put it, 'a power broker and the object of folk hero adoration by his supporters'. The Taukei movement had not anticipated that Rabuka would endorse the recommendations of the Council of Chiefs for a constitution in which Fijians would be represented largely by chiefs and their nominees. 'Though the leaders have compromised for the moment about a republic, it is believed that the movement and its influential group of high-chief backers will eventually force this as the only way to achieve political Fijian dominance.'

'There is madness afoot in the land,' said publisher Philip Harkness of the *Fiji Sun*, the most outspoken newspaper critic of the coup. 'For the past two or three weeks, the people of Fiji have see-sawed back and forth between hope and despair as the militants and the moderates have tried to win ascendancy in the current political struggle.'

Beyond the shores of Fiji, groups of Fiji citizens, students and sympathisers of all races had come together almost overnight in the wake of the coup. At public and private meetings, committees were set up in Auckland, Sydney, Wellington, Melbourne, Vancouver and London – to seek to co-ordinate voluntary efforts to restore democracy in Fiji and to give support to their relatives and friends at home. They had much to reflect upon and much to learn about the ineluctable power of the gun. And of the ambivalence of human response to physical confrontation and terror.

'If you open Pandora's Pacific Box,' said another observer gloomily, 'you don't know what you will find in it, do you? Maybe maggots and leeches sucking the blood of racial tolerance and human dignity. Till it's gone for ever. So that you wonder whether it was ever there in the first place – in a cannibal's land where the victims in war were roasted and eaten.'

As I pondered these potential extremities in the reading room of New Zealand House on an early August day in London, I became aware of a female voice.

'Jeez, George, look here! The price of toilet seats has just gone up at home. That's a bit rough.'

There was silence. And then a slow male response.

'I suppose you will have to go less often.'

The report of the Constitutional Review Committee was not made public until 21 August. As generally expected, there was a majority and a minority report because on fundamental questions there was no real possibility from the beginning of accommodating two widely divergent points of view. The chairman made the resounding announcement that each of its fifty-six recommendations had been agreed by a majority of members. He himself had not voted and thus retained his entrenched position on the fence.

The four nominees of the Great Council of Chiefs, with a degree of reinforcement from the coup leader and of the Alliance nominees of Ratu Mara, did the Council proud. At first sight, there seemed to be little between what the Council had sought and what the Review Committee had recommended. There were differences of emphasis and detail, one significant difference and one important addition.

The committee endorsed the Council's recommendation for a seventy-one-member unicameral parliament with Indian representation limited to twenty-two and General to eight seats. Voting would be on communal rolls and cross-voting abandoned. There would be twenty-eight Fijian members elected through provincial constituencies, a point of departure from the machinery advocated by the Council of Chiefs. Fijians generally would not therefore be disenfranchised; and the Council of Chiefs would not have the power to veto legislation.

There were a variety of other recommendations including the restriction to Fijians of the offices of Prime Minister and the ministers of Foreign Affairs, Finance and Home Affairs; and the nomination of the Governor General by the Great Council of Chiefs for a five-year fixed term. The committee rejected the notion that Fiji become a republic.

The minority report was written by the four nominees of Dr Bavadra (two Fijians and two Indians) with the agreement in the main of two Indian members nominated by the Governor General. It contended that the changes recommended in the majority report would give Fiji Indians the status of third-class citizens; and would condemn Indian elected members of parliament to the Opposition benches for all time. Describing the recommendations of the majority report as 'thoroughly abhorrent', it urged the retention of the 1970 Constitution which, it argued, adequately protected Fijian political interests.

The committee, the minority report went on to say, had been hurriedly assembled, gave limited opportunity for people to put their views and had been conducted in a 'climate of oppression and intimidation' from security forces operating under the state of emergency. Almost daily, while the committee was sitting, there were reports of detentions without charge, particularly of Indians.

151

The minority report made another major criticism of the way in which the business of the committee had been conducted. It contended that the full committee had not attempted a breakdown of changes proposed in the hundreds of submissions received, but focused instead wholly on the submissions from the Great Council of Chiefs. This gave the impression at times 'that those were the only submissions worthy of consideration'. The minority group therefore conducted its own analysis of the submissions and concluded that the overwhelming majority of Indians and more than 60 per cent of the individual Fijians who made submissions, favoured retention of the 1970 Constitution. The minority report concluded that the recommendations of the majority were repugnant on the grounds that they would further segregate the various races in Fiji.

'Indians are taxpayers aren't they?' said Jai Ram Reddy. 'The American War of Independence was all about no taxation without representation. Two hundred years later, it does not seem as if much has been learned. Just change the words to "no taxation without fair representation" and you see just what these misguided proposals are worth.'

The quest for separate Muslim representation in the legislatures of Fiji had been a perennial proposition throughout the development of internal government in the colonial era and into independence. It had consistently got nowhere. Accepted by the Council of Chiefs, now it was raised again 'in an attempt', the minority report argued, 'to divide the Fiji Indian community . . . To project Fiji Muslims as another race is humbug and something most Muslims in Fiji reject. Islam is a religion not a race.' Maybe, but Islam remains an active militant force in world politics emanating from nations which cohere by virtue of the Islamic religion. The Muslim argument in Fiji is, however, essentially weak as seemed to be implied by the unctuous submission put to the Constitutional Review Committee. In accepting that 'Fijian interests should be dominant in their own country' and then asking for four seats reserved for Muslims out of a reduced proportion for Indians in an enlarged legislature, the League was just seizing the opportunity to get seats for the first time, even if this was at the price of supporting overall Fijian numerical supremacy and wider Indian subjugation.

The climate of oppression and intimidation to which the minority report referred was exemplified in the treatment of the local press throughout the time the Review Committee was in session. Harkness, Johnson and their staff at the *Fiji Sun* were having a rough time in July and August. Both the *Sun* and the *Fiji Times* received identical letters dated 14 July 1987 from the Reverend Raikivi, the

Governor General's Adviser for Information, a Taukei movement leader who in appearance and approach resembled no one more than the Reverend Ian Paisley of Northern Ireland. The letter expressed

> 'the serious concern of the Government over the irresponsible, biased and unbalanced reporting of your newspaper during the tense and sensitive period in the country . . . A State of Public Emergency exists in the country and in the interest of public safety and public order, I urge you most sincerely and in the national interest, to discharge press freedom in a responsible manner. The return of the country to parliamentary democracy and normalcy, the restoration of our economy to firmer ground and the maintenance of social stability, cannot be achieved by irresponsible, biased and unbalanced reporting . . .'

The *Sun* published the letter in full and Harkness made the following editorial comment:

> The claim by Rev Tomasi Raikivi, of all people, that both newspapers are guilty of publishing material 'of a racist nature contrary to the Public Order Act' is the epitome of hypocrisy. We let the public be the judge of that.
>
> For our part, we make no apology for our news coverage and editorial opinion of events since May 14.
>
> The *Sun* has made every effort to give all its correspondents a fair chance to express their varied views on the grave situation which exists in Fiji.
>
> We look upon the above letter as another distasteful attempt by those currently in authority to control the Press.
>
> Firstly, the newspapers were closed by the military immediately after the coup. Then we were threatened with censorship. Now we are again being threatened.
>
> This newspaper will continue to publish the news without fear or favour. We will continue to publish, to the best of our ability, true, fair and accurate reports on matters of public interest. Anything less would be a dereliction of responsibility to our readers.
>
> We will not be intimidated.

It was a courageous action on the part of a newspaper which had continued to publish fearlessly in circumstances of mounting harassment and tension. Its days, however, were numbered. The

Sun would soon set and would not rise again. Not before the paper's director, Miles Johnson, had been taken into custody and held like many others in prison cells without charge; and its deputy publisher, Jim Carney, had been deported to his native New Zealand.

17

Laucala Bay was chosen in the early stages of World War II as a maritime advance base for the Royal New Zealand Air Force. With the bombing assault on Pearl Harbor, Honolulu, in December 1941, the Japanese warlords signalled their intentions in the new Pacific theatre of conflict. Pushing east and south by sea and air, they invaded the British Solomon Islands Protectorate, Papua New Guinea, the Gilbert and Ellice Islands and Nauru. Others were taken or merely bypassed. New Zealand Army and Air Force contingents were despatched to Fiji which, together with the New Hebrides, looked to be next in line for Japanese aggression. The colony was placed on a war footing of civil and military preparedness for what seemed then to be the inevitable.

These weighty matters apart, for the men of the RNZAF squadron the Fiji station was a far from disagreeable posting. The Sunderland flying boats were moored inside a protecting jetty which curved out from the wooden landing stage and hardstanding in front of a massive corrugated iron hangar and workshops. On the gentle slopes behind, the general accommodation, messes and officers' quarters were built. All faced into the prevailing south-easterly trades. They were accordingly pleasantly cool when Suva city, just around the peninsula coast and over the hills of Muanikau and Samabula, would be sweltering in heat and humidity. Offshore, in the bay itself, the tiny islands of Nukulau and Makaluva made Sunday picnics and swimming a relaxing feature of station life at Laucala Bay.

When the Japanese advance had been halted and then reversed and the Pacific war had, six months after that in Europe, come to an end, the RNZAF station remained at Laucala Bay to fulfil a general defence surveillance and humanitarian role. As the colonial administering authority, Britain was responsible for the defence of Fiji against external threat or aggression; but Fiji and the United Kingdom were 12,000 miles apart, Fiji and New Zealand a mere 1,200. So, by virtue of a defence agreement between the governments of the United Kingdom and New Zealand and, with the concurrence of the Government of colonial Fiji, New Zealand was made immediately responsible on behalf of Britain for the defence of Fiji. Thus, it retained and maintained the Laucala Bay station, as much in its own defence and foreign policy interest as those of any other country; employed large numbers of Fiji civilians and trained them in trade skills; regularly seconded a New Zealand Army officer as the colonel commanding the Royal Fiji Military Forces; accepted Fiji officers and soldiers for training in New Zealand; and undertook numerous joint military exercises in both countries. The links were close and lasting. The fact of that had a bearing on New Zealand's response when there were cries for armed intervention by New Zealand military forces in the early days after the Fiji coup.

Sunderland flying boats provided the first regular trans-ocean air services between New Zealand and Fiji in the early days after World War II. They were uncomfortable, gruelling journeys with thermos flasks and cold meals. The aircraft were unheated, unpressurised and noisy, but they did yeoman service throughout the South Pacific for twenty years. In mid 1950 Tasman Empire Airways which had earlier inaugurated a service between Auckland and Sydney with Solent flying boats – successors to Sandringhams and with a staircase to an upper deck not unlike that of a Boeing 747 – began a weekly service from Mechanics Bay in Auckland harbour to Laucala Bay in Suva. From there, they went on to establish what became known as the Coral Route – Western Samoa, the Cook Islands, Tahiti and back to Suva and Auckland. The Government of Tonga entered into charter arrangements in 1954 for a four-weekly return service to Nuku'alofa and back and initially paid £125 per flying hour for the privilege. It seemed high at the time; but the Government did get the mail brought in and the limited receipts from passenger and cargo sales.

Throughout all these developments, Laucala Bay was thus both a military and a civilian air/sea operating and South Pacific meteorological control centre. On 1 February 1965 the station was officially closed: the response of the RNZAF in its civilian rescue role to calls for assistance from outlying islands with dangerous reefs and no technical aids for landing on uncharted lagoons had gone 'far beyond the call of any duty,' said the Governor of Fiji, Sir Derek Jakeway. Since 1945 the squadron had flown 164 mercy missions, 92 searches for missing vessels and 17 hurricane investigation flights.

As news of the death sentence for the Sunderland squadron penetrated to the outer island extremities of the South Pacific, the question was frequent – what shall we do now when there is a medical emergency and no seaplane is available?

'The answer,' said the Fiji Director of Medical Services, 'is unfortunately that a lot of people who might previously have been saved may now die.'

Operations at Laucala Bay did not completely come to an end until 31 March 1967. On that day the last Sunderland flew out, accompanied by its replacement – the new land-based Orion. It was the end of an era. A new one, of a quite different nature, was about to begin.

Throughout the 1950s and 1960s increasing numbers of Pacific island students were being equipped for tertiary education. They were to be the future leaders, teachers, lawyers, accountants, engineers, economists and administrators as the winds of political change began to blow across the islands of the South Pacific, large and small. Since there was no institution providing tertiary education in any of the island territories, places were sought and found in the universities of Australia and New Zealand. To those neighbouring countries went increasing numbers of Pacific islanders to be exposed to the new and often disorienting influences and cultural loneliness. As their numbers grew, so the problem of obtaining places grew with them. Both the receiving governments and the universities became restive about their capacity and willingness to protect sufficient places in the right faculties at the right time.

The pressure began, gently at first, for alternatives to be sought. Papua New Guinea, in consultation with and the support of Australia, decided to set up its own university outside Port Moresby. This would cater not only for its own requirements but also for those of its Melanesian neighbours, the Solomon Islands and the New Hebrides. It was unlikely that it would attract either Micronesian or Polynesian students in large numbers. Anyway, from its inception it did not purport to be a regional university.

With the departure of the RNZAF from Fiji the opportunity arose therefore to examine the possible use of the site and what buildings there were as a centre of advanced education not available either in Fiji, its Polynesian neighbours to the east, or in the Micronesian islands to the north. A group of experienced educationalists and education developers from Britain, Australia and New Zealand assembled in Fiji under the chairmanship of the Vice Chancellor of the University of Leeds. At the last minute, I found myself as its Secretary. We went off to view developments in Papua New Guinea and to enquire into needs in Fiji itself, Western Samoa, Tonga, the Gilbert and Ellice Islands, the Cooks, Solomons, Nauru and Niue. The conclusion: that the creation of a regional uni-

versity on the Laucala Bay site was justified and timely; and that
the Pacific island governments concerned should support its establishment by diverting their students from Australasia to Fiji where a
more suitable social and educational environment would be
provided.

This approach did not meet with universal welcome in the region.
Some countries were far from convinced by the arguments for giving
up their traditional university links. It was clear that Fiji itself, which
would provide most students, would have to accept the main regional
share of annual recurrent cost – with an uncertain and burdensome
financial future. The Polynesian nations normally do not mind giving
Fiji its head, so long as Fiji – or some other source – meets the cost.
Benefits they are prepared to accept; costs they are reluctant to face.
For them there *is* such a thing as a free lunch. And they have no
qualms about accepting one.

For them all, there was an important consideration. They were
doubtful about the long-term wisdom of exposing their students to
the radical evils of Suva and the racial peculiarities of Fiji. They
viewed with suspicion participation in an institution which, whatever
it might be called, would become in effect a University of Fiji
dominated by the roundly disliked Indians. This was not their
idea of a true South Pacific environment for the higher education of their chosen sons and daughters; nor of the standards of
academic instruction and recognition likely to be attained. For
them, the prospect was one of even worse adulteration of their
traditions and cultures than either Australia or New Zealand could
achieve.

It was a minor miracle then – and what would now be called
a triumph for diplomacy and negotiation – that the proposal to set
up a regional University of the South Pacific went ahead with
the support and participation of governments. On 2 February
1968 the first 200 students from Fiji and other South Pacific
countries converged upon what was now the Laucala Bay campus
to enrol. The start had been made – two and a half years before
the new flag of independent Fiji was raised at Albert Park in
Suva.

The campus today is unrecognisable from its utilitarian RNZAF
inheritance. The first vice chancellor succeeded to the residence
of the commanding officer. It was a poky colonial-style wooden
bungalow, reflecting public works departmental parsimoniousness
rather than wartime austerity. The enveloping balcony was studded
with rusting metal mosquito netting attached uncertainly to doors
and windows. Inexplicably, the house faced Laucala Bay Road,

deprived of the cooling sea breezes. The noise and dust of passing traffic added to the misery of its occupants.

In June 1987 Geoffrey Caston knew how fortunate he was. The former Registrar of Oxford University occupied a new vice chancellor's residence which is spacious without ostentation and blessed by the breeze. Its Fiji timber floors are a delight in a wood-starved construction age while its beams and ceilings reflect the sensitivity of a designer who has drawn on indigenous styles and techniques.

Two thousand undergraduates from the near and far reaches of the South Pacific basin thronged the internal roads and paths in term time. Their dress, hair styles and debates revealed how far many had gone from the constraints of custom they may have yearned to shed at home and succeeded in doing at USP. Gathering unto itself over the years much of the youthful intelligentsia of Polynesia, Micronesia and indeed Melanesia, the university was a crucible of culture in transition. It had produced its writers, its demagogues, its radicals, its questioners of traditional practices and social structures, and its race and colour debates. This had given a succession of vice chancellors an increasingly hard time: a regional university in a developing country within a manpower-starved region and dependent for survival on the largesse, goodwill and support of its patron countries is forced to adopt a number of roles. Not least is the production of graduates in disciplines that reflect what subscribing island governments believe they will need. Their manpower planning has been chronically weak. Anyway, such a university is – or should be – more than a polytechnic. If it is healthy and active, it will vibrate with new ideas and approaches, often in conflict with given wisdom and tradition. No vice chancellor can prevent this. There are many who would argue that he should encourage it – not least being Geoffrey Caston's wife, an American Civil Rights campaigner and a social scientist of principle and physical courage. Hers may well have been the only white face among hundreds of brown and black who gathered in quiet and orderly appeal at Albert Park in the wake of the coup and the enforced confinement of the Bavadra Government when trouble broke out, as Fijian youths went on the rampage. She was arrested, forcibly removed by soldiers, and taken off in a military truck. For her, the protection of human rights was more precious than personal safety; the harassment and brutality of military power more divisive than race and colour.

With an inflammable campus on his hands, Geoffrey Caston went into early conclave with his Senate about the implications of the coup for the university. It had already been an uneasy year. Staff and students had been deeply split in their support for the Alliance and Coalition parties in the campaign build-up to the April general election. Attitudes had become entrenched; antagonisms created. The student recreation centres seethed with debate and doctrinal divide. Staff members were known to have been directly involved in political campaigns and close advisers to aspirant politicians of both sides.

The Alliance defeat had resulted in heady excitement for some, in disbelief and anger for others. Then the campus began slowly to settle down until the coup placed the university on full alert for trouble. Trouble between whom? Fijians and Indians most likely, as the soldiers came in to search the offices of Coalition sympathisers and supporters, and a bomb exploded, killing its holder, in a car outside the main entrance to the university. The campus was poised for verbal arson. Perhaps worse.

The large outstanding sum owed to the university by the Government of Fiji compounded the problem. Was its policy still to support the university to which it had given shelter and succour for nearly twenty years? Curious too when Caston's immediate predecessor as Vice Chancellor was the peripatetic James Maraj, former citizen of Trinidad now of Fiji and Ratu Mara's Permanent Secretary for Foreign Affairs both under the Alliance Government and its military-inspired interim successor. An article in the *Australian Financial Review* of Tuesday 19 May 1987 said:

RATU MARA TRIES TO TURN THE CLOCK BACK

Before his defeat at the last Fiji elections, Ratu Sir Kamisese Mara told a visiting Australian Liberal MP that the basis of his political problems was the University of the South Pacific in Suva.

Ratu Mara argued it was the establishment of that University in 1970 [sic] at the urging of Britain and New Zealand and with the support of Australia which had slowly but surely undermined his political position by creating dissent at his rule and the intellectual base for the now deposed Fijian Labour Party.

It was a revealing admission by the Fijian power broker for it underlined the deep conservatism which was distancing him from an increasingly educated Fijian electorate.

The ultimate cost of Ratu Mara's alienation from a changing and less racially aligned Fiji was his loss of power to the Labour dominated coalition.

Yet, as the details of the last election showed, Ratu Mara lost not only because of growing dissent and the rise of a Fijian educated class, but the loss of support from the Fijian urban workers who were annoyed at the growing wealth of the Alliance Government.

The shift of voters away from ethnic ties towards regional, economic and class allegiances meant that Alliance support from eastern Fijians and Fijian islanders and villagers was no longer enough to win government. From a core support of Hindu Indians, Indian business people and western Fijians, the Labour coalition's ability to pick up the support of most of the unemployed, the university educated, urban Fijians in Suva and the public service saw it win power.

Now with the haughty Ratu Mara clearly acting to retrieve power via a military coup, he will be attempting to return Fiji to the more racially based, less educated, less complex community which kept him in power for so long.

This aim involves a conservatism of extraordinary dimensions. It literally means turning the clock back – a dangerous and clearly impossible task.

The underlying political reality was that Ratu Mara lost the battle at the last election and to try and regain it by force must throw Fiji into turmoil and conflict.

Within a few days of the 14 May coup, the campus was emptying itself as neighbouring governments instructed their students to abandon Fiji to its self-inflicted agonies and return home. The Government of Tonga despatched its Minister of Education, Langi Kavaliku, to oversee the evacuation of its citizens and to steer them on to chartered Air Pacific flights to Nuku'alofa.

The university's half-year vacation was due to start in three weeks. On Wednesday 21 May the Senate, having debated the current uncertainties, decided to advance the start of the holiday and send virtually everyone off campus. It was a question as to whether there would be a return pilgrimage at the beginning of July. If there was not, the University of the South Pacific as a regional institution might expire. Without the financial support of the Government of Fiji, it certainly would.

By the end of 1987 the whole question of the survival of the university in its original form was beginning to look increasingly academic, so to speak: some fifty expatriate members of staff, from Australia, New Zealand and other South Pacific islands, had gone. The campus was slowly dying. The military regime was achieving its presumed objective at Laucala Bay by doing nothing. A year was to go by before it was to mount an oppressive programme of on-campus intimidation of those academics and undergraduates who were brave enough – or foolhardy enough – to challenge its actions and to seek redress.

18

Every Fijian wants to punch an Indian
– Taukei movement leader

August 1987

In the years ahead, lawyers and students of Pacific history will generate a powerful head of academic steam about the legal and related issues which arise from the Governor General's assumption of executive authority under the Fiji Constitution of 1970 in the wake of the military coup on 14 May, together with his actions which followed. Not least, near the beginning of it all, was the dissolution of Parliament on 20 May. This was the most damaging blow to the prospect of the restoration of Dr Bavadra and his Ministers in office. Whether it was done under duress or not, it had been done, lawfully or otherwise. It was a question as to whether it could be undone even if there was the will so to do. The decision was made by the man who, a short time before, had himself sworn in the members of the new Cabinet at Government House. It was the same man too, who, on the night of the 14 May coup, made the following broadcast in his own voice:

I am deeply disturbed by the events of this morning during a sitting of the National Assembly.

The unlawful seizure of members of my Government and some Members of Parliament has created an unprecedented situation which must not be allowed to continue.

The executive power under the Constitution of Fiji is vested in Her Majesty The Queen, which by law and convention I exercise on her behalf on the advice of the Cabinet.

In the temporary absence of Ministers of the Crown, I have assumed that authority.

I have accordingly issued a proclamation that a state of public emergency exists and I am taking immediate steps to restore the lawful situation.

I wish to emphasise that the Constitution is the supreme law of Fiji and has not been overridden and that all public officers duly appointed as such remain in office.

As Commander-in-Chief in Fiji, I now call upon all officers and men of the Royal Fiji Military Forces, the Royal Fiji Police and members of the Public Service to return to their lawful allegiance in accordance with their oaths of office and their duty of obedience without delay.

For the sake of the peace and prosperity of our beloved country, I command the people of Fiji to respect and obey the Constitution.

The Governor General's recorded message was put out by the commercial radio station, FM 96, and not the three-language Radio Fiji which, throughout the day, transmitted only statements issued by the coup leader. Soon after breakfast, soldiers entered the station and confiscated the tape.

The second indigenous Governor General of independent Fiji, Ratu Sir Penaia Kanatabatu Ganilau, is one of the four great chiefs who emerged as potential successors to Ratu Sir Lala Sukuna, the first national leader of the Fijian people in modern times. The other chiefs were Ratu Sir George Cakobau, the paramount chief and Vunivalu of Bau, the great-grandson of Ratu Seru Cakobau, Tui Viti or King of Fiji; his half-brother Ratu Sir Edward Cakobau, the widely accepted extra-marital son of King George Tupou II of Tonga and Adi Cakobau, Ratu George's mother; and Ratu Sir Kamisese Mara, on whom the mantle of choice was ultimately to fall. Like Ratu Mara, Ratu Penaia was appointed an Administrative Officer in the Fiji Colonial Service, but was equally at home in the army. In the latter capacity, he commanded for a time the Fiji Battalion in Malaya and latterly had paid regular visits to the Fiji military detachment in the Lebanon. A genially generous-hearted man, he was in a sense a reluctant politician, not perhaps ambitious enough for the highest office of political responsibility and not an enthusiast of the electoral hustings. Not infrequently he found hard to resist the call of village life in his Taveuni retreat. He was, none the less, an influential figure in the formation of the Alliance Party and before his elevation as the Queen's representative in Fiji was Deputy Prime Minister in the Mara Alliance Government.

Ratu Penaia's personal links with the Crown were long and apparently enduring. Perhaps they began in a personal sense in 1953 when, on 17 December, the newly crowned Queen of the Colony of Fiji and the Duke of Edinburgh stepped ashore for the first time at Suva from the royal yacht *Gothic*. 'Then,' as Joseph Sykes wrote in his account of the royal visit,

the great moment arrived for Adi Mei Kainona, the little Fijian girl with her bouquet of flowers. She was a chiefly child, for the word 'Adi' means 'Lady', the daughter of Major Ratu Penaia Ganilau, a high chief from the province of Cakaudrove, at present serving as second-in-command of the Fiji Battalion of the Fiji Infantry Regiment in Malaya: she bore a chiefly gift, a posy of the rare tagimaucia, the flower which grows only on the shores of a lake high in a mountain range on the island of Taveuni, the home of the Cakaudrove chiefs. She made her presentation in a truly chiefly manner, to a truly chiefly guest. To the accompaniment of much clicking and whirring of cameras, little Adi Mei advanced slowly and with perfect composure towards Her Majesty and when she was two or three paces away, gravely bowed her dark curly head and offered her bouquet. The Queen smiled, bent down and took the gift. The child, her eyes never leaving the Queen's face, walked slowly backward three paces and then gracefully sank down on the bark cloth carpet and solemnly clapped her hands as a mark of respect. It was a beautiful and moving act performed with the utmost grace and dignity.

For Peni (the informal version of his first name) royal and military honours were to come with prolific regularity: DSO 1956, OBE 1960, CMG 1968, CVO 1970, KBE 1974, ED 1974, KCVO 1982 and GCMG 1983. He lost his first wife, Adi Laisa, after she had borne him five sons and two daughters. In 1975 he married Adi Davila, herself a widow of a former Fiji Legislative Council Member, Ravuama Vunivalu. On her death, he married again in 1985, this time Veniana Bale Cagilaba, the widow of Jonati Mavoa, a long-time minister of the Alliance Government.

At the end of the day it would not be difficult to judge – nor would Ratu Penaia deny – where his basic sympathies lay. Yet, apart from its optimism, no one could fault the strength and courage of his first statement on the night of alarm and confusion that followed the May coup. There was no 'deafening silence' from the Governor General. It was all the more bewildering, therefore, when he dissolved Parliament and thus effectively removed Dr Bavadra and his colleagues from their elected offices, then officially pardoned the instigator of the coup. The cynics said that it was all quite understandable: Lieutenant Colonel Rabuka's first act, the coup accomplished, was to go to Government House. Ratu Penaia was the high chief of the coup leader and thought to be his godfather.

Parliament was dissolved, Dr Bavadra has contended, without prior consultation with himself as Prime Minister of the day. If so, it seemed a witless procedural omission, whether Dr Bavadra was in enforced custody or in his village. Constitutions may not define all the circumstances which may exist when consultation is required with a Prime Minister in a matter of such importance. How could they? The fact remains, Dr Bavadra has argued, that if there was no consultation with him then the dissolution of Parliament was unlawful. On this assumption, the elected Parliament was still in being and he was still Prime Minister.

There was more to it than that. Section 70 of the 1970 Fiji Constitution reads *inter alia* as follows:

(1) The Governor General, acting in accordance with the advice of the Prime Minister, may at any time prorogue or dissolve Parliament, provided that . . .
(b) if the office of Prime Minister is vacant . . . the Governor General, acting in his own deliberate judgment, may dissolve Parliament
(5) If, after a dissolution . . . the Prime Minister advises the Governor General that, owing to . . . a state of emergency, it is necessary to recall Parliament, the Governor General shall summon the Parliament that has been dissolved to meet.

So not just consultation was required with the Prime Minister. The Governor General was empowered to dissolve Parliament only on the advice of the Prime Minister. That would explain the lack of consultation. Dr Bavadra would obviously have advised against dissolution. The only apparent basis for the Governor General's action would thus be that the office of Prime Minister was vacant by virtue of the military takeover of the Government, so he could then act in his own deliberate judgment and dissolve the elected body. Stretching it a bit I would think, since the office of Prime Minister was, before any dissolution, manifestly not vacant.

One other thing is clear, however. The dissolved Parliament could have been recalled under section 70(5) by the Governor General who had himself declared a state of emergency. It was the will to do so that was lacking, not the authority or the means. No wonder the interim government was worried about the outcome of the Bavadra court case and had imported a British barrister to act on its behalf.

To a layman, there did not seem to be too much for the court to determine – if it was permitted to.

Not known to be a man to evade or shirk his duty, Ratu Penaia was none the less in his seventieth year as the crisis mounted in the second half of 1987. He could be forgiven for reflecting that he was being visited by the daemons of Hades as his official life drew to a close. Especially since the Palace, Commonwealth governments and the United States continued to describe him, the Governor General and Queen's representative, as the sole source of legal authority in Fiji. What else could they do? Well, for one thing, they could have been less ambivalent about the destruction of the democratic process, once past the initial reaction of regret and condemnation; and they could have been less legalistic about the status of the deposed Government and given more positive encouragement for its restoration. The continued reiteration of support for the Governor General was insufficient and begged the main question.

On 26 June, I was back metaphorically in Dunedin where in the first blizzards of the South Island winter, four political scientists took a hand to draw attention to the dangers they considered to be implicit in New Zealand Government policy support for the Governor General's position and actions. The four contended and the *Otago Daily Times* reported:

> Once Ratu Sir Penaia sacked the Cabinet, dismissed Parliament and declared himself ruler of Fiji, he lost any claim to be recognised as legitimate guardian of the Constitution and Head of State.
>
> It is the fundamental principle of our system of government that the Constitution is made up of two elements: formal law and constitutional convention.
>
> If we discard convention we have a governor general with the powers of a seventeenth-century despotic English king. Lawyers may be able to argue that the Fijian regime is within formal law, though that is very much open to doubt. No lawyer, however, could argue that the governor general of Fiji acted within the convention of the Constitution. For centuries it has been an unbreakable rule of our system of government that Parliament is supreme and the king, queen or governor general reigns, but cannot rule.
>
> The dangers of present government policy are immense. What a governor general can do in one of the Queen's realms, a governor general could do in another realm.
>
> We should stand firm on the principle that cabinet governs, only cabinet can govern, and that lawful and constitutional government

is possible only if there is a Parliament, the government is account-
able to Parliament and the governor general follows and acts on
the advice of the government. These are ancient and hallowed
rules.

Faced on the one hand with a governor general who backs a
military coup and on the other by a lawfully elected and lawfully
installed government, we should have no hesitation in our response: the only constitutional government of Fiji is that headed
by the Prime Minister Timoci Bavadra.

Whatever the legal polemics, the realities had to be faced. The
realities were the military and the Taukei movement. The Governor
General did, at least, offer the semblance of continuity and one
avenue of hope.

Yet there was never complete certainty for long as to exactly what
the Governor General could do and where he stood in respect of
the grave issues with which he was confronted. As early as the
second half of May he had already back-tracked from his post-coup
broadcast stand; and shown that he was sympathetic to the aims of
the coup, if not to what its leaders had done in carrying it out. He
appeared for a time to take a firm stand when the Chief Justice
and his fellow judges wrote to him declaring the coup to be unlawful
and supporting his efforts to restore democracy. And he was
strengthened by the Queen's message to the Great Council of Chiefs
and by Palace reminders of his duty as the Queen's representative
to uphold democracy. But, throughout those crucial early weeks, he
was in unstable partnership, involuntary or not, with the army
officers who had overthrown the Bavadra Government.

In the five-month period of the battle of wills for Fijian hegemony,
protagonists and antagonists seemed to change their views and
actions with disconcerting frequency. Some of this was understandable and desirable: persuasion, second thoughts, compromise and
dialogue are basic ingredients of responsible public decision-making
– or should be. Where there was movement from extreme positions,
there was a chance of reconciliation and reconstruction. The case
for supporting the Governor General's efforts was that only he could
achieve this. In the absence of elected ministers capable of carrying
out their responsibilities, the Governor General was indeed the
residuum of executive authority derived from the Queen and Constitution – whatever the Dunedin political scientists might say.

It was not long, however, before his stand and his position began
to seem ambivalent. The forgiveness of Rabuka's treasonable sin
by means of a pardon, while legally possible, may have seemed

uncharacteristic. The swearing in of Rabuka as head of government, his promotion in rank to the post of Commander of the Royal Fiji Military Forces were scarcely credible. Ratu Penaia's acceptance of advisers so predominantly pro-Alliance in numbers meant that his former position as Alliance Deputy Prime Minister was recalled. There was an early proposal, much criticised by Dr Bavadra during his visit to London, for a nominated 'parliament' in order to consider and presumably 'legitimise' constitutional changes to the benefit of Fijians and the consequent detriment of other races. His appointment of a Constitutional Review Committee heavily weighted with Alliance Party members; and his failure to ensure that the Coalition members were given proper security protection during a period of grave danger to them, demonstrated that he was not effectively in charge of the internal security whatever pretensions he might have had. The tattered remnants of his control under the emergency powers introduced on the evening of the 14 May coup were clear for all to see. By and large, the racial recommendations of the Great Council of Chiefs were endorsed by the majority of the Constitutional Review Committee. With an Alliance founding father as Chairman, there were those who believed that the committee was just another charade on the way to constitutional change of a quite different kind from that which the committee recommended. So it proved.

With the belated report of the Constitutional Review Committee before him, the Governor General concluded that the next step should be a meeting at Government House with Dr Bavadra and Ratu Mara 'to put Fiji on the road to a government of national unity representing all parties'.

The Alliance parliamentary group met – for the first time in three months it was reported – and agreed its prerequisites. These were that the Bavadra Coalition should accept that amendments (unspecified) must be made to the 1970 Constitution; and that the deposed Prime Minister should agree to discontinue his Supreme Court challenge of the dissolution of Parliament.

Dr Bavadra responded that he was 'content to ignore these conditions. The legal action is before the courts and it is not the business of the Alliance to raise it as an issue. I will be at Government House at the appointed time. I hope the Opposition leader will be there.'

'A government of national unity including both Dr Bavadra and Ratu Mara appears to be gathering support as a way out of Fiji's crisis,' said a NZPA–AAP despatch.

Was it, I wondered? And thousands of others much closer to the problem did likewise.

On 31 August the Governor General made a radio broadcast. He promised 'a solution acceptable to the nation, the Queen and the Commonwealth'. He foreshadowed changes to his 'original path back to democracy. The nominated parliament is now only one option for the way ahead. It may be replaced by other options which will convey the will of the people and at the same time be lawful. They include a temporary caretaker government for the period in which arrangements for a permanent solution are being talked through and finalised.

'The place for agreement to such an arrangement is the forthcoming Council of National Reconciliation' (the third council of one sort or another since the May coup, in addition to the Great Council of Chiefs). 'It will include all members of the dissolved parliament plus the present Council of Advisers' (a total of ninety). 'The final solution will be one arrived at with the agreement of the elected representatives of the people of Fiji under my guidance. The Council of National Reconciliation will be preceded,' the Governor General said, 'by a meeting of delegations of the two main political groupings to consider the recommendations of the Constitutional Review Committee.'

A few days before the Governor General's radio broadcast, the Commonwealth Secretary General was in Wellington. He spoke to journalists at a briefing on the forthcoming Commonwealth Heads of Government meeting in Vancouver. It was due to begin on 13 October. Commonwealth intervention to resolve Fiji's constitutional problems was, Reuter reported, ruled out by Ramphal.

'I do not think,' he said, 'that we should expect the Commonwealth to produce a solution to what is essentially a domestic matter.' Developments in Fiji would not be on the formal agenda for the meeting, but he expected Fiji to be discussed informally.

There were some raised eyebrows among the journalists. Essentially a domestic matter? That was what the upholders of apartheid in South Africa have consistently contended; but, equally consistently, Commonwealth nations and Ramphal have resisted the contention. Hence the initiative in 1985 for the Commonwealth-sponsored Eminent Persons Group visit to South Africa.

'Essentially a domestic matter'? Was Rhodesia? Uganda? Grenada? Is Cyprus? And, outside the Commonwealth, is the Lebanon? New Caledonia? Or the suspension of human rights by governments anywhere? And why is it that when a real issue of significant principle arises, countries with a common inheritance of justice, law and parliamentary institutions may choose to wash their

hands of the problem and thus make it easy for the servants of the
Commonwealth to do likewise? Hence those expedient Cabinet
decisions offering public goodwill and private disengagement where
national self-interest indicates but marginal concern for the problems
of another. In the Caribbean region, the question of Grenada was
a notable exception in this decade.

It was not long before the Secretary General was to say something
quite different about the supposed domesticity of the Fiji political,
constitutional and military crisis.

In a major constitutional dispute, there is but one legitimate recourse
– to the High Court. So Dr Bavadra had instituted the proceedings
to test the legality of the Governor General's action in dissolving
Parliament before he set off for London in mid June. The task of
filing the papers to enable the action to be set in train was given to
a New Zealand lawyer who, for his pains, was speedily deported
home. He was to have his say months later.

To ask the courts to determine this matter was one thing: to get
the case started and heard was another. It was not a question of
procedural delay. Into the equation came an indigenous body of
men and women determined to frustrate the judicial process by
whatever means. And to impose their will upon the people of Fiji
as a whole, irrespective of race. Racialism and militarism were now
effectively to join forces. The possibility of a political rapprochement
was sufficient to unleash a new and fearful element in the struggle
for power.

The Taukei movement had come into being as an active force in
Fiji and Fijian politics in the immediate aftermath of the April 1987
general election with the victory of the Bavadra Labour–Federation
Coalition and the defeat of the Mara Alliance. Its campaign took off
in the weeks after the election with a series of demonstrations
against the new Government, thus providing the trigger for Sitiveni
Rabuka's first military intervention. Its objectives were racially
extreme and its methods disreputable. It was a black Coup-Klux-
Klan.

There is no full equivalent in English for the word 'taukei'.
Fijians may use it to describe themselves in the sense of 'native' or
'indigenous'. The rough and ready alternative employed, at least in
the past, by European and part-European, is 'kai Viti' – a 'person
of Fiji'.

'Taukei' has, however, a wider and deeper significance which
relates to land and the ownership of land. The earliest form of
Fijian society of which there were hints in tradition were those of

171

independent agnatic family groups. They were tillers of the soil. Ties of cognate blood attracted inter-marrying groups to the same locality. Each such unit had its own village, its own defined and recognised arable land and its own leadership authority, the senior male. We are told that in the seventeenth century the groups began, except in the mountains of Vitilevu and Vanualevu, slowly to press westward. When this ceased early in the eighteenth century, the units had become inextricably mixed: it was the starting point of a new way of life and the birth of tribal government. The forces which had driven these families to migrate now compelled them to combine in new and unfamiliar surroundings for the purpose of mutual protection. Tribal leaders emerged and a chiefly structure gradually took hold.

There were, however, disintegrating influences at work. Throughout the eighteenth and nineteenth centuries there were incessant tribal forays and clashes. These in turn led to the emergence of powerful groupings and still higher chiefs. The migratory movements had significant effect on land ownership and usufruct. Individual ownership did not exist. All land was held by a proprietary unit; and the right of ownership over land was absolute and indestructible. An early missionary, the Reverend Lorimer Fison, described it this way:

> It is certain that, though the taukei may be driven from their lands by a stronger tribe, they do not acknowledge the most crushing defeat as the extinction of their title. In fact, they consider their title to be inextinguishable as long as they themselves are not extinguished. It may be held in abeyance but it cannot be destroyed.

In the sophisticated and complex days of the twentieth century, the paramount need to entrench Fijian land ownership and control resulted in the determination of inalienable Fijian reserved land; in the establishment of the Native Lands Commission to decide ownership of Fijian land, to consider inter-Fijian and Fijian-settler disputes and to determine boundaries; and in the creation of a Native Land Trust Board to administer the granting of tenancies of Fijian land and usufruct mainly to Indians. The questions that could arise were time-consuming, complex, deep-seated and potentially injurious. Fiji was, however, far from alone in this. Western Samoa, then a World War I League of Nations mandate administered by New Zealand, set up a special land court and imported a judge to preside over it. The fact is that the unyielding attachment of Pacific islanders to their lands lies deep in the lifeblood of all their societies. Resentment may be dormant, but never disappears – hence the tenacity with which New Zealand Maoris have pursued their efforts to reverse the injustices in respect of land which they believe lie within the 1840 Treaty of Waitangi.

The use, therefore, of the word 'taukei' by the new and militant political movement in modern Fiji goes to the heart of pre-Christian ethos and traditions. So too, it might be added, did some of their words and deeds.

'All we hear from the Taukei movement are threats to burn, riot and kill, in the name of God, for a few more leather-covered seats in Parliament!' Thus wrote Jone Dakuvula, cousin of Sitiveni Rabuka, in the *Fiji Sun* of 17 August.

'The Taukei movement,' said *The Dominion Sunday Times* in Wellington on 6 September, 'has about as much intellectual and political responsibility as Britain's National Front. Fortunately it has won the support of only a minority of the Fijian people.'

It was an oversimplification. Only a few days before, a group of Maori radicals had met with Rabuka in Suva and pledged full support for him and the Taukei movement. They called for the interim Fiji Government to 'get rid of' the New Zealand and Australian High Commissions in Suva for allegedly trying to undermine the Taukei movement.

'We are proud of Rabuka and the Fijian people for their maintenance of Fijian life,' a member of the group told the press. 'We have made enduring ties. The Fijian and Maori struggles for dominance are similar and we look to the time when we can do in New Zealand what Rabuka has done here.'

The regional pot was beginning to simmer. A national leader of a democratically elected government ignores such extremism at his – or her – peril, no matter what security advisers may say about 'vocal minorities' and that 'the vast majority of New Zealanders, Australians and decent citizens reject such statements'. Well they might; but that does not dispose of the problem.

In the fastnesses of Kent, on the night of the fourth of July – a curious, but irrelevant American coincidence – I apparently had a nightmare. Apparently, because I don't remember it.

On normally good authority, however, I am told that in what are usually described as the 'small hours of the morning' I began to shout out:

'Kill . . . Killlllll!'

This not being my normal procedure, I demurred.

173

'Yes you certainly did. I don't know who you had in mind, although I was wondering . . .'

I thought for a minute about such understandable concern.

'I don't think you need be alarmed on this occasion. I suppose it is just preoccupation with the calamities of Fiji; and "kill" is only a stage further, after all, from "punch".'

19

> Civilisation is hideously fragile. There is not much between
> us and the horrors underneath. Just about a coat of varnish
> – C. P. Snow

September 1987

The efforts of the Governor General to get the two opposing political parties and their leaders round the Government House table at the beginning of September were being watched with increasing impatience and distrust by both the military and Taukei movement leaders. On Thursday 3 September Dr Bavadra and Ratu Mara had met with Ratu Penaia for the first time since the 14 May coup. It was essential, many considered, that the sustained pressure on the Governor General for nearly four months be relieved, or at least shared. It had come from the army, the Taukei and the Great Council of Chiefs. Cranking up the rusting political machinery was now imperative – or it could be too late. So it was accepted that the Coalition and Alliance negotiating teams would come together the following day to discuss the formation of the Council of National Reconciliation, which would address itself not least to the Constitution and the recommendations of the review committee. It was no mean achievement. The differences between Ratu Mara and Dr Bavadra had become so profound that at this time dialogue of any kind was well nigh impossible, let alone the addressing of the fundamental issues about which they disagreed. In the end, both Fijian leaders came to Government House with the blessing of their parties to seek a remedy for the open wounds in the body politic of Fiji and thus avert the cataclysmic consequences which the country might well face if they failed. For Fiji, as one observer put it, 'is slowly bleeding to death'.

The New Zealand Herald, in an editorial on Monday 7 September, did not think much of the chances of a satisfactory and lasting outcome:

While an odd glimmer of hope for a speedy and satisfactory return to normality still flickers in Fiji, the likelihood of an agreed solution to the five-month-old crisis must be considered slim. The intractable difficulty is that the Bavadra coalition and those who deposed it are talking about two quite different and barely related concepts.

If the nature of the opposition facing Dr Bavadra was not clear before, it has been graphically enunciated by the group of Maori activists recently returned from Fiji. The ousted leader faces an ethnic revolution that wants to turn back the historical clock with all the myopic fervour of a jihad – and has not thought much past that.

Dr Bavadra and his supporters stalk a conventional political arena, at least for these times. Content that indigenous and traditional rights are already protected, he is concerned for the social issues of health, education, employment and human rights that straddle all racial divisions.

In another time and place politicians from the conventional Left and Right might have struck a compromise. But having happily profited from the coup, the Alliance Party must now follow the agenda of the chiefly elite and the extremist Taukei movement. And that agenda allows no compromise, reconciliation or reasoned argument.

Events in Suva on the preceding Friday had already proved the point, as was intended, beyond question. Beneath the great sculpture of Ratu Sir Lala Sukuna on the lawns in front of the law courts in Suva's Government Buildings, a lovo pit was dug. Common enough in the hotels of the south coast where the old traditional rites of the Fijian people were translated into modern-day pretend cere-monial for the club-carrying blackened warriors of the dance troupes and the fire walkers of Beqa. The hot stones and white ash were used to earth-bake the pork, palusami, fish and root crops of cultural entertainment – while the war cries were uttered with mock menace and the challenge of the spears stopped inches short of the eyes of anxious tourists. It was a ritual that went back, however, into the deep roots of a turbulent society – and cannibalism.

The principal authority on the state of Fijian society when the vavalagi – the strangers from beyond the horizon – first came into contact was the Reverend Thomas Williams. He wrote down what he found and saw and not what he wished to find and see: a singular approach for an untrained early Methodist missionary who served in Fiji from 1840 to 1853 and whose observations only occasionally drifted towards the subjective. In the 1840s he described events after victorious battle in his *Fiji and the Fijians*. First published by Hodder & Stoughton in 1858, his book is the cornerstone of Fijian anthropological studies and remains widely read and respected today:

> Captives are sometimes taken, and are treated with incredible barbarity. Some have been given up to boys of rank, to practise their ingenuity in torture. Some, when stunned, were cast into hot ovens; and when the fierce heat brought them back to consciousness and urged them to fearful struggles to escape, the loud laughter of the spectators bore witness to their joy at the scene. Children have been hung by their feet from the mast-head of a canoe, to be dashed to death, as the rollings of the vessel swung them heavily against the mast.
>
> The return of a victorious party is celebrated with the wildest joy; and if they bring the bodies of the slain foes, the excitement of the women, who go out to welcome the returning warriors, is intense . . .
>
> . . . Dead men or women are tied to the fore-part of the canoe, while on the main deck their murderers, like triumphant fiends, dance madly among the flourishing of clubs and sun shades, and confused din. At intervals they bound upon the deck with a shrill and terrible yell, expressive of unchecked rage and deadly hatred. The corpses, when loosed, are dragged with frantic running and shouts to the temple, where they are offered to the god, before being cooked. On these occasions, the ordinary social restrictions are destroyed, and the unbridled and indiscriminate indulgence of every evil lust and passion completes the scene of abomination . . .

According to the Fiji Museum, the most notorious cannibal in Fiji history was Ra Udreudrei who laid down a stone for each victim: 872 stones in line were seen by the Reverend R. B. Lyth in 1849, some time after Ra's death. His grave can still be seen near the Kings Road in north-west Vitilevu.

The fire for the lovo was lit in Suva on Friday 5 September 1987. Half a mile away up Cakobau Road at Government House, political reconciliation was being attempted. Not so for the Fijians who guarded the lovo in the traditional dress for battle, faces blackened and smeared with ash, and armed with clubs and spears. This was not entertainment for tourists – as Dr Bavadra's spokesman, Richard Naidu, discovered when, going too close, he was recognised, chased and beaten before guests in the Suva Travelodge across Victoria

Parade. He suffered a broken arm, a head wound that needed ten stitches and severe body bruises.

Ratu Meli Vesikula, ex-British Army sergeant-major with twenty-three years' service from 1961 to 1984 in Northern Ireland, Cyprus and Malaysia, was reported as saying:

> This is not for show. One day we will put people in it. There will be more lovo like this if the Fijians don't get their way. The Coalition has shown disrespect by challenging the wishes of the Great Council of Chiefs and by going ahead with a court action against the Governor General challenging his authority to dissolve Parliament and order a state of emergency. The lawsuit by Bavadra against our high chief is an insult to the Fijian people . . . The Taukei movement now warns that there will be no court case. We will not allow it. We warn those opposing our legitimate struggle that you have not seen us in action yet. We are now at that point. Stand prepared.

The putrescence of human flesh is, I suppose, the ultimate obscenity. The stench is unmistakable; and the memory enduring. I came close to it with merciful brevity at an early adult age.

Jerusalem is the confluence of three world religions – Christianity, Judaism and Islam. On 22 July 1946 this polyglot, revered but ambivalent city was the scene of modern history's most skilled, daring and undetected assault on high-security property and staff. It was perpetrated, with classic irony, by sons of the holocaust; and was to set alight for years to come the minds and energies of insurgent disciples across the protesting world.

Part of the King David Hotel had been taken over as the central secretariat of the Government of Palestine and as military head-quarters Middle East Levant. It was heavily guarded. Security checks depend however in the end on human beings – soldiers, policemen or civilian guards – to administer them. And when the routine of routine takes over, slackness will lead to carelessness in respect of the familiar – or apparently familiar – pass holder. So it was that day as a delivery cart with its milk churns and milkmen, dressed as normal and speaking Arabic, were waved through the check points. Once inside the perimeter fences, the 'milkmen' proceeded to the basement of the building, left the day's supply of milk in its usual place and took away the empty churns. But some of the new ones contained not milk, but high explosives.

Two hours later, a vast explosion sliced off a wing of the hotel as a knife goes through a fruit cake. Ninety-one staff members of

178

the Palestine Secretariat died – British, Arab and Jew – in that discriminatingly indiscriminate slaughter.

Smoke and dust still filled the air of the broken building when I arrived from Port Said and El Kantara two days afterwards, somewhat more appreciative than I had been of a ship's engine room breakdown in the Red Sea with a following wind at the height of the Middle East summer and a temperature of 120 degrees Fahrenheit in the shade of the ship's metal shell. With only about half the dead recovered, the work of rescue continued in searing heat and desperate nausea from the acrid putridity. The burned and twisted bodies still trapped beneath the rubble had begun to fester and rot. I counted myself fortunate to be despatched without ceremony to Gaza in place of the induction processes of the wrecked Secretariat to which I had been bound. Over forty years later, the Taukei threats beside the pyre in Suva seemed too real and too menacing to be dismissed as mere words. I had no doubt that Vesikula meant exactly what he said. And was permitted to say without let or hindrance in a public place.

The tension in Suva mounted. Violent incidents erupted in the city. The army was out in force as the hunt began for Coalition supporters who were believed to be planning revenge attacks following the Naidu assault. Armed soldiers gathered outside the Laucala Bay home of Dr Bavadra, ostensibly to prevent further clashes between Taukei movement and Coalition supporters. Shots were fired into the building. The Bavadra family were inside. Fears mounted for their safety. Dr Bavadra emerged on the balcony and shouted 'What are you shooting at? Why don't you shoot me? Isn't it me you want?'

It had been another day of opposition to reconciliation, of extremism against dialogue, of racialism against humanity. Further stock-taking would now be necessary. A minority movement with the support of the guns was no longer just a minority movement. Fear stalked the streets by day and night. It could not now be wished away.

Next day Dr Bavadra set off from his tribulations in Suva for his village home in Veiseisei. There, and at a rally of his supporters in Ba, he took counsel about his next steps in the heightening atmosphere of racial incendiarism. He and his colleagues were urged not to attend further meetings with the Alliance unless their safety could be guaranteed. And that was not going to be easy. There was growing frustration and fear among the Indians of the west. 'There is a limit to everything,' said Bavadra's Deputy Prime Minister Harish Sharma, 'and we will not just sit and watch when torture and harassment exceed the limit.' But the military grip was too strong. There is only one way to fight a monopoly of guns: slowly, by the economy. And that would require patience, sacrifice and, above all, endurance of enhanced levels of harassment and torture. It was difficult to see where 'the limit' would be; and how words could be translated into instant effective action. A demoralised political and racial Coalition, incapable of co-ordinated action, was what the coup and Taukei leaders – and at this stage they were rapidly becoming synonymous – were seeking.

The posturing proceeded. The Governor General guaranteed the safety of Dr Bavadra and his colleagues for their attendance at the second round of reconciliation talks at Government House in Suva on Tuesday 8 September. It was not enough for Dr Bavadra. He pulled out of the meeting, citing death threats against him, his fellow party members and against judges who might hear his Supreme Court action challenging the legality of the dissolution of Parliament in May. Members of the Taukei movement were responsible for the threats, he said. Army and police had watched the assault on Richard Naidu. Two members of the Governor General's Council of Advisers had also been present. The Governor General's previous assurances of safety for him and his staff had been ineffective. Any hope for his participation in the day's talks was dashed when a group of Taukei members, Dr Bavadra told the Governor General, led by former Senator Inoke Tabua, came to his Laucala Bay house on Sunday and, in the presence of witnesses, threatened to burn it down. 'It is a matter of great concern that no arrests have yet been made in connection with these recent incidents, although in Mr Naidu's case, the identity of his assailants is well known.'

The Governor General did his best: he charged the Taukei leaders with provocative attitudes which were not helping him to steer the country back to parliamentary democracy. He called for responsible leadership to prevent further violent or threatening tactics. It was too little too late. Only days afterwards, there was rioting and burning. The torch was put to parts of Suva.

As the overt attempts of cross-party political dialogue faltered, there was a new development. Ratu Mara and Dr Bavadra met secretly at Deuba, a favoured beach resort forty kilometres from Suva. There they patched together what came to be known rather grandly as the Deuba Accord for a power-sharing joint party government of elected members and the retention of Fiji as a Sovereign State.

'Do you think you can trust Ratu Mara?' Dr Bavadra was asked.

'I have to,' he replied. 'What else can I do?' What indeed. 'Anyway he may not think that he can trust me.'

'It is easy to trust you, Dr Bavadra; but it is not sensible to trust a man with a gun. Or the man behind the man with the gun.'

The confidence and the confidentiality did not last. It never does in small places. Especially island communities. Movements can never be concealed, meetings rarely. And not for long. Infidelity and assignations of a sexual nature are secrets hopelessly available to all. Deception is possible but short-lived. Someone is always watching, speculating and reporting. News gets out in strange ways. In official business, it is impossible to control, no matter what security classification you put on a file or minute. My first lesson may have been in Palestine, but I learned it the hard way in Tonga where from 1953 to 1956 I cut my teeth as Secretary to the Government. Leakages were so commonplace that it seemed sensible no longer to resist, but to adjust and use them. I came to terms with the notion that as soon as something was typed, whether for internal or external purposes, news of it would already be in the streets. That accepted, I could plan a bit better. Then came a strange discovery: like many others, I occasionally had ideas in the middle of the night and went off to the Premier's Office in the morning thinking that I would act upon them. They would have been mentioned to no one. Yet the Chief Clerk would come in and say, 'I hear that you are thinking of doing . . . I wouldn't if I were you.' And he would explain why. Worse, when I was stopped by a total stranger as I got out of my car at the office. He strongly advised against a nocturnally chosen, but unrevealed, course of action and said he knew that I intended to take it: raising taxes, perhaps. Very odd. No one has a monopoly of wisdom – or lack of it – I suppose. But I came, after eighteen months, to a firm conclusion: as soon as I had an idea, as soon as it came into my head, I must accept that everyone, both inside the Government and outside it, would know that I had. Before I spoke about it or put it to paper. I got on fine after that. Life was so much easier. There was less to worry about. Any politician advocating open government knows where to find out how it works: the islands of the South Pacific. The people are expert watchers, analysts and gossips – matched only in my knowledge by the penetrating skills of citizens of the smaller Caribbean islands. There they know who you are almost before you know it yourself.

The extremist response to suspected rapprochement between the two Fijian political leaders was immediate and devastating; and it ushered in a period in the second half of September that was to be crucial to the future of Fiji and all its people.

'Indians are greedy, grasping, mercenary, individualistic and selfish. They want to make money in the shortest time.' Thus said a Maori activist who happened to be a lecturer at Auckland University. 'Fiji Indian students should be deported from New Zealand if they disagree with the aims of the coup.' This caused a bit of a stir. The Vice-Chancellor responded on classic lines: 'A university is a place for freedom of thought and expression.' Except perhaps the University of the South Pacific. And a few others.

On Sunday 13 September arsonists and looters moved into the Cumming Street–Waimanu Road area of Suva. It is a tourist-orientated concentration of modest Indian-owned hi-fi stores and tailor shops. A duty-free bargain hunter's mecca. In the early hours of the morning six buildings were set ablaze with petrol bombs in an outburst of racial violence. Shop windows were smashed and goods stolen. Acrid smoke billowed through the streets as firemen from four brigades battled the fires, watched by scores of people who had just left nearby nightclubs at closing time. A service station attendant was struck on the side of the head with an axe by one of several masked men who set the station on fire in the first attack. The petrol station was badly damaged as were four buildings housing shops and the offices of the Fiji Labour Party and the Fiji Trades Union Congress. The buildings had thus not been chosen at random. There was a purpose beyond arson for the sake of arson. Two other shop buildings were gutted, including one that was formerly the Bank of Baroda's headquarters in Suva.

The following day there was another small step down the path to anarchy and chaos. A group calling itself the Taukei Liberation Front claimed responsibility for the burnings and looting. They promised more. Thus a new evil was born and the terminology for such groups in Northern Ireland, in Europe and in the Middle East came to the South Pacific.

'They are, of course, a small minority, a lunatic fringe, not representative,' it was put to me. Maybe so. The modern world is sadly afflicted with a variety of extreme political, racial and religious groups; and their effectiveness can be in direct proportion to their limited numbers. The Irgun Zvai Leumi and the Stern Gang were minority terrorist groups of latter-day Palestine. Their objective was to make the mandate unworkable and get the British out. The success of their operations over many years was to cow much of the Jewish population into submissive silence. The same was true of Eoka in Cyprus. The IRA and its Protestant equivalents survive because they terrorise successfully. They are minority groups with influence and control far beyond their numbers. So are the kidnappers, the hijackers and the car bombers of the various Middle East Arab groups fighting with apparent aimless abandon for causes barely comprehensible to those not directly involved. But with countless silent sympathisers. Terrorists to some are freedom fighters to others.

The emergence in Fiji of a group proclaiming its intention to step up arson, violence and destruction clearly translated to Fiji what successive companies of Fiji's soldiers had seen, absorbed and pondered in the Lebanon.

On Friday 18 September, five days after the first outburst of arson and robbery, soldiers shot one man in the leg and arrested twelve other people after gangs set ablaze several businesses owned by Indians in central Suva. The army sealed off Suva with road blocks and fired on youths who rampaged through the capital looting shops and setting fire to buildings.

With his security and that of his colleagues sufficiently assured by the Governor General to enable him to feel it possible safely to attend the resumption of all-party talks at Government House, Dr Bavadra duly did so on Monday 21 September.

By Wednesday, after an intensive period of negotiation, a chink of optimism began to appear in the darkness of the political scene. There emerged an agreement for the establishment of a bi-partisan caretaker administration under the presiding influence of the Governor General and in which the interests of both the April 1987 victorious but short-lived Coalition Government would be equally represented with the Alliance, which had run the country since independence in 1970. For equal representation on such a body was what the Coalition had consistently sought.

To close observers – and there were many who felt that all hope had long since gone for ever – it was the beginning of a possible return to consensus and stability. For the time being at least, the principles for which Dr Bavadra had fought would remain on the table. His Fijian and Indian supporters would return in some degree from the political and racial wilderness. The Alliance would participate in the policy-making processes of the caretaker government, having accepted what Ratu Mara himself had so long advocated: that inter-racial participation in the affairs of the Fiji state was fundamental to its present and its future. In return, Dr Bavadra agreed to abandon his Supreme Court action to contest the legality of the dissolution of Parliament. It was a major concession.

Two days later Dr Bavadra called at Government House to discuss with the Governor General the final details of the new power-sharing

ministerial portfolios. He was perplexed by what he found: a pre-
occupied and seemingly worried man, a man who was evasive in his
replies and reluctant to discuss the agreed agenda for the meeting.
Gone was the euphoria of the Deuba Accord and the publicised
cake-cutting ceremony which followed it.

When Dr Bavadra took his leave, Ratu Penaia said:

'And give my loloma (warm greetings) to Adi Kuini and the
children.'

'At all our meetings, he had never said that before,' Dr Bavadra
recalled later. 'It seemed a kind of farewell. As if he knew something
and that all had changed.'

'At six o'clock this evening,' said Radio Fiji, 'His Excellency the
Governor General, Ratu Sir Penaia Ganilau, will broadcast to the
nation and will give details of the political agreement reached earlier
this week.' Thus was Ratu Penaia to tell the people that he had
fulfilled the promise he had made on 31 August, three weeks before:
the promise that he would find a solution to the current problems,
a solution which would be acceptable to the Queen, to the Commonwealth and to all the people of Fiji.

It was not to be. At 4 p.m. on Friday 25 September 1987 the road
blocks were up again and the barbed wire was out. Fijian soldiers
again took over Government Buildings, the radio studios, telephone
exchanges, press offices and key points throughout the city. Coup 2
had begun. The Governor General's broadcast was never transmitted. An hour later at 5 p.m. Colonel Sitiveni Rabuka delivered his
own.

Soon after his Government House meeting, Dr Bavadra considered what next he should do. The prudent course was for him to
return forthwith to the security of Veiseisei and the north-west. At
three o'clock he set off from Suva by car. He had passed through
the hills when, at the Navua Bridge thirty kilometres from Suva, his
car was stopped by an army road block. Soldiers surrounded the
vehicle.

'Will you please come with us, sir,' said the officer in charge.

'No. Why should I? You have no right to do this.'

'Please do not make it difficult for us, sir. We are only obeying
orders. Do as I say and get out of your car.'

'And if I refuse?'

'Then we shall take you anyway.'

The door of the car was opened. The soldiers waited. Slowly Dr
Bavadra got out. He stood alone in the centre of the road. As the
soldiers watched, hesitating, uncertain, he removed his shirt until

his chest, shoulders and back were bare. Facing the officer, he said with deliberation:

'Shoot me. That is the best thing for you to do. Shoot me. Do it now, here, and be done with it. Before witnesses.'

The officer lowered his eyes but did not otherwise respond. Then he signalled to his troops and the deposed Prime Minister was hustled into the back of an army truck. The driver started the engine, turned the vehicle round and set off back in the direction of Suva.

The Prime Minister whom the Queen did not see, and who thus could not return to the Pacific with the mana that an audience would have bestowed upon him, was next day placed in solitary confinement in the maximum security prison of Naboro, fifteen kilometres from Suva.

Brought in at the same time and placed in a nearby cell was Jim Carney, co-publisher of the *Fiji Sun*. Bavadra and Carney met for the first time in these macabre circumstances of shared misfortune. Deported to New Zealand some days later, Carney was to describe his impressions of Dr Bavadra in *The New Zealand Herald* on 30 September: 'He is an outstanding man. A man of sincerity. A man of great personal fortitude and charm. A man who is deeply religious.'

Perhaps it is something to do with his name. 'Ba vadra' means a fortress of pandanus. And a pandanus grass fence is one that may bend but will not break.

From the same prison, three days earlier, over one hundred prisoners were permitted to leave with spades and shovels, travel to Suva and to march through the city to Government House for tea with the Queen's representative. It was one of the more bizarre events of a week of darkness and foreboding.

It is not customary to give credence or legitimacy to anonymous letters. None the less, a handwritten letter dated 21 September 1987, supposedly from a senior officer in the security forces, was delivered to the Coalition that day: prior to the Naboro break-out and Coup 2. It proved to contain generally accurate intelligence about Taukei plans for a destabilisation run-up to the second definitive military intervention on 25 September and went some way towards explaining military and police inaction in respect of arson, looting and assault:

21 September 1987
A special meeting was held on Monday evening and plans drawn up. Taukei movement leaders and prominent members took part. Release the Naboro prisoners but first of all light the complex on fire. Get whatever tools available from prison storeroom to fight

and attack with. To be done on Tuesday night 22.9.87 after tea.

1. The earlier the better to enable one group of prisoners to escape inland and hide or try making their way to the Suva area. One group of prisoners to protest to Governor General. Wait until dawn. Show themselves to security forces. Their demands must be met or else. Prison officers supporting the Taukei movement to release them. Let them march to Governor General and also see Rabuka.

2. Night raids and attacks to begin on Wednesday 23.9.87 (mass killing) target Indian community and Bavadra supporters. Prisoners to be supported by gangs at Raiwai, Delainavesi, Samabula, Kinoya and Naboro. Must be a combined effort. Names mentioned Bavadra, Kalou, Navuso, Tavai, Naidu, Siwatibau (Reserve Bank) main targets.

3. The talks held in Deuba to carry on and to approve everything about a caretaker government but when this caretaker government comes into operation sometime next week, more riots and unrest should take place to enable another coup to take place. Excuse is that this caretaker government cannot control the whole situation. No help to be given. Four hours only to be given for the short ruling of the caretaker government.

4. 29.9.87 make another lovo and protest to the Governor General over court case. If Bavadra wins, club him and his supporters and put them into the lovo.

5. This weekend more trouble to take place.

6. 2,000 people from Cakaudrove, Bua and Macuata to come to Suva to be present during the court case on 29.9.87. They prepare a lovo to put Coalition supporters in.

7. Another coup to take place – overthrow of Governor General, shoot Bavadra, Epeli Nailatikau and Coalition supporters.

8. Fiji to be under military regime until 10.10.87 when the country will be declared a republic.

9. All seats to be Fijians, other races not to be given power and decision making.

10. Indian schools next target of attacks. Observation and stories from the security forces heard soldiers helping terrorists; also they have been helping throw petrol bombs at buildings although pretending to protect the public. (Friday incident also Saturday night 12.9.87.)

11. Soldiers and Taukei movement working hand in hand. There is evidence – overheard a police officer saying let them do it, Friday's riot.

12. Not all soldiers, Westerners and other supporters in the army

are merely carrying out our orders but may revolt if they are forced to shoot their own relatives and 'kai vata'. These soldiers and policemen are just working for their bread and butter. Inside there is bitter feeling against Rabuka.

13. Everything happening now is being backed by the Taukei movement leaders who have encouraged youths and ex-criminals. There is evidence that some soldiers and policemen already knew before what would happen on Saturday night 12.9.87 and Friday 18.9.87. On Sunday evening 7.30 p.m. 20.9.87 Rabuka went to the Central Police Station cell and had a private audience with five to eight members of those who were to appear in court on Monday morning 21.9.87 (arsonists). He took them cigarettes and gave them. He had a secret discussion with them. Only him alone, no other member of the security force was to be with them. He ordered that the arsonists be released for a few hours that evening. He apparently entertained them and also briefed them. Please, I hope you won't reveal my identity. We pity Bavadra, Navuso, Nailatikau etc. We are trying to help them. Please take care.

20

25 September–10 October 1987

If Coup 1 was a reaction against a so-called Indian dominated
government and an attempt to reassert or restate the paramountcy
of Fijian control and interests, by the time of Coup 2 the complex
struggle was reproduced on an almost entirely intra-Fijian stage.
The Indians stood on the sidelines as the dynastic power game
unfolded. The four principal characters – Ganilau, Bavadra, Mara
and Rabuka – were all indigenous Fijians locked deep in their own
Pandora's boxes of historical relationships. One of the nearest – not
all that near – Indians to the contest was Jai Ram Reddy, joint author
of the minority report of the Constitutional Review Committee. He
had no delusions of grandeur.

'I am not sure that I am an enthusiast for our early return to
government,' he had said quietly in London in June. 'Why should
we have to take responsibility for cleaning up the mess these other
fellows have made? They've done it. Let them face the consequences.' No great urge to 'dominate' here. But entrenched racial
attitudes die hard and many thought otherwise. Or said they did.

Sitiveni Rabuka had wanted a Friday for his first coup. He couldn't
have it because the Fiji Parliament was not scheduled to meet that
day in the week he wanted. So he did the next best thing and chose
the day before. A Thursday military takeover meant that the security
forces had to contend with only one extra full day of business and
public activity in the towns before government offices and banks
closed for the weekend. For his second definitive intervention it was
'Friday again'.

The Fiji clock is eleven hours ahead of British Summer Time. I heard the news first on BBC Radio 3 at 8 a.m. and on the World Service at 9 a.m. Unlike Coup 1, I was not in Fiji either during or immediately after Coup 2. There were some advantages in the age of the instant international telephone and the fax. With the local press shut down and Radio Fiji using only what it was permitted by the military regime, the people of Fiji were again largely ignorant of and confused by what was happening. Rumour and counter-rumour abounded. Furthermore, as the action shifted first to London and then to Vancouver, Fiji achieved sustained press, radio and TV coverage and comment in Britain. The goings on in a small far-off Commonwealth country were under daily scrutiny in news analysis and comment.

The causes were not far to seek. Not only had that most loyal and monarchically-minded ex-colony gone off the constitutional rails: there was the involvement of the Palace and the implications for the Head of State, Her Majesty the Queen. It was all very well for the erudite to point out in *The Times* that the British Crown was not the same crown as the Fiji Crown; or any other for that matter. The fact was that the same crowned head was wearing it; and she was first and foremost our Queen – of Britain. Why continue this anachronism, it was argued, of the sovereign lady being head of state of other curious pagan places – like Papua New Guinea, the Solomon Islands and Tuvalu. Let alone Australia. It should be stopped, they said: there is a conflict of interest, real or imaginary. Our Queen should not be sucked into the race-stalking of army adventurers in cloud coup-coup land.

So parochialism paraded in the popular press; and Britain heard much about a forthcoming meeting of Commonwealth Heads of Government at which the affairs of a distant group of South Pacific islands would come under examination.

There was in fact good reason. Questions of serious import for the Commonwealth were at stake – and for its principles. Such matters do not, however, often find themselves in the forefront of TV news bulletins and national newspapers. It was the coincidence of happenings in Fiji with the Commonwealth meeting in Vancouver that made for good copy, plus the everlasting newsworthiness of the Queen's role in a modern and changing world.

My daily diary summary of events as they unfolded, not always in consistent or logical sequence, together with key public reactions in the days after Coup 2, was a distillation of various source reports of the developing tragicomedy.

Friday 25 September

The army has carried out another coup in Fiji, the second since May.
The man who led the earlier coup, Colonel Sitiveni Rabuka, said that
he had taken power again because the newly announced caretaker
government was not prepared to alter the Constitution to enshrine
the interests of the indigenous Fijian people. Recent developments
had made it clear that the objectives of his May coup had not
been achieved. The army had again assumed full control of the
government of Fiji to ensure that indigenous Fijians govern Fiji, not
the majority Indians. He would not be deflected from his aim of
giving control to indigenous Fijians. Rabuka's statement replaced
one due to have been made by the Governor General, Ratu Sir
Penaia Ganilau, who was to have made an appeal for co-operation
with the new caretaker government . . .

     . . . The Governor General remains at Government House.
Soldiers remove Dr Bavadra from his house at Laucala Bay in Suva
and fire shots into the ceiling. He is taken to the Central Police
Station. Some twenty others are moved to Naboro maximum security
prison or placed under house arrest. They include two judges, former
ministers of the Coalition Government, trade unionists, the Deputy
Speaker of the House of Representatives, police officers, lawyers,
a university lecturer, newsmen, the Governor General's secretary
and Dr Bavadra's spokesman. A curfew is imposed between 8 p.m.
and 5 a.m. Rabuka bars Sunday cinema and sport so that Fiji can
return to being 'a godly country'. This means effectively banning
Indian sport, trading and recreation. In fact all secular activity.
Church attendance is permitted i.e. mainly for Fijians, but public
transport is prohibited. Radio and press are under military control.
The Governor General is instructed not to comment on the coup or
the political situation. The Government of New Zealand releases
the text of the Governor General's undelivered radio broadcast
about the agreed caretaker government.

Saturday 26 September

Ramphal: 'I have been in touch, of course, with countries in the
region to see if there is anything we can do. The Commonwealth
stands four square against military intervention of this kind which
cannot be justified in any shape or form. This was not military
intervention in response to an ailing political process or a failing
process, it was military intervention that interrupted a successful
political process, a return to parliamentary government . . . It was
compounded of elements that leave grave disquiet: elements of

terrorism, elements of racism, elements of authoritarianism – a veritable witches' brew.

'I know that there will be a very substantial reaction in the Commonwealth to these events . . . The Commonwealth is bound to set its face against this kind of development . . . It is an act of injury and insult to indigenous peoples everywhere. I think it will come to be seen as such and, therefore, to evoke from the Commonwealth a very broadly based expression of regret and of determination to see it defeated. What form that might take is, of course, much too early to say. But the Commonwealth must not, I think, compromise its anxieties, its concerns, its deep offence in terms of the development that has taken place . . .'

Sunday 27 September

Rabuka is determined to push on with his original plans for perpetual political control by indigenous Fijians. He expects to make a formal announcement of a republic on 10 October (the anniversary of the Deed of Cession in 1874 and independence in 1970). He hopes that Fiji can remain a member of the Commonwealth.

Sir Geoffrey Howe, British Foreign Secretary: 'The Fiji coup is deplorable.' The Taukei movement tells the British Foreign Secretary to mind his own business.

Ramphal: 'If Rabuka declares a republic, Fiji will have to apply again for membership of the Commonwealth and this will be refused . . . This would be a serious reverse for all that the Commonwealth stands for, not least an affront to the Queen as Fiji's Head of State and of Her Majesty as the Head of the Commonwealth of forty-nine states.'

Quite so, I reflect, as I hear this; but it is not quite how it will be seen in all quarters in Fiji itself. For, while this indeed is a matter of deep concern and potentially great damage to the Commonwealth concept and what it represents, it is of no immediate significance whatsoever to those who have done violence to the due processes of an elected government and have made the decision to take Fiji to republican status by means of a military coup. Their racial megalomania and economic myopia will now place Fiji among the leper nations.

Monday 28 September

Rabuka again states his intention to declare a republic and to ask the Governor General to be the first President. If Ratu Penaia refuses, he will sack him as Governor General. 'This is the only way to secure the military control of the government. I'm very sorry about the Queen,' he says, 'but if it is a question of loyalty to the Queen or to my people, then my people come first.'

Rabuka later announces that the 1970 Constitution has been abrogated and a new one is being prepared by his legal advisers. He plans to set up a military council and to announce its membership in twenty-four hours. Radio Fiji describes Colonel Rabuka as the head of government and says that he will declare himself as Head of State.

The Queen sends a strong message condemning the coup, emphasising that she continues to regard the Governor General as the sole source of legitimate authority in Fiji, and in effect saying that she remains Head of State. Such a powerful and unprecedented intervention was exactly what was wanted after Coup 1. Too late now – sadly.

Supreme Court Judges: 'We shall discharge our duties only so long as the Governor General continues to exercise his lawful authority.'

Governor General: 'I am still the Queen's representative. The only way I will leave Government House is in irons or dead.'

Ratu David Toganivalu: 'If the Governor General is removed from Government House by force, this country will go up in flames.'

Sir Geoffrey Howe: 'The British Government still regards the Governor General as the sole legitimate source of authority. He has our full support. British aid of some four million pounds is under review.'

Australia cancels aid to Fiji.

The New Zealand Foreign Minister warns that New Zealand may cease all economic aid, withdraw all forms of military co-operation with Fiji and cancel preferential sugar purchasing agreements.

Rabuka: 'New laws and rules will be promulgated to come into effect immediately. If becoming a republic means that Fiji has to leave the Commonwealth, so be it. The Commonwealth is not worth belonging to.'

Ramphal: 'This is a coup against the Queen. It is a coup against the Governor General as the Queen's representative and the legitimate authority of government in Fiji . . . It is a quite dreadful situation and means that Fiji is effectively discharging itself from the Commonwealth. If the republican path is the path that Rabuka has chosen by military means, he has done so because it is the only path left open to him.'

Tuesday 29 September

Rabuka: 'I recognise that my actions constitute a treasonable of-fence.'

Wednesday 30 September

The Commonwealth Secretariat issues a statement on Fiji in response to questions about Fiji's Commonwealth membership:

> The established convention is that if a member country wishes to become a republic and to continue thereafter to be a member of the Commonwealth, it will formally communicate its intentions to the Secretary General to enable him to initiate the necessary consultations with all member governments. The Common-wealth's unanimous concurrence is required for continued mem-bership; such concurrence is neither automatic nor can it be assumed.
>
> While Commonwealth governments continue to regard the Governor General as the only legitimate executive authority in Fiji, there is no change in the status of Fiji and the question of Fiji's membership has not yet arisen.

The deposed Prime Minister Timoci Bavadra is released from solitary confinement at Naboro maximum security prison. He is taken by car to Government House. The Governor General presides over an historic first meeting with Bavadra, Mara and Rabuka. The coup leader appears thereafter to hesitate about declaring Fiji a republic. His plan may have to wait. The journalists conjecture as to why. They are not alone. Has the coup leader been persuaded to negotiate as a result of external condemnation of his actions and pressure in the light of the Governor General's new initiative? Or is his change of tone just to tantalise? Having declared a *de facto* republic, why should he now say it may not be necessary? Is there a first real hint of a basic intra-Fijian struggle for power? A BBC correspondent thinks 'this sudden indecision is astonishing from someone in the driving seat. The influence of the Queen would certainly be one of the main reasons; but pressure from within Fiji is specially important because of the complicated series of relationships which revolve around the tribal nature of Fijian society. By one of those quirks of history, Rabuka is a serving warrior to the Governor General as his paramount chief. Therefore the idea of sacking the Governor General may have recoiled on him.'

No one fails to notice that the influences at work from outside Fiji, as evidenced in statements from Britain, Australia and New

Zealand, are of a more positive kind than those after Coup 1. Reason: the general elections in all three countries have long since passed. The electorally insecure have been electorally resecured. Not so the Governor General. He remains resolute in his irresolution.

Thursday 1 October

Rabuka again announces that the 1970 Constitution has been revoked and declares himself to be Head of State. 'The office of Governor General no longer exists.' He is not satisfied that his meetings with political leaders will result in satisfying the aims of the coup. He will offer the Presidency to Ratu Mara. The *Fiji Times* and the *Fiji Sun* will remain closed. The curfew will continue . . .

The Taukei movement has again succeeded in stiffening Rabuka's resolve. He is not to waver any more – for the present.

Friday 2 October

Bavadra: 'Rabuka has destroyed the Fijian people and seems bent on destroying Fiji as well.'

Supreme Court Judges meet at the residence of the Chief Justice. They decline to recognise the validity of the military decrees abrogating the 1970 Constitution and declaring Rabuka to be Head of State. They reaffirm their support for the Governor General.

Rabuka: 'The judges are all dismissed. I plan to appoint new ones.'

It is announced that the Governor General is to convene a further meeting with Bavadra, Mara and Rabuka on 5 October. This causes anger and resentment among Taukei extremists who step up threats of intimidation and worse if it takes place.

As reserves and revenues plunge, the Reserve Bank comes close to immobilisation. A third devaluation is expected.

Ratu Mara: 'The pockets and stomachs of Fijians will be empty by Christmas.'

Saturday 3 October

Bavadra says that he is not willing to attend the proposed meeting unless his safety is guaranteed and only if the meeting is held out of Suva.

Sunday 4 October

Rabuka again bans all sport, picnics, gardening, taxis, public transport and entertainment, i.e. all Indian recreation and movement.

Bavadra and his son suffer a twenty-mile car chase by police and armed soldiers in balaclavas. They find sanctuary back inside Veiseisei where the soldiers draw back and set up an encampment outside. The village is under military siege. He refuses to attend the Monday meeting unless it is held in Western Vitilevu because he fears for his life.

The Bishop in Polynesia, in a sermon at the Holy Trinity Cathedral in Suva: 'The demon of fear is loose in the country.'

Monday 5 October

The Governor General, the deposed Prime Minister and former Prime Minister and the coup leader meet at the Governor General's western retreat – a chiefly bure in Lautoka, a sugar export centre of western Vitilevu and Fiji's second city. It is ten kilometres from Veiseisei. Point to Bavadra.

The meeting lasts fifty minutes. Rabuka lays on the table his minimum non-negotiable demands for not proceeding with the declaration of a republic:

The Governor General to be nominated by the Great Council of Chiefs and appointed by the Queen (thus always a chiefly Fijian).
The Prime Minister always to be a Fijian.
Fijian permanent parliamentary majority and thus political control.

Ratu Mara: 'These demands are acceptable to me,' it is reported.

Bavadra: 'I am saddened and shocked and not even prepared to discuss them.'

The Governor General: 'I cannot allow this situation to deteriorate still further to cause widespread suffering and hardship and will be announcing my next moves within twenty-four hours.'

Analysis: There is nothing new in Rabuka's request or objectives. Bavadra is being made to look the sole obstacle and the impasse to be entirely due to his intransigence. There is no reported mention of Mara's departure from their agreed power-sharing formula pre-Coup 2.

Prospect: The Governor General will announce acceptance of Rabuka's demands thus isolating Dr Bavadra and leaving him to ponder with his Fijian and Indian colleagues whether he condones a civil disobedience campaign including the burning of sugarcane and pine forest. The Governor General's next step will be to seek to persuade the Palace to endorse the changes sought and then to introduce them by executive authority. Tall order. How will he attempt this?

Ramphal: 'There is a time when an internal matter becomes an external one. And then the world – or in this case initially the Commonwealth – has to take notice.'

Wednesday 7 October

Rabuka formally declares Fiji to be a Republic and appoints himself Minister for Home Affairs. The announcement is made at midnight on Radio Fiji and is a news flash in Britain at 1 p.m. The full text of the declaration is issued in a Gazette Extraordinary (opposite). Maybe no one notices that the old Fiji Coat of Arms still appears at the masthead of the Gazette with its motto, Fear God and Honour the (now deposed) Queen.

A press conference is held later that day by the new self-appointed Head of State:

Rabuka: 'Fijians have a great reverence and love for Her Majesty the Queen, but the decision to proclaim a republic is the only pragmatic way out of the country's crisis . . . The Governor General can stay at Government House as long as he likes. I no longer recognise his authority. In time the world will find that the authority claimed by him cannot be effective.' The coup leader announces a crackdown on trade unions; a Council of Ministers and new judges are to be named shortly. He will be Head of State until elections are held. Fiji will not be represented at the Commonwealth Heads of Government meeting in Vancouver next week.

Prime Minister Hawke re-states Australia's opposition to the Rabuka regime.

Prime Minister Lange of New Zealand does not accept the legality of Rabuka's action.

Thursday 8 October

Ratu Mara leaves Fiji for London via Melbourne and Singapore, as emissary of the Governor General. Reported dual objective: to persuade the Queen to endorse constitutional changes giving Fijians permanent control of the legislature and agreeing that this be done by executive act in Fiji without parliamentary sanction. If agreed, this would mean the preservation of the link with the Crown, the abandonment of the republic and the possible retention of

EXTRAORDINARY

27

FIJI GAZETTE

PUBLISHED BY AUTHORITY OF THE GOVERNMENT OF FIJI

Vol. 1   WEDNESDAY, 7th OCTOBER 1987   No. 5

[23]

DECLARATION—REPUBLIC OF FIJI
DECREE 1987 NO. 8

INTERIM MILITARY GOVERNMENT OF FIJI DECREE NO. 8

In exercise of the powers vested in me as Commander and Head of the Interim Military Government of Fiji I hereby make the following Decree:

1. This Decree may be cited as the Declaration—Republic of Fiji Decree 1987 No. 8.

Whereas the People of Fiji have expressed their desire to have a new Constitution for the advancement of their beliefs, rights and freedoms, and trusting in Almighty God and His blessing upon this Decree I hereby proclaim that as from this day forth Fiji is declared a Republic and that the People of Fiji shall embrace the Constitution that:

    (a) requires that a new Constitution replace the Constitution under which they attained independence on 10th October 1970;

    (b) they freely accept that it is desirous that the Constitution be replaced so that the will of the people may be truly set forth and their hopes, aspirations and goals be achieved and thereby enshrined;

    (c) re-affirm that the indigenous Fijian race is endowed with their lands and the right to govern themselves for their advancement and welfare;

    (d) re-affirm that the Nation is founded upon principles that acknowledge the Deity and the teachings of the Lord Jesus Christ, the importance and place of the family in a free society with free institutions and unalterable and inalienable belief and faith in the fundamental rights and freedoms with which all brethren in the fellowship of men are possessed;

    (e) re-confirm that Fiji is a democratic society in which all peoples may, to the full extent of their capacity play some part in the institutions of the national life and thereby develop and maintain due deference and respect each other and the rule of law;

    (f) re-assert their recognition that the indigenous people of Fiji in respecting the rights of their brethren to live in harmony are entitled to due deference to their customs and traditional way of life.

    (g) reiterate their recognition that people and institutions remain free only when and for so long as freedom is founded upon respect for the spiritual and moral values of each other and a mutual observance of the rule of law.

Dated 7th October 1987.

COLONEL SITIVENI LIGAMAMADA RABUKA, o.b.e. (Mil.)
Commander and Head of the Interim Military Government of Fiji

Price : 15c   I. B. RAVUTU, Government Printer, Suva, Fiji—1987   5/FG/87—1,400

Commonwealth membership. Such proposals are believed to be acceptable to Colonel Rabuka.

It seems a long shot and one which overlooks the Queen's toughness of character and principle which many prime ministers have discovered. Even if the Queen were to be advised and she were to be persuaded – both highly improbable – that she could properly give her consent to executive constitutional change in Fiji without rupture to her position as Head of State, it is inconceivable that the Queen could allow herself to be manoeuvred into a position of appearing to support or permit the virtual disenfranchisement of 50 per cent of her subjects in Fiji by whatever means. Her Majesty and her immediate advisers will regard any attempt to entrench permanent constitutional dominance of one race by another in a country of which the Queen is Head of State as abhorrent to all the Queen has stood for since Her Majesty's coronation and her dedication to the cause of the Commonwealth. Leaving aside events in Sierra Leone in 1967, there is no previous military coup against the Queen. Thus, there is no real precedent for the sovereign's response to the usurpation of the Queen's position as Head of State in a country of the modern Commonwealth. Her decision will create one; and not be one which she will wish to have been compelled to make. A country which had voluntarily entered into a solemn act of cession to the Crown had now severed that link by an act of military violence against the Crown.

Friday 9 October

Ratu Mara arrives at London Heathrow accompanied by his wife, Adi Lala. VIP facilities are extended to him. He is met by the High Commissioner for Fiji in London and leaves in the High Commissioner's official car. He looks grim. There is no dialogue with reporters. He goes to Buckingham Palace in the late morning and meets with Sir William Heseltine for about three quarters of an hour. The Queen's Privy Councillor is not received in audience by Her Majesty. Has the gamble failed?

Both BBC and ITN TV say that the object of the visit is to seek the Queen's support for constitutional change giving Fijians permanent numerical superiority in Parliament, thus avoiding a republic and the severance of Commonwealth membership. There is no statement after the meeting but the general assumption is a royal thumbs down. The High Commissioner says that Ratu Mara will not now be going to Vancouver. The Queen, the Duke of Edinburgh and the Private Secretary leave the Palace shortly after the Mara visit to begin their journey to Canada.

I decline on this occasion to participate in a British Channel 4 News analysis of 'Mara the Man'. It is never certain how an interview of reasonable duration and scope will appear when cut, subedited and its residual seconds placed into a scripted production competing with a variety of world and domestic crises for programme space. The item begins with a dramatic clip of Sakeasi Butadroka, founder of the extremist Fijian Nationalist Party, shouting in a Suva street: 'That bastard Mara.' The rest of the Fiji content indicates where editorial sympathies lie.

A long list of Fiji citizens not permitted to leave the country is compiled. The Trades Union Congress and Civil Service Union offices are closed down and occupied by soldiers. The *Fiji Times* says it will only start publishing again when it can do so without hindrance, harassment and censorship.

Indian senior civil servants are being told to resign (one is the Fiji High Commissioner in New Zealand) so that their posts can be filled by indigenous Fijians.

The Fiji dollar is devalued by 15.25 per cent, that is by 33 per cent since Coup 1 in May.

Rabuka announces his Council of Ministers. There are three army officers; the other nineteen are either Taukei movement activists or former Alliance ministers. One Indian named is Irene Narayan, long-term Federation Party critic of the Alliance Government who defected to join her political adversaries and was soundly beaten for her pains at the April election. She does not attend the swearing-in ceremony and tells Colonel Rabuka that she will not serve on the Council since she was not consulted beforehand. Reports said that she was later to have second thoughts.

The BBC World Service carries the item. One bulletin adds: 'Among the remaining ministers, three have served prison terms for criminal offences including violation of public order, riot, illegal strikes and destruction of property.' This is deleted from later bulletins.

Saturday 10 October

The London *Daily Telegraph* headlines its news item on the Mara visit to the Palace in words that seem familiar:

ROYAL SNUB FOR FIJI EX-PREMIER

India, preparing itself for Vancouver, announces suspension of all trade and technical co-operation with Fiji in protest at the military takeover. A statement from the Foreign Ministry says India is dismayed at attempts to deprive Fiji citizens of Indian descent – about half the population – of their legitimate rights.

Rabuka: 'We can do without India which should stop trying to interfere in our affairs.'

21

12–17 October 1987

Commonwealth Heads of Government have met biennially in exotic showplace arenas over the last two decades – Singapore, Ottawa, Kingston, London, Lusaka, Melbourne, New Delhi, Nassau – and in 1987, amid the British Columbian drizzle-free delights of Vancouver. As the number of countries of the Commonwealth has grown – forty-seven full members that year, plus two special members, Nauru and Tuvalu, who do not attend the Heads of Government meetings – so the difficulties have increased of maintaining the intimacy and informality of the early formative years. Then, as now, the greater value of the occasion is not always in the formal proceedings as in the exchange of experiences, problems, solutions; and in seeking and often discovering common ground among politically elevated colleagues from Africa, the Mediterranean, the Caribbean, Asia, the South Pacific, Britain, Canada and Australasia. If Lee Kuan Yew was wont to complain in the past that the Commonwealth devoted too much time to the problems of the African continent or the Caribbean, then here was his opportunity, which he took in Vancouver, to capture the minds and awareness of his colleagues in respect of the defence, economic and racial hazards facing South-East Asia in the contemporary world. And there is the 'retreat' for forty-eight hours or so which takes place in presidential and prime ministerial purdah away from officials, newsmen and prying lobbyists. The lubricant is language: English can be used exclusively throughout, with all its national and regional permutations and variety.

A convention of Commonwealth meetings is that decisions are reached by a consensus of those present. There is no voting. If there is no recognisable consensus to agree, there may reluctantly be a consensus to disagree; but even then, at ministerial meetings, the Secretariat and the drafting committees work away at a communiqué which has sufficient bite but can still mean something to everybody and has sufficient verbal skill to get past the scrutinising nationalism of each leader and his team of hovering advisers. It is understandably every delegation's objective to go home to capitals claiming success.

So how would the question of Fiji be dealt with in Vancouver and what would be the outcome? Would Ratu Mara have succeeded in holding together the Fiji link with the Crown? Not very likely. Or in holding off the expulsion of Fiji from the Commonwealth? Likely. Inertia usually wins. Own-goals abound. In international assemblies, there are always compelling reasons for not doing something. And Ratu Mara had been attending reunions with the boys every two years since 1971. Not nice to be nasty to an old friend, temporarily in the political wilderness. Better to wait and see. Low key. Play it down. Easier all round, especially back home where you never know what is going to happen in your own volatile political and economic world. The edentate lion won't mind if the goalposts of principle are shifted. Anyway, one country's principle is another's obstinacy. And when you get down to it, who ultimately cares about anything other than what's in one's own backyard or just over the fence? A really good hurricane would fix the whole thing in Fiji. What time's the coffee break, George? . . .

. . . If no man is an island, neither is a country. Figuratively, that is. Even a state of leprosy is curable. In the end. Sooner or later if the reasons are compelling enough, those governments closest to the problem will come to terms and deal with almost any regime, however disagreeable. Expediency will prevail. Given time. The reasons are what make many politicians more interesting as people than civil servants. But not necessarily more likeable or trustworthy, as they properly pontificate about South African white apartheid while at the same time may shy off from denouncing black racialism in Fiji. What did leaders of the African front-line states really think of the racial obfuscation of some of their South Pacific colleagues at Vancouver? It's none of their business, the Tongans would say.

There was a flurry of pre-conference activity as Her Majesty the Queen arrived with the Duke of Edinburgh in Vancouver on Friday 9 October 1987 to spend the weekend on Vancouver Island. The course of decision would have already been charted: a private dinner with the Prime Minister of Canada, the Chairman of the Common-wealth meeting, was an opportunity to take soundings and discuss

timing and presentation. And she would do so with the Commonwealth Secretary General also.

One by one the Heads of Government arrived, giving their own
press briefings and mini-conferences, leaking, hinting, teasing, setting the scene for respective positions on what were becoming the
two main topics for debate: the perennial question of apartheid and
sanctions against South Africa; and Fiji. Not far behind was the
troubled issue of Tamil-Sinhalese violence in Sri Lanka and the
fragile peace-keeping responsibilities of the Indian Army. Rajiv
Gandhi was not going to have an easy time of it. If Toronto has the
largest urban population of Italians outside Italy and Melbourne of
Greeks outside Greece, Vancouver is a haven for Fiji Indians. They,
together with the numbers of anti-Rajiv Sikhs of India, were for
quite different reasons determined to ensure that Commonwealth
Heads of Government would not be allowed to forget the problems
of race and the military destruction of the democratic process in Fiji.
And whether or not race was central to the Taukei-military-inspired
problems of Fiji, then it would be convenient, in Vancouver at least,
to let it be thought so. There was guidance about such things, agreed
in Singapore in 1971 as the Declaration of Commonwealth Principles:

We believe in the liberty of the individual, in equal rights for all
citizens regardless of race, colour, creed or political belief, and in
their inalienable right to participate by means of free and democratic political processes in framing the society in which they live.
We therefore strive to promote in each of our countries those
representative institutions and guarantees for personal freedom
under the law that are our common heritage.

We recognise racial prejudice as a dangerous sickness threatening the healthy development of the human race and racial discrimination as an unmitigated evil of society. Each of us will vigorously
combat this evil within our own nation. No country will afford to
regimes which practise racial discrimination assistance which in its
own judgment directly contributes to the pursuit or consolidation
of this evil policy.

The 1971 Singapore Declaration was reaffirmed and reinforced by
the 1979 Lusaka Declaration against Racism and Racial Discrimination.

Rather bravely and with the degree of impudence that first
spawned and then perpetuated the Edinburgh Festival Fringe, a
Parallel Commonwealth Conference was mounted. Shridath
Ramphal appeared and said that the question of sanctions for

South Africa would not go away, whatever the British Government and Mrs Thatcher might think; and Tupeni Baba called, prudently, for Commonwealth condemnation of the Rabuka regime in Fiji and, less prudently, for a Commonwealth peace-keeping force – a notion which he and his Coalition colleagues had put to the South Pacific Forum in June. It got nowhere there and was assured of meeting a similar fate in the wider Commonwealth context now. Lawyer Vijay Singh, erstwhile Mara supporter, one-time Alliance minister, and now Chairman of the Fiji Sugar Growers Council, applied himself to the legal and constitutional issues of the Queen's position and the on-off republic pronouncements of Colonel Rabuka.

But the sands were already shifting. The South Pacific Forum members convened their own preliminary meeting in Vancouver. It had long since been made clear to both Australian and New Zealand prime ministers that the Melanesian and Polynesian island countries of the South Pacific were tired of patronising pronouncements from Canberra and Wellington about their affairs and problems. 'We support the Melanesians in Fiji,' as one Papua New Guinea High Commission official put it, simplistically, in London. He looked wonderingly at me when I asked 'Which Melanesians?' Keep off, it was said in Vancouver, and let Fiji sort out its own problems. Thus the Fiji Ambassador to the United Nations, irked by the crassness of New Zealand criticism from the same platform the previous day, had urged the General Assembly. The Caribbean approach was not likely to be fundamentally dissimilar. It is not so easy to express concern about events in another man's land without seeming to interfere in what is supposedly not your affair. Ratu Mara had made much of this sort of argument.

With not unexpected ambivalence, Prime Minister Lange had fallen in and out of love with aid and trade restrictions for Fiji; the Kingdom of Tonga appeared to lend support to Colonel Rabuka by recognition of the military-led republic, then recanted or denied any such intention next day; the Prime Minister of Australia had slithered back and forth between condemnation of the coup and backing off from a final close-down on aid and trade. Britain à la Geoffrey Howe was 'consulting with our friends most directly concerned and giving urgent priority to a review of our aid and other commitments to Fiji'.

'Fiji is still a member of the Commonwealth,' said the Secretary General, 'and the seat is available at the Vancouver meeting, although not for Colonel Rabuka.' That seemed strange, given the Secretariat statement of 30 September and the formal declaration of a republic by Colonel Rabuka on 7 October.

It was left to the Canadian Prime Minister Brian Mulroney to say something worth saying on the evening before the Conference opened on 13 October:

> Fiji is an important Commonwealth issue. I do not believe that the Commonwealth can stand idly by and take no action when a democratically elected government is deposed by military force and the Queen is replaced as Head of State in order to establish a republic. If you go on to the discriminatory proposals for racial electoral representation, then you have circumstances which are repugnant to everything the Canadian Government stands for and everything which Canadians believe to be right . . .

Mulroney's indignation also stemmed from the fact that the Queen is also – indeed first after Britain – Queen of Canada, and as the Heads of Government meeting was taking place on Canadian soil, he was the Chairman.

At the meeting itself, Prime Minister Rajiv Gandhi made a statement on similar lines. 'Democracy has to be restored in Fiji. Any counsel of inaction is a mockery of all the Commonwealth stands for.' The backroom boys had done their stuff in Delhi. And while India might not be the least objective observer of events in 1987 Fiji, nor a country with an entirely unblemished record of democratic government, it was none the less timely that the Indian Prime Minister should remove any doubt about the positive nature of his Government's approach.

Crown Prince Tupouto'a, the Tongan Minister for Foreign Affairs, attended the Vancouver meeting in place of his ailing uncle, Prime Minister Prince Tu'ipelehake. He had travelled from Nuku'alofa via Suva where he had met and talked with the Governor General, Ratu Mara, Colonel Rabuka and others including members of the Tongan community there.

He listened while the reactions and arguments about Fiji went back and forth; and as the national interpretations of events demonstrated the largely subjective judgments of others from their own experiences and problems far distant from the South Pacific.

The question was finally put to him. What did His Royal Highness think? He stirred himself to reply with the teasing aristocratic elegance that is his style.

'I may perhaps know more about the real situation in Fiji than anyone else here,' he finally offered to the assembled group of Commonwealth Heads of Government, 'but I'm not disposed to tell you. Tonga and Fiji have lived oceanically side by side for centuries and will no doubt continue to do so in the future. The modern-day question of recognition or non-recognition does not arise.' Tupou-to'a sat back and permitted himself the indulgence of a slight smile. Tongan foreign policy remained happily intact. His journey to Vancouver had been justified.

The most entertaining writer in the last hundred years on the Kingdom of Tonga is Basil Thomson. His *Diversions of a Prime Minister* published in 1894 remains a mine of insight, enlightenment and elegant style. 'The conceited man,' Thomson wrote, 'is he who thinks well of himself and thinks that others do so too; the vain man is he who thinks well of himself and wishes that others thought so too; but the proud man is he who thinks well of himself and does not care a jot whether others think well of him or not.' Upon this exegesis, the Tongan is a proud man.

On 15 October an important announcement was circulated to the assembled Heads of Government. 'The Queen,' the statement said, 'has received the following message from the Governor General of Fiji:

> ". . . Owing to the uncertainty of the political and constitutional situation in Fiji, I have now made up my mind, [wrote Ratu Penaia] to request Your Majesty to relieve me of my appointment as Governor General with immediate effect. This I do with the utmost regret but my endeavours to preserve constitutional government in Fiji have proved in vain and I can see no alternative way forward . . ."
>
> In the light of the Governor General's decision that he can no longer effectively exercise executive authority in Fiji, the Queen has accepted with regret the resignation which Ratu Sir Penaia has tendered. Her Majesty has expressed to him her gratitude for his loyal services and her admiration for his courageous efforts to avert changes to the form of government in Fiji by force.
>
> The Queen accepts that it must be for the people of Fiji to decide their own future and prays that peace may obtain among the people of all races in that country. Her Majesty is sad to think that the ending of Fijian allegiance to the Crown should have been brought about without the people of Fiji being given an opportunity to express their opinion on the proposal.'

Speaking that evening at a banquet for the assembled Presidents and Prime Ministers, the Queen, Head of the Commonwealth, again affirmed that she was greatly saddened by the ending of Fiji's allegiance to the Crown. She 'prayed for the future peace and happiness of all the people of Fiji, whatever their racial origins'. The direct and very special link between the chiefs of Fiji and the Crown, forged on that October day in Levuka in 1874, thus came to an end on another October day in Suva and Vancouver in 1987.

High sentiment and words apart though, could the Commonwealth, personified by its collective Heads of Government meeting together, 'stand idly by and take no action . . .?' The answer was given. It could. And did. Thus proving itself to be 'a mockery of all it stands for'. Or so it can, not unreasonably, be argued.

The Vancouver Communiqué contained the following:

STATEMENT ON FIJI

Commonwealth leaders acknowledge that, on the basis of established Commonwealth conventions, Fiji's membership of the Commonwealth lapsed with the emergence of the Republic on 15 October. They viewed with sadness the developments in Fiji and hoped for a resolution of the problem by the people of Fiji on a basis consistent with the principles that have guided the Commonwealth. They agreed that the Commonwealth would, if requested, be ready to offer its good offices towards such a resolution and, on such basis, if the circumstances warrant, to consider the question of Fiji's membership of the Commonwealth if asked to do so.

Vancouver
16 October 1987

It was a weak and sorry compromise. A credit to none. Not least the national leaders and the Commonwealth Secretary General who had spoken with such passionate conviction and awareness of human injustice in the days before. There was no condemnation of the destruction of both the democratic process and an elected government, of the abrogation of the constitution, of the dismissal of judges, of the violations of human rights, of the deposing as Head of State of the Queen whom all accepted as Head of the very body in whose name they were assembled; no word of abhorrence for violence, imprisonment without charge or trial, and widespread intimidation; no restatement of those hard-won Commonwealth principles about the liberty of the individual and of equal inalienable rights regardless of race, colour, creed or political belief.

'The Commonwealth did not do very well about Fiji at Vancouver.' So, in a cold London November, said an experienced and devoted Commonwealth journalist.

He was being kind. It had been a sustained failure of responsive action since the beginning. A failure of the Commonwealth Secretariat in June to perceive and to respond to need and to Dr Bavadra's request for the only initial intervention with a chance of holding steady the floodgates. A failure of the Palace to galvanise the Secretariat and to act imaginatively beyond protocol and precedent: tea and sympathy with the Private Secretary was insufficient to repair the grievous wound to the democratic body politic in Fiji. A failure by the Commonwealth Secretariat to respond again in July when the alarm bells were ringing loud and clear. A failure of governments to do other than give token support to the tattered remnants of legal authority in the person of a wavering and insecure Queen's representative. A failure of democratic dialogue in Fiji itself. A failure there too of moral leadership, of integrity and of public honesty, Dr Bavadra excepted. A failure in Vancouver of an assembly of those of whom there is much good to be said, but little to praise on this occasion: because they fudged the issue and did not dispense, at the very least, a sharp and unequivocal warning to Fiji that unless a racially balanced Constitution emerged, the republic could have no hope of readmission to Commonwealth membership – should it ever wish to seek it.

So the coup leaders and their associates duly achieved their republic; the Queen ceased to be the Head of State; the membership of Fiji having thus lapsed, no decision to expel was necessary; Colonel Rabuka became interim Head of State and was promoted Brigadier – because of his increased responsibilities, said a Public Service Commission announcement.

Everyone lost. Except, in the short term, the coup leaders and the Taukei extremists. Until the economy runs dry, corruption reigns unchecked and external exploiters of instability have wreaked their havoc in Fiji and thus in the region. The Commonwealth suffered a reverse of credibility and world influence. It lost a member. The fault, at least in part, is that of the Commonwealth itself, when put to the test: Fiji, a fatal flaw in the fine phrases about Commonwealth principles, influence and action.

There were, of course, defenders of this wishy-washy outcome. The British Prime Minister expressed her regret at the severing of Fiji's links with the Commonwealth. 'But you don't desert your friends in their hour of need, you know. We shall see what happens.'

A Commonwealth senior official recalled John Diefenbaker's observation as Canada's Foreign Minister when South Africa left the Commonwealth in 1961: 'A light has been left in the window for [an internationally acceptable] South Africa.' An advance on Duracell, that optimistic light has been burning hopefully for twenty-eight years. Prime Minister Bob Hawke of Australia, recognising shilly-shallying when he saw it, took a different approach: 'Fiji should spend some time in exile.'

Thomas Hobbes, author of *Leviathan*, sought to understand the nature of state power by looking at what would happen if a state fell into collapse. 'Life,' he wrote, would then be 'solitary, poor, nasty, brutish and short.'

On 17 November Ratu Inoke Kubuabola, former Bible Society secretary, Taukei movement leader and now the military republic's Minister of Information, said in New Zealand that the former Governor General, Ratu Sir Penaia Ganilau, had agreed to accept appointment as the first President of the Republic of Fiji. The month-old pre-condition for consideration of such acceptance – a constitution fair to all races in Fiji – was accorded no mention.

The announcement was premature and apparently made without Ratu Penaia's consent. It was none the less the shape of things to come. There were many who thought back to the former Governor General's Radio Fiji broadcast in June, of his detailed plans for the return of Fiji to democracy and representative government. That broadcast had ended:

> I trust in the people of Fiji to see that what I am putting before them is based on what I have judged to be the best path for all of our citizens.
>
> It is a path which will safeguard the security of life, it is a path which will lead to a steady growth in the value of property and business in Fiji, and it is a path which will be within the Laws of Fiji.
>
> Put your trust in the plans I am laying before the nation and I give you my word that your trust will not be misplaced.

22

I've got the world in a jug and the stopper in my hand
– Old blues lyric

October–November 1987

All was not sweetness and light in the new Jerusalem. Within days
of Coup 2, a series of measures was promulgated by the 'Fiji Military
Government' which demonstrated with chilling clarity that the gun
was now the sole law of the land. With the blessing of an ecumenical
Almighty it seemed. For God not only has a lot to answer for. He
has quite a lot to answer to. It cannot be straightforward even for
an all-knowing, all-powerful, all-loving and all-forgiving deity to
proffer oracular support equally to a messianic Methodist military
man, a Roman Catholic patrician politician and a spiritually socialist
physician cum short-term prime minister.

The military decrees dramatically and fundamentally changed
daily life in Fiji and opened the freeway to enhanced harassment,
intimidation, torture and coercion. In Suva, military road blocks of
barbed-wire coils and the regular checking of cars and car registration
numbers soon became a familiar sight. These restrictions, while
intimidatory, did not constitute brutality. What happened to people
in the largely Indian sugar towns of Labasa in Vanualevu and Ba in
western Vitilevu did. Reports smuggled out of the country were used
extensively in Australia, Britain and New Zealand by press, radio
and television. None were transmitted by Radio Fiji so, once again,
external news sources – notably ABC and the BBC which extended
its transmission time to Fiji – became the only means of learning the
focal facts of Fiji life. Colonel Rabuka's friendly coup had been
succeeded by unfriendly rape. The reports assembled by the Fiji
Independent News Service in Sydney listed accounts of the military
forcing people to:

210

- walk naked in the street, sometimes holding human excrement,
- stand for up to twenty-four hours in an iron water tank,
- swim in sewerage ponds filled with human excrement,
- lie or sit naked for hours at a time on hot tar-sealed roads,
- submit to rape and other forms of sexual assault by soldiers, often in uniform and at army check-points,
- walk barefoot in hot mill mud (mill mud is the by-product of the sugar refining process), and
- walk long distances carrying heavy loads while watched by soldiers.

Men and women were lashed upright to a military truck for periods of up to twenty-four hours. Children were subjected to degrading punishment for violating the Sunday edict banning sport, picnics, gardening and swimming: in Ba, children were beaten with sticks until they could no longer stand and then forced to rub their noses on a concrete floor. Others had to wet their faces with fresh cow dung and lick it: a gross violation of Hindu custom and religious belief. In Labasa, the reported victims included farmers, a doctor, a magistrate, a taxi driver and civil servants.

The psychology of these inhumanities had something in common with the concept of village collective punishment, employed to stem violent rebellion during the so-called Arab troubles of 1936–39 in Palestine; and with similar methods later used in Israel itself and the Lebanon.

'The transition of Fiji,' said one writer in the *Sunday Telegraph* at the beginning of November, 'from a model Commonwealth democracy to a military dictatorship has been brought about with a series of decrees whose verbose, pompous style would be amusing if it was not so threatening.' The most draconian of all is the grandly, but misleadingly, entitled 'Fundamental Freedoms Decree 1987 (Decree 12)' which gives the security forces a licence to kill in the line of duty: a member of the armed forces would effectively be immune from prosecution if he killed while making an arrest or preventing escape, suppressing a riot or insurrection, or defending a person or property from violence. There are provisions concerning the restraint of movement and the suspension of the right of freedom of expression, private correspondence and opinions in respect of political activity. All political, industrial (strike) and dissident activity is outlawed and the Civil Service purged of Indians at senior levels. In religious matters, Christianity is given 'the foremost place' and it is 'the duty of the military government of Fiji to protect and foster Christianity'.

In a taped message to the Evatt Foundation Conference on Human Rights in Sydney in mid November, Dr Bavadra said:

> . . . As was to be expected, the coup has polarised Fiji racially. The strength of Fiji's political and economic anatomy lay in multi-racialism. Today, the Indian people are cowed and afraid. Many look on Fijians as army supporters or informers. For them, silence is their only protection, or flight to another country. For the Fijian people, no other event in seventeen years of independence has raised their political consciousness so sharply. In six short months, they have been exposed to the best and worst of democracy – its capacity to change those who govern them for new leaders and its very fragility in the face of organised lawlessness. The fact is that the coup makers, in attempting to unite the Fijians against a common enemy, have left them more divided than ever. The division is political: Coalition against Alliance. It is regional: east against west. It is social: chiefs against commoners . . .

Tropical sunsets blaze and die, remembered by few, mourned by none. The human spirit is less quenchable. It can rise to heights of courage and endurance; fall to depths of degradation and brutality. Then there are the global millions for whom breadline survival is their heroism of the spirit. The only kind they know. Without it they too die. They it is and their children who suffer to survive in the Fiji of today.

There are those who do not doubt that the democratic sun of Fiji will rise again; and that it will come from the west and not from the east.

23

Why some politishun
Not knowin' when to stop?
Seem dat dey are goin'
Downhill to de Top.
–Mighty Whitey, Calypsonian

5 December 1987

The news agencies carried the following item from Fiji:

The former Governor General, Ratu Sir Penaia Ganilau, has been appointed the first President of Fiji, which has become a republic after two military coups.

The announcement was made by the army commander, Brigadier Sitiveni Rabuka.

The new President then announced that he was appointing Ratu Sir Kamisese Mara as Prime Minister.

Sir Kamisese's election defeat sparked off the first coup in May.

So, the Alliance former Prime Minister and Deputy Prime Minister were together again in high office in a Republic of Fiji. The old firm was back in business. By courtesy of the gun. The lessons of the 1959 disturbances had not been forgotten; never mind that one or more of the participants had, in 1987, changed sides. The Governor General was now President; Apisai Tora had conveniently forgotten that he was once Mohammed; and Ratu Mara?

On 25 May Ratu Mara had made an emotional and at times angry speech to the great Council of Chiefs: continuing accusations that he had been behind the military coup on 14 May meant that he would not seek any part in Fiji's future political or public life . . . Well, if you are appointed, that's different.

Three months before, on 18 August, the *Fiji Sun* had recalled Ratu Mara's final pre-election address, broadcast by Radio Fiji on 3 April:

Let there be no doubt in your minds, FIJI is not so much at the turning point as it is AT THE CROSSROADS. If we take the wrong direction, there is no return and no way out. Will we now go the way of so many other countries which, after a promising start in the first decade of independence, stumbled, faltered and eventually came to nought soon after? I recall those torn apart by racial strife and drowning in debt, where basic freedoms are curtailed, universities closed down, the media throttled and dissenters put into jails and camps. Will we too go down that road to rack and ruin? Will we squander the gains of the last sixteen years in the next five? That is the question . . . I urge you in the name of St Paul to think on these things.

Timoci Bavadra heard the news of the coup leader's appointments at home in Veiseisei village. Unlike Kubuabola, he could not depart Fiji for New Zealand or anywhere else for that matter. By military decree, he was prohibited from leaving his country.

The wheel had turned full circle. The eastern chiefs had gained their pyrrhic victory. *Plus ça change* . . . 'A sellout' complained some Taukei leaders in resentment at this regression to high chiefly power. For Dr Bavadra, like other deposed leaders before him, the only game left was the waiting game. He had made the journey from patients to politics. Now there was another: from politics to patience. In the last list of public servants published by the Government of Fiji before independence in 1970, there are the names of 187 medical officers. The 115th entry says simply:

T. U. Bavadra DSM (Fiji) DPH (Otago)
born 22.9.34
salary $F2586
date of appointment: 1.1.60
Seconded to British Solomon Islands Protectorate

Who would have known from that obscure entry how his star was to rise – and fall again – seventeen years later? For the present, the ineluctable gun had indeed prevailed, as Sitiveni Rabuka, with his chiefly and Taukei confederates – or, perhaps, an uneasy chiefly and Taukei alliance, by virtue of the power game of Sitiveni Rabuka – continued their lemming-like descent into human bankruptcy.

People in countries where the democratic process is well entrenched and seemingly secure from risk can be the most apathetic about its virtues. 'The least bad of all systems of government' is about the extent of it. Until the right to choose a government is denied; then it is most coveted. For democracy means asking the people. The essence of democracy is choice. President Cory Aquino knows this – and says so. That is why people want it and why many of their rulers resist it. Successful misappropriation of governmental power and executive authority, whether military or civil, is no measurement of popular consent for its continuing exercise; while the continuance of power without popular consent is an authoritarian denial of *liberté*, *égalité* and a good measure of *fraternité*, wherever in the world it may be exercised and in whatever context.

'I had to do it because if my house is on fire with members of my family inside . . . why should I wait? I must try and rescue them,' Ratu Mara was reported as saying in explanation of his decision to join the Rabuka-led Council of Ministers immediately after Coup 1 in May.

'I would think,' said Mr Justice Govind in a speech to human rights lawyers in Sydney in November, 'that if one's house is on fire, one joins the fire-fighters and not the arsonists.'

In Auckland, at the turn of the year, my New Zealand politics watcher said suddenly:

'I last saw Ratu Mara in 1945. That's forty-three years ago. Easter Monday it was. His head, backside and heels were horizontal; and his arms and legs were spreadeagled – on the floor of the Wellington Town Hall.'

My eyebrows lifted.

'Not, I would have thought,' he went on, 'the accepted thing for a high chiefly son of Fiji.'

Some microfilm research of New Zealand newspapers seemed to be the next step. So, in the reference department of the Auckland Public Library, I tracked down this item in *The New Zealand Herald* of 3 April 1945: 'The finals of the boxing championships at the New Zealand University tournament in Wellington resulted: Heavyweight: A. D. McKenzie (Canterbury) 13 st. 7 lb. beat R. Mara (Otago) 13 st. 12 lb. by a technical knockout in the first round.'

Something like it did not happen again until the surprise electoral defeat of Ratu Mara's Alliance Party in the first campaign of the Labour–National Federation Coalition in April 1987. But soon after that occurrence, a convenient new philosophy emerged: if you can't win by the accepted rules, then change them so that you do.

Even if those rules are ones you have yourself helped to formulate. For, on 30 April 1970, Ratu Mara, Prime Minister designate and leader of the Alliance Party, had reported at a plenary session of the Fiji Constitutional Conference at Marlborough House, London, the agreed conclusions reached at discussions between the Alliance and National Federation delegations:

'The two parties,' Mara said, 'state their belief that the democratic processes of Fiji should be through political parties, each with their own political philosophy and programmes for the economic and social advancement of the people of Fiji, cutting across race, colour and creed; and that all should work to this end . . .'

It was not to be a joyful Christmas in 'Christian' Fiji. On Friday 18 December 1987 Ratu David Toganivalu was dead. The man who, with true chiefly dignity, conceded electoral defeat by Dr Tupeni Baba in April, died, his neck broken, in a car accident. Joint Deputy Prime Minister in the latter years of the Alliance Government, Ratu David had been regarded as the likely heir presumptive of Ratu Mara as leader of the Alliance Party; even more so after his fellow Deputy Prime Minister, Mosese Qionibaravi, was sadly also to die in a Sydney hospital during the year. There is a strong residual element of the mystical and the superstitious in the Fijian psyche; and many would perceive a supernatural hand in these human tragedies. Two men for all seasons were no more; and people of all races in Fiji were the poorer for their loss. For neither had appeared in any of the military-appointed ministerial lists following Coup 1.

Dead too – also killed in a car accident – was the alleged arsonist, former Fijian Senator, Jona Qio.

Sunday morning in early 1988 Suva. The streets are stilled and silent: a Hollywood non-moving set. A solitary stranger strolls across Victoria Parade – soon, he wonders, to be renamed the Avenue of the Republic? He stops on the fringes of Albert Park and gazes at the sporting void.

'What are you doing?' asks a pursuing soldier, fingering his automatic rifle.

'Just breathing,' explains the stranger, his passport and airline return ticket belted to his body.

'What you are doing is forbidden on Sundays by Brigadier Rabuka. If you do not stop, you will be taken into custody for twenty-four hours.'

'Very well. I shall try to stop. But if I have to go on breathing, military custody seems preferable to being clubbed to death, roasted, and you know what.'

'Unless that comes later anyway . . . It may well,' he confides to himself – after the President's decree of 18 January declaring that

Brigadier Rabuka and his Fiji Army are immune from prosecution for the 14 May military coup and the overthrow of the newly elected parliamentary government.

24

29 March 1988

Ratu Mara, Prime Minister of the military regime in Fiji, is again in Britain seeking to drum up some sort of continuing link with the Crown: a 'legitimising' act it would be. He tries the argument that the Queen retain the title of Tui Viti – Queen of Fiji – which was passed to Queen Victoria by Ratu Seru Cakobau on the occasion of Fiji's cession in 1874. Not much chance of that without an acceptable Constitution, the British press make clear. Especially when the seventy-five-year-old direct descendant of Ratu Seru, paramount chief and former Governor General Ratu Sir George Cakobau, announces his opposition to any such notion.

'The title came back to me,' he says in Bau, 'when Fiji became independent in 1970. I have no plans to abdicate. The title is not Ratu Mara's to give away.'

Mara had better luck with Margaret Thatcher when he went to Downing Street the next day. 'A very cordial meeting,' officials said. Britain would be willing to help prepare an acceptable revised Constitution and to resume the training of Fiji Army officers. Curious that, one British observer ruminated: we are apparently going to train officers for an army which committed an act of treason against our Queen, their Head of State and, as it happens, ours too.

14 May 1988

Saturday. The first anniversary of Coup 1. The army and police are on full alert, weapons drawn from armouries, all leave cancelled. Key points and installations are heavily guarded. The towns are silent and sombre, the roads still. At Sukuna Park in central Suva, eighteen persons assemble quietly on foot. They are dressed in black or with black armbands – in mourning, they say, for the death of democracy a year before. There are three Roman Catholic priests – from England, Ireland and New Zealand. Among the rest are women of various races – wives, social workers and academics from the University of the South Pacific. One of them is 'Atu, back from temporary exile in Australia and at the university again since February. All are arrested by the police for holding an unlawful assembly. They are taken to detention cells.

As the tropical night envelops the silent city, the women begin to sing, joining together in whatever songs they can find in common to bolster their spirits as they face the comfortless hours until the dawn. The singing irritates the guards. A police van arrives outside the cells and backs against the cell windows. The engine is left running. The rapid pollution of the air makes breathing difficult and survival uncertain. The detainees drop to the floor, cover their heads as best they can on the cold stone and seek thus to limit the effect of the poisonous carbon monoxide fumes. So they stay throughout the interminable night.

Next day, the demonstrators appear at a preliminary hearing in the magistrates court. The police abandon their earlier opposition to bail. It is the day when an Australian Labour Party delegation with the redoubtable Don Dunstan, QC, as a member, is due to arrive in Fiji. It is some comfort too that senior lawyers who appear on behalf of the eighteen include Constitution Review Committee Chairman and former Alliance Attorney General Sir John Falvey, QC; and President of the Law Society Miles Johnson, director of the silenced *Fiji Sun* and himself not unfamiliar with the deprivations of enforced custody in contemporary Fiji.

31 May 1988

In Sydney harbour, Customs officers seize about twelve tons of Soviet-manufactured arms. They include machine guns, rocket grenades, anti-tank mines, mortar shells and rocket launchers. They are concealed in a container bound for Fiji. The ship *Anro Australia* sailed to Sydney from North Yemen.

'It's enough to start a small war,' says a startled Customs officer. The question is whose.

7 June 1988

In a series of co-ordinated raids, police in Fiji seize a large quantity of arms smuggled earlier through Lautoka, the north-west sugar port of Vitilevu. Some forty people are detained including, once again, the Bavadra Government Foreign Minister Krishna Datt. The arms include over 100 AK 47 automatic rifles with 46,000 rounds of ammunition, machine guns, rocket launchers, some 300 rocket grenades and other items of military equipment. Tension runs high from east to west as Fiji stumbles to the brink of civil war and raw communal violence.

Next day, twenty-two persons are charged with arms offences. They include, it is reported, Ratu Mosese Tuisawau, brother-in-law of Ratu Mara, and a Fijian who for years has sought to bridge the divides of race and culture. Dr Bavadra counsels caution and calm. He condemns what he says is a witch-hunt by the security forces of Indians and supporters of all races of his Coalition Party. Nightly, the windows of cars owned by known Coalition Party supporters are pulverised and panels beaten. Thuggery is unchecked and families are terrorised.

Sitiveni Rabuka's apologia for his military intervention in the parliamentary process is contained in a publication entitled *No Other Way*. A promotional visit is planned to New Zealand and Australia. New Zealand says he would be unwelcome. There is no visit. Prime Minister Bob Hawke intervenes personally in Australia, so the publicity says. There is no visit there either. The active organisations in both countries working for the return of democracy in Fiji breathe a little easier. A public judgment has been given by positive political leadership. The significance cannot be missed.

17 June 1988

It is thirteen months since Fiji ran somewhat short of continuing to qualify as 'the way the world should be'. A new Internal Security Decree, signed by the President and former Governor General, is issued in the government gazette with a new-style Fiji Republic masthead. Still nestling nostalgically on the title page, however, is the old Fiji coat of arms with its now anachronistic motto 'Rerevaka na Kalou ka doka na Tui' – Fear God and honour the Queen.

The model legislation for the decree is thought by some to be that of Malaysia where the retreat from popular democracy has been exceeded in the region only by its uneasy neighbour, Singapore. In both, dissenting debate has been largely stifled and coercion substituted. Fijian links with Malaysia go back to its battalion which served with distinction in the communist emergency of Malaya; and its political party blueprint for Ratu Mara's Alliance. Singapore Prime Minister Lee Kwan Yew has been an occasional golfing companion of Ratu Mara over the years. They have an ideological empathy, it would seem.

The Fiji decree is lifted virtually en bloc from the Internal Security Decree of Singapore of 1960, revised in 1985. The stated objective is to strengthen existing laws on internal security and to counter subversion. It takes some eighteen thousand discomforting words to do this. 'Frightening,' said a Caribbean lawyer to me in July. 'A massive deprivation of accepted human rights. More comprehensive than anything enacted in Jamaica in the violence before the 1983 election. There is no parliament and the courts seem scarcely to exist. Its provisions are paramount.'

Blanket powers of search, seizure and detention are given to Brigadier Rabuka and his security forces. As Minister responsible for Security, he now has wide-ranging powers to

- prohibit quasi-military organisations and uniforms, emblems, banners or flags of any kind.
- prohibit what are judged to be subversive publications, imported or otherwise. There is a heavy fine or imprisonment or both for possession of any such document or publication. Subversive content is apparently assumed unless the contrary can be proved.
- declare any area of Fiji a security area if it is in danger of organised violence.
- declare any part of a security area to be a danger area. Within its boundaries, the security forces have freedom to kill without redress. They may
  - enter and search any premises at any time, day or night, without warrant. A man may search a woman if it is 'impossible' for a woman to do so.
  - search and seize any documents believed to be subversive.
  - control exhibitions, entertainments and movement and require information.
  - take possession of land, buildings, and destroy unoccupied buildings; and
  - arrest and detain suspected persons without warrant.

Any person found guilty of possessing unlawful firearms or explosives in a security area is jailed for life with a mandatory non-parole period of twenty-five years.

There are powers of preventive detention without charge for up to two years – renewable. The Minister's decision on an appeal is final. There is no appeal to any court and no right of habeas corpus. In a number of instances, the burden of proof is switched from the prosecution to the defence: in these cases, an accused person is presumed guilty unless innocence can be proven.

The list goes on: the Minister responsible for Security can close any school or educational institution without consultation or appeal – except to him; order the inspection of bankers' books; order the confiscation or cancellation of passports; determine by right of veto who is appointed or not appointed to the staff of any such institution determined by him; approve or disapprove staff appointments by any legally established body. So civil servants, local government staff and those of statutory bodies are clasped, appealless, in his excluding embrace.

The decree is retrospective to 1 March 1988, thus abandoning at a stroke a fundamental principle of parliamentary lawmaking: that new laws may not impose retroactive penalty provisions. But this is not parliamentary lawmaking. It is military decreemaking.

A week later Christopher Harder, a Canadian lawyer resident in New Zealand and engaged to represent five of the twenty-two persons arrested on arms charges on 7 June, is himself arrested by the poolside of his Suva hotel. He is taken into detention for thirty hours and placed in a tiny cell measuring eleven hand lengths by eight hand lengths. He is said to be claustrophobic. No matter. He is served with an exclusion order stating that his presence in Fiji poses a danger to the peace and good order of the country. Good order? It had perhaps been a shade quixotic of him to write, together with the Secretary of the Fiji Law Society, criticising the internal security decree. Poor timing anyway. None the less . . .

His deportation to New Zealand outrages its lawyer Prime Minister. 'The new Internal Security Decree,' David Lange announces, 'makes Fiji the first police state in the South Pacific. What is clear, is that we have a concept of the rule of law in Fiji which is just totally abhorrent. It amounts to a total destruction of personal rights and liberties. There is now a pattern of arbitrary detention and police violence.'

Warning New Zealanders not to go to Fiji, Mr Lange says the Government's analysis of the decree is that New Zealand's representatives there will be 'very severely restricted in giving assistance to any New Zealand citizen'.

The Dominion is the morning newspaper of the capital city of Wellington. It is thus on the breakfast table of every parliamentarian. On 24 June 1988 it delivered a series of broadsides not unreminiscent of the treatment meted out to the Welsh Rugby Union team by the All Blacks in Auckland a fortnight before:

A DANGEROUS BUFFOON

Fijian politics are now a sinister mixture of tragedy and farce. The Brigadier, making good use of the emergency powers he gave himself last week, has arrested an academic who wrote a critical review of his book. The sensitive author has also given a public blessing to Fijian rugby tours of South Africa, and unblushingly described his own regime as a species of apartheid. He would be merely ridiculous if he were not able to impose his racist and reactionary prejudices on the people of Fiji. As it is, he is an increasingly dangerous buffoon, and what he is doing to his country is no joke at all.

The discovery of an arms cache in Fiji has prompted the Government to issue the Internal Security Decree, giving virtually unlimited powers to the army and the police. The dictator who seized power at the point of a gun now takes a high moral tone with those who would use similar tactics. His Government warns that attempts at armed rebellion 'will seriously impede the speedy return to parliamentary democracy'. But it was Rabuka and his thugs who killed democracy in the first place; and they had shown no convincing signs of wanting to restore it.

Plots to overthrow the Government by force, dangerous and deplorable though they might be, were more or less inevitable in Fiji. In a banana republic – and Fiji has been one since May 14 last year – countercoup follows coup. The normal rules do not apply, as the New Zealand lawyer appointed to defend the alleged plotters has now found. Mr Christopher Harder appears to have acted most unwisely in his dealings with the Rabuka regime. That does not justify his detention or deportation. But this is no longer a state which respects the rule of law or the principles of justice.

In New Zealand, powerful voices have called for 'understanding' and 'tact' in dealing with the dictatorship; and they have prevailed. We have even had the extraordinary spectacle of a retired chief of defence staff reportedly criticising the Government's lack of sympathy for what was probably the most deep-seated worry of the region's indigenous people. This is the tangata whenua argument; and it is utterly specious in relation to Fiji. Rabuka and his mates do not represent the downtrodden Fijian masses. They are merely the military arm of a feudal chiefly clique which saw its powers rapidly fading, and wanted to snatch them back.

Supporters of the Lange Government's policy of appeasement

might now like to ask themselves: exactly what have we gained by snuggling up to the Brig? Have we stopped racial oppression, or halted the slide into economic ruin and political chaos? No, we have not. Rabuka continues his grotesque imitation of Idi Amin; and it seems that some of the dispossessed are prepared to fight fire with fire. Have we, by dint of diplomacy and the resumption of aid, helped encourage Fijian rulers towards social democracy? Of course not: the regime now plans to ask aid donors to meet the cost of replacing its fleet of ministerial cars.

Fiji is going to hell in a handbasket; and the man taking it there is jailing book reviewers and babbling about receiving orders from God. Russell Marshall [the Foreign Minister] murmurs, and wrings his hands, and cannot understand why concern and understanding have such little effect on barbarians.

Some days later on British television, Bishop Huddleston was reflecting on his life-long struggle against apartheid. 'It is,' he said, 'a system based on institutionalised racism.'
South Africa and Fiji make strange and tragic stablemates.

EPILOGUE

4 July 1988

The all-American day of celebration is muted by the awesome culpability of a United States Navy cruiser in the Persian Gulf. One of its missiles is discharged at and destroys an Iran Air airbus which is on a scheduled passenger flight to Dubai. All 290 on board perish. The world ponders whose judgmentally uncertain finger will next tremble above the button of mass destruction.

Across the world in the last remaining South Pacific island kingdom, there are annual celebrations of a different nature also on the fourth of July. On that day, in Tonga, the birthday is marked of King Taufa'ahau Tupou IV; and in 1988 the celebratory day became a week. It was the King's seventieth birthday and Nuku'alofa, the capital, came alive with day and night feasting, singing and dancing. From all over the kingdom came tributes and gifts for a man who many had feared would not reach his half century, let alone the biblical span: for it is a brave airline which asks His Majesty to stand on the check-in scales and to seat him other than in the widest of first-class aircraft seats.

I went by train to London in the late morning. The noticeboard in the entrance hall of the Royal Commonwealth Society had said simply:

FIJI

Address by Professor Asesela Ravuvu,
Director of the Institute of Pacific Studies,
University of the South Pacific, and
Chairman of the Fiji Trade and Investment Board.

The West Indian ticket collectors at Charing Cross Station were in animated off-peak conversation.

'No, man. I always stay to de finish. Specially when we's winnin'. I tink dat mus' be always now. We beat England two time an' one rain draw so far dis series an' today England go out for ninety-t'ree

225

secon' time bat. Our boys on de victory march. I tell you true. Black-wash comin'. Dose fellas at Lords got sometin' to tink 'bout now.'

Indeed they have, I thought, and turned down the steps into Craven Street. A strong voice called my name. As always, London has its surprises. He strode forward, smiling, hand extended.

'On your way to the Commonwealth?'

'Yes.'

'So am I. Just going across the Strand first to order some ski equipment at the Alpine Sports shop.'

'Right. I'll wait.' Was he perhaps really going to the Army Careers Information Office next door?

He was soon back: jaunty, urbane, charming. The larger than life handlebar moustache had gone. So too the military uniform. But the polished presence was unchanged and unmistakable.

'You look and speak more like your father than ever.'

'You think so? That's good.'

We had not met for perhaps eighteen years when, as a young lieutenant, he was an aide-de-camp at Government House in Suva. But I had, of course, seen him more recently: at a distance, some ten months earlier at Nadi Airport when, having been removed in absentia as Commander of the Royal Fiji Military Forces by his Number Three, he returned from Australia to the uncertainties of post-coup Fiji. A commander no longer with an army to command.

Now styled Brigadier General like the coup leader himself, Ratu Epeli Nailatikau – son of Ratu Sir Edward Cakobau and son-in-law of Ratu Sir Kamisese Mara – had but recently arrived, to diplomatic exile, some said, in London. On 9 June the Buckingham Palace Court Circular had announced that on the previous day he had been received in audience by the Queen and had presented his Letters of Credence as Ambassador Extraordinary of the Republic of Fiji to the Court of St James. Extraordinary indeed, bizarre also: the deposed military commander of Her Majesty's forces in the Dominion of Fiji stood before his country's former Head of State – a Head of State deposed by treasonable act of those same forces – as the envoy in Britain of the military-controlled government of the new Republic. But with the brief, I surmised, to promote the resumption of the royal connection, in whatever form might be possible, with Fiji and the Fijians. He had, after all, also been an equerry of the Queen. It was not quite the usual formal presentation of credentials to the sovereign.

'Hullo, Epeli. How are you settling in?' A former incumbent of Government House, Suva, was standing in the entrance hall of the

Commonwealth Society's building in Northumberland Avenue.

'Well, thank you, sir. I've always liked London.'

'While I think of it, what's the state of play with the new Constitution?'

'I believe a draft is on the President's desk right now.'

'Ah. There is just one slight difficulty that I can see.'

'Yes. What's that?'

'The machinery for making it legal doesn't seem to exist. Unless you can do it by military decree. Not quite the thing perhaps. But it is not my business of course. We're all here to learn about what's really going on in Fiji today, aren't we? Pity about that fellow Bavadra. You know what your chaps should have done: offered him a generous enough allowance to go off to Edinburgh to do his FRCS. I imagine he would have bought that, if you'd put it to him at the right moment. It would have kept him quiet for three or four years and you mightn't have had all this fuss and bother.' He laughed. 'Always a good ploy that. We used it from time to time. Shall we go in? After you, Ambassador.'

An hour or so later the address was over. Some desultory questions were answered. We turned to go.

'That,' said the same journalist who had assessed the outcome of the Commonwealth meeting in November, 'was an example of rigid hardline racism!'

'Join the Club,' Epeli said, as we left the Commonwealth Society building. 'That's what they told me.'

'Who?'

'My diplomatic colleagues from Africa and elsewhere when I arrived in London. Sure, I replied. I'll join. Where is it? No, they said. Not that sort of club. There's plenty of those. We mean the Coup Club. We all belong. You're the first member from the South Pacific.'

He paused. 'OK to be first in something, I suppose. No matter what.' And the only head of mission car in London which appears to have the name of the country on its registration plate – FIJI – swept off towards Trafalgar Square and Knightsbridge.

. . . 'There's nothing wrong with English cricket,' said the ITN news bulletin that night in a burst of inspiration, 'except the players, the pitches and the selectors.' And the West Indian fast bowlers, it seemed right to add. They too have all the guns . . . and Marshall law.

A world away in north-west Vitilevu, Dr Bavadra sits with his people, cross-legged and barefooted, on great floor mats in the centre of the village. It is the day of the soqo ni vakasobu duru – the ceremony to mark the laying of the first foundation pillar of a chiefly bure being constructed in Veiseisei for their Prime Minister and his wife.

Timoci Uluivuda Bavadra is the head of the Werecakaca clan. This name is also to be used for the new house being built by customary methods and materials by the men of Noikoro, Navosa in the interior of Vitilevu. For Adi Kuini Vuikaba is the eldest daughter of the high chief of Noikoro, Ratu Qoro Latianara.

As in other chiefly Fijian villages, there are some fine houses and some which are more modest. One of the latter is the timber house of Dr Bavadra. It bears, above the steps to the small verandah, the name Werenitotoge. This means – perhaps not without some significance – the House of Punishment, where in the past were kept those who refused to obey the orders of the high chiefs and were accordingly liable to be beaten with war clubs.

Things may be different in the fine new bure Werecakaca, which Adi Kuini enterprisingly translates as the House of Unconventional Behaviour. This is not quite its literal meaning, but the message is clear.

For one hundred and nine nights, over one hundred men of Noikoro were with the people of Veiseisei until the work of construction was finished. The formal dedication and completion ceremonies took place on 4 August 1988. Some three thousand people journeyed to Veiseisei for that day of joyous celebration, song and dance.

'For us,' Dr Bavadra says, 'and our Coalition supporters, Werecakaca is a symbol of love, hope and democracy.'

'It is,' Ratu Mosese Tuisawau concluded, 'an edifice so imposing in its structure as to symbolise the best traditional and western technologies.'

So do two worlds continue to meet: the customary and the traditional with the present day political and the harsher realities of the Fiji east. They seem to meet in other ways too, for only a few steps away in Veiseisei is a poorish dwelling optimistically labelled Las Vegas.

6 October 1988

'I see from today's *Herald*,' my Auckland correspondent wrote, 'that Rabuka has promoted himself to Major General, which is probably as close to God as he dares place himself.'

Well, for the time being anyway.

* * *

What I have written will, inevitably, be viewed differently by different people, in differing circumstances, in different countries: for there is no single judgment of public events or human folly. It all depends on where you sit. Yet there must surely be a shared compassion for the vulnerable of all races who suffer in the Fiji of today, who have come to know repression, hunger and helplessness, and who thus yearn to escape but do not have the capability to do so or a land of refuge available to them. They are the bricks in the rebuilding that is yet to come by those with the courage and endurance to attempt it.

INDEX